The Post-Colonial Detective

Crime Files Series

General Editor: **Clive Bloom**

Since its invention in the nineteenth century, detective fiction has never been more popular. In novels, short stories, films, radio, television and now in computer games, private detectives and psychopaths, prim poisoners and overworked cops, tommy gun gangsters and cocaine criminals are the very stuff of modern imagination, and their creators one mainstay of popular consciousness. Crime Files is a ground-breaking series offering scholars, students and discerning readers a comprehensive set of guides to the world of crime and detective fiction. Every aspect of crime writing, detective fiction, gangster movie, true-crime exposé, police procedural and post-colonial investigation is explored through clear and informative texts offering comprehensive coverage and theoretical sophistication.

Published titles include:

Crime Files
Series Standing Order ISBN 0–333–71471–7
(*outside North America only*)

You can receive future titles in this series as they are published by placing a standing order. Please contact your bookseller or, in case of difficulty, write to us at the address below with your name and address, the title of the series and the ISBN quoted above.

Customer Services Department, Macmillan Distribution Ltd, Houndmills, Basingstoke, Hampshire RG21 6XS, England

The Post-Colonial Detective

Edited by
Ed Christian

First published 2001 by
PALGRAVE
Houndmills, Basingstoke, Hampshire RG21 6XS and
175 Fifth Avenue, New York, N.Y. 10010
Companies and representatives throughout the world

PALGRAVE is the new global academic imprint of
St. Martin's Press LLC Scholarly and Reference Division and
Palgrave Publishers Ltd (formerly Macmillan Press Ltd).

Outside North America
ISBN 0–333–73895–0

In North America
ISBN 0–312–22831–7

This book is printed on paper suitable for recycling and
made from fully managed and sustained forest sources.

A catalogue record for this book is available
from the British Library.

Library of Congress Cataloging-in-Publication Data
The post-colonial detective / edited by Ed Christian.
    p. cm. — (Crime files series)
Includes bibliographical references and index.
ISBN 0–312–22831–7 (cloth)
1. Detective and mystery stories—History and criticism. 2. Detective
and mystery stories—Developing countries—History and criticism.
3. Postcolonialism—Developing countries. 4. Developing countries—In
literature. 5. Decolonization in literature. I. Series. II. Christian, Ed, 1953–
PN3448.D4 P63 2000
809.3'872 21—dc21
                                                                99–043512

10   9   8   7   6   5   4   3   2   1
10 09 08 07 06 05 04 03 02 01

Printed and bound in Great Britain by
Antony Rowe Ltd, Chippenham, Wiltshire

Contents

Contributors

Deborah Bosi, an award-winning writer, has written for television, cable, theatre, and print. She has a Master's degree from DePaul University and has lectured in both New York City and Chicago. A native New Yorker, Ms Bosi lives in Prospect Heights, Illinois, with her husband, two sons, and three cats.

Roger Célestin is Associate Professor of French and Comparative Literature at the University of Connecticut. He has written on Montaigne, Flaubert, Tournier, travel literature, and detective fiction. He is the author of *From Cannibals to Radicals: Figures and Limits of Exoticism* (Minneapolis: Minnesota UP, 1995), and is co-editor of *Sites: The Journal of 20th Century / Contemporary French Studies*.

Ed Christian is an Assistant Professor of English at Kutztown University of Pennsylvania. He has been teaching detective fiction for a decade, featuring post-colonial detectives whenever possible. He has written or spoken on the detective writers Dorothy L. Sayers, Chester Himes, and Ellis Peters, among many others, and published the book *Joyce Cary's Creative Imagination*. Outside his native country, he has taught English to graduate students in Beijing, served as surgical supervisor of a hospital in Rwanda, and been a Fulbright Scholar at Oxford. In addition to teaching detective fiction, he teaches three popular courses in biblical literature and another in apocalyptic fiction.

José F. Colmeiro is an Associate Professor at Michigan State University. He has a Ph.D. in Hispanic Languages and Literature from the University of California, Berkeley. He has published numerous articles on Spanish literature and cultural studies, and is the author of *La novela policiaca española: Teoría e historia crítica* (Anthropos, 1994) and *Crónica del desencanto: La narrativa de Manuel Vázquez Montalbán* (U Miami, North-South Center, 1996) awarded the 'Letras de Oro' prize for best book-length essay. He has co-edited *Spain Today: Essays on Literature, Culture, Society* (Hanover, NH: Dartmouth College, 1995). His current research interests involve the study of cultural memory and identity in contemporary Spain.

Jorge Hernández Martín teaches in the Department of Spanish and Italian at Middlebury College, Vermont. He received a Ph.D. from Cornell University in 1990. He is the author of *Readers and Labyrinths: Detective Fiction in Borges and Eco* (Hamden, CT: Garland, 1996), and articles on H. Bustos Domecq's parodies of works by classic masters of detective fiction.

Jeffrey C. Kinkley is a Professor of History at St. John's University, New York City. He has written, edited, and translated several books on modern Chinese literature and autobiography, most recently *Imperfect Paradise*, an edited collection of stories by Shen Congwen. He has written a book on 1980s Chinese crime fiction, and is at work on a sequel.

Dean Loganbill is a recovering academic. Having received his Ph.D. from the University of Denver, he spent many years teaching English literature and composition at various colleges and universities. In 1996 he escaped from the ivory tower and is presently hiding out in Salem, Oregon, where he practices martial arts and, as time permits, pursues a life-long ambition to be a hermit. He wrote 'The Savage Among Us' while teaching at Fayetteville State University in North Carolina.

Patrick Quinn, a University of Warwick Ph.D., is Professor of English Literature at University College Northampton. He has previously taught at universities in Canada, the United States, Germany, and Iraq. He is the author of *The Great War and the Missing Muse: The Early Writings of Robert Graves and Siegfried Sassoon* and the recently edited collection *Recharting the Thirties*, a study of neglected writers of the 1930s. Quinn is also the general editor of the twenty-four volume Robert Graves Programme, which will re-publish all of Graves' major works between 1995–2004. He also is the editor of *Gravesiana: The Journal of the Robert Graves Society* and is the President of the International Robert Graves Society. He is currently researching American patriotic literature written during the Great War.

Marilyn Rye, who received her Ph.D. in Comparative Literature, is currently an Assistant Professor of English and Director of Freshman Writing at Fairleigh Dickinson University in Madison, New Jersey. She has contributed articles and essays on detective fiction to *A Critical Survey of Mystery and Detective Fiction*, *Great Women Mystery Writers*, *The Oxford Companion to Crime and Mystery Writing*, *Ngaio Marsh: The Woman and Her Work*, and *Sherlock Holmes: Victorian Sleuth to Modern Hero: 1894–*

1994. In addition to writing on detective fiction, Dr Rye has written on composition theory and pedagogy, contemporary women authors, and American Indian authors. She is the editor of an anthology of readings for teaching composition, *Making Cultural Connections.* At present Dr Rye serves as a board member of the Ngaio Marsh Society International.

Meera Tamaya is Professor of English at Massachusetts College of Liberal Arts, where she teaches Shakespeare and assorted literature courses. She earned her MA at the University of Madras in India and her Ph.D. in English at the University of Massachusetts. The author of the book *Colonial Detection: H. R. F. Keating,* she has published articles on John Sherwood, Kazuo Ishiguro, Margaret Atwood, Barbara Pym, and Shakespeare in scholarly journals. She also contributes book reviews and articles to *The Berkshire Eagle.* She is currently preparing her manuscript, *(Re)cognizing Hamlet: a Cognitive Approach* for publication.

Edward Tomarken is a Professor of English at Miami University of Ohio. He has written several articles and five books on the literature of the Renaissance and the eighteenth century as well as on literary theory. He has published another article on the work of James McClure: 'The Art of Politics in James McClure's *The Artful Egg': Human Rights Quarterly* 5 (1985), 230–39. His most recent publication is *'As You Like It': from 1600 to the Present,* Garland Press, 1997. He is presently writing a work entitled *Genre and Ethics,* a study of how literary methodology bears upon moral problems, that is under contract to the University Press of Kentucky.

1

Introducing the Post-Colonial Detective: Putting Marginality to Work

Ed Christian

The term 'post-colonial' is still evolving. At its narrowest, post-colonial refers to once colonized indigenous people. More often the term is widened to include settlers and their descendents who stay in a colony after independence is granted. Some writers deny post-colonial status to the United States, but others see the US as the first of the modern post-colonial countries and as a model for those which have more recently been granted independence. In its widest sense, the term post-colonial embraces the members of any group – be it national, tribal, ethnic, or otherwise – which has been marginalized or oppressed and is struggling to assert itself. This could include, of course, women or homosexuals or perhaps even teachers of that academically marginalized sub-genre, detective fiction. To use the term in this way reduces its effectiveness when it is narrowly defined, but nevertheless the wide definition can lead to useful critical insights.

Similarly, the term post-colonial literature is sometimes used as a synonym of commonwealth literature, sometimes restricted to writing by indigenous peoples, and sometimes extended to writing by settlers. More often the term includes writers from the former French, Belgian, Dutch, Spanish, and Portuguese colonies, as well, especially when the colonies were African, Asian, or Caribbean. The term is sometimes used in reference to feminist literature, African-American literature, and several more types of writing.[1] The key concept seems to be that post-colonial literature is writing by members of marginalized groups – writers who are struggling to find voices in which to express the world view of their groups, who are struggling to be heard and to be understood, who are struggling against cultural hegemony and assimilation and neo-colonialism.

I. Detecting

Before defining our use of the term 'post-colonial detective,' I'd like to explain what this book is *not*. First, it is not post-colonial criticism. It has been argued (though many critics would disagree) that only those who are themselves post-colonials can adequately comprehend and explain to others the full complexity of feeling and attitude found in post-colonial literature or among post-colonial peoples. It has also been argued that given the long marginalization of these peoples, to appropriate their critical space by pretending to a thorough knowledge of their most valuable cultural insights is in effect to recolonize them. We are unwilling to do that.[2]

How then do we define the post-colonial detective? The answer is somewhat complex, but the following comments present the boundaries within which we have been working. A post-colonial detective is not always the creation of a post-colonial writer. For example, H. R. F. Keating wrote nine of his culturally accurate Inspector Ghote novels before even visiting India. On the other hand, most detective novels set in foreign countries do not qualify as post-colonial detective fiction (I think here, for example, of the novels of Agatha Christie and Elspeth Huxley set in far-away lands they knew quite well). The crucial distinctions are that *post-colonial detectives are always indigenous to or settlers in the countries where they work; they are usually marginalized in some way, which affects their ability to work at their full potential; they are always central and sympathetic characters; and their creators' interest usually lies in an exploration of how these detectives' approaches to criminal investigation are influenced by their cultural attitudes*. Thus, books featuring post-colonial detectives are interesting not only because of their plots and the quality of their writing but because of their revelations of diverse cultures.

A distinctive feature of hard-boiled and police procedural detective fiction is the way detectives frequently proceed from the interrogation of suspects to the interrogation of society. Individual crime comes to be seen as a symptom of, result of, or reaction to basic flaws in the political, social, and industrial systems. Post-colonial detectives, approaching crime with a special sensitivity enhanced by their marginalized positions, are especially quick to notice societal contradictions because they have always been exploited by them. The practical anthropology which is usually present in these books, the revelation of why people are as they are and why there are benefits to being that way, leads to tolerance of diversity and hybridity as it leads to understanding of why people of different cultures act differently than we do (whoever *we* are).

Those contributing to *The Post-Colonial Detective* look at their authors, works, and detectives in one or more of four ways. First, some look at the process and difficulties of detecting in post-colonial countries. They ask how the conventions of the detective novel are modified by police procedure in these countries. They study how such things as a totalitarian or racist regime, a strong army, or police and political corruption interfere with the detective's search for justice. In this volume, this approach is especially useful in a study of such works as James McClure's South African novels, Paco Ignacio Taibo II's Mexican novels, William Marshall's novels set in Hong Kong or the Philippines, and the Chinese writers discussed by Kinkley.

Second, some look at indigenous detectives in post-colonial countries. They ask how these detectives combine their indigenous cultural knowledge with western police methods in solving crimes in which the motivation is based on the local culture. They look at how the ways these detectives approach their cases differ from the conventions of the genre, how they respond to class and ethnic structures, how they get along with detectives or superiors of other classes or ethnic groups, how they treat the local people, and how that treatment differs from the way other authorities treat them. This approach reveals interesting facets about not only the works mentioned above, but also Arthur Upfield's novels about the half-aborigine detective Napoleon Bonaparte.

Third, some contributors look at post-colonial detectives as people struggling to gain power after being without it. This includes people who have traditionally not been allowed or encouraged to become detectives, whether police or private. They look at the extent to which these detectives struggle against racism or against not being taken seriously by the people they meet – colleagues, clients, the authorities – and they study the ways in which authors subvert or use the conventions of the genre. This approach is particularly seen in the essays on Upfield, on McClure, on Marshall's Manila Bay series, and on the writers discussed by Hernández Martín.

Fourth, some concentrate on detective novelists from post-colonial countries. They look at how these writers must fight for acceptance, both in their own countries and in England and America, in all of which they may be marginalized by their nationalities and settings. These essays ask not only how these authors use the conventions of the genre and the local setting, but what kind of detectives they are creating, to what extent the form of the British or American novel is implicitly or explicitly imposed on these post-colonial writers, in effect recolonizing them, and to what extent this imposition is simply due to the demands of popular taste. This approach is useful in a study of writers whose post-colonial detectives are white and superficially similar to most American or English detectives, as in the works of Canadians Eric Wright and Howard Engel. (The Canadian critic Robert Kroestch has written about how English appears to be his own language, yet isn't, leaving him in a quasi-post-colonial position.) It also lends itself to a study of indigenous writers whose work is never published in the US or UK or is available only by special order, as discussed in the essays by Colmeiro, Hernández Martín, Tam, Célestin, and Kinkley.

The essays in this volume raise a number of questions which deserve the reader's consideration and may serve to inspire further critical work. What are we to make of the fact that most of these novels, though set in post-colonial countries, are written by white males, have male detectives, and have detectives who are members of a police force (even when they are not police procedurals in the usual sense)? Why is the English tradition of the 'cozy' mystery virtually non-existent among post-colonial novelists (excluding expatriate colonials such as Ngaio Marsh), and the amateur or private detective rare? To what extent does the market for detective fiction (whether local or world-wide) influence the development of characters and the choice of generic conventions? For example, would Upfield's Australian audience (and publisher) have accepted a full-blooded Aborigine rather than the handsome half-breed Napoleon Bonaparte as a detective hero in 1928, when the first Bonaparte novel was published? Would William Marshall's *Yellowthread Street* series have been accepted in the US had all the detectives been indigenous Chinese? Would a Chinese audience today accept a Miss Marple-like detective who is a 'public security auntie,' one of the million or so old women who keep an eye on everyone in their neighborhood and report to the police (see Kinkley's discussion of the novel *Public Security Spirits*)? Would a non-Chinese audience be interested in such a book?

We might also consider the extent to which the post-colonial detective novel promotes tolerance of cultural diversity, especially among a group of readers not always eager to accept it. Is the post-colonial detective novel in general written by writers who are more open to the other than most detective novelists? Are characters in post-colonial detective novels stereotypes or do they reveal the authors' careful study and understanding of cultural characteristics? Does this make up for the authors' being white males? Do outsiders find it easier to notice cultural peculiarities and work them into their plots? Do cultural peculiarities and characteristics actually exist, or does it somehow recolonize the post-colonial to point to them? *The Post-Colonial Detective* does not offer a complete answer to these questions, but rather suggests approaches to them.

Some readers may wonder why there are not more post-colonial authors included. Unfortunately, although detective fiction is extremely popular, a large percentage of readers of detective fiction seem uninterested in books set in (much less written by authors from) lands other than England or the United States (preferably New York or Los Angeles). This is astonishing, but it is true. There is much more popular interest in cats as detectives than in, say, Catalans, or Koreans, or Columbians.

Detective fiction is popular in many countries, and often those countries have indigenous authors of detective fiction who have established large followings. In my own country, however, because most of these books are not available in English translations distributed by major American publishers carried by the major bookstore chains, the only Americans who read them are scholars who learn the indigenous languages, go to those countries to study, and are interested in detective fiction in those languages. (Jeffrey Kinkley is a good example of such a person.)

Note the many levels of marginalization and cultural hegemony here. Post-colonial detective fiction by post-colonial authors is marginalized (especially in terms of sales and income) when it is not available in English. Even if it is written and printed in English, it is not generally sold in the major markets unless published there, and it won't be published there unless editors think it will sell. It is marginalized because detective fiction is often considered unworthy of a country's best writers (Schleh explains how this has happened in Africa). It is marginalized because readers – both indigenous and not – expect detective fiction to follow the conventions of the English or American forms of the genre – an excellent example of hegemony (Langer shows how the Australian Peter Corris has been forced to follow the hard-boiled conventions). It is marginalized because most critics consider it undeserving of study. It is marginalized because there is a tradition of poor international sales.

This is not to imply that the authors discussed here are of marginal quality. William Marshall, for example, has the most fertile imagination in the history of detective fiction. His combination of the horrifying and the comic and the absurd in a post-modern narrative style is astonishing and deserves study. James McClure and H. R. F. Keating are also very fine writers. Upfield is a lesser writer than these three, but his Australian settings are interesting.

Some of the books discussed have never been translated into English. Perhaps this volume will lead to their translation and publication. Others are never seen in the major bookstores. It would be nice to see a volume entirely on post-colonial detectives by post-colonial authors. Kinkley's essay shows that they do exist in China, and they have modified the conventions of the genre to fit the needs, interests, and conditions of that country. Are there indigenous schools of detective fiction in, say, Pakistan, or the Philippines, or Iraq or Turkey or Angola, Venezuela or Jamaica or the Ukraine? The difficulty is that unless the books show up in English in our own countries, we don't know about them. It may be that there are some fascinating mystery writers undiscovered by us because of the marginalization caused by language and culture.

On the other hand, what makes a good crime writer? The genre of detective fiction, like all genres, has conventions from which writers depart only with care (the conventions of detective fiction are simply more closely defined than with, say, 'the modern novel,' which also follows certain conventions; Cawelti clearly explains these conventions of the mystery). In fact, the conventions are constantly being pushed as authors look for new angles, but if the conventions are simply ignored, or are pushed too hard, the audience will turn elsewhere. For example, Sara Paretsky transgressed the boundaries of the hard-boiled detective novel in several ways, most obviously by creating a hard-boiled woman detective, but her success would have been unlikely had she not treated most of the conventions with respect. These conventions are inescapably western, developed primarily in Britain and the US, and yet if a post-colonial writer were to avoid them, the work would be difficult to recognize as detective fiction. This means that a true post-colonial literature of detection will probably be a syncretic hybrid. This is not, of course, meant to be pejorative – I would argue that the result could well be more interesting than the original western forms.

Many writers of 'serious' fiction have tried to write mysteries yet failed, and this failure is nearly always due to their lack of respect for or understanding of the conventions of the genre. A great post-colonial example of this is *Petals of Blood*, by the noted Kenyan novelist Ngugi wa Thiong'o. As Stephen R. Carter writes,

> Ngugi turned the classic detective novel with its conservative social values into an anti-detective novel with a radical social vision. Through his construction and resolution of the mystery in *Petals of Blood*, Ngugi reveals and rejects most of the fundamental principles

underlying classic detective fiction, including glorification of individual heroism and the effectiveness of individual effort, belief in the European social order and overwhelming value of civilization (meaning, of course, European civilization), idealization of the puzzle-solving intellect, and the conviction that facts have a high value in themselves divorced from their complex human context...Ngugi also repudiates such underpinnings of classic detective fiction as the belief in a system of ethics founded on either traditional western sources (including Protestantism, Catholicism, and English and American democratic ideals) or an individual code and the belief in the fixity of human nature (75).

It seems to me that while *Petals of Blood* is an important novel, it is not a successful detective novel. Rather than pushing against the conventions and appropriating them, Ngugi simply uprooted them. In detective fiction, experience shows, this is about as successful as trying to write *terza rima* with four line stanzas. A similar failure by a noted novelist who ignored the conventions is Mario Vargas Llosa's *Who Killed Palomino Molero?* The theorist Umberto Eco was able to write what is perhaps the greatest detective novel of all time, *The Name of the Rose*, because he stood on the foundations of convention and leaped far above them. When authors tear down the conventions in the name of ideology, the remnant may be remarkable, but it is not really detective fiction.

Even when writers try to follow the conventions, the result is not necessarily good detective fiction. Mary Lou Quinn and Eugene Schleh have written on a series of mysteries by Kenyans and Nigerians published in Africa by the Macmillan Education Program in the 1980s. These books were published solely for the African market, but Schleh kindly loaned his copies to me. As popular culture, the books were very interesting, revealing a popular fascination with western cars, clothes, and luxury goods seldom seen in the works of the more noted African authors. As fiction or as detective fiction, the quality of the writing was very low, far below both the work of the African authors we know and love and the level of even the most conventional mystery published in the west. Perhaps the many African authors of talent have other concerns than detection. Are we wrong to judge genuinely post-colonial literature on the basis of the quality of writing, whether or not the conventions are followed? Surely not.

The International Association of Crime Writers, founded in 1987, may help remedy the problem of access to these works. Paco Ignacio Taibo II, for example, discussed in this volume, has served as President. The

IACW has sponsored an anthology called *The New Mystery*, which includes stories by several authors rarely seen in print in the US Ironically, though, of the thirteen authors listed on the cover, the only two not from the US are Jorge Luis Borges and Joyce Carol Oates, not as crime writers.

II. Theorizing

Most of the contributors to this book, though informed by theory, have chosen to observe their post-colonial detectives without resort to explicit theorizing, thus avoiding the metonymic gap between the priests and priestesses of theory and the common reader.[4] This has, at times, compromised their ability to explain the effects of post-coloniality in their detectives as precisely as possible, but the increased accessibility is a benefit.

Those wanting a comprehensive introduction to post-colonial theory should read *Key Concepts in Post-Colonial Studies*, by Bill Ashcroft, Gareth Griffiths, and Helen Tiffin, and *An Introduction to Post-Colonial Theory*, by Peter Childs and Patrick Williams. The first is in the form of a dictionary, the writing is unusually accessible, and the bibliography is selective, but large and current. The latter provides more depth, organizing the field by way of a few major concepts and theorists, but bringing in hundreds more in the comprehensive notes, and is particularly useful in not only introducing ideas and theorists but critiquing them in the light of how other critics have seen them. (The most incisive observer of the weaknesses of post-colonial theory, often quoted by Childs and Williams, is Robert Young, in his books *White Mythologies* and *Colonial Desire*.) Those who would like to read the criticism without intermediation would do well to begin with two collections: *The Post-Colonial Studies Reader*, by Ashcroft, Griffiths, and Tiffin, which offers a panoramic view of the field, and *Colonial Discourse and Post-Colonial Theory: A Reader*, by Laura Chrisman and Patrick Williams, which offers more depth.

Nevertheless, some readers who know little about post-colonial theory might appreciate a very brief introduction to the field and its implications for detective fiction. Ashcroft, Griffiths, and Tiffin, in a very influential book, *The Empire Writes Back*, have extended the post-colonial to cover 'all the culture from the moment of colonization to the present' (2). which is to say, after the beginning of colonialism rather than after the end. More commonly, its starting point is taken as the time when overt colonial rulership of a country ends. Peter Hulme has suggested, helpfully, that the term post-colonial refers 'to a *process* of disengagement from the whole colonial syndrome,' a process that occurs not only in the once-colonized countries but also at the center of empire (246). The use of the word post-colonial to refer to works of literature being written in cultures recently freed from colonial control goes back to about 1977,[5] and the term gradually gained in currency, probably because of its connotations of resistance to colonialism and determination to forge a new literature.

Post-colonial theory has been strongly influenced, like many other theories, by Lacan, Foucault, and Althusser, and to a lesser extent by Bakhtin and Gramsci. These names are frequently mentioned in the literature. Among post-colonial theorists, three names stand out among the many: Edward Said, from Egypt, and Gayatri Chakravorty Spivak and Homi Bhabha, both from India.

An important aspect of post-colonial literature is that, as Ashcroft et al. indicate in the title of their book, *The Empire Writes Back*, post-colonial writers do not write only for their own peoples, but for the seat of empire, what is called the metropolis or metropole, with the aim of transforming it. It is significant that Said, Spivak, and Bhabha are all academics in western universities, because one result of colonialism's end is a diaspora of post-colonial peoples to the metropolis. Paris, London, New York, Los Angeles, Honolulu, and more have been greatly affected in the past fifty years by the immigration of the post-colonial, as have most western universities. This diaspora to the metropole amounts to a virtual reverse colonization, though in this case the power of the colonizers comes not from troops with guns but from a willingness to work and a determination to prosper. (On the other hand, when the colonial powers fill their universities with post-colonial graduate students, they are exercising a superficially benign hegemony which will, they hope, foster neo-colonialism in the name of commerce and trade.)

Edward Said's most influential books have been *Orientalism* (1978) and *Culture and Imperialism* (1993). In the first book, Said argues that the colonial understanding of the orient produced by those westerners who studied it and wrote about it drew on ancient stereotypes, often untrue, and overwhelmingly negative. As Childs and Williams write, 'The cruelty, decadence, and sensuality of Oriental culture, the laziness, mendacity, and irrationality of its inhabitants, the violence and disorder of its societies: these were some of the staples of Orientalist knowledge' (100). Said writes, 'Orientals were rarely seen or looked at: they were seen through, analysed not as citizens, or even people, but as problems to be solved or confined, or – as the colonial powers openly coveted their territory – taken over' (207). In *Culture and Imperialism*, Said explains a crucial distinction between the imperial powers and others: 'All cultures tend to make representations of foreign cultures, the better to master or in some way control them. Yet not all cultures make representations of foreign cultures *and* in fact master or control them. This is the distinction, I believe, of modern Western cultures' (120). (The histories of representation, conquest and colonization by ancient Egypt, Babylonia, Persia, and Greece, China, India, and others suggest that Said's last sentence is mistaken.)

In his book *The World, The Text, and the Critic*, Said has elaborated the difference between what he calls filiation and affiliation. The filiative is passed down through the call of blood and culture, by tradition. The affiliative is a view of the individual within the society which interposes between the person and the tradition, offering new ways of imagining the self within the group. The colonial is at first affiliative, drawing people away from what is passed down and offering them new categories of definition. However, it eventually leads to new filiation as the colonized come to see themselves within the western tradition – of freedom, of culture, of law, of human rights, of empire. Thus, affiliation is both liberating and colonizing. This tension between filiation and affiliation is often seen in post-colonial detectives. It is their affiliation that frees them to detect, but it is their filiation which makes them better detectives than those from the west who have taught them, who have imposed the methods of detection on them.

Gayatri Chakravorty Spivak, in interviews and essays collected in *The Post-Colonial Critic: Interviews, Strategies, Dialogues* and *In Other Worlds: Essays in Cultural Politics* and in her influential article 'Can the Subaltern Speak? Speculations on Widow Sacrifice,' makes several points worth considering before we look at our post-colonial detectives. A major interest for Spivak is the position and voice of the subaltern, to use Antonio Gramsci's term, those who, because of their class or caste or ethnic group or occupation, are unheard in history and culture. She cautions critics that while they may study and write about the subaltern, they should avoid trying to speak for these powerless people. Post-colonial detectives, however, are not subalterns. Even though they may be resisting the colonial past or the effects of the neo-colonial effort, and even though there may be many ranks of power and office above them, they still have, by force of office, a power and respect that sets them apart from the subaltern. There are places in which these authors include the subaltern in their books – for example, H. R. F. Keating has members of the 'untouchable' caste in some of his novels set in India – but though these characters sometimes speak, they are not speaking *for* their people but are simply part of the plot mechanism. They are treated with dignity, without condescension, and their inclusion is not for local color but for accuracy and inclusion. This is an important difference between the creators of post-colonial detectives and those who have merely set novels in 'the colonies' (Abdul R. Jan-Mohamed has written insightfully about what he calls the 'Manichean dualism' in the varieties of colonial and colonizing literature, the stark division between the good and the bad, the known and the other).

As Childs and Williams write, 'Spivak always foregrounds specificity and maintains that as a teacher she is combating the homogenizing moves of "liberal-nationalist-universalist humanism" together with such claims as the autonomy of art and of the author' (157). She warns scholars to avoid the 'epistemic violence' of imposing their views of a people on that people, whatever those views may be. For example, in her essay 'French Feminism in an International Frame,' she writes, 'My point has been that there is something equally wrong in our most sophisticated research, our most benevolent impulses' (*In Other Worlds*, 50). The creators of post-colonial detectives, however benevolent their impulses, however accurate their observations, do unavoidable violence to the people they *imagine* and write about. They are, however, at this stage of the post-colonial project, when actual post-colonial detective novelists are not yet effectively 'writing back' to the metropole, serving, I would argue, as valuable intermediaries between cultures – perhaps not the real thing, yet preferable to silence.

The post-colonial critic whose work is most useful in understanding the post-colonial detective is Homi Bhabha. Many of his most important essays are collected in *The Location of Culture* and *Nation and Narration*. One term used by Bhabha is liminality, the condition of being within a space made by the meeting of two borders, a space which serves as a threshold between the two (*Location* 4). Often, the post-colonial detective *is* this space, this area of overlap, this space of meeting. In the detective the colonizer and the colonized collide, the oppressor and the resistor struggle for space. The detective has the power to oppress given by western police methods and the detective's place within society, often on the police force, but also the power to resist oppression given by filiation, by education, and by access to power. Police methods are one of the most obvious forms of colonial control, and these methods have not necessarily grown less repressive in post-colonial societies. By adopting these methods, the post-colonial detective risks recolonizing the people. Because the detective has closer contact with the colonizing or neo-colonizing power, the detective risks, as do the various other post-colonial elites, such as academics, becoming part of the comprador class implicated in the superficially benign neo-colonial hegemony. This is not a problem post-colonial detectives have necessarily solved, but they tend to be aware of it.

Bhabha has also written about mimicry, the tendency of the colonized to mimic the colonizers in order to be like them. However, as he points out, the better the colonized understand the colonizers – the better they understand the weaknesses of the colonizers – the closer their mimicry grows at times to mockery, and as the colonizers look at this mimicry, they come to see themselves in a disturbing light. This mimicry is often seen in post-colonial detectives. For example, in James McClure's South African novels, the Afrikaner Lieutenant Kramer expects his Bantu partner Sergeant Zondi to emulate him, yet Zondi's mimicry is always slightly ironic, even though polite and uncomplaining, for he knows he is the better detective, and when he occasionally mocks Kramer – usually by strict adherence to rules, Kramer winces as he recognizes himself.

Robert Young has written, in *Colonial Desire: Hybridity in Theory, Culture and Race*, about the ambivalence of the colonial position. The colonizer is both attracted and repulsed by the alterity or otherness of the colonized, whether physically, philosophically, culturally, or spiritually (161). Bhabha has made good use of this idea in examining the bilateral ambivalence in colonial and post-colonial societies. Both the colonizer and the colonized are attracted, yet both are also repulsed. This too is frequently seen in the post-colonial detectives discussed in this book.

One thing which makes Bhabha's work especially useful in examining the post-colonial detective is his optimism about the benefits of post-coloniality. Where many theorists (discussed in Childs and Williams, *Introduction*, chap. 1) have followed the lead of Frantz Fanon, Leopold Sedar Senghor, Aimé Césaire, Ngugi wa Thiong'o, Gandhi, Nehru, and others in urging continual resistance to the colonial, whether by physical resistance, by separation, by writing in the indigenous language, or by rejecting western conventions of writing, Bhabha, while not rejecting resistance in some forms, points to an inevitable *hybridity* which results as the colonizer and the colonized meet, beginning in the liminal space and expanding to both societies. The result of the conflict between the two, for Bhabha, is, finally, not the depowering of one or the other, but a decentering of power, a sharing of power. As both the colonizer and the colonized learn from each other, they become more like each other, whether they want to or not, whether they realize it or not, and the result is the strengthening of both peoples, even though the process may have led to suffering, to the violent wresting of culture away from its owners and the enforced replacement by another one. Bhabha insists that this hybridity goes both ways and that, though painful, it is beneficial. The effect of the post-colonial world on the metropolis, as more and more post-colonial peoples move to the metropolis and make themselves essential to it, is readily seen in may large western cities.

Hybridity is an essential component of most of the post-colonial detectives discussed in this book. Some are angrier than others. Some are more resistant than others. But they are themselves sites of hybridity. They are themselves blendings of western police methods and indigenous cultural knowledge, and their abilities are greater because of this hybridity. They have appropriated what is useful from the empire, but transformed it. As with post-coloniality in general, the post-colonial detective is a work in progress. These detectives are in process, they are learning, adjusting, changing, compromising, rejecting, resisting. They are not heroes of the resistance, out to destroy the oppressor. They are all employed, whether publically or privately – they answer to employers.

Is their agency limited by their complicity with the colonial project? The post-colonial detectives are not entirely free agents, but their freedom to act is perhaps greater than most, for they have power. They must decide whether to act within the law (which is the law of their post-colonial country, even if borrowed from western law) or to circumvent it. They must decide always between justice and mercy, making adjustments in the law where it unjustly oppresses. They may think, resent, encourage, speak (with caution), and sometimes act. Ashcroft, Griffiths, and Tiffin have written that '[o]ne of the most powerful strategies of imperial dominance is that of surveillance, or observation, because it implies a viewer with an elevated vantage point, it suggests the power to process and understand that which is seen, . . .' (*Key*, 226). The primary work of the post-colonial detective is surveillance, the surveillance of that which is suspect. Part of that surveillance, as this book shows, is the observation of both the empire and the indigenous culture, the observation of disparities, of ironies, of hybridities, of contradictions. Now the surveillance is not for imperial dominance, though, but for the restoration of what is right.

The field of post-colonial theory is still in flux, to some extent. The dominant positions have shifted from what they were when this book was begun, though the earlier ideas, more insistent on resistance, are still held by many. As Ashcroft, Griffiths, and Tiffin write:

It is likely that the . . . increasingly detailed archival work done on all aspects of colonial/post-colonial culture will continue to correct the more simplistic generalizations that characterize early formulations of the field without overthrowing the validity of a general, comparative methodology in framing important questions that a strictly local materialist analysis alone could neither pose nor answer (192).

As the field matures, it will have more to say about the post-colonial detective, as well. My hope is that in another decade or two the metropolis will have access to a wide range of the best detective novels by truly post-colonial authors from around the world.

Notes

1. 'But like all labels, *postcolonial* has created complications of its own, complications that involve the historical and national contexts in which literature is produced and received, as well as the gender, class, religious, and racial specificities of colonial (and imperial) experiences. . . . As the essays in this issue of *PMLA* show, some of the preoccupations of postcolonial theory intersect (without replicating) those of contemporaneous and equally problematic theoretical discourses such as postmodernist, feminist, lesbian, and gay or queer studies' (Hutcheon 8, 9).
2. I thank Priscilla Walton Carleton University in Ottawa for helping me understand this and helping me develop these caveats. Satya P. Mohanty writes, 'The claim is that our location is an objective feature of the world in which we live, the world as it is constituted precisely by various "positions" of power and powerlessness. As such, *our location is causally significant: it shapes our experiences and our ways of knowing. It can limit the possibilities available to us, since it helps frame our choices by organizing the habitual patterns through which we perceive ourselves and our world*' (109–10; emphasis added). Later, though, responding to those who question the possibility of cross-cultural critical understanding, he writes, 'The version of multiculturalism that demands that we suspend judgment on purely a priori grounds offers at best a weak pluralist scenario of noninterference and peaceful coexistence that is based on the abstract notion that everything about the other culture is (equally) valuable. Given the lack of understanding or knowledge of the other, however, the ascription of value (and of equality among cultures) is either meaningless or patronizing. Genuine respect depends on a judgment based on understanding, arrived at through difficult epistemic and ethical negotiations' (113).
3. Langer used the term in print and in a paper given in Australia in 1990, though I did not discover this until she responded to my call for papers. I'm not aware of any earlier use.
4. See W. D. Ashcroft's ' "Is that the Congo?" Language as metonymy in the post-colonial text.'
5. See W. D. Ashcroft, et al., *New Literature Review*.

Bibliography

Ashcroft, Bill, Gareth Griffiths, and Helen Tiffin. *The Empire Writes Back: Theory and Practice in Post-Colonial Literatures*. London: Routledge, 1989.

———. *Key Concepts in Post-Colonial Studies*. London: Routledge, 1998.

———, ed. *The Post-Colonial Studies Reader*. London: Routledge, 1995.

Ashcroft, W. D. 'Is that the Congo? Language as metonymy in the post-colonial text.' *World Literature Written in English* 29.2 (Autumn 1989).

———, M. Cotter, J. Docker, and S. Nandan, ed. *New Literature Review*, 2 (1977) 'Special issue: post-colonial literature.'

Bhaba, Homi. *The Location of Culture*. London: Routledge, 1994.

———. *Nation and Narration*. London and New York: Routledge, 1990.

Carter, Stephen R. 'Decolonization and Detective Fiction: Ngugi wa Thiong'o's *Petals of Blood*.' *Clues*, 8.1 (Spring/Summer 1987); rpt. in Schleh: 72–91.

Cawelti, John G. *Adventure, Mystery, and Romance : Formula Stories As Art and Popular Culture*. Chicago: U Chicago P, 1977.

Charyn, Jerome, ed. *The New Mystery*. New York: Dutton, 1993.

Childs, Peter, and Patrick Williams. *An Introduction to Post-Colonial Theory*. London and New York: Prentice Hall/Harvester Wheatsheaf, 1997.

Chrisman, Laura and Patrick Williams, ed. *Colonial Discourse and Post-colonial Theory: A Reader*. London and New York: Prentice Hall/Harvester Wheatsheaf, 1993.

Gugelberger, Georg M. 'Postcolonial Cultural Studies.' *The Johns Hopkins Guide to Literary Theory and Criticism*. Ed. Michael Groden and Martin Kreiswirth. Baltimore: Johns Hopkins UP, 1994. 581–85.

Hall, Stuart. 'When was "the Post-colonial"? Thinking at the Limit.' Iain Chambers and Lidia Curti, ed. *The Post-Colonial Question: Common Skies, Divided Horizons*. London: Routledge, 1996.

Hulme, Peter. 'Including America.' *Ariel*, 26, 1, 1995.

Hutcheon, Linda. 'Colonialism and the Postcolonial Condition: Complexities Abounding.' *PMLA* 110.1 (January 1995): 7–16.

JanMohammed, Abdul R. *Manichean Aesthetics: The Politics of Literature in Colonial Africa*. Amherst: U Massachusetts P, 1983.

Kroestch, Robert. 'Unhiding the hidden: recent Canadian fiction.' *Journal of Canadian Fiction*, 3.3 (1974): 394–396.

Langer, Beryl. 'The Real Thing: Cliff Hardy and Cocacola-nisation.' *Span: The Journal of the South Pacific Association for Commonwealth Literature and Language Studies*. 31 (February 1991): 29–44.

McClintock, Anne. 'The Angel of Progress: Pitfalls of the Term "Post-colonialism."' *Social Text* 31–32 (1992): 1–15.

McGee, Patrick. *Telling the Other: The Question of Value in Modern and Postcolonial Writing*. Ithaca: Cornell UP, 1992.

Mohanty, Satya P. 'Colonial Legacies, Multicultural Futures: Relativism, Objectivity, and the Challenge of Otherness.' *PMLA* 110.1 (January 1995): 108–18.

Quinn, Mary Lou and Eugene P. A. Schleh. 'Popular Crime in Africa: The Macmillan Education Program.' Schleh, 39–49.

Rahn, B. J. *Murder is Academic: A Collection of Crime Fiction Course Syllabi*. New York: n.p., 1993.

Said, Edward. *Culture and Imperialism*. New York: Knopf, 1993.

———. *Orientalism: Western Conceptions of the Orient*. New York: Vintage, 1979.

———. *The World, The Text, and the Critic*. Cambridge, MA: Harvard UP, 1983.

Schleh, Eugene, ed. *Mysteries of Africa*. Bowling Green, OH: Bowling Green U Popular P, 1991.

Spivak, Gayatri Chakravorty. 'Can the subaltern speak? Speculations on widow sacrifice.' *Wedge* 7.8 (Winter/Spring, 1985).

———. *In Other Worlds: Essays in Cultural Politics*. New York: Methuen, 1987.

———. *The Post-colonial Critic: Interviews, Strategies, Dialogues*. Ed. Sarah Harasym. New York: Routledge, 1990.

Walton, Priscilla L. 'Paretsky's V. I. as P. I.: Revising the Script and Recasting the Dick.' *Literature, Interpretation, Theory*, 4 (1993): 203–213.

Young, Robert. *Colonial Desire: Hybridity in Theory, Culture and Race*. London: Routledge, 1995.

———. *White Mythologies: Writing History and the West*. London: Routledge, 1990.

2
Keating's Inspector Ghote: Post-Colonial Detective?

Meera Tamaya

In an essay describing the genesis of his Indian detective, Inspector Ghote, H. R. F. Keating assumes the point of view of Ghote's disgruntled colleague who speculates on the dubious origins of his famous rival: 'Mr. Keating in the beginning saw a pair of shoulders only, thin and bony shoulders with a burden always upon them . . . I do not believe the fellow altogether knows what like are Ghote's feet . . .' ('Inspector' 113). It would be all too easy to argue that the 'burden' on Ghote's shoulders is that of his post-colonial status: a true-blue Hindu working in a Bombay police force modeled on Scotland Yard, legacy of the erstwhile British Raj. It would be equally easy to argue that Ghote's 'thin and bony shoulders' are bowed under the political incorrectness of being sired by a true Brit, H. R. F. Keating, who dared to write about a country he had not visited – the first nine Ghote novels were written before Keating visited India. Indeed, Keating writing from an Indian's point of view is roughly analogous to Prospero rewriting *The Tempest* with Caliban as the protagonist.

Perhaps Ghote's shoulders slumped even more when his prophetic soul foresaw literary theorists tying themselves into knots trying to sort out the different strands in his psyche. Aren't theorists, pursuing the bread and butter of their profession, obliged to toss around such terms as post-structuralist, post-colonial, post-modern, etc., making Ghote's already beleaguered life even more problematic? And as surely as the Bombay monsoon follows the long hot summer, post-anything will surely trail behind it such politically hip terms as center/margin, sabotage, subversion, subaltern, and plurality, all of which signal a 'radical' (not-so) sub-text: dismantle old imperial centers of authority, usher in the new utopia composed of the voices of the oppressed, the colonized, and the marginalized. Above all, the said dismantling or

17

deconstructing should be done by Caliban himself; not, heaven forfend, by Prospero.

The political incorrectness becomes even more convoluted: for here I am, an Indian woman academic domiciled in America, writing about an Indian detective authored by an Englishman. The very hip title, 'Inspector Ghote as Post-Colonial Detective,' implies, no shouts, a semi-noble political agenda. But alas, any academic, like any writer, often has a publish or perish motive. And Keating's stated reason for writing the Ghote novels was no less venal. He has described how his first few traditional whodunits, set in England, enjoyed only a modest success because, as one publisher informed him, they were too British. Casting about for an exotic locale which would make them more marketable, he thought of India because 'India was in that year.' Amplifying this remark he goes on to say, 'India, certainly in the British press, was held up as being a fine example of neutrality. People thought, can there be a way out of the cold war and India a line between' (Interview 1983).

Keating is talking about the early sixties; his first India novel, *The Perfect Murder*, was published in 1964. Before considering how India's special features suited Keating's needs as a writer, we must examine England's cultural and historical situation which made India particularly attractive to its citizens. The '60s were a time of cultural upheaval. On the level of popular culture, the Beatles put working class talents and panache on the map. In the realm of 'high' culture, French theorists were aiming their missiles at the ivory towers of academia. As they deconstructed the canon as well as Ian Fleming, the lines between high- and lowbrow literature were blurred. On the political front, Britain found itself relegated to the status of a minor power in the cold war between the superpowers America and the Soviet Union. The nationalization of the Suez Canal in 1956 by Egypt's President Nasser marked the decisive end of England's long reign as the world's foremost imperial power.

Even as England suffered the final spasms of its imperial *delirium tremens*, it was seized by a feverish nostalgia for all the exotica associated with its colonies. The Beatles levitated towards India seeking spiritual sustenance and ended up creating a market for Nehru jackets. The influx of immigrants from the disintegrating empire also changed the provincial face of English cities. London's Holmesian fog was dispersing in the winds of spicy ethnic cooking. Living as he does in Notting Hill Gate, it was inevitable that Keating should capture the *zeitgeist*, create Inspector Ghote, and set him on his peregrinations through the varied landscape of India.

Keating's Ghote novels belong in the mystery genre, but they also have to be considered in the broader perspective of British writing on India. From Kipling to Paul Scott, India has provided raw material for the British imagination even as it supplied natural resources – cotton is just one example – to its ever-hungry factories, with the finished product, English chintz, sold back to India at extortionate prices. When Queen Victoria declared herself Empress of India, the brightest jewel on her crown was literally the diamond, the Kohinoor, from India. Incidentally, Paul Scott's novel chronicling the death throes of the empire bore the eponymous title, *The Jewel in the Crown*, thus encapsulating the literal and metaphoric wealth that the British derived and continue to derive from India.

In his monumental study of British and French representations of the Orient titled, *Orientalism*, Edward Said points out that 'When Disraeli said in his novel *Tancred* that the East was a career, he meant that to be interested in the East was something bright young Westerners would find to be a consuming passion; he should not be interpreted as saying that the East was only a career for Westerners' (3). For Keating, however, interest in India did start out as a profitable career move, but it soon became a passion, not so much for the country as for *knowledge* of it.

In Foucaultian terms, acquisition of knowledge is a precondition for control. In Keating's case, with the passing of empire, it is one way of retaining imaginative, if not political, control. Having set his novels in an exotic locale he had never visited, he must have been driven to compensate for his lack of firsthand experience by learning about India from every possible source. He has talked about his exhaustive research and tireless observation of Indian immigrants in London. He studied, among other things, Indian telephone books and railway guides to get a feel for Indian names as well as places (Interview 1983).

Indeed, when I first discovered the Ghote novels in the early seventies, soon after my arrival in the United States, I was drawn to them mainly because of their felt authenticity of detail. Here was an author who did not talk about a generic Indian, as many do, but understood the immense cultural and linguistic gulf that exists between Indians from different states and different castes. The differences are invariably manifested in the details of dress, manners, speech, and nomenclature. Keating gets these details right, thus avoiding the mistake many seasoned India observers like Ruth Prawer Jhabvala make, of writing about India as if it were a homogenized whole, as if there is such a thing as an Indian psyche, a subject of much ethnocentric generalization by the West.

Visitors to India often see selected parts of India, mostly erstwhile princely states in the north and the major cities – Delhi, Bombay, and Calcutta – and blithely proceed to make assumptions about the whole. What many writers fail to take into account is that India is a loose federation of states, divided along linguistic lines, each with a distinct culture. Added to these often irreconcilable regional differences are the nearly rigid lines drawn according to the intricate caste system which functions like the class system in the West. Thus, talking about the typical Indian character is rather like trying to describe a typical European without taking into account the enormous differences, for example, between the French and the Germans. Keating is perhaps the only Western writer I know whose Indian characters are sharply individualized according to their place of origin and their caste.

The most immediately obvious regional and caste differences are to be found in the many varieties of English spoken in India. From the very start of Britain's global colonial enterprise, one major instrument of colonization has been the imposition of English on its subjugated peoples. When Thomas Babington Macauley proposed an English education for Indians, he recognized that the consolidation of the empire necessitated that the bureaucracy, the army, the police, etc., needed to learn just enough English to obey and carry out the dictates of the British government. An authoritative and imaginative use of the language was not part of the bargain. Indians were expected to know enough English to serve as bureaucrats who could oil the engines of quotidian life. This they did while at the same time stamping their newly acquired English with the imprint of a distinctively native syntax, diction and accent. The latter varies according to the region and the social class of the speaker. Thus, an Indian with advanced degrees, especially in the humanities, from the prestigious cosmopolitan universities of Delhi, Calcutta, Bombay, and Madras tends to speak fluent, idiomatic English, while those who receive a technical education from provincial universities bear the strongest influence of their native tongues.

Here the distinction proposed by Ashcroft, Griffiths, and Tiffin between English and english is very useful:

> In order to focus on the complex ways in which the English Language has been used in these societies, and to indicate their own sense of differences, we distinguish in this account between the 'standard' British English inherited from the empire and the english which the language has become in post-colonial countries . . . We need to distinguish between what is proposed as a standard code, English (the

language of the erstwhile imperial centre), and the linguistic code, english, which has been transformed and subverted into several distinctive varieties throughout the world. (*Empire* 8)

Keating has a remarkable ear for the different varieties of english spoken in India, which differ according to region, caste and profession. As far as I know, no other writer has reproduced the multiplicity of english 'dialects' which are imprinted by native languages in terms of accent, syntax, and idiom with such accuracy.

Besides regional differences, the greatest divisive forces in India are rooted in caste distinctions. There are four major castes, with subcastes too numerous to mention here. They are: the Brahmins, the priestly classes; the Kshatriyas, the ruling or military classes; the Vaishyas, the business classes; the Shudras, the lowest, traditionally called the untouchable, classes. These castes, with their rigid hierarchy of power and status, are analogous to the British class system. This is one of the reasons that the British were able to engraft their class consciousness into native soil, with such lamentable results.

Roughly the Brahmins, like the priestly classes everywhere, are the moral arbiters of culture and therefore also receive the mostly scholarly education. The ruling classes acquire enough, usually Western, education to wield economic and military power. The Vaishyas use enough english to successfully conduct business, while the Shudras, relegated to menial labor, are traditionally illiterate. There are a great many other distinctions to be made, and there can be a degree of social mobility between subcastes, but these cannot be gone into in this paper.

Keating's representations of these issues is varied and accurate. For example, in *Inspector Ghote Breaks an Egg*, an early novel written before he visited India, there is a heated exchange between a guru and Ghote, who has dared to bring a box of eggs into the *sanctum sanctorum*: 'It is enough that I have said. Now go. While you are in the room I will fast. Fast to death' (59). The guru obviously regards his utterances as royal proclamations – 'I have said' – which are to be obeyed unquestioningly. As priests, Brahmin gurus wield great power: over men's souls. However, Ghote has enlisted the aid of a Sikh doctor to prevent the guru from fasting to death and causing a religious riot. The Sikh speaks like an upper class British twit, a Bertie Wooster; for example: 'Give me a hand old boy, and we will have something in him in a jiffy. We'd better mix it with a bit of water, digests easier that way' (170).

Then there is a Moslem judge whose precise cadences express an almost Holmesian faith in empirical data, 'I had allowed myself to hope that the expression of plain facts, however few the ears that heard them, would do some good in these hard times, that with lies and corruption all around us a few grains of truth would show up like specks of white in the universal blackness' (*Line* 29). The antithesis of the aristocratic judge is Mr Ramaswamy, a mere cog in India's vast bureaucratic machinery whose stilted formality and whose 'intrusive "e" in front of words beginning with an "s"' proclaim him a Southerner from Madras:

> That is precisely the nature of my occupation. I travel all around the area of the Central Railway and sometimes make forays in other areas, and e-Sir, I inspect the forms kept at my station I choose to descend upon. And of course, the stationary. It is you will agree a curious form of existence. (*Train* 81)

Ghote's own english is a major source of his chronic sense of inadequacy. In *The Sheriff of Bombay*, Ghote is saddled with an aging British film star who wants a tour of the infamous red light district. Douglas Kerr plays the schoolmaster, constantly correcting Ghote's english:

> 'Is it you are pleased to be back once more in India, Mr. Douglas Kerr?'
> 'Prefer to be called Carr, if you don't mind, old boy. Pronounced Carr. Surprised you don't know that, if you are so much a fan of my work as you said you were.'
> 'Oh, yes, indeed, Mr. Douglas Kerr – Mr. Carr. I was always a very, very great admirer of your many feats.'
> 'Only two, old boy.'
> 'Only two feats? But I am thinking...'
> 'Feet. Feet, old boy. Things you have on the end of your legs, don't you know.'
> In a moment or little longer, Ghote had got the joke. He laughed. (7–8)

Any authority that Ghote might possess is constantly undermined by Kerr's schoolmasterish attitude, and Ghote is reduced to playing the role of a bumbling schoolboy. It is a well-known colonial attitude: all natives are to be treated like children. Nearly thirty years after independence, Ghote reprises the role of his forefathers. It never seems to occur to the British that if *they* bothered to learn native languages, which they seldom did, *they* would become the butts of comedy. Keating's representations of India's multitudinous english voices approximate the Russian critic Bakhtin's formulations of 'dialogic' or 'heteroglossic' discourses. According to Bakhtin, the novel form often contains a polyphony of competing or conflicting voices which effectively negate a totalizing, authoritarian 'meaning.' The cultural phenomenon of carnival, in his view, is the theatricalization/ritualization of the interplay of such subversive voices which he terms dialogism. It is during carnival that the marginalized and the powerless act out, through bawdy songs, dances, masquerades and practical jokes, subversive parodies of institutionalized authority. In the American celebration of Halloween, for example, children are allowed to roam about in disguise and indulge in pranks – squashing pumpkins, squirting shaving cream, throwing eggs, etc. – against adults without fear of punishment. It is their one day of freedom from adult authority. Keating depicts such licensed misrule in his portrayal of Diwali, the festival of lights, which celebrates the vanquishing of evil by the god Rama. At the climax of the protracted battle between the demon Ravana and god Rama, a day is set aside for Holi – carnivalesque misrule. During Holi the lower classes and children mock the upper classes and adults, squirt colored powder and water at those who are their social superiors/oppressors. Appropriately enough, Ghote, as the representative of law and order, is pounced on by the revellers:

> Tossing powder by the handful, squirting ink by the bicycle pumpful, they came at him from every side. In seconds he was through, red wet, blue wet, yellow wet. And on to the wetness their colored powders, pink turquoise and orange, clung and smeared. . . . I have deserved this he thought. This is a fit punishment for coming here with my money and telling people how to live their lives. Exactly fit.
> (*Crusade* 226)

This scene, of a police officer becoming an object of derision and, what is more, accepting it as part of licensed anarchy and a 'just' punishment for his own arrogance, is unthinkable in a traditional British mystery. The great detectives – Holmes, Poirot and their descendants – are not exactly known for their humility. Holmes is the epitome of British imperial arrogance: his deification of deductive powers, and his upperclass, very British assumptions, are never shaken by self-doubts. His literary descendants, from Peter Wimsey to Adam Dalgliesh, share Holmes' unquestioned sense of superiority meliorated in varying degrees only by their good manners.

Perhaps Keating's greatest innovation in the direction of post-modernist democratization is the figure of Inspector Ghote. Although he is enshrined in the pantheon of great detectives of literature – Otto Penzler has included an essay by Keating in his book *The Great Detectives* – Ghote's very presence among the heroes of detection like Sherlock Holmes, Lord Peter Wimsey and Roderick Alleyn redefines the concept of greatness. For great in the old traditional sense Ghote is most definitely not. He does not have an imposing physical presence like Holmes, nor is he aristocratic like Wimsey, nor outré in appearance like Poirot. Not only is Ghote's physical presence innocuous, even his intellect does not inspire awe in the reader, his colleagues, or his wife. In fact, everyone Ghote meets tends to have the upper hand over him; he is a much put-upon man. How then has Ghote managed to take his place among the colorful, showy, great detectives of fiction? Ghote is great because he is so intensely, ordinarily human, with all the self-doubts, personal inadequacies, and failures that make up 'humanness' for the majority of people.

Working in a police force modeled on Scotland Yard, forever thumbing through his bible, Hans Gross' *Criminal Investigation*, bullied by his boss, nagged by his wife, perched on that precarious foothold of respectability – the middle class – struggling with an inadequate salary to be a good provider for his elegant wife and a son seduced by western advertisements, hobbled by a cumbersome bureaucracy, pulled in different directions by India's traditional insistence on the primacy of caste and family loyalties, Ghote consistently tries to maintain his integrity as a policeman and as a human being.

But alas, his attempts to define himself as a policeman often run counter to his innate compassion and empathy for the downtrodden. The Indian police force, hamstrung by rigid orthodoxy and antediluvian codes of behavior, requires Ghote to maintain the image of brutal toughness, and Ghote is always afraid of being found too soft-hearted. Thus in the opening chapter of *Inspector Ghote Trusts the Heart*, Ghote has just succumbed to the whiny machinations of a little beggar boy with a withered leg:

> He pulled out the two-paise piece and pressed it hastily, stealthily into the boy's thin-fleshed hard, little expectant hand. There. It was done. Freed of a burden, he swung sharply away and prepared to mount the steps at a trot. 'Ah. It is Ghote. Inspector Ghote.' A cold lurch of dismay froze him into stillness. Spotted. Found out. A hard-hearted inspector of the Bombay C.I.D. seen falling for the totally transparent wiles of a mere boy of a beggar.   (*Heart* 2)

Towards the end of the novel, Ghote solves the case by following up on his own intuition, risking the wrath of his boss, the Commissioner of Police, who had ordered Ghote not to pursue the investigation any further. Ghote is dismissed for insubordination, for 'trusting his heart.' But he manages to find some personal redemption by establishing a brief, human contact with the little boy he had rescued from the kidnappers. He buys a bobbing red balloon and puts it in the hand of the little boy in an attempt to rouse him from his apathy:

> As the ambulance driver waited for his companion to open the back door of their vehicle, Ghote saw the tailor put out a tentative hand to his son and gently touch him. And then at last Pidku smiled. Ghote felt his lethargic gloom sliding away like great, stiff, cakes of dust under the first rain of the monsoon.   (*Heart* 200–1)

Over and over again, Keating registers every twitch of Ghote's psyche as he struggles to retain his humanity and integrity in a brutalizing and corrupt police force. All this intricate construction of Ghote's subjectivity by Keating should make it obvious that Keating is writing, as he has admitted, in E.M. Forster's humanistic tradition: the individual is regarded as the vehicle for resistance and subversion, working *within* what Althusser calls the repressive state apparatus comprising the police force, the judicial system, et al. (Interview 1992). Not for Keating, although writing in the '60s and its aftermath, the post-modern fragmentation of the subject. According to Ihab Hassan, terms beloved of post-modern theory, such as:

> deconstruction, decentering, disappearance, dissemination, demystification, discontinuity, differences, dispersion, etc.... express an ontological rejection of the traditional full subject, the cogito of western philosophy. They express, too, an epistemological obsession with fragments or fractures, and a corresponding ideological commitment to minorities in politics, sex and language. (Hassan 55–6)

Keating, far from rejecting the 'traditional full subject, the cogito of western philosophy,' represents it in all its individualistic, humanistic, liberal avatars. It could be argued that for the colonial subject the post-colonial enterprise *is* recovery: of the cogito, capable of making minimal choices or at least the illusion of choices, an illusion needed to preserve Ghote's sanity and survival. It must be noted that Keating's depiction of a plurality of voices and cultural constructions does not represent any sort of political commitment to minorities *per se*. Rather, it is a derivative of the good old-fashioned Keatsian negative capability, the capacity for the empathetic imagining of the Other.

According to Edward Said, western formulations of the Orient were based on the perception of its colonies as the shadowy Other, the repository of its own darkest fantasies. This perception provided the justification for savage colonial oppression and exploitation. Writing nearly a quarter century after India gained its independence in 1947, Keating's first novel, set in India, originated in the British tradition of using its colonies as a metaphor for its own perceived imperfections. Describing the genesis of his first novel, *The Perfect Murder*, Keating says that the theme of perfection was something he wanted to explore because:

> I am a perfectionist in aspiration but in achievement I am a second best. I am born with a conscience; determined always to do the right thing. So perfection comes from that. So this was one of the possible likenesses that was in my mind. I am sorry to say that I thought of India as being marvelously imperfect, which in many ways it is.
>
> (Interview 1983)

Obviously, Keating balked at using his own country as a metaphor for imperfection. However, to do him justice, Keating has Ghote visit the much idealized England in *Inspector Ghote Hunts the Peacock* only to find that the real England is very different from his romanticized notions of the country, notions based on his reading of English literature. He is bitterly disillusioned by the racism, the police brutality, the general muddle which exists in England. Finally, Keating's post-colonial sensibilities emerge triumphant in his constant spoofing of the conventions of the Golden Age mysteries.

Besides the character of Ghote being the very antithesis of the lofty British detective, Keating's notable innovations lie in parodying the form of the detective novel. While almost every novel has parodic elements, I'll focus on two, one the earliest, *The Perfect Murder*, and the other, *The Body in the Billiard Room*, one of his most recent, in which Keating engages in a complex subversion of the essentially monological, authoritarian form of the traditional whodunit. Linda Hutcheon elucidates the role of parody in rethinking the past:

> Modern artists seem to have recognized that change entails continuity, and have offered us a model for the process of transfer and

reorganization of the past. Their double voiced parodic forms play on the tensions created by historical awareness. They signal less an acknowledgement of the 'inadequacy of the definable forms' of their predecessors (Martin 1980, 666) than their own desire to 'refunction those forms to their needs.' (4)

I suggest that in deciding to transpose his fiction from England to India in the pursuit of a wider market, Keating 'refunctioned' the mystery form to suit his needs as well as India's cultural imperatives. The most notable change lies in Keating's inversion of the conventions of the form, which often follow this pattern: a murder is committed, a body is found, an investigator is called in and questions a limited number of suspects, and after fruitlessly pursuing a number of red herrings, finally solves the crime and exposes the criminal. An upper-class detective often displays a god-like authority about disposing of the criminal. He may decide to let the law take its due course, or if the culprit is socially privileged, let him take his own life in order to prevent the kind of public disgrace that lesser mortals are routinely subjected to.

In *The Perfect Murder*, by contrast, there is no murder. Ghote is called in because the victim has been hit on the head with the proverbial blunt instrument, but in 'imperfect,' notoriously inefficient India, even the attempted murder is botched and the victim lives on, albeit in a coma. Ghote's investigation of this crime is equally wacky, because although Ghote does his best to follow the rules of police procedure, no one respects or obeys him. In this endlessly imperfect world the victim bears the improbable, comically uneponymous name Perfect. He is secretary to a gross, wealthy businessman, Lala Varde, who considers himself above the obligations of ordinary citizens. His imperious wife, Laxmi, and all the other suspects obstruct Ghote at every step for their own devious reasons. As if all these obstacles were not enough, Ghote is entrusted with another case – a laughable one concerning the disappearance of one rupee (about 10 cents) from the desk of a stern minister of the government who treats Ghote like a personal lackey. The final straw that threatens to break poor Ghote's bony back is the fact that a great big Swede, Axel Svenson, from UNESCO attaches himself to Ghote in order to study Indian police methods.

Svenson blunders after Ghote like a bumbling St Bernard, adding to Ghote's problems, but a genuine friendship develops between them when Ghote risks being a little late for an appointment with the fanatically punctual Minister for Police Affairs in order to help his Watson/ Svenson – thus once again putting humanness above an abstract idea.

Nature plays its own inexorable role, adding to the general muddle in India: a heat wave is on, a prelude to the spectacular tropical thunderstorm which, when it breaks, clears the muddle in Ghote's own mind, and helps, in a burst of brilliant insight, to solve the case. The solution, like the crime, is absurd in its imperfection, but the very imperfection is responsible for saving a life. Keating's consistent parodying of the British whodunit works on a structural level to highlight his philosophical theme that relating to a fellow human being is more important than a mechanical perfection and efficiency.

Keating's love of spoofing the conventions of detective fiction reaches its comic apotheosis in *The Body in the Billiard Room*. As the title indicates, the novel is ostensibly in the tradition of the golden age of mystery fiction, suggesting neatly murdered bodies behind closed doors in an upper-class sporty setting, much given to displays of hunting, fishing, and snooker trophies. Ghote is sent by his boss to the very British hill resort of Ooty in South India, where the relics of the British empire huddle together in an exclusive club, warming themselves at the embers of rituals left over from the heyday of the Raj.

When Ghote arrives in Ooty after a long, carefully described bus journey through the winding hills, he realizes he has come to a fairytale world which could be either, in his words, 'paradise Ooty, hell Ooty' (24). It feels like paradise because the cool air of the hill station reminds him that he has escaped the 'heat of the turbid plains' into a magical world which seems ye olde world England, full of neat little tiled cottages covered with climbing roses, with names like Glen View, Harrow-on-the-Hill, Woodbriar, Stella Cottage, Dahlia Bank, Clifton Villa, and so on, with all its attendant sense of law and order of which the British like to think they are the very source and fount. At the station, he is met by a former Ambassador, His Excellency Surinder Mehta, who had asked for Ghote's services on the strength of the praises sung about him by that 'fool of a British writer' (10) who had once watched him at work. This sly reference to Keating occurs again later on in the novel when one of Keating's own mysteries, published under the pseudonym Evelyn Hervey, becomes instrumental in providing Ghote with an important clue.

This self-referential spoofing of mystery fiction provides the deep structure of the novel, the rigid spine of which is His Excellency, Surinder Mehta, an ardent fan of the genre who can not only quote chapter and verse from the golden age of detective fiction, but constantly confuses the reality of murder with the fantasies of crime spun by mystery writers. Ghote, whose knowledge of detective fiction is sketchy at best, is forced into a role which, given his innate realism and modesty, makes him very uncomfortable – the role alternately of Sherlock Holmes or Hercule Poirot, with the former Ambassador as his Dr Watson or In-spector Lestrade. In the topsy-turvy world of Ooty where fiction and reality overlap, the roles of detective and sidekick are also reversed, with Mr Mehta in his role of Watson directing the precise moves to be made by his superior, Holmes.

Ghote's sense of unreality is further heightened when he is informed that nothing is to be gained by the normal police procedures of search-ing the murder site for clues. The body of Picchu, the billiards marker, had been found the day before, carefully laid out on the billiard table, with only a neat little stab wound indicating that he was not merely in an alcohol-induced sleep. To Ghote's consternation, he learns that the local Inspector had not only summarily removed the body, careless of any clues, but in addition, had not ordered a post mortem and had declared that the murder was committed during a robbery, or in Indian parlance, a decoity, of the silver sporting trophies which it was part of Picchu's duties to guard. But Mr Mehta insists that it could not have been a run-of-the-mill robbery because of the orderliness with which the murder was committed and the body disposed on the table. Playing his self-appointed role as the Great Detective's stooge, Mehta has found out that Picchu was a nasty piece of goods and, judging from his luxurious possessions, a blackmailer as well. So Mehta is determined that the murder should conform exactly to the pattern used over and over again by Dame Agatha Christie: 'Yes. Just like in the books. The circum-stances that make it clear that only a limited number of suspects could have committed the crime.... The situation here is precisely that of a Christie story' (22–3). Mr Mehta also insists on seeing the club as a snowbound manor house as in Christie's *Sittaford Mystery* and its mem-bers as the seven suspects in a Michael Innes novel.

Ghote tries to retain his sanity in this inspired craziness by stubbornly clinging to the humdrum police procedures of interviewing the suspects and applying logic to what turns out to be a tangled web of irrational, thoroughly human, unpredictable behavior by the club members. *The Body in the Billiard Room* does not pretend to be a fully-fleshed, realistic novel. Its characters are not merely stereotypes; rather, they are broadly drawn caricatures, milked for all their comic potential. There is the Maharajah of Pratapgadh who insists on making Ghote his golfing partner, and who cheats blatantly, counting on Ghote's ignorance of the rules of the game. His luscious but bitchy wife, the Maharani, carries on an affair with an indigent student in a sordid hotel and is self-righteously indignant when she learns about her husband's liaison with a well-known film star. There is the corpulent Moslem Habidulla, who eats only dessert – roly-poly pudding – and nothing else. There is Miss Lucy Trayling who thinks of England as home but stays on to nurse her ailing ayah, exhibiting the self-proclaimed British traits of loyalty and courage in the face of adversity. Then there is Major Bell, the winner of a coveted award for his prowess in snooker, who lives alone with his decrepit dog in a decrepit house. Then there is Mr Iyer, the secretary who recalls P.G. Wodehouse's fictional character, the efficient Baxter. Finally, there is the Professor of English literature, named, tongue in cheek, Godbole, after the character in E.M. Forster's *A Passage to India*, who discourses learnedly on the archetypal nature of the Great Detective: 'Holmes is a person, a super-person one might say, of a unique sort. He is a man able to combine at the highest level the intuitive powers of the poet with the powers of logical analysis of the mathematician' (77).

It is Godbole, professor and high priest, who educates the empirical, logical policeman, Ghote, to entertain the heady freedom of poetic insights. Ghote, stubbornly resistant to intuitive flights, thanks to his British police training, admits defeat after deductive analysis of all the tortuous trails of shameful secrets and blackmail and other evidence fails to solve the identity of the murderer. On the verge of giving up and returning to crowded, chaotic, but very real Bombay, Ghote is persuaded to attend a lecture on the Great Detective by Godbole. Ghote finds himself listening to his words with fascinated concentration:

'We are, are we not,' the little Brahmin said, favouring his scattered audience with a sharply wicked grin, 'each one of us trapped? Trapped within our own personalities. Over the years we build up in our minds a picture of ourselves. A picture of a person we can bear to live with, perhaps often a person of whom we are secretly proud...but a picture that we create for ourselves in this way has a most terrible effect. It places round us limits. It lays down for us rules, rules we dare not break even though they are rules we alone have devised. But the Great Detective...Ah the Great Detective, he – or sometimes she – in the pages of those books we delight to read, can by the force of genius show us these rules being broken. He shows us that the prisons we make for ourselves can be escaped from...Yes, the Great Detectives, whilst we read with simple pleasure of the triumphs, can teach us by the secret ways of imaginative writing that it is possible to escape from the prisons, the locked rooms, imposed on us by our own egos. Now, what is one of the ways, perhaps the most striking in which this lesson is presented to us? Why, by the simple, and always intriguing device of disguise. In that notable tale *A Scandal in Bohemia* we read of Mr Sherlock Holmes disguising himself as a drunken groom, making himself – note – wholly into a person smelling equally of the horse and the bottle. And we realize then, without realizing that we have realized it, that other people exist . . . He has to recognize, for himself and for us also, that the whole outside world is there. A world beyond him, a world of the other.' (196–7)

Godbole's speech has a galvanizing effect on Ghote's spirits. He sets out to put himself in the proper meditative frame of mind suitable for sparking the intuitive leap which transcends the built-in limitations of logic. To do this he has a choice of two techniques – Indian and Western. Indian by birth and upbringing but Western by virtue of his police training, Ghote can choose either the Hindu discipline of yoga or some of the techniques of Sherlock Holmes: both are aids to achieving a trance-like state of mind conducive to free association.

There are comic descriptions of Ghote sitting in the lotus position and concentrating on the tip of his nose – as recommended by Dr Joshi in his book on yoga. Having failed to achieve *dharana* or yogic trance, Ghote decides to try the 'Great Detective way' – smoking a pipe à la Sherlock Holmes. Ghote buys a cheap pipe and tobacco (because Spencer's Stores is 'Sunday-closed') from a street vendor and doggedly puffs away as he strolls around Ooty wondering, 'Should he try combining pipe yoga with Dr Joshi's? Concentrating perhaps, not on the tip of his nose, but on the smoke-curling bowl of his pipe?' (229). Nothing happens except that after leaving the town, he wanders into more rugged country where 'wooded ravines,' and a 'silver stream' put him in mind of wild beasts. A combination of cheap tobacco and rarefied mountain air make him feel giddy and nauseous. Pausing to rest on a rock, throwing away the pipe in disgust, he again savors bitter defeat. Finally, wandering back to the town, his mind empty of thought, he hears the chimes of St Stephen's Church. Standing still in appreciation, he realizes that he has experienced the 'Great Detective's trance' and 'the knowledge of who it was who had been Picchu's poisoner had flowered in his mind. Everything had mysteriously come together at the very back of his head, in the innermost recesses' (229).

Ghote lays his chain of largely circumstantial evidence before the Ambassador and, because he has no actual proof that would hold up in a court of law, decides to confront the murderer and extract a confession. In true implausible British mystery fiction manner, the murderer, a true Brit to the last, acknowledges his guilt and obligingly shoots himself. A dignified exit in British upper-class tradition, immortalized by Shakespeare in his description of the traitor Thane of Cawdor's conduct during his execution: 'Nothing in his life became him like the leaving of it' (*Macbeth* i.iv. 7–8). Of course, such dignity in death is not allowed the lower orders, who are unceremoniously hauled off to be tried and hanged.

In real life there are several less noble, more plausible solutions to upper-class crime: first, it is very seldom that a crime is brought home to a member of the ruling class, and second, even if it is, his peers ensure that it is covered up so that the dignity of the individual and, by extension, of the whole class is preserved intact. They have the education and writing skills to construct an elaborate mythology which ensures not only the maintenance of their status quo but the very self-aggrandizing myths which help them to stay in power and exploit the masses. However, to apply the constraints of painful social realities to such a frothy concoction as *The Body in the Billiard Room* is, according to the Bard, to taste with a distempered appetite and mistake bird bolts for cannon bullets. Indeed, in Keating's hands, the rigid format of the classic detective novel becomes capable of yielding extraordinary flights of fancy and imagination which ironically yield greater, if fitful illuminations into the dark, often impenetrable interstices of life. As a parody of all the elements of the classic British mystery, *The Body in the Billiard Room* perfectly captures not only the coexistence of British and Indian cultures but also their mutual transformations, the sea changes resulting from the collision of east and west.

Finally, and perhaps most important of all, Keating's Ghote novels, while liberating the genre and the detective from its British stereotype, manage to convey the felt authenticity of how people manage to live out their daily lives, relating to fellow human beings in all their flawed humanity in spite of intolerable historical forces not of their own making. For surely, for the majority of human beings, history is not experienced as 'history' i.e., a succession of events shaped by forces beyond their control, but as it affects the fabric and texture of daily life and relationships. As Raymond Williams has pointed out, 'Every aspect of personal life is radically affected by the quality of the general life, yet the general life is seen at its most important in completely personal terms.'

And Keating is able to see general life in India in personal terms because, rather than imagining the colonial 'other,' Keating identifies with Ghote. As he has admitted in a recent interview with me, Keating places before Ghote moral dilemmas he would like to explore and 'asked myself what I would do in a terrible dilemma...I know that I wouldn't do necessarily the right thing' (Interview 90). In other words, Ghote responds as Keating would, to a specific moral problem. When I pointed out during the interview that he had made 'a clear identification between your [his] psychological make-up and Ghote's,' Keating's reply was an unambiguous 'Yes, I think it is there.'

Keating's decision to write about India from an Indian's point is problematic in the best as well as the worst sense. It *is* an act of hubris after all for the descendant of colonizers to think that he can write from the point of view of the formerly colonized. This is analogous to William Styron's decision to write from the point of view of an insurgent black slave, Nat Turner. However, I would argue that to discount an author's ability to imagine the other from the inside is too simplistic and places an unwarranted constriction on the artistic process itself. We would have to disregard the great female characters created by men, from Chaucer's *Wife of Bath* and Shakespeare's *Cleopatra* down to Joyce's Molly Bloom. Surely, the test is how well an author can imagine the other, and hubris can be forgiven if he/she pulls it off, as it were.

Well, Keating does. That is primarily because, as he has admitted in his interview with me, he *identifies* with Ghote. Not only does Keating explore philosophical/moral themes through Ghote, but Ghote embodies the distinctly unheroic social self not admissible in a detective/protagonist in traditional mysteries. In British self-representations, the so-called heroic virtues are class-related. Style, elegance, stiff upper-lipped self-mastery, and its corollary, imperial mastery of others, are all British upper-class attributes. Wherever diffidence, self-consciousness, a personal sense of inadequacy and its comic possibilities appear, they are represented as attributes of the underclass. On the British social map, they are classed as failures.

It is tempting to speculate that Keating's self-perception as a 'gentle failure' was partly responsible for his identification with Ghote, who, though very successful as a detective, would still be counted as a social failure by British upper-class standards. In other words, the creation of Ghote liberated Keating psychologically, politically, and, perhaps most important, artistically.

Keating may not have made these innovations in form and theme if he had stuck to England and an English detective. A Holmesian, insular, homogeneity is impossible in a country like India which, despite a hundred years of British rule and the legacy of its judicial, educational, and parliamentary systems, has managed to retain its hydra-headed identity. It is this multiplicity and its paradoxical yet distinct unitary identity, forged mainly in *opposition* to the west, that Keating has grasped and portrayed. The multitudinous voices, the varieties of english spoken by Ghote and his fellow countrymen and women transform the linear, totalizing, hegemonic logic of the traditional British novel into its post-colonial avatars.

This is not to say, however, that hierarchy, marginalization, etc., do not re-form with a distinctively Indian face. To hear theorists talk, post-colonial fiction and, by implication, the worlds it represents, has done away with the center, with hierarchy and marginalization. This is utopian wishful thinking fuelled by fashionable winds blowing in the top echelons of academia, itself a class-ridden, highly hierarchized place both in its left and right wings. Lived reality is different. The evils of colonialism are often mimicked by the evils of post-colonialism. This is analogous to the way theoreticians in academia couch their 'radical' theories in such esoteric jargon that it functions like a code by which the initiated retain their exclusive membership and exclude those who would benefit most from their supposedly equalizing agenda. After all, Caliban learned Prospero's language so well he re-enacted his master's script with Stephano and Triniculo. The burden of post-colonial theoretical jargon might just turn out to be the final straw on poor Ghote's 'thin and bony shoulders.' Have I just laid it on him? Oh well, I was asked to contribute this paper, and the *praxis* of my profession has to take precedence over his.

Bibliography

Althusser, Louis. *Lenin and Philosophy*. Trans. Ben Brewster. New York: Monthly Review P, 1971.

Ashcroft, Bill, Gareth Griffiths, and Helen Tiffin. *The Empire Writes Back*. London: Routledge Kegan Paul, 1989.

Bakhtin, Mikhail. *Rabelais and His World*. Trans. Helane Iswolsky. Cambridge, Mass: MIT P, 1968.

———. *The Dialogic Imagination*. Trans. Caryl Emerson, Michael Holquist, ed. Austin, Texas: U of Texas P, 1981.

Forster, E.M. *A Passage to India*. New York: Harcourt Brace, 1924.

Foucault, Michel. *The Archaeology of Knowledge*. Trans. Alan Sheridan. New York: Pantheon, 1972.

Hassan, Ihab. 'The Critic as Innovator: The Tutzing Statement in X Frames.' *Amerikastudien* 22.1 (1977): 47–63. Qtd. in Patrick Brantlinger. *Crusoe's Footprints*. London: Routledge Chapman Hall, 1990.

Hutcheon, Linda. *A Theory of Parody*. New York: Methuen, 1985.

Keating, H. R. F. *The Body in the Billiard Room*. New York: Viking, 1987.

——. 'Inspector Ghote and the British Author.' *Winter Crimes* 7. Ed. George Hardinge. London: Macmillan, 1975.

——. Interview by Meera Tamaya. *Clues* 4.2 (Fall/Winter 1983). Rpt. Tamaya 1993. 105–33.

——. Interview by Meera Tamaya. *Clues* 13.2 (Spring/Summer 1992). Rpt. Tamaya 1993: 135–51.

——. *Inspector Ghote Breaks an Egg*. New York: Doubleday, 1971.

——. *Inspector Ghote Draws a Line*. New York: Doubleday, 1979.

——. *Inspector Ghote Goes by Train*. New York: Doubleday, 1972.

——. *Inspector Ghote's Good Crusade*. New York: Dutton, 1966.

——. *Inspector Ghote Trusts the Heart*. New York: Doubleday, 1972.

——. *The Perfect Murder*. New York: Dutton, 1965.

——. *The Sheriff of Bombay*. New York: Doubleday, 1984.

Said, Edward. *Orientalism*. New York: Pantheon Books, 1978.

Scott, Paul. *The Jewel in the Crown*. London: Pan Books, Heinemann, 1966.

Tamaya, Meera. 'H. R. F. Keating.' Ed. Earl F. Bargainnier. *Twelve Englishmen of Mystery*. Bowling Green, OH: Bowling Green U Popular P, 1984. 276–301.

——. *H. R. F. Keating: Post-Colonial Detection: A Critical Study*. Bowling Green, OH: Bowling Green U Popular P, 1993.

Williams, Raymond. 'Realism and the Contemporary Novel.' *Partisan Review* 20.1: 200–13.

Mystery Novels by H. R. F. Keating:

Death and the Visiting Firemen. Gollancz, 1959.
Zen There Was Murder. Gollancz, 1960, Penguin, 1963.
A Rush on the Ultimate. Gollancz, 1961, rep. Doubleday, 1982.
The Dog It Was that Died. Gollancz, 1962, Penguin, 1968.
Death of a Fat God. Collins, 1963, Dutton, 1966.
The Perfect Murder. Collins, 1964, Dutton, 1965, rep. Academy Chicago, 1983.
Is Skin-Deep, Is Fatal. Dutton, 1966.
Inspector Ghote's Good Crusade. Dutton, 1966.
Inspector Ghote Caught in Meshes. Collins, 1967, Dutton, 1968, rep. Academy Chicago, 1985.
Inspector Ghote Hunts the Peacock, Dutton, 1968, rep. Academy Chicago, 1985.
Inspector Ghote Breaks an Egg. Collins, 1970, Doubleday, 1971, rep. Academy Chicago, 1985.
Inspector Ghote Goes by Train. Collins, 1971, Doubleday, 1972.
Inspector Ghote Trusts the Heart. Collins, 1972, Doubleday, 1973.
Bats Fly Up for Inspector Ghote. Collins, 1974, Doubleday, 1975.
A Remarkable Case of Burglary. Collins, 1975, Doubleday, 1976.
Filmi, Filmi, Inspector Ghote. Collins, 1976, Doubleday, 1977.
Inspector Ghote Draws a Line. Doubleday, 1979.
The Murder of the Maharajah. Doubleday, 1980.
Go West, Inspector Ghote. Doubleday, 1981.
The Sheriff of Bombay. Doubleday, 1984.
Mrs Craggs: Crimes Cleared Up. Buchan & Enright, 1985.
Under a Monsoon Cloud. Viking, 1986.
The Body in the Billiard Room. Hutchinson, 1987.

Dead on Time: An Inspector Ghote Mystery. Mysterious P, 1989.
The Iciest Sin. Mysterious P, 1990.
The Rich Detective. Mysterious P, 1993.
Cheating Death. Mysterious P, 1994.
Doing Wrong. Penzler, 1994.
The Good Detective. Scribner, 1995.
The Bad Questions. Macmillan, 1996.
Asking Questions. St. Martin's P, 1997.
In Kensington Gardens Once. Crippen and Landen, 1997.
(Keating has also published at least seven other novels, eight volumes of non-
    fiction, including *Inspector Ghote, His Life and Crimes,* edited at least four books,
    written radio and screen plays, and contributed to many collections and maga-
    zines.)

3

James McClure's Mickey Zondi: The Partner of Apartheid

Edward Tomarken

James McClure's most recent police procedural involving the partnership of the South African police detectives Tromp Kramer and Mickey Zondi, *The Song Dog* (1991), is a 'prequel,' according to the book cover, because although the most recent of the series, it takes place when the partnership was first formed. In fact, *The Song Dog* can be understood as an explanation of how and why Kramer and Zondi got together. This partnership, which has served McClure for the past 20 years as a vehicle for exposing apartheid, has in this latest narrative become itself a focal point. The reason for this new interest is, I would speculate, that the Kramer–Zondi relationship suggests how Whites and Blacks can maintain their difference from one another while working together for the improvement of South African culture. I therefore propose to follow McClure's insight – that the biggest lie of apartheid is that Blacks and Whites can be understood apart from one another – and analyze Zondi in terms of his relationship to Kramer.

I shall begin at the end with *The Song Dog*, the story of how the partnership began, and then examine how this relationship progresses in the earlier stories, keeping in mind that the recent publication date of *The Song Dog* indicates that what for McClure had been a means has now become an end in itself. *The Song Dog* is roughly divided into two halves, the first half in which Kramer and Zondi, working apart, are led astray, and the second section beginning with the formation of the partnership and ending with the solution of both of the crimes. Yet these two crimes are completely unrelated, a fact made clear in apartheid terms in that one is being investigated by a White and the other by a Black. A young detective with little experience outside the big city, Kramer has been sent to the 'bush,' where an Afrikaner detective like himself and a white woman married to an English-speaker have been murdered in suspicious circumstances. Zondi, on the other hand, has come to the same location in pursuit of a Black, also like himself: Matthew Mslope attended missionary school with Zondi, where they were taught that Christian virtue would right the world's wrongs. Disillusionment led to Mslope's murdering a nun, and Zondi, disguised as one of the locals, is searching for him.

Working apart, neither has made much progress. Kramer has been misled by the local police protecting the reputation of one of their own, and Zondi is little closer to the trail of Mslope. When by accident their paths cross and Kramer discovers that Zondi is an undercover policeman who may be useful to him, they begin to make progress on both fronts. At this point, the reader might expect the two crimes to come together, that a 'revolutionary' like Matthew Mslope might well murder a white policeman and a white female establishment member, like the victims of Kramer's case. But, typical of McClure, these initial expectations are thwarted. In fact, the victims in Kramer's case turn out to have been involved in adulterous sex when they were murdered by a jealous white Afrikaner policeman. Here McClure is exposing the complications of the hierarchy among the Whites, the fact that the Afrikaner with most of the political and social power lacks the social cachet of the English speaker. Zondi's case also thwarts traditional expectations. Mslope is not really on the run; he is haunted by the Zulu belief that the unavenged murderer poisons the spirits of his ancestors. Zondi arranges to dispatch Mslope under the guise of self-defense in order to put his former schoolmate out of his misery and free the spirits of his relatives.

If it now seems that Kramer's and Zondi's worlds are inevitably separate, that is precisely McClure's point. On the surface, that would appear to be the case, but a deeper analysis reveals a subtle relationship. Neither detective can solve his case without the direct interference of the other. When Kramer finally realizes that the crime has been committed by a fellow Afrikaner policeman, he is held at gunpoint by the murderer and has to be rescued by Zondi's marksmanship. But after this episode, since Zondi has just shot one man, Kramer offers his gun to Zondi for the execution of Mslope so that the second death will be attributed to Kramer and no questions will arise about two recent fatal shootings being connected to Zondi – particularly as one of the victims was a white man. Distinction remains but requires co-operation: collaboration respects rather than erases difference. McClure makes this point most vividly in one of the most hilarious scenes of *The Song Dog*, Zondi's visit to the songoma, the Zulu prophetess. Here McClure makes clear how

Black and White cultures overlap in South Africa without loss of difference. The Afrikaner policeman victim of the crime assigned to Kramer is
known to have received important information from the songoma, but
Kramer is not familiar enough with Zulu customs to risk such a visit.
Instead he sends Zondi, who 'had been greatly relieved, because visiting
a *songoma*, more especially one of such extraordinary repute as Mama
Pelapela, called for a show of respect that most Whites would find too
humiliating even to attempt, thus jeopardizing everything' (170). Zondi
gains access to the songoma, who is vividly described as 'gap-toothed,
face wrinkled like the knee of a rhino, flat withered breasts, three
inflated bladders knotted above her left ear, a long black skirt, and
dozens of copper rings around her swollen ankles. She was eating sar-
dines and condensed milk, mixed, from a tin plate with a dessert spoon'
(172). Zondi manages to extract the necessary information from this
bizarre prophetess with a compliment: ' "you have the light in your eyes
of a young maiden, compelling me to see you with breasts ripe and full,
and your thighs plump and shiny" ' (174). Even when the information
has been translated by Zondi for Kramer, it requires interpretation to be
properly understood. The songoma had told the policeman to be beware
of his own kind; Zondi understands from the songoma that this information was received by the murder victim not with surprise but with a
shock of recognition, something he already knew but had been trying to
avoid facing. This vital clue suggests to Kramer and Zondi that the
murderer is a colleague of the victim, not a Black revolutionary like
Matthew Mslope. Kramer has enough intelligence and self-possession
to defer to Zondi's superior knowledge, a rare quality among white
South Africans. By contrast, a white priest who treats Zondi with typical
condescension is outwitted by the black detective. In search of Mslope,
Zondi has car trouble and asks assistance of a priest on horseback in the
traditional way. ' "Would it be possible for the master to assist me by
holding the jack in place a moment?" ' While holding the jack, Father
O'Hara corrects Zondi's terms of address, ' "[I] am not your master – only
the Good Lord is that," ' giving Zondi enough time to steal his horse in
pursuit of Mslope (261).

Yet Zondi also needs Kramer's help, a point most succinctly made by
McClure at the climactic point when the Zulu detective saves Kramer's
life. As Zondi raises his pistol Kramer warns the murderer to look back,
but the criminal replies that he is too wise to fall for that old trick.
Kramer quips, ' "Ja, but same as old dogs, it's not easy to teach certain
kinds of people any new ones, hey?" ' Zondi answers, ' "*Hau*, how very
true, Boss," ' causing the murderer to turn and receive his fatal wound in

the front, not the back. By this means the black detective can claim that he shot the white policeman in self-defense. For McClure, the Zondi–Kramer relationship is a microcosm of South African apartheid culture of the 1970s, since he makes clear that the action of this novel takes place when Kramer was a 'rookie.' A marriage of difference, Zondi and Kramer need one another as do the Black and White segments of South African society, but *The Song Dog* ends on an ominous and ambiguous note. Kramer and Zondi make reference to the songoma's prediction that they will 'stand arm in arm in a black township wearing red necklaces' (274). Is this a reference to the method of execution used by Blacks on those whom they consider to have betrayed their own kind? Kramer and Zondi are in a precarious position. They must maintain the outward appearance of separation, while covertly forming a bond of co-operation that enables them to do their job successfully. But the slightest hint of this bond could result in Zondi's being seen as a turncoat or Kramer as a 'nigger-lover.' Apartheid is their best and only protection from the discovery of the opposite, a partnership of mutual respect. Now, in 1998, as ex-prisoner and now-President, Nelson Mandela struggles to relieve centuries of South African tribal and racial tensions and prevent a Rwanda-like explosion, the Kramer–Zondi relationship seems an appropriate focal point for fiction that points to history.

How did the Kramer–Zondi relationship progress from means to ends? To answer that question we have to go back to the first novel, *The Steam Pig* (1971), and analyse how this series of police procedurals culminates with *The Song Dog* (1991). At the outset of *The Steam Pig* the two South African worlds overlap: the murder victim appears to be a white woman who has been executed by way of a bicycle spoke, a method favored by black gangs. We are introduced to Zondi when he sneaks a look at the picture of the corpse of the victim – illegal since at this time Blacks were not permitted to see photographs of naked Whites – with a description of his Frank Sinatra-like demeanor and his uncanny laugh when Kramer quips, ' "Cheeky Black bastard." ' In this terse manner, McClure indicates that Kramer extends special privileges to Zondi. In the next chapter we discover why Kramer permits this risky behavior. Zondi discovers important new evidence at the victim's flat, a discovery he alone is able to make because of his previous experience as a 'houseboy.' But Zondi is equally adept with those of his own kind who have become petty criminals. In the course of questioning a Zulu petty criminal, Zondi reveals his ability to maneuver within this illicit realm. 'Gershwin nodded – then, noticing a quick movement, used his heel to grind the tobacco into the ground. A black urchin, who made his living by rolling smokes out of stubs, slunk back onto the courthouse verandah' (70). While Gershwin is providing vital information to the case, Zondi is able to show that he knows that Gershwin is trying to maintain his position above the 'black urchin,' and when the interrogation is over Zondi tips a packet of cigarettes within reach of the little 'scavenger' who had been thwarted by Gershwin. Zondi recognizes that his ability to extract information from the likes of Gershwin is dependent upon his maintaining the upper hand. Thus McClure introduces us to two separate South African cultures that surreptitiously overlap in the private context of Kramer's office.

It is therefore particularly appropriate that the murder victim is a woman who is killed because she tried to cross the color line. Theresa le Roux was a child of a reclassified family. Born white, she was reclassified when her father was discovered to have 'black blood.' She decides to use specially tinted contact lenses to change her eye-color – the only outward appearance of her 'colored' status – and becomes a white prostitute much sought after by members of the white establishment. When her brother, who has been unable to cross the color line, jealously reveals the truth about his sister, the Whites panic because it may be revealed that they have crossed the color line. At the end it is revealed that the term steam pig was the code name used by the Whites for Miss Le Roux, who carried on her trade by using music at once to cover up the sound and to set the pace of her rhythmical 'chuff, chuff.' *The Steam Pig* is the story of the fate of one who is discovered trying to cross the color line, an explanation of why Kramer and Zondi must maintain their proper place in their respective hierarchies and be extremely discreet about their private disregard for this pigment barrier. Ironically, McClure makes clear, they would never have been able to solve the crime had they not themselves crossed the color line and been aware of how common such occurrences are, particularly because there is a sexual thrill attached to it. Where political and sexual repression coincide, great danger lurks: Kramer and Zondi are walking a fine line. For although together they manage to outwit the brother of the murder victim who had her murdered – and it should be emphasized that it takes both of them, one to distract while the other completes the task – the real culprits remain at large. The members of the town council who have been enjoying Theresa's body in return for approval of building contracts will not be prosecuted. As Kramer points out, there will not be a 'scrap of evidence' when they 'see their lawyers and lose their memories.' The big lie must remain unexposed, allowing the establishment to stay in power: even together Kramer and Zondi have no chance against that sort of political power. At this early point in his career, McClure recognizes that Kramer's and Zondi's crossing of the color line has no political significance. They are able to outwit the murderer of Theresa, but that in large part is because he is her brother and, like her, a victim of reclassification. Those in charge of classification are as much a threat to Kramer and Zondi as they were to Theresa and her brother. At this point McClure seems to be employing Kramer and Zondi to expose the big lie to the reader.

For this reason, McClure turns, in his next novel, from the middle of the society, the level of the 'colored' people, to the top, the English-speaking Whites. *The Caterpillar Cop* (1972) begins with a quintessential upper-crust scene, two young country-clubbers engaging in their first sex. A young Afrikaner has been brutally murdered and castrated on the grounds of a posh country club. Zondi would seem to be completely out of his element here, but in fact as usual he is invaluable, and his presence enables McClure to suggest the relationship between the highest and lowest in the society. Zondi first proves his worth by finding out from black servants that the young murder victim was hated by his servants because he checked their passes, thus leading Kramer to discover that the young man had been a member of an amateur police detective club which functioned for the young Afrikaners like the country club for their English-speaking superiors. By contrast, the reader is given a rare glimpse of Zondi's home life. In a two-room shack shared by seven people, Zondi sleeps on a bed shared by four others, without electricity, indoor plumbing, or telephone. Not only are Black South Africans denied the rudiments of civilization, they are thought not to need them. On his day off, Zondi is asked by his wife to 'put a plank across the bottom of the lavatory door outside. How does the corporation think a modest woman likes to be on that squat pan with everyone looking in under?" (92). The implicit assumption of the Whites is that the Blacks lack modesty, a misunderstanding that undoubtedly stems from the difference in sexual mores. The Whites of South Africa, like those of most other societies, assume that Blacks are more permissive about sexual matters. Difference is classified as less 'civilized,' more 'primitive.' One result is that each level of society is fascinated by the seeming increase in sexual license below them while the level above offers increased prestige. The love/hate complex so obvious between Blacks and Whites is also seen in subtler forms within the white hierarchy. The Afrikaner murder victim had become enamored with an English-speaking girl who as a 'plain Jane' had to stoop below her class. The problem is not merely social but also sexual. Different customs lead to misunderstandings, a point made humorously on Zondi's level.

A witch doctor is refused service in a black bordello when his genitals reveal that he is a health hazard. Enraged, he returns to exact his revenge: the local black constable, Argyle, armed with a spear, is unable to subdue the customer and calls on Zondi for help, but both are nearly overcome until Kramer arrives. 'The beast's [the witch doctor's] massive body lay on its side in a heap, heaving in spasm, with its tail sticking out straight. Not a tail at all, but the shaft of Argyle's spear' (117). But as Zondi points out, Argyle himself was incapable of launching the spear, having had his arm broken by the witch doctor. Clearly, Kramer decided to use the native weapon to avoid 'statements and inquests.' No questions will be asked about Blacks involved in violent and passionate actions in a whore house. Yet we know that the mêlée resulted from this particular black prostitute being more hygienic than many of her white counterparts.

McClure demonstrates that there is a clear correlation between white assumptions about black sexual behavior and hygiene. When Zondi visits Argyle in hospital even he is shocked at the neglect of the black patients. In fact, he places a blood-stained sheet over one of the sleeping patients, knowing that it will be some time before they discover that the body beneath the sheet is warm not cold. Black bodily functions are treated by Whites like plumbing fixtures. By contrast, white genitalia are covered up, and in the white culture their functions are repressed.

The crime in this tale relates to a 'randy' young English-speaking housewife having sex with a friend of her daughter's, but because she is not in the traditional missionary position, an Afrikaner voyeur mistakes the act of sex for one of violence, particularly after his Dutch Reformed priest has reinforced his assumption that respectable white women are always on the bottom. Kramer and Zondi can only solve this crime by mediating between the sexual/hygiene conventions of the black and white cultures. Zondi finds out from the servants that the daughter's guest had been unsuccessful with the daughter and caused a row between the parents. Kramer recognizes that the 'aristocracy' discreetly engages in sexual acts 'unthinkable' to a well-brought up Afrikaner boy and cracks the case by playing upon the upper-crust repression that produces these aberrations. The title, *The Caterpillar Cop*, refers to the fact that biological evidence, the chrysalis of a caterpillar, first directed them to the murderer. McClure's point is biological, for science connects sex and the rest of the body, genetic and somatic cells. White abuse of the black body is symptomatic of their misunderstanding of black sexual conventions and of white 'respectability' that in turn results in white repression.

Zondi and Kramer again combine insights to resolve the case. Zondi sees the connection between the lack of a proper door provided for his wife's outside privy and the neglect of black patients like Argyle. Kramer extracts a confession from the murderer by using a shock technique, knowing that eruption is frequently so triggered among the highly repressed. In anticipation of the question how do Zondi and Kramer gain knowledge of the realm of the culture beyond them, the answer is in their ability to use discrimination for their own purposes. The condescension toward the 'Boers' of the English-speaker who is the murderer reveals a vulnerability that Kramer exploits to extract a confession. And Zondi profits from an unexpected lesson at the mission school: he has a photographic memory because 'the mission where he had been educated could never afford to issue textbooks' (136).

Sex is a constant in McClure's Kramer–Zondi stories because it is the central drive that at once unites and separates Whites and Blacks. *The Steam Pig* shows the socio-political consequences of sexual repression: racial classification leads to prostitution and family murder. *The Caterpillar Cop* demonstrates that the basis of this repression is biological, fear and neglect of the body. *The Gooseberry Fool* (1974) suggests how perverse sexuality is at the base of apartheid. The murder victim in this tale has been equipped with a sophisticated eavesdropping device that enables him to overhear confession in a Catholic church where the priest is suspected of subversion. Although this government spy is unable to produce a shred of evidence for a legal case, he manages to string along the police until he has accumulated enough embarrassing personal/sexual information to blackmail some members of the church. Police paranoia is the source of this 'gooseberry' being eventually murdered by one of those he has been blackmailing.

Meanwhile, Kramer and Zondi are led on a wild goose chase by the authorities, who do not want them exposing an intelligence operation that was illegal and unsuccessful. They are sent after a black servant of the victim who has retreated to one of the black homelands, enabling McClure to give us a glimpse of the hinterlands from which Zondi emerged. Upon his rearrival, Zondi recalls his past:

> The scent of eucalyptus from the blue gums was evocative, taking him back many years to his own mission school in a remote valley in Zululand. There the best dreams of his life had been dreamt; all you had to do, the white nuns had said, was to learn your lessons well,

and then when you grew up, you could be anything you wanted to be. They had been wrong, those stupid, kind women, who believed that all men were brothers, totally wrong, but Zondi could not feel bitter. Unlike his classmate, Matthew Mslope, who had gone back with a mob to burn, pillage, and rape. But Matthew had been wrong too, and Zondi had arrested him, had him hanged. Which was how he met the Lieutenant. And now two wrongs could make a right, whatever Sister Theresa had said. (49)

[Astute readers will note that in *The Song Dog* Mslope is shot, not hanged.] Here McClure is not only preparing the way for *The Song Dog* but also indicating that this story – since this scene occurs early in the narrative – will be devoted to the world of Zondi's origin. We soon learn why Mslope was wrong to turn on the nuns, who were also wrong. Zondi is at first surprised by the demeanour of the people. 'His immediate reaction was instinctive: a prickling along the spine, a tightening of sinew that halted him in his tracks. Then he realized there was nothing ominous in this for not a head turned to inspect him – these were people lost in themselves and totally listless' (71). It soon becomes clear that in this wasteland, the Blacks are totally dependent upon outside government sources for food and water; they are kept listless by a low supply of both. Moreover, even if they were tempted to settle in the dust and attempt to raise their own crops, they are regularly moved without notice. The strongest and ablest workers are in any case sent off to the city to be servants.

So [it was] a natural enough assumption on her part to suppose that the policy with regard to the movement of Africans in and out of white areas could make Shabalala's unsanctioned homecoming a hazardous undertaking. Zondi knew that at the stroke of a clerk's pen, a man could be endorsed out of a city in which he was born to a homeland hundreds of miles away – and that this applied even to such a man as the business tycoon who headed an official township council but was officially classified as a casual labourer. (80)

Even Kramer, who has no political axe to grind, is appalled at the treatment Zondi gets in hospital. 'Here was this bloody little puppy, sitting on his fat arse letting a kaffir run errands for him instead of being there at Zondi's bedside himself, doing all he could. But he would have to be careful' (118). Fortunately, Kramer is wrong about the 'kaffir' in charge of Zondi. He turns out to be a well-educated and competent doctor who quickly recognizes that the problem is 'who shall guard the guard,' more specifically who polices the police. McClure implies that the best guards of the guards are identified by their response to the dilemma of Zondi. The Widow Fourie, Kramer's 'friend,' for instance, upon hearing that Zondi is in hospital, organizes a carload of useful items donated by her neighbors to tide over Zondi's family. By contrast, the wife of one of those responsible for the spying activity is described as follows:

> the colonel's wife, Popsie, [was] a pinch-faced nympho who looked out on the world from between her fine legs. Alas for poor Popsie, her efforts on behalf of her spouse had finally placed her with him on a pedestal where no sane man, whatever his motive, would dare venture. Which had a moral: bitches in heat should never climb lamp-posts, some get stranded and miss all the fun. (123)

Popsie, like the 'gooseberry,' is a product of the sexual conventions of the typical Afrikaner policeman. The result varies from nymphomania to paranoia. McClure's point is that the means of enforcement of the South African racial policy designed to prevent intercourse between Blacks and Whites in fact manifests a fear of sexuality. Hence, the police informer naturally gravitates from spy to voyeur/blackmailer. Nevertheless, McClure does not exempt the English-speaking from his sexual critique; we saw some of their problems in *The Caterpillar Cop*. Here he focuses on the question of who guards the guards, how their enforcement procedures affect their own family lives and, in a more physical way, those of the Blacks who are feared because they are more at ease with their bodily functions.

Snake (1975) moves on from the white policeman to the ordinary Whites. Eve, an Afrikaner soft-porn strip-teaser who performs with a python, is found murdered with her own snake. This opening image announces an exposé of white sexual conventions. Indeed, in the brief conversation before death Eve makes clear that even her immodesty has limits. 'In front of *natives*? That'll be the day!' (11). Actually Eve is murdered by an English-speaker who first killed the python and then used it to strangle her. True to her name, Eve lured on the murderer, then refused his final advances, leading to his frustrated anger and her death. But the appearance here of a separate white sexual realm is, as ever in McClure, illusory; the murderer was raised, particularly in the first five years of his life, not by his own mother but by the black servant. Prohibited from using any overt corporal punishment on her young master, the black woman tried to nurture and discipline him but worried about his peculiar sexual habits. McClure explains his problem by way of a conversation between Kramer and the Widow Fourie concerning her son's Oedipal drives. 'Oedipus is only part of psychopathetics, and it's to do with their consciences. They don't feel guilty and they don't feel sorry for others – why? Because they don't have a mum's care and attention when they are small' (95). Those, on the other hand, who receive proper maternal concern pass through the oedipal phase to normality. Similarly, Zondi and his wife are shown providing the proper kind of nurturing for their children. 'Then he put six handfuls of maize porridge in a pot on the Primus stove, found the bowl, and hunted for the golden syrup. He discovered it in a tin inside another tin that had water in the bottom to keep the ants off. Miriam was a resourceful wife, as her lacy tablecloth of cleverly scissored newspaper showed. And, having domestic details now forced upon him by circumstance, Zondi also admired how she had fashioned a new handle for her flatiron from cotton reels. Miriam, who took in washing and mending, hoped one day – when the electricity was put in – to have saved enough for a steam presser' (46). In spite of the difficult circumstances, Zondi and Miriam provide the requirements for their young: care, nourishment, and a clear sense of responsibility for the children, encouraging them to become responsible to and for others.

In a sense, the image of Eve strangled by her own snake – now that we know that the agent of death was not the snake but the murderer using the snake – is highly appropriate. Eve and the murderer are both the victims of sex without love. She offers it in her nightly performances and he seeks it as a surrogate. The snake coiled, head-to-tail, is a traditional symbol of self-defeating activity. Eve, the tease, dies by way of her own lure, while the murderer kills the object of his desire.

Meanwhile, in the subplot, a group of black revolutionaries is finally exposed because they violate the families of their own followers. For McClure, the family is the crucial unit, particularly if one recalls that the black servant is often a surrogate parent in the white households. Apartheid in this respect divorces children from those who function as their parents – the murderer's family being, in this regard, typical. But even Eve's last thoughts are of her father: 'Pa had always cautioned that one day she would go too far with one of her acts, do something to a man she wouldn't believe possible' (19). If the Afrikaner dies because she toys with animality, the English-speaking murderer kills her out of fear of animality. But the animal here is not the snake but man and woman, who both in their different ways use the snake.

Learning to live with the animal in ourselves, Kramer and Zondi demonstrate, is to respect, not fear our bodies, and to employ, not exploit our basic drives. Apartheid, from this perspective, is much more than the separation of races; it is men and women divided from themselves, an attitude that enables sex to become degraded to a snake and attraction to take the form of murder.

In *The Sunday Hangman* (1977), McClure turns from the town to the country, the veld, to examine the grass roots support of Apartheid, the Boers or farmers in the fields. Here again we see that what appears to be a political position is in fact based upon sex drives and family feelings, less an ideology than frustrated desires that are sublimated by the state machinery. The crime here involves a state machine in a literal sense. The murderer, a comfortable, respectable Afrikaner farmer widower with a daughter, rigs up his own mobile gallows and ritually executes those whom he believes have slipped through the net of the law. Getting his information from foreign books and hearsay from witnesses – since description of the South African official hanging procedure is forbidden by law – the murderer becomes in his own view the agent of the state. The executions are meticulously carried out at the proper official time and with all the expertise and efficiency of the eighteenth-century British hangman. Until the very end, the victims are criminals, in the eyes of the police, and their deaths are attributed to other criminals and of little interest. But Kramer and Zondi discover that this vigilante of justice is in fact working out revenge for his illegitimate child, who was executed by the state on the false testimony of a petty criminal who is one of the early victims of the Sunday hangman. The murderer turns out to be a deeply introverted man who had a sexual relationship with a mother-figure during the war. Many years later, after he had married and fathered a daughter, he was informed that his illegitimate son was in trouble with the law. Anonymously, he hired the best lawyer, but the testimony of the other accused was accepted by the court. After his son was hanged, the reserved farmer took the law into his own hands.

But the real nature of his motivation becomes clear when Kramer meets the murderer's daughter. Home from boarding school and relegated to her room as punishment, a regular occurrence it would seem, this teenager makes such an overt sexual invitation as to embarrass even Kramer. The entire house exudes repression of all sorts, the murderer's obsession about the death of a son he has not seen in 20 years has little to do with the son himself and more to do with his conception, one of the farmer's rare moments of direct sexual expression. By this means McClure is able to suggest that state executions – ironically one of the few instances where apartheid is not practiced, even though most of the victims are black – are, under the cover of justice, really expressions of deep frustrations, suggested by the secret and ritualistic characteristics. The separation from the self, we have already seen, is sanctioned by the state.

At the same time, McClure does not want to suggest that Afrikaners, or even those of the veld, are alone responsible for this situation. The murderer's friend is a foil figure: brought up in the same situation as the murderer, this farmer is a decent, upright, sensitive soul who is kind to his servants and even gives some consideration to those he calls 'abolitionists.' The murderer represents a perversion of the solid Afrikaner-farmer's values, respectable family people who respect the land, its crops and animals, and worship its Creator. Kramer, after all, is of this stock, and he suggests that these sorts of values can go both ways.

Zondi's part in this tale is somewhat truncated. Conveniently, he has been injured at the outset and is for the most part temporarily replaced by a local white policeman until the end. Of course, these farmers have their black servants; Zondi is most useful in communicating with them. Interestingly, he acquires important information from the female servants by using sexual jokes to gain their confidence. ' "You are a wicked woman," he whispered, giving her arm a coarse nudge. "Can you not see how your lustful talk has put ideas into the minds of the young ones?" ' (147). Zondi gains their confidence by showing that he shares with them something not shared in their white masters' homes, an ease and freedom with sexual matters.

In this way McClure is able to suggest that the grass roots for apartheid derive not from unfeeling people who are unaffected by the pain and anguish that their state policies produce. Rather, it should be understood as a strange manifestation of the perversity of those very feelings, the empathy that makes most Afrikaner farmers loyal friends, dependable members of the community, and responsible as well as loving family members. Yet in the end it is Zondi, not Kramer, who saves the life of the young Afrikaner who is to have been the last victim of the Sunday Hangman. Before overturning the mobile gallows, he reflects: 'Perhaps all that theorizing had been too fanciful, too reverent about executions in the way white people often were, trying to turn killing into pulling teeth' (250). Somewhat impulsively, Zondi recklessly turns the steering wheel and ends up not only saving the life of the man in a noose in the rear of the van but also breaking his own leg.

Behind the facade of justice with its cool appearance of impartiality is buried human desire, with which Zondi is in closer touch even than

Kramer, in spite of Kramer's regular visits to the Widow Fourie. Here we need to recall that Zondi first suspects the murderer when he finds that the man's black servant, who knows too much, has been bribed with lovely furniture and special privileges. In a tacit way, even the Afrikaner murderer recognizes that his own black servant is in touch with his deepest motivating forces. Probably for that reason McClure demonstrates that the young Afrikaner who temporarily replaces Zondi – when his bullet wound becomes infected – has himself to be saved by Zondi. The white man – however enlightened and anomalous like Kramer himself – is acculturated to a certain amount of sexual repression not required of the black man. Ordinarily, the result of this distinction in South Africa is that Blacks are thought to be less 'civilized,' less modest, less in need of amenities like a door for the privy. But it is typical of Zondi to exploit such a misunderstanding and make good use of his relative lack of inhibition about drives common to us all.

In *The Blood of an Englishman* (1980), McClure turns to an English-speaking equivalent of the Sunday Hangman. Passion on this upper level of South African society is either totally masked or markedly overt. The former is exemplified by the murderer. In order to keep his reputation intact, he kills one of his fellow RAF pilots who discovers that his colleague's survival was secured by turning in a family of British sympathizers to the Germans. The latter is exemplified by the young woman who manages to lure Kramer into her bed, much to his police partner's disapproval, and who tries unsuccessfully to coax Zondi to call her, not Madam, but Tish. These 'aristocrats' can either attempt to maintain complete discretion or scandalize the middle class. But the price paid for either form of privilege is severe. The murderer and his wife turn to drink and a general numbing of the senses. He becomes a staunch backer of apartheid, as becomes clear from his explanation of the murder victim's background:

> 'fiery little devil Edward...Couldn't wait until we had got things sorted out here, so off he went. Joined the RAF in Rhodesia, got his wings, and that was the last my wife's family saw of him; rather selfish, I thought...came back here and blotted his copybook by starting the Torch Commando...War veterans, y'know. It'd all gone a bit to their heads, this business of having Blacks out there in the desert with them, doing the cooking and the ambulance driving and that. They tried to nip the Nats' plan to implement apartheid in the bud, but not too surprisingly came unstuck.' (92)

The conversation continues with reference to a famous Afrikaner RAF pilot, another member of the Torch Commandos, who was refused a military funeral on the grounds that he had fought for a 'foreign power.' The dramatic split among the Whites after the war is here concisely clarified: those in favor of apartheid also separated themselves from the British allies and eventually formed an alliance with neo-Nazis. The others found themselves aliens in their own country. The female aspect of this division is vividly seen in the contrast between the murderer's wife and Tish. The former, usually in an alcoholic haze, is attracted to the burly earthiness of Kramer and his kind; when she is told that her husband has murdered her brother she finds consolation in the arms of the Colonel, an Afrikaner who is the equivalent of our chief of police. The enforcers of apartheid are thus seen to protect the English-speaking from their own family members and from themselves. Tish, on the other hand, finally returns to England; the explanation is provided succinctly by Zondi's inner response to her request that she call her by her first name, 'impossible.' The subversion inherent in Tish's behavior, her sexual freedom, cannot be sustained in this society.

By contrast, Zondi takes us to a black brothel where a crime has recently been committed. Here we learn some of the subtleties of black sexuality. Since this is one of the best of the black brothels, Zondi expects to see one of the 'true Zulu beauties: a sturdy young heifer with golden-brown skin, full breasts, wide hips and big strong thighs with plenty of lift in them.' Instead he sees a woman who is 'skinny, flat-chested and narrow-hipped as a white woman, and topped it all off with an absurd yellow wig.' This strange creature, Zondi is told, is the favorite, not of the factory workers and laborers, but of the cook boys, garden boys, and drivers who are clearly imitating the taste of their superiors. But in either case, the Blacks are here openly expressing their sexual desires – in marked contrast to the white murderer and his wife. Indeed, Zondi discovers that the crime that has been committed at the brothel is related to the Black's murderer's particular problem that inhibits his sexual satisfaction.

But McClure's point is that the exception in the black community is the rule in the English-speaking white one. The inability of the society to sustain Tish – who only wishes to have a sexual fling with Kramer and be a friend on equal terms with Zondi – is what makes the dilemma of the English-speaker special. The Widow Fourie, as an Afrikaner, can maintain her respectability and carry on a liaison with Kramer. The South African society needs English-speakers at the top of the society to lend an aura of 'poshness' and 'civilization' in an attempt to justify apartheid to the rest of the world. It cannot, however, permit its upper crust the freedom of subversion, restricting not only sexual dalliance but also humor, the sort used by McClure himself.

In *The Artful Egg* (1984), McClure explains indirectly why he lives in England while writing about South Africa. Since I have analyzed this novel in detail elsewhere my remarks here can be brief. The murder victim is a female writer who lives in South Africa while writing against apartheid, a Nadine Gordimer type. She is not only murdered because of her subversive ideas but also because naively she has been supporting artists who pose as subverters in order not to change the society but to tap the lucrative sources of anti-apartheid money. Apparently, many Whites appease their consciences by supporting so-called 'subversives.' McClure's point is that only action distinguishes genuine opposition from such posturing, actions which in all likelihood will result in imprisonment and/or censorship for the writer. Gordimer's international reputation makes her the exception: what about the others, promising writers who were silenced before they achieved any notoriety?

The Artful Egg is pertinent to my subject here in two respects. It explains why South Africa cultivates its English-speakers even if they are paper subversives, and it vividly presents the role of the 'coloured' or mixed race that appears in the South African hierarchy between the Afrikaners and the Blacks. In fact, there is an unexpected relationship between this relatively low caste of people and those at the top. And it should be pointed out that McClure's novels are well populated with Indians and other Asians. The murderers cleverly disguise their crime by way of a red herring involving references to Hamlet. Kramer and Zondi are perplexed; the allusions are explained to them by a professor. Shakespeare epitomizes the culture of the English-speaker, a realm revered by and at one remove from South Africa. Kramer and Zondi, their feet firmly implanted on South African soil, shrewdly see through this subterfuge. But many South Africans never do, like the artful egg. 'Bespectacled, standing five-two-and-a-quarter, slightly bow-legged and as spare as a sparrow's drumstick' (8), Ramjut Pillay, Asiatic Postman 2nd Class, is answerable to his Afrikaner boss but thinks and speaks in relation to the English-speaking culture. His pet phrase in his frequent bouts of frustration, 'There's the rubbing,' is characteristic. Similarly, Ramjut's aspirations are, by way of a correspondence course, to be not a policeman, a position appropriate to an Afrikaner, but a detective, a sleuth in the tradition of Sherlock Holmes. In this role Pillay gets involved in the case to no purpose: he in fact pursues the red herring. In the end, even though he has broken the law, Kramer releases him like a harmless bird. Pillay believes in the culture of Shakespeare which contributes to his being above Zondi in the social hierarchy while remaining below Kramer and powerless. Probably one reason the 'coloureds' were given their own legislature and the vote was because their high 'British' aspirations help make them content or at least not overtly dissatisfied with their nearly powerless position. In short, McClure demonstrates that apartheid uses English-speaking culture in precisely the way the murderers tried to use allusions to *Hamlet*, as a distraction from the grim reality. Indeed, the 'coloured' or 'mixed blood' Parliament is itself a distraction from politics; the vote there is an empty one since it has no effect upon the conduct of affairs.

For this reason, Pillay's detection to no purpose, his chicken-like scurryings, contrast with Zondi's actions. When one of the murderers addresses Zondi as 'nigger' and 'boy' and physically attacks him, the Zulu detective uses his razor to remove two of the gunman's fingers. In the end, Zondi and Kramer overcome the English-speaking murderers by physical means. Their lack of understanding of this high culture – the web that entangles Ramjut Pillay – enables them to bring to justice criminals who regard their opponents as a 'nigger' and a 'kaffir-lover.' And McClure is left with Kramer and Zondi as the subject of his latest story because he has made clear that South Africa must make its own culture, even if it be, like all others, a combination of its predecessors. But the genuine nature of any culture must be related to its soil and indigenes, not the product of another land. Why then are we not left with only Zondi, since he is the only real indigene? McClure once explained in a conversation we had a number of years ago that the English-speakers can always go back to the old country, as he has done. But the Afrikaner has no home but South Africa; he does not belong and would not be welcomed in Holland. Moreover, the Boers, a term that means farmer, have become a part of the land and have developed a culture – however unjust and incomplete – from and upon the land. Therefore, McClure believes that the hope for a peaceful end to apartheid is something for the Afrikaner and Black to work out. Present-day political events suggest he was right. The question remains as to whether or not these ethnic groups can work out in larger political terms what Kramer and Zondi have negotiated between one another as individuals.

We come then to Zondi's dream at the end of *The Song Dog*. 'The Song Dog also warned that one far-off night, Lieutenant, you and me would stand alone together, arm in arm in a black township, wearing red necklaces as bright as petrol flames' (274). Is this the promise of a sequel, a tale of a new crime to be solved, or does it presage the black community turning on Zondi and Kramer for their refusal to abide by racial boundaries? Is the relationship between these two South African policemen merely an anomaly that has survived by way of discretion and luck or is it a microcosm of the society as a whole if it is to evolve out of apartheid intact? The end is Zondi's dream/nightmare, in that the future of South Africa involves just such a choice. No one will dispute that the future cannot maintain the status quo. McClure's rebuttal is to assert that those on the far right who say, as did one of its spokesmen recently, 'we will share the land with the Blacks but not the power,' are laboring under a delusion. Some power has always been shared, even if it is heavily masked. The Zondi–Kramer partnership shows us that the society would not have been able to maintain law and order without some tacit sharing. Moreover, the reserve power of the ghetto, that of the burning necklace, is an ever-present threat and reminder of the power that, for the most part, has been restrained and shared in an unequal partnership.

McClure's last two police procedurals conclude by focusing on his own means as a writer, the reason for his own choice of exile and the function of the Zondi-Kramer partnership, because they represent the viable option for South Africa, the alternative to civil war and anarchy. Those who dwell within must be brought to recognize that the problem is less antagonism between the races and more ignorance concerning the bond between them that has enabled apartheid to survive and that can also expedite its peaceful demise. For McClure, Kramer and Zondi represent the microcosm of the best of South Africa, that which is redemptive and redeemable. But it remains to be seen whether or not their bond will be recognized as a promise or a threat, whether the red necklaces are flowers or fire.

Bibliography

McClure, James. *The Artful Egg*. 1984. New York: Pantheon, 1985.
——. *The Blood of an Englishman*. 1980. New York: Pantheon, 1982.
——. *The Caterpillar Cop*. New York: Pantheon, 1972.
——. *The Gooseberry Fool*. 1974. Harmondsworth: Penguin, 1974.
——. *Snake*. New York: Pantheon, 1975.
——. *The Song Dog*. 1991. New York: Mysterious P, 1992.
——. *The Steam Pig*. 1971. New York: Pantheon, 1982.
——. *The Sunday Hangman*. New York: Pantheon, 1977.
Tomarken, Edward. 'The Art of Politics in James McClure's *The Artful Egg*.' Human Rights Quarterly 5 (1985): 230–9.

4
Upfield's Napoleon Bonaparte: Post-Colonial Detective Prototype as Cultural Mediator

Marilyn Rye

Like his namesake, Inspector Napoleon Bonaparte conquers all who come before him: criminals, law-abiding white Australians, the official police bureaucracy, Aborigines of the Australian outback and all readers who follow his adventures. Named for a Frenchman, modeled on the fictional English detective Sherlock Holmes as well as a half-caste Aborigine tracker met in the outback, Upfield's detective functions on many levels as an argument for cultural integration. By creating a heroic detective who is a man of two races, half Aboriginal, half English, Upfield acknowledged that both races have much to contribute to Australian culture. But since Upfield himself was not a man of both races, he was not a truly neutral observer. Moreover, because he was writing in the traditional genre of detective fiction, Upfield ultimately placed a greater value on 'reason,' which becomes associated both with English culture and the detective tradition.

In his Inspector Napoleon Bonaparte series, written between 1929 and 1964, Arthur Upfield created an early prototype of the post-colonial detective. Although not a post-colonial subject, Upfield approached the task that indigenous writers would undertake as their society and literature transformed the cultural inheritance of the colonialist power. Upfield imagined a detective of mixed cultural background – born of an English father and an Aboriginal mother – who would struggle with the reconciliation of two cultures. Upfield's conception of this character came from his imagination, observation, and experience in the Australian outback, but not from a personal connection with the indigenous culture he described. As a white man his cultural inheritance came from England, where he was born. Therefore, his depiction of Aboriginal culture rested upon his observations as an informed outsider. In most cases, the sum of the anthropologically correct details and observations that Upfield wove into his story did not result in either a realistic or complete picture of Aboriginal culture (Pierson 24). As an outsider, Upfield either idealized the Aborigines into a symbol of the superior state of man when unspoiled by a decadent white civilization or turned them into a symbol of the bestiality of man when unchecked by that same civilization. While Upfield's ambivalent attitudes did not recognize the reality of the Aborigine, by strange coincidence his ambivalence did produce a psychologically accurate portrait of the conflict often internalized by indigenous inhabitants coming to terms with the culture of the European colonizer. In his recognition of this conflict, his appreciation of the culture of the Aborigines, his concern for the historical consequences of the process of colonization in Australia, and his insistence that Australia should not define itself as an Anglo-White society, Upfield articulated many of the concerns pursued by post-colonial indigenous writers, including writers of detective fiction.

Unquestionably, the most decisive moment in both Upfield's and his character Napoleon Bonaparte's careers occurred when Upfield decided to rewrite the draft of his first novel, *The Barrakee Mystery* (1929), changing the character of his detective from full-blooded white man into a man of Aborigine and English parentage. While it is easy to identify the repositioning of author in relation to his subject at this moment, the cause behind this repositioning is less easy to identify. Ray Browne, in his pioneer study of Upfield, attributes Upfield's decision to a 'stroke of inspiration' and a desire to make the novels as Australian as possible (32). Browne notes that Upfield actually knew a half-caste tracker named Tracker Leon and that after Upfield's second encounter with Tracker Leon, when they exchanged books, including Abbot's *Life of Napoleon Bonaparte*, Upfield radically reshaped his detective hero (32). The incorporation of Tracker Leon's biography into Upfield's character's history suggests the accuracy of this account, as does Bonaparte's own explanation of his name. For Upfield's detective, familiarly called Bony, explains that he was named by the matron of a mission after she found him gnawing on Abbot's work (*Sands* 2). Even agreeing with Browne's assessment of this moment as inspired, inspiration and the actual presence of Tracker Leon do not explain Upfield's decision to make this crucial choice. Rather, his decision reflects his own identification with the position of an outsider and his realization that an outsider can play an important role as an observer and intermediary. His choice offers the key to understanding his interest in transforming his work from a simple mystery or adventure story into a more complicated discussion of the issues of race and class. A half-caste figure allowed Upfield to work out in terms of his characters' lives the more complex historical process he was interested in examining. Thus, as Browne notes, the novels became as Australian as possible, since they incorporated Australian landscape and characters. Even more importantly, they became Australian because in them Upfield recognized the particular historical meeting of the two races on the Australian continent and the important role this meeting would play in defining the Australian society of the future.

Upfield's radical choice of a figure who was an outsider to two cultures reflected the circumstances of his own life. In his novels, Upfield created a literary construct based on the materials at hand – in this case the tracker Leon – that represented his own sense of being an outsider. He transformed his personal experience into a means of understanding the process of cultural displacement. He was able to empathize with the position of an outcast of both societies because at an early age his English family had thrust this status upon him. While very young Upfield was sent to live with both sets of grandparents, although his brothers remained at home with his parents. He returned home for short visits only to be shipped out again (Browne 4). This process of rejection culminated in Upfield's being sent to Australia at 22 because his father thought him nothing but trouble and believed 'that [he] would never amount to any good' (Browne 5). As Browne notes, this treatment was 'an act of expulsion ... [that] must have cut deeply into ... [his] person-ality and left permanent scars,' especially since lack of money would most likely make this a permanent exile (4). Even in Australia, Upfield assumed the status of an outsider, since he was attracted to the fringes, the outback instead of the cities, and the disappearing older generation of pioneer homesteaders instead of the more 'civilized' city dwellers. As a writer, Upfield again experienced the sense of being an outsider, since he never made it into the Australian literary elite. Although his critical reception can't explain his initial choice of an outsider as a main char-acter, his position outside the literary pale confirms the lifelong pattern of his experience. Thus Upfield's own history made him sensitive and aware of the presence of the Aborigines, also outsiders in Anglo-Australia. It helped him imagine the attraction and rejection a half-caste Australian might alternately feel when defining his relationship to both cultures. His detective is post-colonial in his ability to observe white society from the vantage point of a non-white character with indigenous blood and to use both of his cultural backgrounds in his detection.

Even though Upfield could not duplicate the experience of an indi-genous subject, he went much further than most of his contemporaries in his recognition and appreciation of Aboriginal culture. In his novels he introduced that culture to his Anglo-Australian readers. Through his character of Bony, Upfield placed a value on Aboriginal culture that suggested Aborigines could no longer be conceived as exotic extensions of the landscape. Upfield placed a human value upon them and recognized the complexity and uniqueness of their culture. The stories he wrote focused attention on the indigenous culture in the same way that Bony's discussion of the culture often presented it to the Anglo-Australian characters in the novels. Upfield inscribed the process of cultural mediation in his text through the character of his detective and repeated this process in the relationship of text to reader. Through his presentation of a heroic man descending from two races, Upfield required that readers adopt the same attitude towards the Aboriginal race that the enlightened white characters in the novels adopted towards Bony. Bony's exploits convince readers as well that he is '[t]he man who had so often proved that aboriginal blood and brains were equal to those of the white man' (*Bone* 30). With this conclusion, Upfield invites a reversal of the assumption that Aborigines are inferior. And in his novels he gives many examples of the way Bony's Aboriginal heritage contributes to his superior talent.

In every novel Bony must explain his dual ancestry to some other character in the book, thus raising the question of the relationship between the two races. His initial impulse, especially when speaking to others, is to place an equal value on both races and to suggest that his background defines his function as a bridge between the races in Australia.

> 'I see a problem I've often come across...the gulf between the mind of the white man and the mind of the Australian black man. As the mind of the Occidental differs widely from that of the Oriental, so differs as widely the minds of the Australian black tracker and the Australian white policeman. My birth and training fashion me into a bridge spanning the gulf between them.'   (*Widows* 93)

Bony often describes himself as a bridge between two cultures, although other narrative references sometimes use metaphors suggesting conflict to define the same relationship. When Bony describes himself as a bridge, he is emphasizing the way the superior qualities of each race combine in him to make him a superior detective. The circumstances of his birth allow him to state that 'I have the white man's reasoning powers and the black man's eyesight and knowledge of the bush. The bush will give up its secrets to me' (*Death* 26). Upfield's narrative often suggests that Bony stands midway between the races as a neutral judge who is 'able to look dispassionately on the white man and the black...' (*Wings* 122). While Bony ultimately abandons this neutrality, this position introduces an unusual toleration for non-Anglo culture.

Bony's Aboriginal inheritance gives him tracking skills, knowledge of the bush country, and an understanding of Aboriginal society. The traits inherited from his mother are all geared towards survival in a harsh landscape. Thus, as he turns his indigenous knowledge towards the solution of crime, his non-traditional methods make him a superior detective. As Bonaparte often stresses, his cases are not set in the traditional English library (*Sands* 57) but in the outback where his superior tracking skills give him an advantage over the white policemen assigned to a difficult case. Bony's knowledge of the Australian bush and its inhabitants allows him to read a landscape which would be illegible to a more traditional detective figure. For example, in *Man of Two Tribes* Bony uses a dead bushman's diary to locate the unknown spot where a missing person vanished. The dead man recorded the arrival of an airplane in a remote spot identifiable only through descriptions of the landscape. Bony recreates the man's path of nomadic wanderings, matching descriptive phrases from the diary with features of the actual landscape. As Bony reads both diary and landscape he demonstrates his bilingualism in the texts of both cultures and his superiority in interpreting both. The novels support Bony's contention that he can read the landscape like 'a white man reads a newspaper' (*Wings* 122).

Every novel set in the outback demonstrates Bony's tracking skills through original and ingenious examples. Like Sherlock Holmes, Bony can recreate complete stories from shreds of evidence such as wool fibers or strands of silk. He can distinguish between the tracks of wild or partly civilized Aborigines. The value that Bonaparte attaches to the importance of this skill in his work becomes clear when he compliments a man he considers an equally successful tracker in a different environment. The highest praise Bony can offer for a superior sailor tracking a lost boat at sea is 'you're a man after my own heart, for you can track as well at sea as I can track on land' (*Mystery* 90). By demonstrating the value of Aboriginal survival skills, Upfield encourages his audiences to accept the fact of the Aborigine's superior talent and accomplishments.

Upfield also suggests that Bonaparte is a sign of Aboriginal presence and cultural duality in another way. Bonaparte does not dismiss the activities of Aborigines as senseless, as do many of the whites. Instead, he reads the Aborigines' messages to each other about events that have passed and considers their observations about white behavior. He shows a cultural logic behind their actions which has its equivalent in white society. As a man between two worlds, Bony must establish a connection to the ritualistic practices and ceremonies of both worlds in order to establish relationships with the inhabitants of each. He partakes of tea with the white ranchers and policemen because he moves easily in that world of polite gestures and conversation. But when Bony needs to get information from Aborigines, he establishes his connection to them through the fact of his own Aboriginal blood and inheritance.

The novel *The Sinister Stones* provides an excellent example of his ability to obtain and integrate knowledge from Aboriginal sources. First he confirms his connection to Aborginal culture by removing his shirt, the covering of civilization, to let the Aborigines see the cicatrices and initiation marks that tie him to their culture and rituals. Clothed or unclothed, English or Aborigine, Bony's ability to be accepted in either culture marks his function as an intermediary. At the same time, for the reader, Bony is a sign of the presence of the Aboriginal figure in the Australian landscape and a predictor of the transformation of Australian society. While the Aborigines are busy marking the clan and status occupied by Bony, he reads them in reciprocal fashion: for him they are more than just features of the landscape as they would be for white settlers. Bony credits them with intelligence. Because he takes their actions seriously, Bony pays attention to messages sent in their 'smokes,' believes in mental telepathy, and in the mental powers possessed by many tribesmen. Upfield weaves these beliefs into his plots, validating them by making the mysteries' solutions rest upon events that cannot always be explained within the logical solutions of western rationalism.

Two novels particularly lend credence to the value of Aborigine beliefs in arriving at knowledge as they educate readers in some approximation of Aboriginal life. In *The Sinister Stones*, Bony concludes that a horse is somehow connected with a murdered man's body, even though he can't give a rational explanation to support his conclusion. Instead, his belief rests upon his interpretation of smoke signals he has watched send messages across the landscape. Although no witnesses observed the murder and no one has found the body, the natives have used mental telepathy to establish that murder was committed. Bony accepts the messages as factual. Bony also believes the Aboriginal system of justice equal to the white man's since both indict the same man. Although he can't read the markings made by Aboriginal medicine men, he believes that the Aboriginal ritual will identify the stone with the murderer's name on it. And in fact, the narrative establishes that the supernatural ritual of the Aborigines and Bony's logical reasoning lead to the identification of the same man as murderer. The narrative adds weight to the Aboriginal presence by respecting the Aboriginal belief system and equating the effectiveness of Aboriginal and Australian justice.

In *The Bushman Who Came Back*, Bonaparte also credits the Aborigines with extraordinary telepathic powers and participates in the process of gaining knowledge through telepathy. In this novel, Bony approaches a gathering of local Aborigines to gather information about the 'spirit' dolls belonging to a missing child. Bony's knowledge of Aboriginal legends allows him to hear the Aboriginal flute, the didjeridoo, 'tell' the legends and gain a description of the scene of a crime. When Bony leaves the camp, he has a clear mental picture of the body of a local woman who has been murdered. No one has described the scene to him, so his vision of this woman with a wound like a question mark on her back has only been conveyed through the music of the old and blind tribal chief, Canute. Bony uses this information, as well as his observation of Aboriginal behavior in the case, to solve the crime.

Furthermore, Upfield invites the reader to reread Australian history from a point of view sympathetic to the Aborigines. By invoking the history of colonization, its effect on the unspoiled earlier civilization, and the unfavorable position of the Aborigine in a modern Australia that devalues and destroys their culture, Bony's speeches again raise the issue of the colonists' treatment of the Aborigines. Upfield's detective, who evaluates the Aboriginal culture in a positive way, blames the destruction of that culture on white civilization. In *The Bone Is Pointed*, for example, a novel which highlights the problem of the destruction of the Aboriginal way of life, Bony's response to a request to identify himself as Aboriginal or Australian indicates his pride in his Aboriginal ancestry. He replies, 'I am Australian, at least on my mother's side. It is better to be half Australian than not Australian at all' (51). His words suggest the white Australian is the outsider. In addition to defining Australian in an original way, he expresses his pride in belonging to a race that has achieved a higher state of civilization.

> There is a very great number of people who regard the Australian aboriginal as standing on the lowest rung of the human ladder. Because they have found no traces of a previous aboriginal civilization, no settlement, no building, no industry, they say that he always

has been a man of a very low type. Yet, for all that, he has possessed for many centuries that which the white race is constantly trying to obtain . . . Contented Happiness. . . . Yet the blackfellow possessed culture when the white man ate raw flesh.   (*Sands* 99)

In *The Bone Is Pointed*, Bony admires the Gordons, who have tried to protect 'their' Aborigines from the devastating effects of western civilization which would disrupt their culture. Like Bony himself, this family acts as a mediator to shield the Aborigines from the outside world, although not the influences of westernization. For Upfield and Bony, the worst effect of the westernization process seems to be the power of money to disrupt the native economy and turn the Aborigines from independent tribesmen living in nature to dependent hangers-on in western settlements. Bony approves of the Gordons because they have managed to keep the Aborigines around them free from state control and help them manage their money. Putting money in the bank for the tribe as a whole keeps the individuals of the tribe from direct contact with currency; thus, their values are not corrupted. They do not develop the meaner traits of whites but can remain proud and generous. Upfield uses Bony's values to criticize capitalism more than contact with western civilization. Mrs Gordon argues that her family helps the tribesmen who continue to practice 'the Christian Socialism . . . [they] practised centuries before Christ was born' (*Bone* 119). Thus, the Gordons can only understand the Aborigines by viewing them in terms of known European culture; they cannot step outside their culture to appreciate the Aboriginal society. As Bony's reactions frequently reveal the same context of evaluation, his approval of the Gordons' attitudes is not surprising. Through their interventions, the Gordons help the Kalchut avoid the fate of other tribes. Upfield places a very impassioned defense of the Aborigines and a sharp critique of their conditions into the mouth of Mary Gordon, whom Bony admires. Her address really raises the issue of the Aborigines' place for white readers, although it is addressed to Bony in the novel.

And now the shadow of civilization falls upon them although they don't know it. Civilization comes to shoot them down, to poison them like old dogs, and then, to excuse itself, to depict the victims of its curse as half-wits in its comic papers, to sneer at them as naked savages, to confine them to reserves and compounds. It has taken away their natural food and feeds them on poison in tins labeled 'food'.   (*Bone* 119).

Obviously, Bony would know all of this history. But explaining it to him serves to validate Mrs Gordon as a character who avoids the prejudice at large in Australian society. In her speech she simultaneously addresses Bonaparte and the white Australian reader, thus suggesting an equation between the two. Like many characters, she ultimately accepts Bony as a member of her class and society. Bony often casts himself in a similar role to Mrs Gordon's because he takes on the responsibility of explaining the Aborigines to white men. Thus he aligns himself with the liberal whites who recognize the fact of Aboriginal culture, who demonstrate positive attitudes towards it, but who can only see it existing within the framework of the Anglo-Australian value structure.

Bonaparte's distance from his Aboriginal heritage and his closer identification with his English heritage appears in the early novels when he credits success to his ability to improve Aboriginal skills by applying his English inheritance of logic to them. At one point he explains that 'my aborigine mentors found me a good student because I inherited the white man's ability to reason more clearly and more quickly than they' (*Bone* 104). His use of a framework of western culture appears also in his viewing Aborigine culture through the eyes of the settlers' descendants. As the narrative often makes clear, he distances himself from the Aborigines when discussing them. In the following example, Bonaparte's use of the pronoun 'we' suggests he is aligning himself with the white policeman listening to his explanation.

They're full of knowledge and helpful in their own country and are nervous and suspicious when away from it. We feed them and clothe them, and we bring them to understand enough of our language to communicate. They smoke our tobacco and ride our horses; many of them drive our cars and trucks and are able to repair wind mills and pumps. Nevertheless, they retain their tribal customs. (*Sinister* 84)

In *The Bone Is Pointed*, both Bony and the Gordons recognize the power of Aboriginal customs, but they regard some of them in a negative light. The Gordons forbid certain traditional practices, like 'pointing the bone.' They are afraid of the political ramifications of this practice, which causes death through symbolic magic and mind control. They know the culture can exist only if it does not pose a threat to the Australian sense of law and order with its belief in a rational process of justice. When the bone is pointed at Bony he almost dies because his Aboriginal blood makes him susceptible to Aboriginal ceremonies. Symbolically, when Bonaparte's maternal heritage takes control over his logical western mind, he becomes susceptible to terror and is almost extinguished as a logical thinking human being. Bonaparte sees his destruction in the possibity of the failure of his reason, whether manifested in an inability to solve any case or an inability to exercise his reason against the power of the primitive physical world of Aboriginal power. His reaction to the boning is to resolve that, '[h]e would fight it with all the strength of his mind, and again he would triumph over his aboriginal ancestry as he had so often done before . . . Was he a savage: Was he an ignorant nomad of the bush?' (140).

Even though the Aborigines in this book are not assimilated, Upfield's novel diffuses any perceived threat caused by their presence. He presents them as loyal to white benefactors. John Gordon and Jimmy Partner, his Aboriginal foster brother, have a strong mutual allegiance; their loyalty in the face of a racist white man precipitates his murder. Jimmy kills the white man who is torturing his foster brother, John, because John stands up for Aborigines. The protection of the Aborigines is repaid by their loyalty, since the tribe points the bone at Bony out of loyalty towards the Gordons.

One of the most interesting features of Upfield's attitude towards Aborigines is his reassuring message that they can accommodate their presence to white Australian society. Upfield's works validate Aboriginal culture, present it to the inspection of Anglo-Australians, and defuse the idea that it could prove threatening to the established order. *The Bone Is Pointed*, like many other novels in this series, helps familiarize white Australians with the culture of the 'other,' while at the same time reassuring them that the indigenous race will not challenge their basic assumptions about themselves. Partner's loyalty to Gordon is paradigmatic of Bony's relationship to the state he serves. Bony's whole identity is tied up in his service to the white police force, dependent upon its recognition of him as superior, and rests on his belief that his superiority includes an ability to be more civilized than those who accept him. He may praise his Aboriginal heritage, but his psychological identification is clearly with the white society that hires him to protect it from the criminals who violate the tenets of a stable social order. Bony's identification with whites eventually causes him to devalue Aborigines and the part of himself that is Aborigine, an attitude that reflects Upfield's probably ambivalent feelings about Aboriginal culture. Even while admiring it, his identity as a white man may have led him to hold unconscious assumptions about the superiority of white culture. Yet even Upfield's recreation of his own ambivalence in Bony's ambivalent attitude comes across less as racist than an accurate picture of the ambivalence of an educated native who has been raised to accept English culture as superior.

Upfield creates a very credible past for his character that explains Bony's deepest urges to identify with English culture, the culture of his father. Like many post-colonial detectives, Bony has a love-hate relationship with the West. Bony, who resembles other indigenous people educated by colonialists, identifies more closely with the culture that educates him. Upfield writes that after his mother's tribesmen killed her and abandoned him, Bony was rescued and raised at a mission school, where his intelligence and coloring won him a superior status. In *The Sands of Windee*, Bony gives a remarkable insight into his earliest and enduring identification with English culture as he confides his view of his experience:

> He had been born with the white man's blood in him and as is sometimes the case, a skin as white as his father's. From an early age he had felt his superiority over the other little boys at the mission station, most of whom were black, or of that dark putty color there is no mistaking. At eighteen years . . . [w]ith the inevitability of fate his long-dead black mother claimed him from the grave, claimed him and held him. He was bathing with several companions . . . and one remarked how peculiar it was that his legs were darker in colour than the upper part of his body. The horror, the agony, the knowledge that, after all, when he had been so certain that the black strain would never show, it was at last asserting itself. (174)

Like many post-colonials, Bony has been educated into accepting English values as superior. He has no understanding of his Aboriginal heritage until later, when an uncontrollable instinct surges in his blood and draws him back to the bush and his mother's tribe. But his Aboriginal blood cannot keep him there because he needs to return to 'civilization' to reaffirm that he still remains superior and is accepted as such.

Bony's defining characteristic is his sense of superiority, first over blacks, then over blacks and whites. Yet instead of bolstering the assumption that Bony is ideologically neutral, his sense of superiority betrays the idea that both cultures carry the same weight. His accomplishment of having reached the apex of a hierarchy where Aborigines are on the bottom and whites higher up gives him a sense of superiority. Bony has no illusions about how he holds his place in this society. He dryly comments that 'In this country colour is no bar to a keen man's progress, providing that he has twice the ability of his rivals' (*Bone* 52).

His dress, his intellect, his attitudes towards his colleagues, and his perfect record of solving crimes (if not handing over the murderer) impress the fact of his superiority on those around him.

In short, Bony provides his white colleagues with a model of accomplishment they can imitate but not achieve. The policemen who work under him idealize him for his accomplishments and for his refusal to pull rank. Repeatedly Bony insists that they call him by his first name, a privilege he grants to his friends. When Bony finds a worthy but unappreciated colleague like Sergeant Telfer in *The Mystery of Swordfish Reef*, he gives him the credit for the arrest and arranges his promotion. Bony's behavior suggests that an Aborigine would not be a threat to the advancement of the white man. Instead, Bony serves his colleagues and the state and makes the system of criminal justice run more efficiently. 'Unlike many of his fellow members of the C.I.B., Bonaparte did not adopt an attitude of lofty superiority towards uniformed men. Consequently, he never failed to get their generous support and cooperation' (*Mystery* 68). Bony thus acquires an unthreatening moral superiority.

The clothes that identify Bony as a member of white Australian society also are a visible mark of his superiority, his membership in an elite class of natural aristocracy. When not disguised as a horsebreaker or derelict, Bony's appearance differs sharply from that of his colleagues, and he is proud that he doesn't look like a police inspector. While on occasion, often a private occasion, Bony dresses with a sartorial splendor that overwhelms his colleagues, his public appearance suggests a more elegant and restrained taste. He is even perceived as princely by one observer in Bermagui where he adopts the cover of a rich man who has come to pursue swordfish. This inhabitant, Blade, 'experience[ed an] awe of this visitor... who was so immaculate, so easy in his manner, and still so unusual. He was not unlike an Indian Prince' (*Mystery* 45). Bony has a wardrobe of light gray tweeds with matching shirts, ties, and hats, white canvas shoes, creased drill pants, and silk shirts (*Wings*; *Sinister*). In private he is flamboyant, as if his most private apparel expresses the flair of his inner thought processes. Neither colleague nor reader will forget Bony's elegant yellow and green silk pajamas or his dressing gown of 'pastel blue with yellow collar and cuffs and a large bright red pocket' (*Sinister* 212, 214).

Bony is an intellectual dandy as well, whose university education has helped him develop a superior intellect that few whites can match. Indeed, those same settlers' descendants who might consider the Aborigines uneducated and illiterate demonstrate their intellectual poverty when compared to Bony's. In *The Sands of Windee*, when Bonaparte borrows works by Virgil and Marcus Aurelius from a local priest, his Sergeant wants to know 'Who the devil are they?' Bony replies, 'They are, I think, strangers in Mount Lion' (118).

As Bonaparte's experience demonstrates, the process of adapting to the colonialists' culture, particularly as that adaptation is accomplished through education, makes neutral attitudes towards an inhabitant's indigenous culture almost impossible. Bony is not exposed to his maternal culture until after his university education, and by then, western values are embedded in Bonaparte's mind. Bony recalls that at 22,

> my body craved for complete freedom from the white man's clothes. I wanted to go ahunting as my mother's father had hunted, and I wanted to eat flesh, raw flesh, and feast on tree grubs . . . this is what I wanted to do; but reason, the trained white man's reason, caused me to behave a little less primitively, and in the end, the white and the black blood in me called a truce. (*Sands* 65)

Upfield's melodramatic statement implies that culture is grounded in genetics as well as education. Because Bony's craving for these foods probably causes most readers to shudder, they most likely would applaud the reason that restrains Bonaparte's initial 'primitive' responses. But in reality, as the novels consistently show, because no truce exists, the narratives demonstrate that Bonaparte usually resolves the inner conflict in favor of his white, patriarchal, and logical inheritance. While Bonaparte is willing to learn a great deal from his tribe's medicine man, Illawalli, Bony refuses the conditions attached for learning the secrets of more mysterious powers: acceptance of a leadership position as Illawalli's heir. Instead, Bony prefers his position as a police inspector to leadership and power in the tribe (*Sands* 107). When forced to choose, he ultimately rejects his maternal, Aboriginal inheritance that so closely connects him to the physical world. This division and preference is clear in the observation about Bonaparte's dual heritage:

> From his white father Bony had inherited the precious gift of reason, and from his mother the equally precious gift of patience. Reason and patience, developed by an undying passion for knowledge, produced in this half-caste a force for good seldom found among the white races and almost never among the black (*Down* 68).

Whenever Bony abandons this 'reason' or behavior perceived as reasonable, he feels intense shame at the stripping away of the trappings of civilization and its accompanying forces for good. Two incidents occur in *The Mystery of Swordfish Reef* that demonstrate how lack of reason becomes identified with dangerous and beastly behavior. The imagery in Upfield's description of Bonaparte at these moments suggests his character's 'bestial' and 'savage' nature. In the first incident, when Bony is attacked and beaten up by two henchmen of the arch-villain, the intense anger which darkens his appearance and distorts his features transforms him from light to dark, from human to animal.

> The heat in his brain had become too fierce for longer control, and abruptly his mother's blood took charge of him, made him one with her and her people... Bony's face had become jet-black in color, his eyes glaring blue orbs set in seas of white, while his teeth reflected the light like the fangs of a young dog... Never before in his life had his aboriginal instincts so controlled Napoleon Bonaparte to the exclusion of that complex part of him inherited from his father on which was based so magnificent a pride. Reason had fled before the primitive lust to destroy. (204–5)

A later scene in this novel confirms the extent to which rage transforms Bonaparte from reasonable man to animal. In a second scene, he goes berserk. While in some novels, like *The Will of the Tribe*, Upfield invests the shedding of clothes with a positive connotation of reversion to an uncorrupted past, here the shedding of clothing is equated with a complete reversion to a savage state. Surrendering to his anger, Bony becomes unrecognizable, at least as a civilized counterpart to the white citizens and fellow policemen:

> His general appearance was the antithesis of that... known to his colleagues. The veneer of civilization, so thin in the most gently nurtured of us, was entirely absent. He was wearing nothing... His hair was matted with blood.... His lips were widely parted, revealing his teeth like the fangs of a young dog (241–2).

In the final analysis, neither Upfield nor Bonaparte successfully reconcile their attitudes towards the hero's position between two different cultures. Although later indigenous detectives might place more value on the native culture of their birth, Bonaparte remains trapped between an ideal of unspoiled Aboriginal culture and the white culture that judges that culture as inferior. His inability to resolve his dilemma, especially in view of the destruction of Aborigine culture due to the process of white settlement, reflects Upfield's inability to imagine how these two cultures could exist harmoniously in a modern Australian state. The detective figure Upfield created is very much an Australian version of the 'noble savage,' domesticating the terror of the unknown with the criticism of the known. The idea of the unspoiled savage, living in an Edenic and pre-civilized state, has always functioned as a model of noble behavior that 'showed civilized men [what] they were not and must not be' (Pearce 5). Bonaparte is 'noble' and 'savage' simultaneously. He presents the ideal of the unspoiled Aborigine whose best characteristics should serve as a model for white behavior. Upfield suggests that this most civilized behavior confirms civilized man's ability to extricate himself from the worst aspects of his civilization and from brute nature.

The conventions of detective fiction provide the only possible means of reconciling the opposing halves of Bonaparte's personality. This reconciliation suggests a plan along which the two halves of Australian society can also be reconciled. As a detective, Bonaparte must identify with the highest moral order. Because of his dual heritage, he faces the difficult task of locating the moral order in one of two cultures – in the uncorrupted Aboriginal past which no longer exists or in Anglo-Australian society which is marred by its racism. Less by coincidence than design, in Upfield's novels the worst villains are often racist and the virtuous people are whites who accept and appreciate Bonaparte's superiority. Significantly, in *Murder Down Under*, Mrs Loftus, who has murdered her husband and hidden his body under a haystack, will not invite a thirsty Bony in for tea, but sends him back to the well. However, both the descendants of heroic white settlers and his white colleagues treat Bony as an equal or their superior, inviting him into their homes and serving him at their tables. His own superior in the police hierarchy, Colonel Spender, values Bony the most and is most important in establishing Bony's sense of his own worth and his self-esteem. Bonaparte both internalizes Spender's voice, mimicking his comments on Bonaparte's behavior, and is ecstatic when Spender personally comes to retrieve him from a death by boning (*Bone* 97, 270).

Upfield uses his character of Bonaparte to posit an ideal for Australian society. If Bonaparte can win the recognition and respect of the Anglo-Australian society for Aboriginal culture, he can give his allegiance to a progressive Australian society. Upfield obviously hopes to win the reader's acceptance as well. Since Bonaparte identifies closely with the legal and moral order of the Australian state, and less closely with his maternal heritage, he is not in the strictest sense of the word a 'mediator.' While he often explains Aboriginal culture to white Australians, he does not function in the reverse fashion to explain white society to the Aborigines except in terms of attributing his own superior authority to his position in white society. But in terms of Upfield's narrative construction of character, Bonaparte mediates between white Australian society and Aboriginal culture. He demands that white readers recognize the existence of Aboriginal culture by so presenting it in his text.

In his heroic figure of Napoleon Bonaparte, Upfield has created a character who is a sign of Aboriginal presence, if not an accurate representation of its reality. In every novel Upfield raises the issue of race and the need to consider the relation between the two cultures of the Australian continent. Because Upfield does not deal in realities but poses a primitive and unspoiled state against a modern and imperfect one, he leaves his detective little choice but to throw in with modern westernized society. What detective could choose to live in a condition of harmony which excludes the possibility of an interesting crime? The lack of a good crime to solve drove Sherlock Holmes to cocaine. Offered a similar choice, Bonaparte also prefers a world where the existence of crime provides an interesting puzzle. As he says in *The Bone Is Pointed*,

> 'Just think if the world were as pure and life as simple as it was in Australia before ever Dampier saw it. Ah, but then, I should not have been happy, I suppose. There was no crime higher than the elementary crime of stealing your neighbour's wife. No, no! After all, I think I prefer the shadow in which crime and bestiality thrives.' (120)

Rather than judge Upfield's work according to his ability to present an accurate and neutral depiction of Aboriginal culture, we can look at it in terms of what Genette describes as 'the history of literary function' (76). Upfield's novels' function, as they make us aware, is to reshape the society they describe. Upfield's novels foreshadow the work of later indigenous writers because Upfield struggles against the simplistic and naive attitudes the writer Chinua Achebe felt the Europeans always brought with them. In an interview with J. O. J. Nwachukwu-Agbada, Achebe decried the limited vision of the whites. His criticism pointed out that 'the white man comes, claiming to be the way, the light, the truth: nothing works except him. Now this kind of thinking, this kind of simplicity and self-righteousness . . . is dangerous because it is one of the basic causes of distress to mankind today' (282). The inspired creation of Inspector Napoleon Bonaparte proves that Upfield valued the cultures of both the colonizer and the colonized. Upfield wrote to lessen the distress to mankind.

Bibliography

Browne, Ray B. *The Spirit of Australia: The Crime Fiction of Arthur W. Upfield.* Bowling Green, OH: Bowling Green State U. Popular P., 1988.

Genette, Gérard. *Narrative Discourse: An Essay in Method.* Trans. Jane E. Lewin. Ithaca, NY: Cornell UP, 1980.

Nwachukwa-Agbada, J. O. J. 'Interview with Chinua Achebe.' *Massachusetts Review.* 28:2 (Summer 1987): 273–285.

Pearce, Roy Harvey. *Savagism and Civilization: A Study of the Indian and the American Mind.* 1953 as *The Savages of America.* Berkeley and Los Angeles: U California P, 1988.

Pierson, James C. 'Mystery Literature and Ethnography: Fictional Detectives as Anthropologists.' *Literature and Anthropology.* Eds. Philip A. Dennis and Wendell Aycock. Lubbock: Texas UP, 1989.

Upfield, Arthur W. *The Bone Is Pointed.* 1947. New York: Scribner's, 1985.

——. *The Bushman Who Came Back.* 1957. New York: Scribner's, 1984.

——. *Death of a Swagman.* 1945. New York: Scribner's, 1984.

——. *Man of Two Tribes.* 1956. New York: Scribner's, 1986.

——. *Murder Down Under.* 1937. New York: Scribner's, 1983.

——. *The Mystery of Swordfish Reef.* 1943. New York: Scribner's, 1985.

——. *The Sands of Windee.* 1931. New York: Scribner's, 1988.

——. *The Sinister Stones.* 1954. New York, Scribner's, 1983.

——. *The Widows of Broome.* 1950. New York: Scribner's, 1985.

——. *The Will of the Tribe.* 1962. New York: Scribner's, 1984.

——. *Wings Above the Diamantina.* 1936. New York: Scribner's, 1986.

Arthur W. Upfield's The Inspector Napoleon Bonaparte Novels

The Barrakee Mystery. 1929 (US title: *The Lure of the Bush.* 1965)
The Sands of Windee. 1931
Wings Above the Diamantina. 1936 (US title: *Wings Above the Claypan.* 1943)
Mr Jelly's Business. 1937 (US title: *Murder Down Under*)
Winds of Evil. 1937
The Bone Is Pointed. 1938
The Mystery of Swordfish Reef. 1939
Bushranger of the Skies. 1940 (US title: *No Footprints in the Bush.* 1944)
Death of a Swagman. 1945
The Devil's Steps. 1946
An Author Bites the Dust. 1948
The Mountains Have a Secret. 1948
The Bachelors of Broken Hill. 1950
The Widows of Broome. 1950
The New Shoe. 1951 (Also titled *The Clue of the New Shoe.* 1974)
Venom House. 1952
Murder Must Wait. 1953

Death of a Lake. 1954
Sinister Stones. 1954 (English title: *The Cake in the Hatbox*. 1955)
The Battling Prophet. 1956
The Man of Two Tribes. 1956
Bony Buys a Woman. 1957 (US title: *The Bushman Who Came Back*)
Bony and the Black Virgin. 1959 (Also titled: *The Torn Branch*. 1986)
Bony and the Mouse. 1959 (US title: *Journey to the Hangman*)
Bony and the Kelly Gang. 1960 (US title: *Valley of Smugglers*)
Bony and the White Savage. 1961 (US title: *The White Savage*)
The Will of the Tribe. 1962
Madman's Bend. 1963 (US title: *The Body at Madman's Bend*)
The Lake Frome Monster. 1966 (completed by J.L. Price and Dorothy Strange)

5

A Crane among Chickens:* The Search for Place in William Marshall's Yellowthread Street Novels

Deborah Bosi

At the threshold of every installment to the Yellowthread Street novels, author William Marshall introduces what is essential to every mystery: fear. After considering the Hong Kong phenomenon – a European-leased Asian city-state that depends on Communist China for its drinking water – Marshall beckons his reader into the Hong Bay district of Hong Kong with this caution: 'Hong Bay is on the southern side of the island, and the tourist brochures advise you not to go there after dark.'

By 1997, this capitalist society will be 'returned' to mainland China, which has promised to retain Hong Kong's free-wheeling, free-enterprise lifestyle. In the meantime, as Great Britain relaxes its grip on its Asian charge, Hong Kong becomes an exciting window of literary opportunity as both native orientals and natives of European descent examine the racial dynamics of past and present Hong Kong. In this way, Marshall's detective series, The *Yellowthread Street* Mysteries, adds yet another aspect to the canon of post-colonial literature. Marshall, though Australian by birth, lived in Hong Kong for several years. As a citizen of another former British colony, his position is unusual: he can emote empathy for both Hong Kong's aboriginal and transplanted citizenry. He understands the dilemma each struggles with: the clashing cultural heritages, the deep rooted desire to belong; for the Chinese culture it is the need for acknowledgment of their culture as the primary one; for those of colonial heritage, it is the need to be regarded as members of the community, not despised as oppressors. As we shall discover, Marshall explores these conflicts through his cast of characters,

---

* An old Chinese saying that bespeaks the aspirations Chinese parents have for their children. In ironic terms, it also applies to the non-Asian living in Hong Kong.

the detectives of the Yellowthread Street police precinct, and particularly through Chief Inspector Harry Feiffer, a Hong Kong native of European descent.

We return to our feckless reader who, as the page turns, crosses the threshold into Hong Bay. There is a sense now that there is no turning back. Greeted with Marshall's vision of reality, the reader finds a Hong Kong never to be found in travelogues: irresistible, frightening; a world colliding with itself, within itself; a world where modern man and superstition, ancient rituals and 20th-century economics vie for first place. The British paved this world for international economic success, but in their wake, the Asian approach has subverted Western methods, surreptitiously reinstituting 'the Chinese way' into this steel and glass success story. The result is a microcosm of the post-colonial mentality; native culture struggling to re-establish itself, its past, its future. Marshall ushers the unsuspecting reader into this struggle; to hear the crash of the Chinese psyche as it hurls itself against the outside world.

By setting his detective series in post-colonial Hong Kong, William Marshall provides his reader and his Western characters with an opportunity to examine the detective-in-his-society in a manner not previously possible. Traditional detectives are portrayed as anti-heroes. The traditional methods and philosophies inherent to the occupation exclude the detective from society and convention. Detectives trust no one, discount nothing. Overwhelmed by a steady display of corruption, cruelty, and evil, the detective nevertheless perseveres through the moral sludge, hoping to disprove the reality of his experience. It is the burden of this knowledge that separates the detective from those he protects. However, the non-Asian detective in Hong Kong is further isolated by his race, his Western straightforward approach and logical mind-set. While Marshall's detectives are generally not portrayed as anti-heroes – in fact, they often speak fluent Chinese and are sympathetic to Chinese concerns – they are nevertheless regarded as outside the Asian community in which they live.

What follows is an examination of selections from the Yellowthread Street series illustrating how conflicting philosophical approaches and identity crises among non-Asians in an Eastern culture underscore the tensions of modern-day life and police work.

In its traditional form, the detective genre features a hero who is a creation of the plot's criminals. That is, the sleuth exists to restore the fragile peace society once enjoyed but now finds fragmented by the crime. Once the crime is solved, the need for the detective usually vanishes and the story ends. Yellowthread Street detectives are, rather, a creation of their location. No one particular crime or criminal brings this tiny squad of detectives to life: it is the dynamics of their precinct boundaries that keep Chief Inspector Harry Feiffer and his staff vigorous and vigilant. The dynamics of tradition and heritage, as in *The Perfect End*; the explosion of third world bigotry in *Gelignite*; the haunting lessons found when ancient beliefs meet with greed and deceit in *Out of Nowhere*; this is the lifeblood of the Yellowthread Street police precinct. These detectives then, are a creation of Hong Kong. Their ability to fit into an Asian society and the obstacles that confront these detectives in making that adjustment is what gives each of the Yellowthread Street detectives their identity (Van Meter). The racial insecurities, fear of public disdain, the deep-rooted need of the Caucasian and Asian detectives for acceptance within the Chinese community are all a result of the fractured society in which the citizens, as well as the police, of Hong Kong live. Marshall highlights these emotional needs by making his detectives racial minorities, his uniformed policemen, Oriental. This technique not only emphasizes the distance between characters, who otherwise enjoy a harmonious relationship, but further delineates the relationship of the detective to the reader, for the reader is now drawn into a complex consciousness of conflicting loyalties. Traditionally accustomed to identifying with the detective-as-hero, the reader now becomes increasingly aware of his/her own ethnic heritage as it differs or conforms to that of the protagonist. While playing upon reader sympathy, the post-colonial detective format simultaneously reinforces the position of reader-as-outsider. And if we suppose the audience is of a non-Asian culture, this technique deftly solidifies reader identification with the protagonist.

One obvious way to stress this sense of otherness is through the use of English. While many of the Chinese in Hong Kong speak English, the reverse is not necessarily true. Chief Inspector Harry Feiffer speaks perfect Cantonese, easily slipping from English to Chinese as needed. The ability of a white police officer to do so is noted with continuous amazement by many of the Chinese characters. In *Out of Nowhere*, a Chinese ambulance driver speaks Cantonese to Feiffer who responds in turn: 'He looked hard at Feiffer. The ambulance man said softly, "Your Cantonese is perfect"' (17). While Feiffer regards himself as no more European than any other Hong Kong-born citizen would, he is constantly viewed as one by civilians and policemen alike. An exchange with his friend and colleague Detective Inspector Christopher O'Yee, an Irish-Chinese immigrant from San Francisco, illustrates the crisis of racial identity that exists in Hong Kong:

> 'Bloody European!' [said Christopher O'Yee.]
> 'I'm not a European. I was born in Hong Kong. The nearest I've been to Europe was a package tour to Singapore.'
> 'Well, you look bloody European.'
> 'So do you.'
> 'I look bloody Chinese. I don't want to be a bloody European! I want to be a bloody Chinese – I want to be what I am; half and bloody half!'   (*Out of Nowhere* 67)

As a policeman, Feiffer is viewed with distrust, echoing the poor regard in which the Chinese hold their government officials. As a Caucasian, Feiffer is regarded as the eternal outsider, despite his birthplace, his perfect Cantonese. Yet his life and sensibilities are undoubtedly touched, if not transformed, by his contact with Chinese society and culture.

Refusing to accept his fate as an outsider to his society, Feiffer is continually disproving his stereotype, constantly attempting to create a relationship between self and place. In *Gelignite*, while searching for a letter bomber, an elderly shop owner is suspected of assassinating his partner. Feiffer finds the elderly man, Tam, seated in a darkened one-room apartment overlooking an exclusive cemetery. His questions are distractedly answered; the old man never turns his gaze from the window. As Feiffer approaches the man, he immediately recognizes the smell of a leper. Instead of continuing his investigation in a style which would be consistent with a Western approach – direct, progressive questions – Feiffer takes what clearly is a more intuitive, almost Eastern approach:

> 'Where's your family's tomb?'
> 'On the other side of the hill.'
> 'Overlooking the water.'
> 'Yes.'
> Feiffer said, 'The best shui is probably over there.'
> Mr Tam said, 'It is.' He asked, 'Did I tell you a man was brought all the way from Canton to divine the site?'
> [Despite the fact that this was previously mentioned three times, Feiffer replies:] 'No...I envy your place.' (53)

While many non-Asian detectives might have been aware of Chinese burial customs and the superstitious folk custom of feng shui, few would have recognized the importance of incorporating that awareness into a police interrogation.

At times O'Yee, who describes himself as an 'American by birth, Chinese by inclination,' is shunned for the same reasons Feiffer is. In *Frogmouth*, a Feng Shui Man is summoned by Constable Lim to determine the cause of some mysterious sounds in the precinct walls. As the Feng Shui Man explains to them, it's 'just a matter of rearranging the tiger's tail of heaven where it sometimes drops over the edge of the world.' Noticing O'Yee is not 100 per cent Chinese, the Feng Shui Man gestures to Lim who explains O'Yee is Eurasian. Thinking that O'Yee cannot understand Chinese, the Feng Shui Man sighs and says in Cantonese, 'Bad luck.' As he attempts to explain feng shui philosophy to O'Yee, the Feng Shui Man separates himself from O'Yee as he lectures about what 'we Chinese believe in . . .'

Yet because O'Yee is Chinese by 'inclination,' he has developed an approach to police work that is influenced more by Eastern mysticism than by the police procedurals of Western logic. Manning the phones during a particularly hectic period of crank callers in *Out of Nowhere*, O'Yee uses a variety of word association techniques not only to rid himself of the lunatics, but to diffuse their violent impulses. One caller who calls himself 'Chang, the Total Annihilator,' is completely disarmed by O'Yee's recitation of Wen I-To's poetry (' . . . We are a pair of red candles . . . Quietly burning away our lives . . . ') Chang breaks down and explains his frustration; he is living with his mother-in-law and has few moments alone with his wife. In thanks, Chang turns to the traditional Chinese custom of payment for a favor with a modern-day touch: offering O'Yee his Mastercard.

Despite his inclinations, the ways of the Orient can be overwhelming for American-born O'Yee. 'This is getting a little too Chinese for me,' he thinks, as he converses with millionaire Conway Kan in *Gelignite*. Kan has invited O'Yee to his home to discuss an off-duty assignment. Their conversation begins with great ceremony, intricate mannerisms, then suddenly switches from Cantonese to Mandarin, a dialect considered more refined in the Chinese-speaking community. While Marshall handles this stiff exchange between strangers with his typical humor, he simultaneously underscores the social alienation and inferiority O'Yee feels with a polished and urbane Chinese. In appreciation for O'Yee's assistance in locating a family heirloom – a stuffed toucan – Kan mentions an art auction in which a particularly valuable piece could be purchased inexpensively. As Kan explains:

'I mention it in passing because I, alas, will be disposed by illness at the time of the sale and will not therefore be able to bid on the work.

The auction will be held in three to four weeks time.' O'Yee paused. He tried being Chinese. 'I'm sorry to hear about your future illness.' (32)

As an outsider trying to fit in, O'Yee's position often parallels the reader's. Though his Chinese heritage gives him some advantage over his Caucasian colleagues, O'Yee sits astride two cultures. Even his name connotes his ambiguous position with its mixture of Gaelic and Oriental traditions. By agreeing to read the novel, the reader accepts this precarious position. Therefore, the environment of the novel, though non-Western, may increasingly be viewed as non-threatening, perhaps even desirable. Yet the reader is forced to remain an eternal outsider, outside the embrace of Hong Bay and the lives of the people who inhabit it. Like O'Yee and Feiffer, the reader can never be anything more than someone whose presence is temporarily accepted.

Marshall demonstrates this struggle most effectively through O'Yee. In *Perfect End*, O'Yee has decided to reject modern-day society and become a backwoodsman because, as he explains to Feiffer, '...like all true-born Americans of middle-age, I feel the great outdoors calling to me.' Modeling himself after the Chinese frontiersman, Pine Cone Pin, O'Yee begins to shave with a knife and dreams of living off the land. As he reads his Boy Scout manual, O'Yee struggles once more to understand his position in a culture that is, for him, within sight but beyond integration. Feiffer and the other Caucasian detectives use Western-style techniques to apprehend the Fade Street cop-killer; questioning shopkeepers, looking for witnesses, clues. O'Yee relies on his woodsman-inspired intuitive instincts; stalking the killer from a cemetery back to the deserted Fade St. police station. Though both Feiffer and O'Yee come to the same conclusion regarding the identity of the killer, each arrive by a set of procedures dictated by their cultural disposition. Though time and again O'Yee struggles with his dual mind-set – Oriental intuition and Western logic – at times rejecting it, hating it, misunderstanding it, it is this very same sensibility that O'Yee must use to recreate his origins and identity. It is his key to creating for himself a place in Hong Kong.

At times, O'Yee's struggle is serious and disturbing. A search for all the remains of a dismembered male corpse found in the Bay embroils O'Yee in a moral dilemma. The police search is halted once all but a missing leg is recovered. O'Yee, recalling the Chinese belief that a person must be buried with all body parts or be denied entry into heaven, hesitates before a crowd of watchful Chinese bystanders. Should he ask for their assistance?:

Maybe it's the European side of me trying to be so goddammed Chinese...If I do call them and they don't know what I mean, I'll look foolish. It'd be a loss of face, Chinese or no. I have to make them take me seriously as a policeman or I'll be finished...The European part of me says that's a load of crap. The Chinese don't know what they're talking about...On balance, I prefer the Western side of my background. (7, 15)

Yet he argues over continuing the search for the missing limb with Feiffer, who appears unaware of the cultural importance of burying the corpse intact. In mid-argument, and to his great relief, O'Yee inadvertently recovers it. Later in the novel, O'Yee muses about himself and the onlookers at the beach:

...People like me who don't know what side of the fence they're supposed to perch on.... All I want is for someone to say to me, 'You're a real Chinese and you were right, they really do care about things like that. (*Gelignite* 179)

While Marshall handles the intricacies of Asian manners with good humor, the East–West tensions are depicted with a mixture of absurdity and seriousness that catch both reader and characters off-balance. In *Hatchet Man*, Constable Yan calls upon Eton-educated Detective Spenser for assistance; an old woman, believing she is in 1930 Shanghai, has entered the police station demanding to see the British Consul. Spenser, annoyed, responds:

'Can't you people handle something like this?'...Yan looked at him [Spenser]. [Yan] said, suddenly acid, 'The lady wants a white man.' He added something Spenser had read about on a sign on a beach somewhere in China in the thirties and forties, 'No Chinese or dogs allowed.' (33)

When Spenser approaches the woman, she is assured by his British public-schoolboy looks. She tells him:

'Tell these filthy little Chinks to go away.' Spenser turned to Sun and Yan and Minnie Oh. He said, 'Go away you filthy little Chinks.' He smiled at them. Nobody smiled back...After she had gone, Spenser turned to the two Chinese Constables and Minnie Oh and thought he would say something funny about filthy little Chinks. He looked at their faces and changed his mind. (34–5)

In order to effectively illustrate how exceptional a post-colonial detective is in an Asian world, an atmosphere with a heightened degree of texture is essential. The author must go beyond stereotyped portraits of Hong Kong-estion; tiny shops, curved streets, untranslated Chinese phrases as is found in second-rate romance novels. The reader must be able to experience this world alongside the detectives. We will examine Marshall's literary choices, subtleties and tones to see just what kind of Hong Bay he envisions.

> '...That's the city of Hong Kong! Look! Look at it! There are no trees or birds or animals or wishes there,' cries the owner of a children's petting zoo to Feiffer. (*Frogmouth* 24)

While Marshall's Hong Kong is not a society beyond repair, it is a place where souls are lost through the crush of everyday life. Marshall's Hong Kong is a place where terrible events occur and time suddenly breaks rhythm, losing itself to the weight of tragedy:

> There were two bodies covered in rubber sheets by the sitting man. He looked at them without saying a word. At one end of the lane there was a woman and a child lying dead in a blanket of red curry powder from the Indian provisions shop. A pall of faintly acrid smoke hung over the lane . . . Feiffer saw Doctor MacArthur and another man by the upturned car. There was a heavy humming in the air and the chinking of bits of glass falling from the smashed frames and the soft hissing of something like gas or an overheated car radiator, and apart from that, nothing. (*Gelignite* 124)

There is no explanation, no commentary to Marshall's language. It is non-judgmental with simply constructed sentences. The emotional language is minimal, resulting ironically in a powerfully emotive scene that is tragic, human, ephemeral. Marshall focuses on small, almost inconsequential acts, constructing them into meaningful actions by the attention and shape he brings to them. Continuing at the same site where a bomb has just exploded, Marshall observes:

> There was hardly any sound. The ambulance moved quietly as if on silent electric motors. No one was screaming. People looked at each other without expressions on their faces. Nobody made a sound above the hissing and the glass chinks. Matsu Lane was very quiet. Two Indians came out of what was left of the Indian provisions shop

and looked at the blanket of red curry powder and the two dead people. There was brilliant sunshine in the street coming down in almost direct arcs between the high buildings, and it made the curry look very bright. One of the Indians said something to the other one and the other one nodded. The other Indian looked up the street to the public cordons. He didn't know what to do. He went back inside his shop and came out with a broad mat and he and his friend laid it over the dead woman and the dead child. (*Gelignite* 124–5)

Once again the dramatic impact is heightened in simple visual terms. The scene is sharply focused for the reader; its misery, its honor and, at the same time, its seeming unimportance, is honed to a crisp edge. It is this precision that renders the scene so poignant; Marshall has squeezed the brutality out of the crime and spoons it into his reader's mouth. The feeling of insignificance, the anonymity of the victims is intensified by their lack of physical description. Yet Marshall heightens their stature by concentrating on the survivors' actions and gestures. In the classic tradition of detective fiction, Marshall provides a sense of universal good and the hope that society can heal itself.

The scene described above, similar in construction to its earlier counterpart, is made doubly effective when we consider the scene Marshall illustrated previous to the explosion: an illiterate Chinese man arguing with a smug Indian translator over a letter-reading fee. The scene is full of irritation and tension and racial jingoism. Marshall extends forgiveness to them both by conceiving of an Indian shopkeeper who acts with respect and reverence to the memory of the dead Chinese woman and her child. Turning again to *Gelignite*, the reader accompanies Detective Feiffer down a slum street as he searches for Mr Tam:

Soochow St is a coffin open at both ends for the extinct, and it has that distinctive smell of death and extinction that is composed of coldness and greyness and mould. Soochow St always looks as if there has just been rain and the wooden walls of the buildings on either side of it are always wet and clammy to the touch. (49)

Is there a more perfect place to find a dying leper than Soochow Street?

While William Marshall's Hong Kong is home to Northern and Southern Chinese, Indians, Eurasians, Koreans, Malaysians and several other nationalities, a Chinese sense of philosophy pervades the atmosphere. And to a great extent, that philosophy dominates the behavior of all the characters, Chinese or not. At times, it is almost unnoticeable, as when

Constable Yan, standing in the Fade St. police station, gently touches his good luck jade ring, hoping to ward off the ghosts of his fellow police officers. Or, when investigating a major highway accident, an earth god tablet, symbol of the protector of the former village, is discovered on the median. When Feiffer and Hansell search the apartment of the victims, we are provided with yet another glimpse of Chinese lifestyles: non-smokers (too expensive); 'middle quality' furniture (so as to have a larger estate to leave the family); statuette of Kwan Jin (goddess of mercy); evidence of few things purchased on credit (caution with money). Marshall's subtle introduction of this couple's values suggests an attempt to link at least some of the mores and standards of this closed culture with those of Westerners; to diminish the sense of otherness and to create some parity of sameness between the two groups.

Thus the source of the tension in Marshall's post-colonial detective world is markedly dissimilar from post-colonial literature in which subtle but continued exploitation of the aboriginal citizenry by the diminishing colonial infrastructure is exposed. There is no moral posturing on Yellowthread Street. The series' purpose is not to shame the non-Asian detectives or the non-Asian reader into a higher consciousness. In fact, Asian/non-Asian encounters often provide the reader with opportunities to view Fieffer, O'Yee and Spenser not as post-colonial dominators, but as human beings struggling to stretch beyond their cultural limits. The tension lies in the immediacy of the circumstances; the tragedies that bring the two worlds together prevents the victims from ever expanding the horizons of their myopic visions of Europeans. Caught up in their grief, the surviving Asian crime victims view the European police officers as simply that.

What occurs in Hong Bay is far more subtle than intentional discrimination or even prejudice perpetrated through ignorance. The tensions within the tensions within the Yellowthread Street mysteries derive from a discerning disclosure of opposing mind-sets and, ironically, the attempts both Europeans and Asians make towards harmonious accommodations. The witnessing of these struggles by the reader is far more potent than any Sunday pulpit lecture. It is these emotional fumblings, revealed in all their contrary posturings – denial and acceptance, fear and fragile pinnings – that entangles the reader in the daily, dark struggle for identity and humanity. The Yellowthread Street police precinct is a demonstration of the struggle to be a conscious human being in a world that offers few rewards for the effort. These are the elements that distinguish this body of work both within its own genre and in post-colonial literature. Marshall has not only added to the detective genre, but elevated it.

Bibliography

Ashcroft, Bill, Gareth Griffins, Helen Tiffin. *The Empire Writes Back: Theory and Practice in Post-Colonial Literatures*. London: Routledge, 1989.

Auden, W.H. 'The Guilty Vicarage.' *Detective Fiction: A Collection of Critical Essays*. Ed. Robin Winks. Englewood, N.J.: Prentice Hall, 1980.

Cawelti, John G. 'The Study of Literary Formulas.' *Detective Fiction: A Collection of Critical Essays*. Ed. Robin Winks. Englewood, N.J.: Prentice Hall, 1980.

Dove, George N. 'The Criticism of Detective Fiction.' *Detective Fiction: A Collection of Critical Essays*. Ed. Robin Winks. Englewood, N.J.: Prentice Hall, 1980.

Marshall, William. *Perfect End*. New York: Holt, Rinehart & Winston, 1981.

——. *Gelignite*. New York: Holt, Rinehart & Winston, 1977.

——. *Hatchet Man*. New York: Holt, Rinehart & Winston, 1977.

——. *Frogmouth*. New York: Mysterious Press, 1987.

——. *Out of Nowhere*. New York: Mysterious Press, 1988.

Palmer, Jerry. 'Thrillers.' *Popular Fiction and Social Change*. Ed. Christopher Pawling. New York: St. Martin's Press, 1984.

Thompson, Jon. *Fiction Crime and Empire*. Illinois: University of Illinois Press. 1993.

Van Meter, Jan R. 'Sophocles and the Rest of the Boys in the Pulps: Myth & the Detective Novel.' *Dimensions of Detective Criticism*., 15. Bowling Green: Bowling Green University Press, 1976.

The Yellowthread Street Novels include:

Yellowthread Street, 1975
The Hatchet Man , 1976
Gelignite, 1976
Thin Air, 1977
Skullduggery, 1979
Sci-Fi, 1981
Perfect End, 1981
War Machine, 1982
The Far Away Man, 1984
Roadshow, 1985
Head First, 1986
Out of Nowhere, 1988
Inches, 1995
To the End, 1998

6
The Savage among Us: The Post-Colonial Detective in William Marshall's Manila Bay Novels

Dean Loganbill

It is often difficult to rationalize the mental and spiritual pleasures of mystery reading to the more earnest of one's friends, who tend to see such activities as a waste of time. It is much akin to the older problem of justifying novel reading to earnest Victorians. Ideally, one chooses a purposive justification which matches their earnestness. By properly guilt tripping them for not understanding the sociology of the mystery in question, one can get them hooked and hear nothing more of the matter. The Post-Colonial Detective provides an ideal vehicle for such a strategy.

Without a doubt, independence is the dream of nearly all colonial peoples, the operative idea being that it is better to make one's own decisions even if they are sometimes wrong than to have them made by someone else, no matter how qualified or well intentioned. Anyone who is still young enough to have even vague recollections of adolescence recognizes the feeling immediately. This fact explains, at least in part, why the post-colonial detective novel commands such a broad audience: it expresses this universal delight in a newly won sense of independence. The thrill of that newly found independence generates – in addition to the usual appeal of the quest for truth, or the thrill of the chase – an energy and enthusiasm, the quick shock or sudden delight of a novel solution, that is frequently lacking in more standard forms of the detective genre. Then, of course, there is that hook to ensnare the imaginations of the earnest.

Though he probably never intended to do so, William Marshall has created a veritable sociological study of the Post-Colonial Detective in his two Manila Bay novels. The three police detectives – Felix Elizalde, Jesus-Vincente Ambrosio, and Baptiste Bontoc – who are featured in both *Manila Bay* and *Whisper* represent three levels of Post-Colonial

Philippine society. Each is faced with problems and prejudices that are unique to his own position and background. The question becomes not simply how to solve the mystery but how a particular detective is to use his own position and background to solve the mystery and what insights into himself and his culture the solving of the mystery will provide the detective. One may, one argues to one's earnest friends, ignore the social aspects of these novels, but insofar as plot and character development are informed by those social aspects, it would require a shallow reading indeed to overlook them.

Baptiste Bontoc is a prime example of an outsider in a society of outsiders. He might even be thought of as a post-colonial post-colonial, standing out as he does even in the polyglot society of the modern-day Philippines. Let us take a brief look at one of the most interesting and unusual characters in all of detective fiction: the headhunter turned detective.

Baptiste Bontoc is a member of a primitive or at least recently post-primitive tribe of headhunters called the Bontocs, hence his last name. He is shorter than most Philippino men, five feet one and a half, and dark skinned. Racially he is a Negrito, most closely related to the African pygmies. He does not even speak Pilipino, the national language derived from Tagalog. He speaks Bontoc, of course, but also English. He was schooled by an American missionary teacher named Miss Thomasina, who, along with his Uncle Apo, was the greatest early influence on him. It is obviously she who is responsible for his given name, Baptiste. Her influence is largely positive, especially considering the limited number of openings for headhunters, at least those who take their jobs literally, in today's society. She is also responsible for the continued development of his intellect – he has an MBA from Harvard, even though in Manila he is a low-level police detective. Baptiste Bontoc, then, is a divided man, the two sides symbolized by his divided name.

On the surface it would seem that his education would be sufficient to make of him a fully modern individual, but the task is made more difficult by the prejudice of others. It is a benign sort of prejudice as such things go: his superiors, and others, simply do not know quite what to do with him. What they do do is to give him the jobs no one else will do. In *Manila Bay*, for example, they send him out to play headhunter! It seems that someone has been digging up the Children's Stone Dinosaur Park at night. The authorities think it is Japanese tourists looking for ancestral bones from World War II. They do not want to arrest these old enemies because the country needs the tourist dollars. Therefore, they send Bontoc to lurk about at night disguised as a headhunter. 'You will appear,' says item six of his typed instruction sheet, 'with your cultural background and primitive life-way-experience (headhunting and massacres), to be a frightening, uncontrollable figure loose in the area of the park (Children's Stone Dinosaur Section). You will appear to be aggressive and angry' (15).

The suggestion here that the Bontoc side of Bontoc can or even might be likely to assert itself at any moment is shared by others as well. Bontoc reassures the gardener at the park. 'Don't worry. All I'm going to do is scare them off.... We don't want to cause an incident' (10). But the gardener is not convinced of the harmlessness of this fellow who, apart from manicured fingernails, 'looked like a man who knew how to use a head-axe' (10). He wants to stay on his good side.

> Maybe it was decades since the Bontocs had taken heads. The gardener, nodding, said, 'Right.' The gardener, nodding, said, 'I've got a lot of time for cultural minorities like the Bontocs and the mountain people. I think it's a good thing that people like you –' He looked at the axe and tried to think of something polite 'that people like you are integrating themselves into the cities and bringing the best of your –' He again tried to think of something polite, 'of your life-ways to Manila to enrich us.' (10)

As usual in such cases, the attempt to bridge the awkwardness only makes things worse. The gardener's approach to Bontoc the headhunter – he does not see Bontoc the Harvard MBA – is typical of those conversing with perceived inferiors. He is patronizing, yet fearful, and thus conciliatory, grasping for the 'spells' of cultural acceptance: superficial civility which will disarm this unknown quantity. The gardener himself is a post-colonial, yet his attitudes are identical to racial majority attitudes everywhere. 'No one in the Bontoc tribe has taken a head for weeks' (10), responds Bontoc darkly.

Despite the external difficulties created by such attitudes on the part of Bontoc's compatriots, Marshall makes it clear that the internal Baptiste/Bontoc split in Bontoc's psyche is very real. Though Bontoc tries to argue that he is like everyone else – ' "They have credit cards! The Bontocs these days, have credit cards!" he shouts, "No one is listening"(30). It is not much of an argument, not when Uncle Apo and Miss Thomasina each has a voice living right inside his head. 'Some people had their mothers,' explains Marshall, others their wives or psychiatrists, some people even had God (so did the Bontocs, but as Intutungtso: the General Idea Above ... up there ... somewhere ... kind of ... more or less ... he was the sort of deity you talked about the weather with more than your problems) – but everybody, everybody had to have somebody.

In the Roman's case they were called alter egos. In Bontoc's they were called Uncle Apo Bontoc and Miss Thomasina Landsborough. They were his spirits. (69)

The verbal sparring between the two is very funny, but seen as the objectification of inner conflicts, it is more serious. Uncle Apo is simple and direct; Miss Thomasina is theoretical and idealistic. In Freudian terms, he is pure id, she pure super-ego.

Uncle Apo Bontoc said, 'Kill!' He had the biggest collection of heads in the district. Uncle Apo said, 'Bontoc *kill* enemy!' He spoke broken English and, for that matter, broken Bontoc. Uncle Apo said, 'Find enemy. Take head. Head on pile. Problem gone. Much honor. Huh!'

Miss Thomasina said quietly, 'Well, Baptiste, that certainly is one way of looking at it' – she was nothing if not a real Christian – 'But will it bring lasting happiness in the end?'

He had loved her. Bontoc said, nodding, 'You're right.'

Uncle Apo fell silent. When Uncle Apo fell silent bodies fell head-less.

Bontoc said quickly, '– probably!' Bontoc steadying himself on the tree and grasping his axe in his hand to keep Uncle happy said, 'I'm a *ukom*, Uncle – a white collar worker – I can't go around chopping people's heads off!' He heard Uncle Apo there in his head go 'Hrrmm!' – 'even as much as I might want to . . .' He sought Miss Thomasina's help, 'And apart from that, it's illegal!' Bontoc said, 'Right, Miss Thomasina?'

'And also against God's law, Baptiste.'

Bontoc said, 'And the government's!' With Uncle Apo you didn't reason, you ducked. (69–70)

In his present situation, Bontoc inclines toward the role models favored by Uncle Apo, even though he recognizes the dangers of doing so, for the dangers of giving in to the urgings of Uncle Apo are the dangers of giving in to the atavistic urgings of the id. Still, he tries lurking in a tree. It does not work. The tree falls over.

The falling tree is part of the mystery, which grows ever more bizarre, but now he knows he is not looking for Japanese tourists. The culprits he must apprehend speak Pilipino. What can they possibly be doing in the dinosaur garden? Given the circumstances, Uncle Apo's heroes, like his arguments, have a certain simple, logical appeal. There is himself, there is General Macarthur (second only to Intutungtso), 'MACARTHUR SAYS JAP HEADS GOOD!' shouts Uncle Apo (70). Since he is no longer looking for Japanese tourists, the authority of the good general is somewhat weakened, but Miss Thomasina is not much help here either. When Uncle Apo says, 'John Wayne! Good fellow!' she loses her temper. 'Shut up you old fart!' she suggests (94). Again, following Uncle Apo, Bontoc buries himself in the ground and waits . . . He catches the wrong man, the gardener. Now the gardener is more certain than ever that Bontoc is dangerous, though now he thinks he is incompetent as well. Nevertheless Bontoc has come a step closer to solving the mystery.

When he does solve it, the gardener does not understand the solution, but Bontoc knows he is right. It seems significant that throughout the mystery the gardener remains willing to help, and it is he who saves Bontoc from being buried alive by the villain. Baptiste Bontoc's conclusion regarding himself is also significant: 'I'm not really a headhunter. I've never taken a head in my life. I'm an intellectual' (150). By solving the mystery through unorthodox means, thanks to Uncle Apo, Bontoc has symbolically enriched the Philippine society of which he is now a member. Through the restraint taught him by Miss Thomasina he has in a sense tamed Uncle Apo and made of him an asset rather than a liability to civilized society. Properly he thanks both his mentors, but in a strange way, they should also thank him. His task has been, again from the standpoint of Freudian symbolism, to develop his own ego as a kind of moderator between id and super-ego. In so doing he consolidates his position in the greater Philippine society, thereby giving greater meaning to the teachings of both his mentors. He has also gained greater self-knowledge. From that point of view, Bontoc no longer seems so odd. Rather, his is the story of every young person finding his place in society. It is true that he is fortunate in his mentors, but he is a good student.

The second of Marshall's Manila Bay detectives, Sergeant Jesus-Vincente Ambrosio, occupies a different rung on the post-colonial ladder. Because, to change the metaphor, he lies in the main stream of Philippine society, he lacks many of the obvious identity problems that plague Bontoc. Ambrosio is the sort of young man one expects to find everywhere once the colonial fetters are removed: enthusiastic, optimistic, determined to work hard and work smart and do whatever it takes to get ahead. When we first meet him, he has just finished his detective sergeant's course. Because of it he radiates confidence. 'He was Mr Cool. He was fresh from his Detective Sergeant's Course. The course was called Socio-Public Relationship Officers' Orientation Group (SPROOG)/Intermediate General Leadership Level(IGLL). . . . (after SPROOG and IGLL you took on the mantle of imperturbability)' (*Manila Bay* 11).

He has the blind faith of the innocent in the efficacy of knowledge to manipulate the environment. A little learning is a dangerous thing, and as an alert reader might suspect, the fabric of Ambrosio's mantle of imperturbability is about to be seriously rent. His task is to apprehend a most vile villain, a durian bomber!

'The durian,' as Marshall describes it,

> was the vilest fruit on the face of the earth. Closed, on the tree, a member of the jackfruit family, it resembled a spiky melon. Open, cut into slices for the enjoyment of its connoisseurs, it still resembled a melon. It smelled, however, like a year old sewer after a herd of water buffalos had used it as a rutting hole and then, getting sick of it, had pissed all over it . . . (11)

It seems the bomber is going up to taxis occupied by people with expensive looking packages and throwing glass vials of durian juice into the back seat. During the ensuing moments of chaos, the bomber escapes with the packages. As with Baptiste Bontoc the name is once again significant. Jesus-Vincente=Jesus-victorious, and Ambrosio=ambrosia, with its associations of good taste and good smell, must first persuade a cab driver to jeopardize his cab – and therefore his living – by using it as a decoy and then must subdue the foulest villain in all of detective fiction. The question for the reader becomes, will Ambrosio's name prove to be prophetic or ironic?

Martinez, the third taxi driver Ambrosio approaches, is representative of the first problem. He is too much like Ambrosio, an entrepreneur; he asks too many questions; he cannot be manipulated. Quickly he finishes undoing Ambrosio's police training. Ambrosio's mood plummets from, 'With SPROOG and IGLL you were on your way UP (Urban Promotions). NSC (Next Stop Commissioner)' (11), to ' "If I don't get someone soon I'll be ruined." The working stiff appeal, the fellow laborers in the vineyard of civilization approach. The desperate soon to be demoted to patrolman, non-SPROOG, non-IGLL falling on the knees and grovelling . . .'(14).

The interesting thing here is that, painful as this damage to his new picture of himself may be to Ambrosio, it reveals an inner toughness and a willingness to do what is necessary to get the job done. It is the essence of the post-colonial spirit, tough, resourceful, and peculiarly creative. The continuing interaction between Martinez and Ambrosio illustrates it well.

> Ambrosio said, 'And you can –' He was grovelling. He was grovell-
> ing to a mere Manila taxi driver. Ambrosio said in one last, final,
> humiliating, non-SPROOG, non-IGLL gasp (all that was over...)...-
> Where were the hopes of yesteryear? Or even two hours ago?
>   Ambrosio, crushed, broken, finished, done, the epitome of the
> rotten cop, said in that worst incitement to crime in the entire
> history and entity of Asia, 'And – and –'
>   Martinez said, 'Yes?' His eyes glittered.
>   Ambrosio said, 'And you can –'
>   Ambrosio said, 'And you can *speed*!...'
>   He took no time thinking about it at all.
>   His eyes glittered. He was convinced.
>   Martinez said as an order, 'Get in!' (16)

Ambrosio is paying a high price in dignity. He is also about to take the most frightening ride of his life, trapped in the back seat of a cab driven by a maniac taxi driver whom he has unleashed on the unsuspecting world, simply because he intends to get the job done. One would not wish to be in the shoes of the durian bomber when Ambrosio catches him. The reader begins to suspect that the name Jesus-Vincente Ambrosio may be a prophetic name, though perhaps not without irony.

So far we have seen the entrepreneurial creativity of the post-colonial ideal manifest itself in the form of the post-colonial detective and the post-colonial taxi driver. Now we see it manifested in the form of the post-colonial criminal. Certainly the concept of the durian bomber is unique, but as Ambrosio discovers, this is not the end of his ingenuity.

The bomber does indeed fall upon the decoy cab. He runs for his life with Ambrosio hot on his trail. There is no way he can escape. Even if Ambrosio loses sight of him, Ambrosio's highly sensitive police nose will not lose the scent of him. Ambrosio has visions of his nose on permanent display before posterity in the police museum. At last, spurred on by anger and frustration, Ambrosio runs him to earth. The culprit turns. He has a gun! Ambrosio comes to a screaming halt. He is out of breath, and his own gun is in an ankle holster out of reach. He trips himself reaching for it. The durian bomber raises his own gun . . . and points it at himself. It's a squirt gun. He sprays himself with the scent of pine. The stench of durian vanishes, and so does he, into a labyrinthine apartment block.

The encounter changes Ambrosio. He reverts to the principles of SPROOG and IGLL. 'SPROOG and IGLL teach you to face issues. I have faced this one' (146). He no longer asks, he gives orders. However, this time there is a difference. This time he has taken the principles of his training and creatively modified them to fit the unique situation in which he finds himself. Considering Ambrosio in terms of the same Freudian symbolism as Bontoc, one might say that for Ambrosio, SPROOG and IGLL represent the super-ego. But just as with Bontoc, the superego alone does not provide adequate direction. For Ambrosio, however, there is less counterweight from the id. His experience, arising from a more secure position in society, makes the task of Ambrosio's ego less a matter of balancing between super-ego and id than of modifying the teachings of the super-ego to fit the real world. Once he has done that, we can see that what had previously passed as confidence proved more akin to hubris. Now he is more genuinely confident, but his problems are not over.

Ambrosio knows the bomber will return because,

He had done a course in SPROOG in Human Interface Behavior Prediction (Reference Amerasian/Latin Male, Philippines) and he needed only God's good clear sinuses, a steady hand, a resolute heart, his MANILA POLICE baseball cap, his ools and his honed brain and Good would inevitably triumph. Ambrosio said, 'He'll come. He'll come because it is in the nature of the Amerasian male not not to come and he'll come. . . . He'll come out from his rat hole in Parker Mansions thinking he'll do another hit on Roxas Boulevard and he'll see us here with all our bags full of – he'll presume – riches he won't be able to pass up and, even if he thinks he should pass up such riches – he'll hit us as a point of honor. . . . The average Philippino, once he gets an idea fixed in his head, will pursue it to the bitter end, even if it means his destruction and the destruction of those around him.'
Martinez said nervously, 'Right.' That was exactly what he was worried about. (156)

The taxi driver who is caught in the middle here is recognizing, as Ambrosio doubtless does not, the irony of Ambrosio's remarks. Ambrosio is a Philippino too. He has an idea fixed in his head; the bomber may still be more sly than Ambrosio expects. In fact, he is, but fortunately for the taxi driver, still not sly enough. Good triumphs inevitably.

> 'You're early! You're too goddamned early! And you changed your goddamned clothes!'
> He saw the man reel back.
> He saw fear in his eyes.
> Ego restoration: it washed over him in a single, wonderful flood-gate-opening surge....
> Professionalism, training, competency, efficiency, method, that was what he had learned in Police College.
> Revenge: that is what he had learned in life. (158)

Ambrosio's revenge is diabolical though in a sense poetic. His weapons are ools, hollowed out duck eggs filled with durian juice. He has enough of them to outlast the pine scent supply of any squirt gun.

> The mugger was about to give up. Ambrosio saw him open his mouth to surrender.
> Ambrosio let him have an ool in the face and the mouth closed again. (162)

But when he has captured the mugger and cleaned him up with the last remnants of pine scent, Ambrosio finds there is none left to clean himself. It seems his underlying kindness has betrayed him. Too much super-ego?

> The mugger, smiling, said, 'Thanks very much for cleaning me up.'
> He asked with an evil grin, 'Empty is it?'
> Ambrosio said, '*Neeeyagh!*'
> He had the single usable ool left for the museum.
> In a wonderful, joyous, liberating example of good old veteran, vintage, non-sociological, basic, primeval, police brutality that, for the first time in a long time, thrilled him to the soul, Ambrosio, at point blank range, used it. (163)

So in Ambrosio the id is alive and well, or, at least it is there when he needs it. Because of the difference in social position between Ambrosio and Bontoc, Ambrosio's ego is stronger. Consequently, he dares to unleash the power of the id, and the result is funny rather than deadly.

But, in fact, it is his ego which saves him, for it is his ego strength which prompts him to use his imagination to compensate for the limitations of his formal training. He has been told that his SPROOG/IGILL courses, clearly based on Western police procedures, are true. At best they are seriously inadequate. Without his ego strength he would have admitted failure rather than resorting to his native Philippine 'street smarts' to provide the edge needed for victory.

Eventually, as Bontoc's ego strength grows, he even considers getting rid of Uncle Apo. When in *Whisper* Uncle Apo pleads with Bontoc not to banish him, the scene is touching and illustrates the extent of the control Bontoc has gained over the powers of his own id. Later he finds anger justified and also, incidentally, useful, as he finds himself 'wishing Uncle Apo were here to kill something' (164). But if the balance of Freudian subconscious entities remains a little toward the id in Bontoc, and a little toward the ego in Ambrosio, it lies a little toward the super-ego in Felix Elizalde, the third of Marshall's *Manila Bay* detectives.

Elizalde's post-colonial social position is an interesting one. Because of his Spanish background, he is a member of the former ruling class. Thus he has inherited some 350 years' worth of attitudes and prerogatives of authority. But he is also an honest man who understands what it feels like to be among the ruled in a colonial society. Elizalde is, therefore, in a position to see a broader picture than either Bontoc or Ambrosio, who serve under him. He is governed to a greater degree by his super-ego, and that fact becomes apparent in his interactions with others.

It has often been said that to whom more is given, of him more will be required. This aphorism certainly proves true in Elizalde's case. Of the three detectives he must track down by far the greatest or at least the most insane and reprehensible villains. Yet at the end of *Manila Bay*, when Elizalde has tracked down his quarry and with Bontoc and Ambrosio cornered him in a decaying old mansion, it is not anger or a thirst for revenge that drives him, but fear and the horror of what man may become. Up to this point in his career, though he has been wounded himself, he has never killed another man. Now, as he faces a deranged adversary, he hesitates in a very non-macho way, not wanting to kill another human being, but fearing the monster and reliving his own pain.

> 'Quintero!' ... He saw the man turn – he saw him as a shadow – he saw the gun move, turn onto him. He felt the awful, tearing wound in his stomach again and again. He felt again what it was like to be shot. The gun was coming around to him. He saw, in the light from the far

room, Quintero's face turn to see him. He heard Quintero say in a gasp, 'You!' He had been shot before. He felt again the feeling. Elizalde, trying to hold himself upright, trying to keep the pistol out in front of him, said,"Stop. Stop...Stop...!' (205)

It is in no way a happy or satisfying experience for Elizalde, let alone for Quintero.

> He shot him. In an instant, pulling once at the trigger of his PPK, Elizalde shot him. He had never shot anyone before in his life, but he shot someone now. He shot him in the chest. He saw him stagger and he shot him again. He saw the Armalite waver, he saw it seem to move in a wide arc down towards the stairs, and standing there, in full view of the man as he looked at him, Elizalde shot him again and again until he fell.
> He had thought the worst thing in the world – the thing of all his nightmares – was the terrible, awful moment when he had been shot in the stomach, when, in that moment, he had thought that he was dying and that everything he had done had been wrong and selfish and for himself alone. He had never taken life seriously until the instant when it was fading for him and he thought –
> It was not the worst thing in the world. The worst thing in the world was not to be killed, but to kill someone else. (206)

Here is an epiphany rare indeed in the annals of detection. Nor does killing become easier for Elizalde. In *Whisper* he never does manage to pull the trigger. Nevertheless, he waits so long that Cafiero, another policeman, does the job for him.

It is in *Whisper* that Elizalde begins to learn about the poor of Manila. Early in the book, for example, we learn of his compassion for a poor policeman, officer Gil, who works under him. Officer Gil, we learn, is so poor that all he can afford is a rusty gun. Even worse, he cannot even afford shoes that fit, a serious deficiency in an officer on foot patrol. Gil has stopped and removed his shoes and socks to relieve the pain in his bleeding feet when he hears automatic weapon fire. Before he can get his shoes back on he is confronted with what looks like a woman from the bario engaged in an apparent terrorist attack on two local businessmen.

> She saw him. She stopped.
> He saw her bring up the gun.

His gun was rusty and the oil each day was not like the bluing people without children could afford to buy.

He heard her yell. He knew, outside in the plaza, there were dead people.

He looked for a single mad, sad, humiliated moment at his red, raw feet sticking out under his rolled-up khaki trousers like a clown.

He had never, never thought if it came it would be like this.

He saw the gun come up. Gil said sadly, broken, all his manhood gone in a single moment, 'Oh . . .'

He wept. As he did it he wept.

He wept.

With a single shot to the center of the forehead that smashed her back down the colonnaded arcade like a fragile, bony doll, aiming his rusty revolver with both hands, Patrolman Gil killed her where she stood. (63)

But even this traumatizing experience does not bring relief from the fears of officer Gil. He is out of uniform. According to regulations he could lose his job. Then what would become of his wife and children? He waits in agony for the arrival of higher authority.

In the Casa Manila arcade Elizalde said quietly, 'Go to the coroner's wagon and tell the driver to give you a pair of surgical boots to put on. Carry your shoes and socks. Tell anyone who asks that your shoes had blood on them and I ordered you to take them off so you wouldn't compromise the crime scene.' (77)

Elizalde then sends Gil home by taxi and later backs him up before still higher authority. As a good detective, Elizalde has looked at the evidence regarding Gil's actions at the scene of the crime and arrived at the right conclusion, not that Gil has been derelict, but that Gil is a good man.

This act of compassion, empathy and justice is done with so little discussion or fanfare that it clearly represents an integral part of Elizalde's character. Elizalde's behavior may thus be seen as a model for how authority figures ought to behave toward others. It is no surprise, then, that as he learns more about the poor, he becomes more determined to help them.

Throughout the Manila Bay novels the values of hard work and devotion to duty are asserted at all levels. We can take it for granted that Elizalde would go to the bario if necessary to get the job done, but as his previous behavior has shown, there is more to him than a work ethic. He has never thought of himself as rich, but he comes to realize that compared to the residents of the bario he is just that. They have nothing. He concludes that the Manila poor do not fear death, because it is always near them, but what they do fear is *desaparecido*, which translates from the Spanish which the bario dwellers do not speak as vanished. Someone is making them vanish and using the fear thereby engendered, a fear made even more terrible by the use of this subversively sinister foreign word, to manipulate them into committing acts of suicidal violence.

The bario dwellers have also been persuaded that the police are their enemies – not a very difficult task – and that the police are part of the conspiracy that is making their neighbors and family members vanish. Elizalde recognizes that they have been manipulated, but that does not alter the fact that many of them have been guilty of violent acts and that the potential for much more violence exists. In order to find out who is manipulating them and why, he must go to the bario and ask them. Under the circumstances most officers in his position would probably go armed and in force. They would put down any violence, and if they could not find the answers they needed, they would let the matter drop. There is even some justice in such a position, and certainly a lot more safety. The poor never have very much real power, and there are always plenty of them to spare. Elizalde does not see things this way, however. Again he looks at the evidence and reaches a just conclusion. These are people. They are worth saving. He goes alone. He goes unarmed. Even when Ambrosio and Bontoc and Cafiero arrive, he tells them to put away their guns.

The confrontation is a difficult one. How can Elizalde convince the leaders that he is telling the truth, that he, not the man who gives them guns and a list of targets, is there to help them; that he, the policeman, is their friend?

> His eyes held Elizalde's. Emilio said coldly, suddenly, 'Are you prepared to die? Are you afraid?' Emilio said, 'Give us your life and we will believe you!' (225)

How is he to respond? ' "All I have in my life is my wife. She is what I hold precious" '(226). He tells them how they can find her.

> In the silence, in the hush, Mrs. Barrera asked Elizalde directly, 'Is all you say true?'

Elizalde said, 'Yes, it is all true.' Elizalde said softly, unable to swallow, 'Now, like you, I have nothing. Now like you –'
Mang Eleuterio asked quietly, 'What is it you want?'
He had lost everything. All he wanted now was what the poor wanted. There was nothing else to hope for. He waited. He looked at Emilio's face and could not read what was there. It was all he had left. Elizalde said in a whisper, 'A miracle.' (227)

Elizalde gets his miracle. In so doing he learns what Bontoc and Ambrosio have also learned. To win you must first be willing to lose everything. With an armed mob of the poor at his back, Elizalde confronts the villain, a man like Elizalde, born to a degree of power and influence, but a man gone awry through the misused influence of yet another. Still it is not for Elizalde to extract the revenge of the poor. It is fitting that the fatal shots are fired by Cafiero, a fellow policeman who, having struggled his way painfully out of the bario, acknowledges his roots and by his action affirms Elizalde's desire to at least give them back their lives. There will be no more *desaparecidos*.

The behaviors of all three detectives imply their opposites. Like Elizalde, Bontoc and Ambrosio are called upon to pursue evildoers who to some extent represent themselves gone wrong. Ambrosio's nemesis, the durian bomber of *Manila Bay*, has much more in common with Ambrosio than Ambrosio would probably care to admit. The dwarves that Bontoc is sent to protect in *Whisper*, who resort to crime out of fear, give us a hint of what Bontoc might face had he not benefitted from the mentoring of Uncle Apo and Miss Thomasina.

On this post-colonial stage, then, we see characters dealing with psychological conflicts, cultural conflicts, and political conflicts. What more could the earnest reader ask? The Manila Bay books provide us with years of education through vicarious experience enhanced by the use of humor and suspense. By trope and symbol and paradigm they admonish us to believe that the truth is worth pursuing, that sacrifice is not wasted, and that compassion is justified. They suggest not only ways of thinking but ways of living, and they do it all without in any way diminishing the importance of being earnest.

Bibliography

Marshall, William. *Manila Bay*. 1986. New York: Penguin, 1988.
——. *Whisper*. 1988. New York: Penguin, 1989.

7
Post-Colonial Problems in the Canadian Detective Novels of Eric Wright and Howard Engel

Patrick Quinn

Canada has an inferiority complex. And why not? She sits in the shadow of Great Britain and the United States. The nation prides itself on its liberal immigration and social policies, but while proudly espousing the success of the vertical mosaic – as distinct from the American melting pot – she secretly laments that no sense of real Canadian culture has emerged in her century and a quarter of nationhood. Pricking at this thought is the depressing realisation that the one unique element of this nation, the French-Canadian culture, is rapidly being eroded by the onslaught of Anglo-North American incursions into Québec. The response of the radical French residents of the province is to leave the Confederation before Québec City becomes another Calgary, where quiet bistros become 'all-nite donut' shops and the ubiquitous french fry wagons become Radio Shack outlets. That which is uniquely Canadian seems to have been reduced to images of heavily padded warriors belting hockey pucks and red-coated men in odd-looking hats astride horses in a 'magical ride' through various exhibition grounds on hot Canadian summer evenings.

That Canada has produced important writers and poets in the last years is not in dispute: Leonard Cohen, Margaret Atwood, and Robertson Davies have become names well known outside Canada, but once discovered and famous outside the country, they somehow dilute their Canadian vision to make it almost undiscernible to foreign readers who might be excused for thinking Canada the 51st state. Even Robertson Davies in his *Rebel Angels*, that most Canadian of novels, depicts the College of St John and the Holy Ghost at the University of Toronto as an amalgam of Oxford and Harvard instead of collegiate life as it exists at Canada's premier university.

The problem is that Anglo-Canada cannot escape its bifurcated love/hate affair with its British past and American present. Struggling to free itself from these dominant influences, Canadian culture has turned to its indigenous population, its immigrant ethnic heritage, and its natural beauty for ways to manifest that which is uniquely Canadian. The results are mixed: the exploitation of the native peoples has led to anger and resentment; the inter- and intra-racial tensions among the different Islamic sects, Serbs and Croats, Vietnamese and Caribbean groups have made Canada's larger cities vulnerable to the same problems which faced American cities in the early '70s; and the acid rain and misguided hydro-electric projects have significantly eroded much of Canada's accessible natural beauty. The 'Great North proud and free' is no longer proud; certainly, nothing is free in overtaxed Canada.

The Canadian detective novel is a further example of the country's struggle to find a national identity and to shake off the American and British influences which have to date dominated the genre. The two writers with whom this paper is concerned, Howard Engel and Eric Wright, serve to illustrate this confrontation within the genre of detective fiction. Their struggle is clearly discernible in the dustcover selling hype of publishing companies like Penguin and the language they choose to use to market their books to a Canadian audience. On the jacket of *Murder Sees the Light* (1984), a Benny Cooperman novel written by Howard Engel, the description of Benny serves to underline this point: 'Whether gamely gutting a fish he accidentally caught or unearthing (literally) evidence of illicit mining, murder and diabolism, he is flip, wry and somehow all-Canadian.'

Is this then the definition of what makes a Canadian? Someone who is able to gut a fish, yet remain glib in the face of adversity? Of course not, but the character of Benny Cooperman in the seven novels that Howard Engel has written since 1980 does give us a glimpse of a Canadian hero whose personality has doubtlessly been influenced both by tough guy Sam Spade and the cerebral and witty Philip Marlowe, but who remains discernibly different from his American models.

Benny Cooperman, in fact, was created by Engel with a view to accentuating the differences between a Canadian detective and his American counterpart. Benny comes from Grantham, a small fictional Canadian city in southern Ontario, thinly disguised St Catharines, the town where Engel grew up. Benny is a traditional, struggling gumshoe who once made a livable wage dredging up unsavory muck for his divorce-bent clients but who, with the liberalization of Canadian divorce laws, must take whatever assignments he can get to stay alive and pay his annual private investigator license fees. His mother and father still live in the same town, but Benny chooses to live at the slightly seedy City Hotel on King Street [he is forced to leave his preferred home in *A Victim Must Be Found* (1988)]. Benny's office is 28 steps from the ground floor and on the same floor as the business premises of the alcoholic and sexually ambiguous Irish chiropodist Dr Frank Bushmill. Benny eats his chopped egg on white (the Canadian version of 'hard-boiled') at the United Cigar Store, where all the waitresses seem surly and uncommunicative. This slightly unsavory atmosphere becomes part of the fabric of the series' flavor much in the way that San Francisco evokes the Continental Op of Dashiell Hammett.

Clearly, Engel is parodying the style of Hammett and Spillane; the descriptions of characters are brisk and to the point. Describing his interview with his once missing client in *Murder on Location* (1982), Benny says, 'Billie Mason walked into the restaurant alone, looking more attractive than her eight-by-ten glossy three-quarter view. I've never seen blue like the blue of her eyes and her neck was like a note held at the end of a song' (75). Of Marvin Raxlin, the film producer from the same book, Engel reports, 'Raxlin was a man in his mid-thirties. He looked like a chartered accountant candidate who'd not made the grade. He was dressed from head to toe in imitation fabrics, the kind that never wear out, they just turn yellow and roll over' (61). Benny has the ability to size up his clients and acquaintances in a style very reminiscent of Sam Spade or Mike Hammer.

No one would deny, least of all Engel, that the necessity of following the American school of hard-boiled detectives is also *de rigueur* in order to have a detective novel published in North America. Still, Engel is able to have fun playing with the expectations of this genre and manages to impart a Canadian flavour to some of his more outrageous metaphors. His description of the sartorial inelegance of Raxlin, for example, which evokes the dying of a ground hog amidst the Canadian autumn foliage, would be quite out of keeping in the tale of a street-wise Los Angeles detective. In fact, Benny's rather slow and methodical approach to life in general, typified by his meditative shaving and endless showers, sets the Canadian sleuth apart from his American colleagues: no one beneath the 49th parallel would take as much time as Benny to do anything!

Like his American counterparts, however, Benny has a weakness for a particular type of woman, the kind of woman who comes to mind when one hears Humphrey Bogart use the word 'dame.' Throughout the Cooperman series, Benny is attracted to and is largely successful with a number of sexually exciting women, for reasons which seem to surprise him as much as they do the reader. The scene is set in Grantham, Ontario in the 1980s, yet Engel still manages to evoke the American detective novel of the 1930s with, for example, the introduction of the soon-to-be widowed Myrna Yates: Benny is sitting in his office listening to the clinking of high heels climbing his 28 stairs when he glimpses a shadowy silhouette through the frosted glass of his door. He calls for the figure to enter:

> She was the sort of woman that made you wish you'd stayed in the shower for an extra minute or taken another three minutes shaving. I felt a little undressed in my own office. She had what you could call a tailored look. Everything was so understated it screamed. I could hear the echo bouncing off the bank across the street.
>
> She took a chair on the other side of my bleached oak desk and played around with her handbag. It matched her shoes, and I thought the car outside probably matched the rest of the outfit. Sitting in the sunlight, with the shadow of the letters of my sign caressing her trim figure, she looked about thirty, but I put part of that down to decent treatment, regular meals, baths and trips to Miami, things like that. When she raised her eyes to look at me, they were grey. (*The Suicide Murders* 9)

What further distinguishes Benny from the Sam Spade school of detectives is his Jewishness. Indeed, the mix of Benny's Jewishness and his Canadian identity work to subvert the American formula of the morose, solitary detective so popular in the American detective canon. Benny is a not a particularly fervent Jew: in *A City Called July* (1986), when he is visited by Rabbi Meltzer and Mr Tepperman, the President of the B'nai Sholom Congregation, whose aim is to locate the shady lawyer who has absconded with half of the congregation's investments, Benny has to admit that 'It had been some time since [he'd] seen either one of them, but [he] remembered the occasions the way a headstone remembers the name chiseled into its face' (3). Still, it is Benny's essential Jewishness that turns the hard-boiled detective soft. His tussles at home with his larger-than-life Jewish mother, who tries in *Murder on Location* to fix him up with a nice Jewish girl or who in *A City Called July* refuses to talk to her ungrateful son after he misses Friday dinner because he had been kidnapped and held at gunpoint are the stuff of Jewish comedy. Benny's close relationship with his gin-rummy playing father, who often knows more about the less salubrious side of Grantham than Benny, offers some touching moments of paternal guidance.

Benny's constant unfavourable comparison to his brother Sam, the doctor, psychologically exposes the hard-boiled detective's vulnerability. The Jewish family relationship and the interaction of Benny's relatives are vital to the fabric of the novels.

Not surprisingly, the setting of Engel's novels serves notice that this is a Canadian story. In fact, five out of the seven Cooperman novels are set in the St Catharine's area of southern Ontario. Clearly, St Catharine's and Niagara Falls bear little resemblance to San Francisco and Los Angeles, but one never forgets the physical and psychological proximity of the United States. Indeed, *Murder on Location*, Engel's first Cooperman novel, is set in the most Americanized of all Canadian towns: the once exotic honeymoon haven, Niagara Falls. The gaudy setting of the Niagara District attracted Engel to the genre of detective fiction in the first place, and except for James Nablo's *The Long November*, no other writer has exploited the potential of this border town.

Murder on Location is an interesting novel from a number of perspectives, but most importantly it brings together the high powered world of American cinema and small town Canada, with its local hoodlums and artists. We are reminded of the backdrop of the amoral and majestic Falls throughout the novel; the ominous sounds of dashing water thunder continuously, and mammoth daggers of frozen water hang precariously over the filming. The film being made, *The Ice Bridge* is set on the Canadian side of the Falls. The final chase scene (strongly reminiscent of the winter chase scene in *Uncle Tom's Cabin*) is played out on the ice floes beneath the Falls; rough justice is meted out by the raging torrents to the villain Neil Furlong, a Canadian local who has sold out to American materialist interests, not unlike the city of Niagara Falls, Ontario.

While he is searching for information about Furlong, Benny crosses the Rainbow Bridge into New York state. Interestingly, Engel's description of Benny's journey across the border offers the reader an insight into a seldom articulated aspect of the Canadian identity: that is, an aversion to and fear of things American. After crossing the border (we hear the ever familiar American greeting, 'have a good day'), Benny experiences a culture shock that both disconcerts and depresses him:

> The whole place looked like it had been hit by a fire-raid and the rebuilding had stopped when the job was only half done.... I followed a street of brick and wooden two-and three-story buildings across a railway track, with dirty snowdrifts high between the rails. More shopworn snow leaned up against the sides of dog-eared stores and walk-up apartments.... At the corner not far from the railway

track I saw the neon sign advertising Schlitz Beer. The sign above the door, looking faded and tired, read Surf Lounge. (*Murder* 128)

The interior of the bar is dark, and the ambience cold and unwelcoming in comparison to the cheery lounges on the Canadian side (the 'Colonel John', for example). The surly bartender reminds Benny of Mr Punch ('His nose and chin were conspiring to meet at a later date'). When he eventually discovers all he needs to know, Benny is pleased to be leaving. In this world, he is a stranger in a strange land, an alien visitor who longs for his own planet only a few yards away across the safety of the 'magical' Rainbow Bridge.

Murder Sees the Light takes the reader into the Canadian wilderness, which has been contaminated by the return of ex-Canadian Norbert E. Patten, a television evangelist who has come to Algonquin Park (a large provincial park in eastern Ontario) to avoid a legal action. (His church faces a possible $400 million class action suit if the US Supreme Court rules against him.) During his stay in Canada, Patten must kill one of the locals, who threatens to expose the evangelist's past participation in a satanic cult. The sub-text here allows for little obfuscation. The effect of Americanization on Patten is complete corruption. Not only has he realized that the American ethic of materialistic religion can be used to exploit the not-so-canny consumer (shades of Chaucer's Pardoner?), but his brash, arrogant manner sets him apart from the Canadian characters. Patten has set up a religious franchise using an amalgam 'of Zen, Spiritualism, and the old-time religion of the American Bible Belt' (4). His Ultimate Church is described as a super cult, and its leader as a megalomaniac who wants to rule the world, but is unable to beat our Canadian hero in a chess match. Benny, of course, cottons on to the motivation and method of murder, and in a dramatic hospital confrontation is able to correctly explain to Patten the sequence of his nefarious actions. Patten's over-confident reaction is right out of Chandler:

'So long, fella. Don't take getting whipped so hard. The deck was stacked against you. No witnesses, no fingerprints, and I've got a steel-edged alibi. Lorca and the boys will back me up on that. You see, I couldn't let that dim-witted yokel ruin things for me and just at a time when I needed to keep a very low profile. No hard feelings, Benny?' (231)

What Benny and Patten do not know is that Sergeant LePage of the Ontario Provincial Police has anticipated this exchange and has planted a tape recorder in the hospital room to record Patten's confession as evidence, which may or may not be admissible in the Canadian court of law. At this point the villain appears to have been checked; the Canadian judiciary system must now find a way of bringing the American evangelist to justice. As the plot moves on and the American cancer has been removed from the Canadian wilderness, Benny's last observation confirms that nature has returned to normal and 'the beavers were up to their old tricks' (240). Or could it be that the underestimated Canadians have outwitted the clever Yanks again?

Eric Wright's Charlie Salter springs from a tradition completely alien to Benny Cooperman. Charlie inhabits a world written in the tradition of what Eric Wright calls the 'decent copper school of police procedural' which includes among its number Ruth Rendell's Chief Inspector Reginald Wexford and Colin Dexter's Chief Inspector Morse. Like them, Salter is involved in sorting out all the potential criminals from the actual murderer by slowly piecing together clues and eliminating all but the actual perpetrator. The focus is on mental acuity as opposed to action, but the Canadian Salter lacks the powerful personality of Wexford or the cultural background of Oxford-educated Morse. In fact, unlike his more eccentric English colleagues, Charlie Salter is unusually down-to-earth (like the salt) and tends to prefer blending in with a crowd as opposed to bringing attention to himself, a trait which might be applied generally to Canadians.

Salter is a working-class Torontonian in his late 40s; he was born in Cabbagetown and has moved upmarket to the 'Anglo-Saxon ghetto off the Oriole Parkway' (*Night* 12). He is married to the daughter of a historically prominent and well-connected Loyalist family from Prince Edward Island, Annie Montagu, whose values and independent judgements often cause an interesting undercurrent of tension in the novels. Salter has two teenage sons, Seth and Angus, neither of whom he understands very well, although occasionally father and sons do fish, golf, or chop Christmas trees together.

When Wright's Salter series opens in 1983, Charlie, in *The Night the Gods Smiled*, is a disgruntled police officer of the Metro Toronto Police department. He has supported the wrong candidate for Deputy Chief and has been given a bare desk and uncarpeted floor in some dismal corner of the police headquarters in charge of the General Duties section. Charlie's problems involve a number of post-modern dilemmas; he cannot communicate with his family, he is passing through a mid-life crisis, he sees his once homogenous Toronto taking on the guises of the large impersonal metropolis, he finds his bosses do not value him as a person, and he is unsure how he feels about love, loyalty, lust, and lies.

Although the settings of the novels shift considerably, Toronto is the center of Salter's world, and here Wright is at his strongest capturing the nuances of Canada's largest city. And Toronto is lovingly brought to life in his works, for the reader gains a sense of a uniquely blended Canadian city spread out from the lush tennis clubs lining Lake Ontario to the sprawling suburbs where even the pinnacles of the soaring CN Tower can be glimpsed only on a clear day.

Wright's ambiguous depiction of sleek silver high-rises and European-style shops, bistros, and coffee-houses that proliferate throughout the city suggest an uneasiness with the tension between Canadian and European values. Obviously, Charlie, himself, is somewhat ill at ease in this ultra-modern chic that Toronto has become. In *A Question of Murder* (1988), Wright uses the old hippy area of Yorkville as a backdrop for the murder of a gentrified dope peddler; ironically, the social class of the victim is reflected in the Yuppie marketplace that Yorkville has become. The dingy coffee-houses and psychedelic paraphernalia shops of the '60s have been 'replaced by couturiers and clothing designers' (16). As Salter wanders through the village during his investigations, he comes upon the typical Yorkville shop, a boutique known as Vera's, with a 'grey-and-white picture-frame window through which could be seen a single silk dress hanging in an antique pine wardrobe' (17). The simple elegance of Toronto's stylish, almost European, image can be heard in this description. For Charlie, the 'new' Yorkville resembles a movie backdrop; he is never comfortable in the artificial ambience of the *nouveau riche*, and he has difficulty sharing their values.

Salter clearly feels no place for himself amidst the architectural splendours and conspicuous wealth of gentrified Yorkville, and he also finds the aimless rapid expansion of his city disturbing. When he goes to interview potential suspects at Douglas College in *The Night the Gods Smiled*, for example, he finds his way barred by phalanxes of security people and wonders where these hordes have come from. The populations of Toronto and Douglas College have burgeoned since the late '60s, and the college's patrolled hallways and the campus security operations are part of Canada's dues for entering the group of seven industrial nations.

Charlie must not only accept the post-modern Canadian urban artificiality and blight; he must also struggle against the outmoded colonial English traditions that inundate his wife's family. The origins of Annie's family traditions are lost in the twilight of Prince Edward Island's past, but those traditions are familiar to anyone familiar with the English aristocratic detective genre. The post-colonial awareness has not touched the core of Salter homelife: the family silver comes out on Sunday; the heavy, dark polished furniture dominates the rooms; and porridge is served for breakfast on Saturday. All the men in the Montagu family (Annie's maiden name), including Charlie's two sons, attend Upper Canada College, one of the last bastions of Anglican education in the country. Instead of talking about the latest Blue Jays' victory, Charlie's sons confuse their poor father by playing and talking about cricket. Furthermore, every summer the Salters spend their summer holiday in the safe precincts of English heritage, Prince Edward Island. Wright takes advantage of this anachronistic colonial setting in *A Body Surrounded by Water* (1987), a double wordplay on the island itself and the fate of the murder victim.

While on the Island, Canadian Salter finds himself straining to conform to the bourgeois expectations inherent in the English traditions of Annie's family. For example, Annie's family are all good sailors, but Salter has not had much opportunity to learn to sail growing up in the shadow of warehouses in Cabbagetown. There exists a mixture of insouciance and insensitivity in the Montagu family's expectations of Charlie, and he is largely ignored till the mystery develops. The crux of the mystery centers on the rediscovery, by Annie's father, and subsequent theft, of the Great Silver Seal of Prince Edward Island, an important Loyalist artifact which had initially been looted by some freebooting American while blockading Charlottetown (the capital of the province) during the American War of Independence. The theft may suggest an early example of American cultural imperialism, but Charlie has more sympathy with the freebooter than the insufferable 'good families' he meets on the case. Perhaps justifiably, the stolen seal is never found even after the murder is cleared up, but the Toronto cop gains the grudging respect of the local RCMP detachment as well as his in-laws by piecing together the clues, discovering the murderers, and learning to fly-fish in the interim. Fly-fishing is a far more acceptable pastime than boating for a democratic Canadian.

Some of Charlie's frustration with the remnants of English colonial attitude are reflected in *A Question of Murder* (1988), where the visit of 'a royal princess' (no doubt Diana) has thrown the Special Affairs Department (to which Charlie has been promoted) into a flurry of activity because the entire police force has been marshalled to guard the Princess from her well-wishers. When the Princess comes through Yorkville, Charlie is in close contact with her bodyguards and admits to a certain territorial friction between the RCMP, Ontario Provincial Police, and Metropolitan Police (the Canadian contingent) and the English body-guards 'who saw themselves as experts' (56). When a van is blown up and the driver killed near the Princess's route through Yorkville, a crime which the British agents come to investigate, their dismissal is rather cavalier. Speaking of the bomb: 'So it wasn't meant for throwing and it wasn't meant to bother us. . . . A little local bother. Seen enough, Neville?' (68). The two experts walk immediately away and wash their hands of the Canadian spot of trouble as if the violent death was beneath their notice. How reminiscent of British colonial rule through-out the last three centuries.

It is England and Englishness that Salter has to overcome, and in *Death in the Old Country* (1985) Wright takes his hero into the heartland of the enemy. From the standpoint of plot, the novel is predictable; Charlie and his wife go to England for a much-needed holiday, and as a result of a car accident are forced to spend a few days in the pictur-esque Cotswold village of Tokesbury Mallet. The landlord of the hotel in which they are staying is found stabbed soon after their arrival, follow-ing which Salter unravels an elaborate blackmailing scheme which has him following up clues in Florence and Toronto to bring the murderer, who is kicked and felled by a riderless horse on a steeplechase course while trying to escape his pursuers, to justice. In Sayers-like fashion, Wright produces a number of possible suspects who have good reasons to have killed the mysterious landlord, a list which is fascinating as well as diverse: the young American student, the Canadian Miss Rundstedt, the voluptuous Italian wife and her slick brother, Mario; the voyeur Gregory, and the mysterious prowler who tickles women's toes. From this menagerie of characters, Salter slowly builds his case and fires a few shots at the paternalistic homeland.

More than a mystery novel, *Death in the Old Country* is a lovingly developed take-off of British life. From the beginning, when the Salters are travelling on a rainy afternoon down a narrow road heavy with English traffic looking hopefully for an inn-keeper who will not swindle them, we know that the old country will be mercilessly satirized. Within a page of the opening, Salter is meditating on the number of words the English have for raining, 'Spitting, drizzling, a few drops, damp out' (10). Indeed, the rain becomes a partial cause of the accident which acts as the *deus ex machina* for the Salters' sojourn in the village hotel. The choice of hotel opens the door for a comic harangue on British accommodations. Here all the stereotypes of this aspect of English life are exposed:

Their first experience was in a two-star hotel in a resort on the coast of Dorset. . . . The landlord showed them a huge, dank bedroom with two double beds and two cots.

'It's a family room,' said the owner. A small pot-bellied man with an RAF moustache, cavalry twill trousers, and egg stains on his check-ered waistcoat. 'You can have it for the price of a double' (21).

The room, with its chipped paint and all, is a tatty but fitting surround for a hostelry where hand-written notices impose time limits on the enjoyment of every activity. The double bed turns out to be two singles lashed together, the point at which they join forming an uncomfortable ridge; dinner is a horrid affair of tinned food and dessert of 'some crusts of bread soaked in milk in which some raisins were floating' (23). And the infernal rain never lets up for the duration of the novel.

English life as portrayed here is mordantly sordid, cheap, and dreary. When Salter tries to purchase some apples at the local market before heading off to the steeplechases, he notes that the shiny ones he wants are for display only, and is offered instead a lesser variety which he refuses to take. The only rooms he finds habitable in England are, ironically, those situated in an Italian-run hotel. So where is this English gentility to which Canadians show such deference? One begins to wonder if Salter will find it in the professional ranks, such as the police force.

Salter's encounters with the British police give Wright a wonderful opportunity to parody this famous British institution. Inspector Churcher, the slightly insecure and therefore highly nervous man in charge of the constabulary of Tokesbury Mallet, evidently sees Salter as a lesser professional, referring to him constantly as a 'colonial colleague' and a 'colleague from the Dominions' (a term *only* 50 years out of date). When the inevitable murder is discovered, Churcher is nonplussed by the supposed murderer's lack of knowledge about the whereabouts of the murder weapon and the inconsistencies of her confession, but all the same brusquely dismisses Salter's nagging inquiries:

'Well Charles, a little story for you to take back to Toronto. But I imagine you get a lot of this with such a high percentage of foreigners.'

Salter's splendid rejoinder reflects his irritation with his British counterpart:

'Yes, it's the interesting English-type murders we miss. The ones where some railway clerk has fourteen middle-aged women buried in the basement.' (67)

The condescension of Churcher in this and the subsequent interviews annoys Salter, but it is Churcher's superior, the weatherbeaten upper-class Superintendent Wylie Hamilton, who represents the squirearchy of English police departments, who irritates Salter more. It is obvious that Hamilton recognizes Churcher's incompetence; he turns therefore to the only available alternative, the Canadian Salter, whom he uses as a sounding board for his investigation. His attitude towards Salter, however, is patronizing; he claims in mock disbelief that he does not know how crimes are solved in Saskatchewan, and ignoring Salter's protests that Hamilton has his geographic facts wrong, calls him the diminutive 'laddie.' This patriarchal treatment of a competent detective spurs Charlie into action.

Of course, it is necessary that the colonial hero should best the English pretentiousness (this is a Canadian novel), and Salter ultimately wins a pyrrhic victory. After the criminal has been discovered and exposed, the Englishman and the Canadian drive to Stratford. On the way, Hamilton begins giggling to himself:

'My game, I think,' Hamilton said.
Salter said, 'Bullshit. You wouldn't have got there today without me.'
'Right,' Hamilton conceded. 'Your point all right.' 'And I got Rundstedt first, remember.' (206)

The Canadian pushes home his advantage, refusing to knuckle under to the Brit's argument that all would have been solved without his interference, but not until Salter sends Hamilton a brief letter dubbing him a 'jammy bastard' does the Canadian feel completely vindicated.

Charlie Salter, then, is a post-colonial detective attempting to expose the absurdity of his country's dependence on the British heritage and culture and to establish a pride in things Torontonian, and by extension Canadian. To do so, however, he is constantly contending against the intrusive English legacy (represented by his wife's family and the latent prejudices within the monied class of Toronto life). The discord between the two antagonists in *The Night the Gods Smiled*, described by a Douglas College professor as 'some dreadful secret that kept them apart while it linked them in silent bondage . . . Like a theme for a Conrad story' (30), seems to mirror the dissonance between the reality of English/Canadian antagonism. The easing of this animosity is deftly handled in the conclusion of *The Man Who Changed His Name* (1986) when Christmas celebrations force together Salter's working class proto-Canadian father and Annie's bourgeois England-worshipping parents. During dinner in the revolving restaurant on the top of the CN tower above the glittering city, the two cultures meet in neutral space to abandon temporarily their cultural difference and to enjoy the festive season together. After the success of bringing off this holiday coup, the truce between warring factions allows the always sexually responsive Charlie Salter to jump into bed beside his wife and celebrate their joint victory in the season of peace and tranquillity.

Both of the authors of these novels, Eric Wright and Howard Engel, recognized the '80s as a watershed when Canadians finally were ready to accept detective novels set in Canada with Canadian heroes. Both writers consciously tried to make their respective heroes distinctively Canadian while following the American or English detective genre, but ironically the tensions that develop out of their forcing Canadian characters into this mold are what set these works apart from the traditional American or English detective novel. Like Canada itself, Benny Cooperman and Charlie Salter are endeavoring to shatter the stereotyped image which has been foisted on them by a conformist culture which is unable to see their individualism for the trees. From the perspective of popular culture, Benny and Charlie symbolize the Canadian dilemma very well – how to find a Canadian selfhood when the surrounding colonial forces dictate what Canadians can or cannot be.

Biliography

(Includes Engel and Wright books not cited.)

Engel, Howard. *Murder on Location*. Toronto: Seal, 1984.
——. *Murder Sees the Light*. Markham: Penguin, 1985.
——. *The Suicide Murders*. New York: Penguin, 1985.
——. *A City Called July*. Markham: Penguin, 1986.
——. *A Victim Must Be Found*. Markham: Penguin, 1988.
——. *Ransom Game*. Markham: Viking, 1989.
——. *Dead and Buried*. Markham: Viking, 1990.
——. *There Was an Old Woman*. Toronto: Viking, 1993.
——. *Getting Away With Murder*. Toronto: Viking, 1995.
——. *Lord High Executioner: An Unashamed Look at Hangmen, Headsmen, and the Kind*. Key Porter, 1996.

Wright, Eric. *The Night the Gods Smiled*. Toronto: Collins, 1983.
——. *Smoke Detector*. New York: Scribner, 1984.

——. *A Single Death*. Toronto: Collins, 1986.
——. *The Man Who Changed His Name*. New York: Scribner, 1986.
——. *Death in the Old Country*. Toronto: Collins, 1987.
——. *A Body Surrounded by Water*. Toronto: Collins, 1987.
——. *A Question of Murder*. Toronto: Collins, 1988.
——. *A Sensitive Case*. London: Collins, 1990.
——. *Final Cut*. Toronto: Collins, 1991.
——. *A Fine Italian Hand*. Toronto: Worldwide, 1992.
——. *Death By Degrees*. Toronto: Worldwide, 1993.
——. *Death of a Sunday Writer*. Foul Play, 1997.
——. *Buried in Stone*. Toronto: Worldwide, 1998.

8

The Post-Colonial Detective in People's China

Jeffrey C. Kinkley

Although the thaw in Chinese literature since the death of Mao has led to an explosion of critical studies commensurate with the reawakening of Chinese creativity, the new literary works have seldom been called 'post-colonial.'[1] Chinese were colonized by the West only in Macao, Hong Kong, and Southeast Asia; by Japan only in Taiwan and, for a time, in Manchuria. Proud of this history, Chinese have been heard to scorn British India as a nation of 'slaves' (Hay 240).

From a Chinese viewpoint, China, not the West, has from ancient times been the core of universal empire and culture – a country calling itself the Central Kingdom, axis of the cosmos. Even in this century, after imperialism so undermined Chinese sovereignty, China could be viewed by its citizenry as the first nation in Asia, including Russia, to stage a successful republican revolution; the bearer of modern nationalism to Korea and Vietnam; and, since the 1960s, the world socialist vanguard and leader of the Third World, without quite having to belong to it.

Unbridled nationalism, interwoven with what enthusiasts of post-colonial writing might disapprovingly term cultural and linguistic 'essentialism,'[2] stifled post-colonial and all other discourse with the West after the Communist revolution. Conditions were ripe for Hong Kong to create a fully post-colonial literature in English, but only Singapore did.[3] In People's China it was unfashionable, if not dangerous, to know English; by the late 1960s, it was dangerous even to know Russian.

Yet, Sun Yat-sen himself called all China a 'hypo-colony': a realm suffering from the ill effects of colonialism and reaping none of its infrastructure-building advantages (2: 106–8). Raising the pitch of anti-imperialist rhetoric to unprecedented levels, socialist China designated all Chinese history from 1840 to 1949 as 'semi-colonial' – that is, manipulated from afar by economic and political forces let in by the 'Unequal Treaties.' If the propaganda rang hollow, the 1950s expropriations of foreign property were impressive both in magnitude and symbolism. China's soul had been wounded, and the West knew the reason why.

Resistance to the idea of Chinese literature as post-colonial perhaps owes less to the uniqueness of Chinese history than to the fact that post-colonial anger is most evident in the sub-literature of the Mao era. Few Chinese, not to speak of Westerners, can bear to read those works today, and not only because they repeat themselves, but because they echo sentiments not just of resistance, but of hate.

Post-colonial dialogue with the West is, however, visible in China's new literature of the 1980s – China's post-post-colonial literature, if you will. Subject to buffeting by the capitalist world economic system again, China sees itself as a backward country once more, groping its way out of cultural desertification left by the Cultural Revolution. Like post-colonial Africans who have seen that independence is not enough, the Chinese have decided that autarchy is not freedom (Lazarus 3–5). Psychologically, the post-colonial idea is all too relevant to the new Chinese literature, whose authors hang on foreign critics' every word (Owen 28–32; Jenner 177–227); one has only to dig, as an archeologist, through all the layers of withdrawal and denial.

Although Chinese citizens are continually being reminded, by their leaders and by external forces, that their nation is a 'developing country,' they still call their country *Zhongguo*, 'the central nation,' and deep inside perhaps still feel themselves to be at the hub of the spinning planet. To them, China's reversal of fortune under colonial institutions is always qualified by an idea of China being the core, in the past and in the future, if not in the present. To the Chinese, then, China might be thought of as a *'former core*, post-colonial' nation (or 'ex-core, post post-semicolonial' nation, to the quibbler).

Enter the post-colonial detective: in People's China, a policeman, symbol of power, with all the ambivalence power evokes. And among literary detectives, only cops have a 'recognizable counterpart in real life,' George Dove notes, for few of us have met a private investigator, and no one has witnessed the brilliance of a Sherlock Holmes (Dove 3). American ambivalence toward power is the reason for the relatively late appearance of police heroes in our own fiction, some suggest; curiously, one of the earliest was of Chinese ancestry: Charlie Chan (Bargainnier 1). But is the people's police power today not itself traceable to China's semicolonial past? Indeed. Moreover, all this literature about Chinese cops (plus all that literature about Western *private* eyes) is a reminder of the absolute nature of the Chinese cop's power. He monopolizes every imaginative, solipsistic possibility of the sleuth. There are no private investigators in China, and this, to some readers, is bound to symbolize the precariousness of the whole private sphere.

China's detective fiction is thus post-colonial in at least three respects: its literary form, the heavily policed social reality on which it draws, and even the resistance to that social reality that some authors manage to work into their texts. Pre-modern China had police, sophisticated theories limiting the power of the sovereign, and literary heroes famous for their powers of detection. But China's modern police system, human rights discourse, even its contemporary detective fiction, are the offspring of twentieth-century models imported from the West. That China preceded Japan and the West in these cultural manifestations renders all the more painful the realization that China's native forms have been displaced – 'modernized.'

And China's old police, civil society, and literary culture were all displaced at the behest of 'the people.' The new police were installed by the Communist 'masses' themselves. The recent democracy movement comes from a minority of scholars and students, but their authority to speak for the masses is legitimated by tradition. As for detective fiction, not just writers, but the great majority of readers have voted with their pocketbooks for new, Western genres – and translations from abroad.

A unique predicament of the literature, compared with the police apparatus, is that it still has to compete on Chinese soil with fresh imports from Japan and the West. The Japanese are as good at writing detective stories as they are at manufacturing autos; in the absence of 'protective legislation,' competition from Japanese and other foreign detective fiction in Chinese translation seems already to have nearly squelched the growth of a major native detective fiction on Taiwan.[4] How mainland China took drastic measures to prevent a similar outcome is a story to be told shortly – for it was the Chinese police themselves who intervened.

True, post-colonialism in recent Chinese detective fiction is 'all in the mind'; the literary works analysed below are not fresh linguistic or thematic renderings of China as a 'new place,' nor are they expressly preoccupied with the legacy of European imperial aggression, as are so many post-colonial works in English. Perhaps this display of Chinese detachment goes with the genre. World detective fiction has long eschewed politics and found 'new places' close at hand, whether in mysterious niches at home or treasure troves from the colonies. Let us then explore the hidden historical dimensions of Chinese post-coloniality, and then proceed to our main concern: how China developed quite Western genres, only to 'write back,' in the end, to the core, with modifications of Chinese descent.[5]

China's 'Ex-core Post-colonial' Police Culture, in Fact and Fiction

The origins of policing in China have been little studied, but research by Alison Dray-Novey finds that the Qing dynasty (1644–1911) organized a complex, territorial system of watches to patrol all Peking long before such systems existed in the West, and thus well in advance of industrialization. Even so, the Chinese police system of today traces its ancestry to a wholly revamped, modern institution of largely Japanese inspiration (which in turn was influenced by continental European models) introduced into China at the end of the Qing. The police system established after the Communist revolution (rule of urban areas was a relatively new challenge for Mao's rural-based Communist Party) was organized around police substations (*paichusuo*) quite similar to Japanese patrol boxes (*koban*).[6] There were also patently Western totalitarian influences from the Soviet Union, and, in the 1980s, active US–China exchanges of 'police delegations' and Chinese importation of American and Japanese technology, from surveillance camera systems to stun guns.

What exactly the Chinese police mean to China's urban masses today is anyone's guess, after the anti-authoritarian movements of the late 1980s – though many Peking police identified with the democracy movement of April–May 1989, and freethinking Yu Haocheng, head of the Masses' Press (the official publishing house of the Ministry of Public Security, which publishes so many works of fiction and nonfiction about crime), was put under house arrest in the subsequent crackdown. Even in Chinese fiction published by the police, 'the masses' are typically depicted as thinking the police rough and undereducated, an auxiliary of the People's Liberation Army (PLA) more attuned to the use of force than the niceties of law (which after all was codified only in 1979) (Leng). Apart from the age-old social consensus that only 'bad people' ever have to deal with the police, widespread fear and loathing of them dates back at least to the era of Chiang Kai-shek's mob-related operatives, and the undisciplined warlord paramilitary units that preceded and coexisted with them. The post-'49 People's Police were most particularly discredited during the Cultural Revolution, which labeled them an instrument of the bourgeoisie needing to be 'smashed.' Police powers assumed by other ad hoc groups at the time, and uniformed police who enforced the Cultural Revolution dictatorship and continued to serve in Deng Xiaoping's regime, left the force severely compromised even in its own self-image, as recent books by police authors clearly attest.

Yet the all too Orwellian People's Police, as sanitized in fiction, are in some ways comfortingly old-fashioned and 'Chinese' in comparison with the violent police and busybody private detectives of foreign fiction and film. The 'watchman' (as opposed to 'legalistic') style of policing, a sociological ideal type described in James Q. Wilson's classic *Varieties of Police Behavior*, is virtually an explicit ideal in People's China, which has had relatively little crime and, as we noted, 'no laws' until 1979, and yet was deathly afraid of political and spontaneous mob violence well before the Tiananmen massacre.[7] Wilson's 'watchman' police do not seek actively to enforce the law for its own sake or to build large arrest records, but concentrate on keeping the peace and preventing mass outbreaks of violence. Viewing the public in terms of groups, they 'distribute' justice according to what each group 'deserves,' often letting families and other authorities administer punishment.

This was the style of the old Peking police, Dray-Novey finds, and it is so still today. Writes sociologist Ezra Vogel of the term 'public security' as used in post-'49 China, 'It symbolizes a particular approach to controlling deviance in society, an approach that stresses the maintenance of public security and public order over the preservation of law' (75). The police do much surveillance and a lot of patrolling (China has a household registration police service that makes periodic household visits), they handle 'serious' crimes that could have a social impact, and they develop auxiliary networks of 'eyes and ears,' from ex-criminals to 'KGB in tiny bound feet,' the neighborhood association grannies and grannies' deputies who check all comings and goings. The watchman style had its apotheosis in the concept of 'preventive justice,' a legal counterpart to Maoist preventive medicine: better to stop a crime before it happens than investigate one after the fact; more important, in fact, to interview and do ideological work on people who saw someone get away with a crime than to track down the culprit. Novels written by policemen entrenched in the norms of their profession still assume that crime is to be combated not for the sake of abstract justice, but because of its social effect.

In this light, the classic Western detective is simply a snoop. He (maybe even she!) pries into things that in China are 'secrets' – information routinely tracked not even by the police, but by the family and its surrogate, the 'unit' (the factory, school, store, or neighborhood committee in which the individual works or belongs, which keeps his dossier – and tracks her menstrual period). The old Chinese judge might trap a person with supernatural powers, but that was the justice of the cosmos. The Western detective turns physical reality itself against the unsuspecting. Yet, everybody wants to overhear 'secrets'; the Western genre gives the Chinese reader an experience of 'playing policeman' that is quite exceptional.[8] If the already powerful and paternalistic Chinese police were in reality to become still more technologically omnipotent, and more aggressive, from the Western virus, *that* would be cause for alarm.

Ancient China also had, through its state doctrine of Confucianism, limits on the power of the sovereign, particularly on his evil and oppressive laws and taxes. The emperor was committed to an ideology of the Mandate of Heaven, to enacting policies suggested by men of virtue, listening to remonstrators, and keeping precedents set by virtuous dynasts of old, particularly his ancestors.

Such anti-authoritarian ideals, though long-lived in the popular mind, lost relevance when the Confucian ideology and the idea of virtuous kingship it enshrined were overthrown in 1911. China's new legal codes again came from Japan and the West; the human rights discourse of today, with such icons as 'separation of powers' and a Chinese Statue of Liberty, is hardly more than a decade old.

On the other hand, since China remains a bureaucratic country, its anti-bureaucratic criticism taps traditional springs of discourse. Some of it may even contradict the Westernizing trend toward legalism [ironically promoted by the Ministry of Public Security (in *Fazhi*), more as a way of avoiding anarchy than making Chinese into 'legal animals']. Because 'law' is still regarded by many as simply the penal law of the tyrant, one sees some of the stories appeal instead to human 'feelings' as a way of reordering society, as if to transcend Western legalism. This seems a despairing manifestation of post-colonial frustration. Anti-police-power sentiments being so complicated in provenance, and so muted in a literature heavily under police surveillance, we shall save comment on them for the end of this chapter.

The road traveled by detective *fiction* has been even more crooked, if not quite so rocky. For the better part of a millennium, China has had fiction with elements of what we now call the 'classical detective genre,' such as an interesting crime and a generously detailed physical and human landscape rich in local color, if not explicitly clues and red herrings. There was above all a wise judge as the detective, a man like Judge Bao Zheng or Di Renjie, who transcended any one literary work by appearing in a series, or by being legendary among the folk. Lord Bao was – and is – worshipped in temples as a god (Kinkley 1985, 1988).

Despite such similarities as a scholar or critic can pick out, the old Chinese works were not self-evidently within the genre of the classical detective story of Poe, Conan Doyle, Agatha Christie, and the Chinese writer Cheng Xiaoqing. The old works were in the tradition of Yuan dramas (operas) or chapter-driven 'popular fiction,' the latter tending by the nineteenth century more and more toward martial arts adventures, with the judge as a *deus ex machina*. And the languages were different: archaic, Ming-Qing 'vernacular' in the old works, and twentieth-century Peking colloquial language in the twentieth-century ones. The judges in the old stories triumphed by probity – and judicial torture – as much as by their wits. The criminal's confession and punishment, and outright sermonizing by the judge, took center stage instead of 'the solution' of the crime. The epistemological universes inhabited by the two kinds of detective were simply incompatible; the old judges could solve cases by supernatural means and sometimes knew the culprit from the start. Or justice could be achieved in the next life. Modern Chinese detective stories, being written in the modern vernacular and having so many urban bourgeois characters dealing with topical Chinese national problems such as the doings of foreigners and the trustworthiness of insurance companies, were inevitably perceived as part of the whole Westernizing thrust of the May Fourth movement. As if this were not enough, twentieth-century Chinese practitioners of the Chinese detective story, as King-fai Tam's chapter describes, gave their great Chinese detectives Western habits, idiosyncrasies, and methods of solving rather Western, genre-driven puzzles in an urban, bourgeois setting. (This is not a criticism – for does not the formula reader, as described by John Cawelti, choose his titles for certain familiar kinds of 'exotic' pleasures, as does the Englishman who habitually travels to the Wild West via Louis L'Amour?) Despite a strong native tradition, twentieth-century China once more 'modernized,' even abandoned, an old tradition in favor of Western models.

The Westernization of modern Chinese detective fiction put the genre in a very bad light during the years of Mao's communism, particularly since crime itself was seldom acknowledged to exist. A detective interest was retained in 'anti-spy' (*fante*) and 'liquidating counter-revolutionaries' (*sufan*) stories, but in them detectives canny about class loyalties and the treachery of the KGB probe social conspiracies, not ordinary crime. The detective story as we know it died; even the spy story was confined to the subgenre of socialist spy story, heavily influenced by Soviet models.

The classical 'Anglo-American' detective story was reborn, quickly and fully developed, when China opened up in the late 1970s, in stories with intricate plots, myriad apolitical red herrings, and countless misleading clues, as if Chinese authors had been writing in the genre all along, just waiting for the day when the works at the bottoms of their drawers could be published. But the main reinfusion of the Anglo-American tradition came from reprints of the foreign classics in Chinese. The two major authors were Conan Doyle (8 450 000 copies printed by all Chinese presses in 1980–81) and Agatha Christie (8 200 000 copies of 32 titles printed by all Chinese presses in 1980–81) (Ye, Interview). Classics from the past – Cheng Xiaoqing – were made available again, too (a print run of 80 000 for volume 1 in a Ministry of Public Security reprint series; 17 000 for the final, 13th volume). Although most of the reprints came from presses of the Ministry of Public Security, which coveted the profits, the Ministry grew alarmed at the unrestricted – and competing – reprints of popular Western detective authors by presses all over the country. Domestic crime fiction seemed in danger of being swamped. The Ministry determined to put a lid on the phenomenon and produce a 'healthy' police-detective fiction, giving voice to its own ideals, and expression to the many 'literary talents' in or close to its own ranks. Chinese fiction, in the detective genre as well as outside of it, was branching out into all sorts of social exposure, as well as alleged sensationalism and pornography. It was the Ministry's duty to protect public morals, particularly in the 1983 campaign against 'spiritual pollution,' which authorized just such crackdowns.

In the reorganizations of 1983–84, dissident magazines were disciplined and the Ministry of Public Security, seconded by provincial-level public security (i.e., police) and judicial organs, began publishing police and detective magazines to provide 'leadership.' The flagship was the Ministry's own journal *Zhuomuniao* (Woodpecker; a bird that pecks out vermin), founded by Yu Haocheng. The wayward genre was, in theory, brought under control. Yet even ex-and practicing policemen, publishing in police-run magazines, continued to peck away at the system itself – to join in the post-colonial discourse about human rights and police misconduct.

Naturally the new, state-supervised police fiction had the mission of refurbishing public images of the police, instilling respect for socialist 'rule of law' (the genre came to be known as *fazhi wenxue*, 'legal system literature'), and even promoting 'socialist spiritual civilization.' Some police writers wrote police fantasies into their works – about respected policemen laboring tirelessly for ever-appreciative Chinese masses and so forth – and the prestige of Chinese detective fiction, never high, plummeted to new lows. Yet, to sell copies, police authors (and non-police authors, who vied with them to publish in journals such as *Woodpecker, Sword and Shield*, and *The World of Police*, whose high circulation provided good pay scales) continued to accommodate two other kinds of taste. One was 'Westernized taste,' including both the modernist tendencies that had entered 'serious' fiction, and the genre attributes of the Anglo-American detective story that so many Chinese readers had grown to love; the other was old-fashioned taste, including plot types, techniques, heroes, even certain themes, from the old novels like *Shuihuzhuan* (*Outlaws of the Marsh*, also translated as *Water Margin* and *All Men Are Brothers*) and *Xiyouji* (*Journey to the West*, also known as *Monkey*).

As it wends its way between all these alternative kinds of taste and narrative strategy, and between conflicting social missions, not to mention alternative visions of ideal police behavior and values, Chinese detective fiction today has become a mediator of alternative worlds. If the political values are becoming more Westernized, reflecting the irresistible cultural power of the Western core's democratic ideals, the literary values are turning back to the premodern Chinese novel, to express differences of language and place within a still largely Western genre. Let us observe these conflicts up close, in representative novels from three periods: the turn of the '80s, the mid-'80s, and the late '80s. Our focus will be on the detectives, their methods, the worlds they inhabit, and the plots that accommodate them.

The 'Classic' Puzzler of the Turn of the '80s

The worst offense of the detective story is dullness, a danger all too real for Chinese authors just thawing out from the Cultural Revolution. Not far beneath the surface are memories of socialist realism, which preferred that all problems be solved by comradely teams rather than individual geniuses.

George Dove, however, finds that the emphasis on routines and teamwork is characteristic of the police procedural worldwide. So is the likelihood that the story, as in China, was written by someone with close connections to the police, for the public expects a certain realism in the police procedural that the classical and hard-boiled detective genres are free to replace with myth. 'One problem that every writer of police procedurals must face is the necessity for making cop-work, the ordinary routines of tailings, stakeouts, lab analysis, and the like, so enthralling and full of suspense that the reader will follow the action with the same degree of interest generated by the legal acrobatics of Perry Mason or the hard-fisted penetration of Mike Hammer' (1–6, 47–55, 56).

And so, when in 1978–81 the first batch of Chinese authors to write detective stories since the Cultural Revolution took up the genre, the formula they resumed was not the police procedural as such but the classical Anglo-American formula. [This omits the many thrillers in which a good cop fights a conspiracy of malefactors, often including evil cops influenced by the Gang of Four, but these are melodramas, not detective stories, descended from 'anti-spy' stories except with the class politics reversed, if not directly descended from socialist realism (Kinkley, *After Mao* 118–27 for a description).] And the new heroes in the genre, though police detectives, are not proceduralists at all, but puzzle-solving 'amateur professionals' (Binyon 79, 91; Dove 2–3,54), virtual Sherlock Holmeses busting out of their drab uniforms, pretending to be 'serving the people' and training the next socialist generation when in fact they are showing off, like Holmes before Watson or Poirot before Hastings.

Hence the detectives in these works, whose story titles typically contain the words 'The Case of the,' are frequently compared by their departments or by the public with Sherlock Holmes, never with Judge Bao, who was frighteningly stern and used torture. They often have a slower-witted sidekick as a foil for their intelligence. They deduce obscure, perfectly irrelevant facts about a person or thing as a sort of 'preamble' to establish their deductive powers before the main investigation gets underway. They escape from locked rooms, gather all their suspects in a single room, solve crimes with railroad timetables, and ratiocinate in a rapture, 'eyebrows dancing and face radiant,' sometimes even keeping to themselves 'some of the magician's tricks of the trade.'[9]

These policemen are so clearly part of a tradition that lives only in books that their extraordinary powers evoke no apprehensions about or really any comparisons with police behavior in the real world. Nor do they spend much time criticizing social ills, for that is a distraction the formula can ill afford. Indeed, for all the Chinese local color and solutions of 'whodunit' according to discriminations between different brands of Chinese cigarettes and facial creams, the world is startlingly un-Chinese in feel, for the cops never think in political terms or even use political terminology to lecture criminals. Likewise, few of the suspects – hardly ever the real perpetrators – seem to be political animals in any way. Corrupt cadres appear not as perpetrators but as red herrings, an ironic, quite conscious bending of the Maoist literary tradition. As in the Anglo-American classics, the world they inhabit is a positivist, 'scientific' one in which clues and physical evidence are omnipresent and yet finite, for either they are discovered, as by the hero, or overlooked, as by the Watson or bumbling 'inspector' who came before. This is a very nineteenth-century world, before 'reality' became too dull to write about.

It may be that this literary evocation of a world of science perfectly fitted the mood of China's students and workers at the turn of the '80s, when television, visions of the developed West, and popular mechanics books about lasers and space travel all suddenly came upon the public unawares. The epitome and saturation point of this trend was reached in the Jin Ming novels of the popular Shanghai science fiction writer, Ye Yonglie. Ye's own background was in science and popular science writing rather than police work, but he forged close links with the Ministry of Public Security. The Ministry published his works, sought his counsel on how to sell crime stories to the public, and made real case files available to him on which to base his mysteries – though with limitations, as we shall see.

Jin Ming is one of the few Chinese police detectives who has established an identity within a whole series of books: a half-dozen novels of 1979–83 that sold the better part of a million copies, and a handful of *policier* comic books that had a total circulation of seven million. Detective Jin Ming (the given name, 'Ming,' meaning 'bright,' or 'enlightened') is affectionately nicknamed 'the scientific Sherlock Holmes,' 'Dr Policeman,' and 'the Ph.D. of policedom' by the characters and narrators of his books. He makes a point of applying knowledge of scientific minutiae to the solution of every crime and mystery; he does not just operate on the basis of lab reports, but explains the different blood types to his sidekick (and the reader), as if the purpose of the novel were to popularize science – which, in Ye Yonglie's mind, it very well may be.[10] But, lest the novel turn didactic, Ye often telescopes time, letting Jin Ming deduce in seconds scientific facts that ought to require days of testing, having him authenticate a previously unknown mosquito species at a glance, and so forth. He uses computers extensively, but not to explain the hardware, rather to assemble from the files of world history all sorts of fascinating irrelevancies that in the end help him solve the case. Outdoing even the Soviet detective story writer

Julian Semyonov, whose heroes dispense titbits from famous people's memoirs that in their time were unknown to the Russians, about the private lives of Khrushchev, Stalin, and the Kennedys (mixed with fantasies about West German and US corporations arming Mao Zedong with atom bombs), Ye Yonglie cranks into the plot any little thing that might interest his information-starved post-Cultural Revolution audience (Laquer). Often his tidbits and factoids cater to the naive (typically young) reader's literary curiosity. In the novel *The Black Shadow*, for instance, the computer pulls up Samuel Pepys's diary when Jin Ming comes across a mysterious coded book written by a hermit, and *Robinson Crusoe* when he seeks to understand hermit psychology (*Hei ying*).

And that is not all. The Jin Ming books mix in science fiction – not enough to compromise the primary interest in solving the case, but just enough to speed the plot and remove the story from present-day reality. Jin Ming sneaks up on his hermit in a silent atomic helicopter, wearing a camouflage suit that changes color like a chameleon. Why? Ye Yonglie explains that by *inventing* the finer points of his criminological technology, he did not have to worry about running foul of his sources at the Ministry of Public Security, who are professionally leery of giving away secrets (Ye, Interview). So the repressive side of Chinese life operated quite consciously to make this 'police' fiction other-worldly. Even more remarkably, Jin Ming makes no comment on Chinese police forces and their procedures because he and his sidekick fly in to the scene and solve their cases alone. It is almost as if they did not belong to a department. They are free cop spirits, created by the imagination of a scientist.

Police Procedurals of the Mid-'80s

When the Ministry of Public Security intervened in 1984 to curb the untrammeled 'unhealthy' tendencies and create a new police literature through magazines, literary contests, and a cadre of public security writers under its own leadership, the tone of the Chinese detective story changed substantially. One line of interpretation might be that the post-colonial detective story was replaced with a nationalistic police story. That would be too simple. The predominant genre was still in the detective story category; the Ministry of Public Security was anxious enough to sell its product that it was not so foolish as to throw out wonderfully awful crimes and all the suspense leading up to their solution, which could only reflect credit on their profession. (To be sure, novels about the reformation of juvenile delinquents and so forth were sponsored also – yet another genre, as it turned out, by the late '80s, that could lead to 'unhealthy' tendencies.)[11] And yet China's typical detective stories were now genuine police procedurals, in which teams of good but quite human cops solved their crimes through teamwork, painstaking procedure, long hours, accurate knowledge of China's new society under Deng Xiaoping's reforms, and dedicated efforts to understand the motives and 'psychology' of the objects of their pursuit. The new stories by and of the police succumbed to self-congratulation often enough, yet the Ministry of Public Security (and its new literary competitor, the Ministry of Justice, which published as its flagship magazine *Zhongguo Fazhi Wenxue*, or *Chinese Legal System Literature*), being aware of image problems with the public and Deng Xiaoping's commitment to reform, and having publishers like Yu Haocheng at the helm, also gave their authors a mandate to expose internal and external 'problems.'

The Chinese 'legal system' writing profession above all tried to elevate the detective story with the 'realism,' social consciousness, psychological character development, and modern narrative techniques that were viewed as giving 'serious fiction,' fiction outside the genre, its prestige. An emphasis on providing motivation 'even for the criminal' fitted current police trends of explaining crime by psychology and social conditions rather than by class standing, and another natural outcome was full-length detective *novels*, the most prestigious form among China's 'serious' writers. Many detective protagonists in these novels almost too clearly 'develop' by learning a lesson or overcoming a particular shortcoming. Unfortunately the doctrinal obsession with realism, which deterred imaginative writing in 'serious' genres also (Lee 160–1), was perhaps an even greater impediment to good police writing than the police supervisors. Many of China's most accomplished detective writers, public security cadres and civilians alike, were getting their 'materials' straight out of ministry files. Privileged to read these confidential case histories, they felt constrained to be faithful to the 'social reality' they contained. Thus, quite unlike Ye Yonglie and his cohort of pioneers, they became leery of invention. That the socially conscious police procedural detective story can in fact be quite imaginative is however proved by the success particularly of Japanese writers in this genre (a good example is Matsumoto). Given the many translations available, including those in magazines such as *Woodpecker*, one cannot even rule out Japanese influence.

This might then seem a devolution from a second-nature post-colonial detective fiction developing the Anglo-American formula to a more muted but more self-conscious post-colonial obeisance to the tradition of nineteenth-century French and Russian realism, as well as a reaction – a turn toward a more familiar, *Chinese*, ideal police image. But there is another peculiarity about these stories. The mystery-solving police are not just a team, but, rather incongruously, an army, *fighting* criminals as they would a foreign invader. This mentality, already disruptive in the Mao era, when war was waged on class 'enemies,' is a throwback not just to China's political past, but to the continuing paramilitary self-conception of the police, and the fact that many of its comrades are demobilized soldiers. It is a police work style in contradiction not only with the 'amateur professional' style of Jin Ming, but with the comfortingly Chinese, paternalistic 'watchman' style. The military style of the PLA is an inherently anti-traditional, 'old-fashioned' (Maoist) post-colonial manifestation.

Like a good soldier, then, the typical detective hero in this story *sacrifices* – his time, his health, his social relations, his marriage – although not his life (the last goes generally for army fiction, too). He is intelligent, but not all-seeing – rather, *professional*; cool, experienced, willing to track down all leads and examine all motivations, more attuned to the 'complicated' nature of people and the necessity of winning their confidence than to the multifarious nature of physical reality. He does not, like Poirot, need to recharge his little gray cells with sleep. He is also, of course, incorruptible, worried about trends in the broader society, and a family man. There are, for the first time, even a few intelligent policewomen, created by young women writers such as Wang Yonghong, although these policewomen are in subordinate roles. They are idealized portraits of the police taken from life.

Wang Yonghong, a protégé of Yu Haocheng, was a uniformed Ministry of Public Security cadre – deputy editor of *Woodpecker* – until she went into exile in Canada in 1987. She offers an interesting point of comparison with her story 'Forensics Policeman Yang Bo' (1984), for her hero, as the title implies, is a man of scientific (medical) training not unlike the Sherlockian Jin Ming (Wang Yonghong). Yang Bo is confronted with a peasant who claims accidentally to have shot his wife in the head with a shotgun on the very threshold of their cottage. Good 'scientist' that he is, Yang notes that the cleanness and angle of the head wound do not conform to the proffered murder weapon. In a seemingly pro-science, anti-traditional swipe at China's ancient treasury of herbal medicines, the *Bencao gangmu* (*Materia medica*), the author adds that Yang Bo, performing an experiment of his own, once disproved one of its entries.

But there the comparison with the Anglo-American 'amateur professional' ends. Yang Bo is an experienced and socially savvy cop, and that counts for more. Like Columbo, he zeroes in on the evidence that is missing, the neatness of the killer's story, and the abundant motivating factors for the peasant to have murdered his wife on purpose, as well as for the commune head, his father, to have covered up for him. All too convenient. He tackles the mystery through procedure. Further, he insinuates himself into village society by spending time listening to the complaints of its people, some of whom dislike the police; they make a world of possible motivations known to *him*, once he overcomes their superstitious fears of exhuming a body and their male-chauvinist prejudices against letting their wives come forward to give evidence.

The forensics cop of course prevails because he is dedicated and hard-working. He bicycles ten miles to the scene of the crime, up in the mountains, the day the killing is announced, without even finishing his breakfast. He neglects to go home to his wife in her village for two months; his salary cannot pay for the sewing machine she wants, and in a poignant moment later on, she (realistically enough) confronts him with the fact that she has bought one with her own superior earnings from the newly bustling free-enterprise farm economy. Meanwhile, Yang must risk his career and appeal to higher authority in the province to get an exhumation, for his superior is covering for the commune head and the head's murderous son, since he knows the former to be a war buddy of the county Party secretary, the only one who can save this bad cop from a demotion for his past misdeeds during the Cultural Revolution. Ultimately, Yang Bo and the truth prevail because of his probity, the purity of the highest authority when appealed to – and the teamwork of other good cops who stick with Yang Bo, lending him moral and material support despite orders from the corrupt immediate superior.

This story is very socially conscious compared to any in the Anglo-American subgenre, Ye Yonglie's Jin Ming tales included. There is exposure – not only of police affairs, but of rural superstition, the subordinate position of women, the rural power structure, and other facets of life, as the story splays out in many different directions at once. Even the portrait of Yang Bo's domesticity is a vehicle for Wang Yonghong's feminism; she takes care to note that when the good cop goes home and finds his wife absent, he makes dinner himself.

Most post-colonial aspects of the story are buried rather deep, in the institutional past of the People's Police, but Wang Yonghong sounds two particularly jarring notes. Fighting crime is not just a profession, but war, Yang Bo thinks in an interior monologue: 'Yes, to be a public security warrior (*zhanshi*, fighting man), struggling face to face with evil criminal elements to the end of one's days, one must be prepared to sacrifice one's own flesh and blood at any time' (463). And, in a quintessentially post-colonial moment, Wang Yonghong as narrator, bemoaning village resistance to the miracles of modern forensic medicine, points out that China, the one-time core, printed a book on the subject in the Song dynasty. 'This great work was produced in 1247. Europe had forensic medicine only in the sixteenth century, 300 years later than our country!' (469)

If the detectives and methods in China's police procedurals of the mid-1980s have a certain uniformity and crudeness of conception owing to their police provenance, their characterization is far more developed than in the pure puzzler stories of the turn of the '80s. The interest in elevating the genre into a form critiquing all society, like the serious stories, has led the Chinese police procedural into some interesting variations, with consequences for their depictions of police behavior. One of the most popular police procedurals of the entire Deng Xiaoping era was a novel (even more popular after it was filmed) by Lü Haiyan, a former police prison guard who for several years has been in the hotel management business. The hero of his masterpiece, *The Plainclothes Policeman*, is a young rookie cop – a bungler, really, who plays something of a Watson to the superior genius of one Department Head Duan. He lets a foreign agent get away from him early on, is thrown into prison for treason when he destroys police photos of his friends taken with secret army spy cameras at a protest rally (a rally later judged 'politically correct'), and is the butt of sarcasm among young men and women of his generation, who consider cops uneducated automatons. The rookie, Zhou Zhiming, is himself just a high school graduate, though his father was a professor; he entered the force because the PLA wouldn't take him. Nevertheless he is rock-steady in his incorruptibility and grows up before the reader's eyes, using in the end his innate suspiciousness – sometimes a weakness as much as a strength, Department Head Duan points out – to crack an impossible case and redeem himself ([Lü] Haiyan).

The strained family life and high divorce rate of police officers is the subject of 'The Soliloquies of a Head Patrolman and a Murderer' (1984) by Wei Dongsheng, a young public security cadre on the staff of *Woodpecker* who is himself divorced and leads the slightly counter-cultural lifestyle of his generation. Through cinematic crosscutting between the soliloquies of the cop and the criminal, both of whom have had marital problems, a certain existential equivalence is suggested (Weiren). Li Di's *The Woman Who Knocked at Dusk* takes the deep-structure equivalence of detective and murderer a big step further.[12] The story is told from the point of view of Liang Zi, a preliminary hearing interrogator. In an inherently unsympathetic role to begin with, this uniformed public security cadre (who gets a crack at the suspects before the formal 'arrest') solves the crime virtually from within the departmental 'locked room' in which it is his duty to grind down the resistance of detainees, in this case chiefly a woman, a physician named Dr Ouyang who is far more educated than he. The compensatory advantages he enjoys over her include not only the investigative reports of others on the force, but the classified dossier on each suspect, dutifully turned over to him by the suspect's work unit. He, too, considers the person across the table 'the enemy.' And he gloats: ' "Have you ever had contact with Manager Wang?" [I asked her] . . . I chose that word "contact," correct enough as it goes but having another meaning too, just to get her to think about it, so I could proceed from there and penetrate deeper.' (8) In the end he breaks Dr Ouyang – induces her to commit suicide out of shame by uncovering her secret affair with the decedent – and yet, she was not the murderer. The real murderer is Dr Ouyang's other lover, who comes to light from a lucky break, in this story based on a true case history. The interrogator is humanized, as Li Di's police editors might have instructed, indeed saved from damnation (driving an innocent to sui-cide is especially reprehensible in China; in imperial times it could be a crime) by having, in his stream of consciousness, subconscious guilt feelings.

The detectives of these police procedurals of the mid-'80s make an ambivalent contribution to China's post-colonial fears and hopes about the police. Though inevitably more 'Chinese' than Jin Ming and his ilk, if only because these detectives are rounded instead of flat, they in their very realism conjure up images of police omnipotence and penetration that lead back to the totalitarian tradition of the West and pre-war Japan. Fortunately their authors had the presence of mind, as literary creators, to endow their police with a sense of human limits and even guilt. They have not only 'humanized' the model police heroes, but they have humanized the police system – or its self-image.

The pieces by Wei Dongsheng and Li Di, both of which were awarded prizes, are notable also for their experimental narrative art. Wei Dong-shen disorients the reader's conceptions of time, character, and motiva-tion with his cross-cutting between wholly unexplained alternate, but strangely parallel, streams of consciousness. The identity of the mur-derer is known at the outset. The mystery is, whom did he murder, and what does he have to do with the patrolman? More, it seems, than just the crossing of their paths because of the crime. Li Di reveals his interrogator's subconscious reservations about 'hunting' Dr Ouyang with cross-cutting of his own – periodic flashbacks to a recurring dream, recalling how Liang Zi became obsessed hunting a fox during his youth rustication in the frozen wilds of Manchuria. These works bring the interest in Western modernism that was blossoming in the 'pure literature' journals into the genre literature.

China 'Writes Back' to ... Its Ancestors

The novels by Wei Dongsheng and Li Di, and many others rather self-consciously published by the police in the mid-'80s, no longer aspire to be 'merely popular.' By the end of the 1980s, there is yet another kind of detective, clearly aimed at the *popular* reader. This type of hero is post-colonial in the deepest sense; a creation by writers fully conscious of history – willing to use all the Western traditions, and yet anxious to 'write back' to the West, the new core from which the modern detective genre sprang – and to the old core, China itself. China's own traditions, in literature and in life, have by now contributed not only different kinds of detectives, but different styles of policing, and distinctively Chinese plots.

The detective in this genre is a watchful, protective, *paternal* police-man who taps deep seams of the Chinese mythic imagination rather than the traditions of European writers or the pious hopes of Chinese bureaucratic modernizers. He presides over a great cosmic design that lets criminals expose and destroy themselves in the fullness of time, while the great detective waits, like a Daoist, neither concerned to dis-play his powers of discernment nor to solve the decade's social pro-blems. Liu Zongdai's creation Huangfu Yu, chief of detectives, is such a hero, notably in *Public Security Spirit* (1988), though he has now been featured in a number of stories.[13] His character well fits China's ideal, non-totalitarian self-conception of police behavior.

Detectives in China's puzzler stories are compared to Sherlock Holmes, and those in police melodramas and procedurals in which they try to reform society are compared to Judge Bao. Huangfu Yu is unique, nicknamed after a deity. The masses call him 'a living Zhong Kui,' after a god who, with his presentiments of evil, protected human beings from ghosts and even 'caught' them, like a good policeman. Like any 'realistic' but ideal head cop in a mid-'80s police procedural pub-lished in *Woodpecker*, Huangfu is superior in intelligence, bravery, and experience. He is cool and detached (*lengjing*; the word is used dozens of times in *Public Security Spirit*), expert at the martial arts, knowledgeable about the law, and yet sensitive to the needs and nuances of human relations. And he has a weakness. He is too 'busy,' perhaps still too emotionally wounded by the death of his beautiful artist-wife during the Cultural Revolution, to remarry and re-establish himself as a family man, a fault in this usually morally conservative genre (Knight). (Two good women – both artists of sorts – fall in love with him in the course of the investigation, providing a love interest. Which one will he choose, if either?) On the other hand, this novel puts conventional detective interests to full use. The plot revolves around one traditional and three conventional puzzler mysteries that must be solved by the end of the book: the appearance of 'ghosts' at No. 13, Gospel Road; a counterfeiting operation later discovered to be going on there in a secret room; and two murders perpetrated as part of the cover-up, amid a whole courtyard full of weak or suspicious neighbors who serve as possible suspects in one crime or another (No. 13 is the address of an old-style, multi-family compound).

Huangfu Yu's deductions are conspicuous but not divine. More central is his role as chief of detectives, conscientiously directing his subordinates to interview neighbors, collect lab reports, go under cover, set up stakeouts, and perform all manner of other procedures. Again, everything is run competently and marvelously, but not really miraculously or with egregiously modernizing effect, except perhaps for the use of an infra-red camera to photograph a 'ghost' in the act. Huangfu's supremacy is rather in his role as a Zhong Kui, an all-seeing protector and moral force in a society that is always in social flux, and still subject to eternal retribution.

Though he at times still uses conventional public security warfare terminology to speak of his role in dealing with the criminal 'enemy,' Huangfu symbolizes the paternalistic reassurance that neighborhood watchmen and wise judges (traditionally known as *fumu guan*, 'officials who are fathers and mothers to the people') have long provided in Chinese consciousness. Familial patterns so penetrate the story that Huangfu's chief operatives are a young husband-and-wife team, Wu Zhikui (a brawny lad with thick eyebrows, sometimes rashly and hot-headedly rushing in to his boss's defense, playing Zhang Fei to Huangfu's Liu Bei) and the pretty Ms Wang Lei, referred to by children living in No. 13 as 'the auntie upstairs'; after her cover is blown, as 'the public security auntie upstairs,' an on-the-scene protector who despite her power and previously incognito status is inherently sympathetic because one night she is beaten up and sent to the hospital by a mal-evolent, prowling 'ghost.' Huangfu's role is to co-ordinate their investigations and those of others, and to worry, as their surrogate father, about whether they will be unmasked and subjected to further danger.

Meanwhile Huangfu is firmly situated within his own family. Whole chapters dramatize the relationship of this orphan cop (now in his 40s) with his surrogate mother – his elder sister, who continually worries that he is not taking care of himself and will never get married. The plot thickens when she, acting on rumors and substituting hopes for facts, collaborates with one of the women who loves Huangfu to bring the two together. Fortunately this woman – an unemployed dancer turned nurse in the public security hospital – is equally nurturing. She makes her apartment into a safe house for Huangfu when he has to go on the lam, and purposely takes a bullet meant for him by his old nemesis from an earlier novel, Black Panther. This conveniently clears the way for Huangfu to marry the older, better matched, artist woman.

Huangfu has a surrogate father, too: Huang Tai, chief of police, who introduced him to his now deceased wife, and worries, with Huangfu's sister, about getting him remarried. The father–son relationship is particularly implicit in old Huang Tai's sacrificial hanging on, when he could retire, until he can be sure that Huangfu will be assigned as his replacement, instead of the scheming and power-hungry bad cop Geng Wenjie, deputy chief of police. (The evil Geng's name is an ironic audio-visual pun on the name of the legendary judge from China's premodern 'detective' fiction, Di Renjie.)[14] When Geng manages to remove Huangfu from the case by framing him for raping, and later for murdering, the young woman at No. 13 who first brought the strange doings of the ghosts to light, Chief Huang Tai not only provides for Huangfu's safety, but orders him to punch out his own protégé, Wu Zhikui, en route to prison, and make a getaway so that he can escape persecution and even continue directing the investigations while on the lam! This staple of American cop (and superhero) movies, the hero-hiding-from-the-law-so-he-can-prove-his-innocence scenario, is thus injected into the Chinese police world by the only legitimation possible – the hero has turned fugitive on secret orders from the top. Despite his individual authority, then, Huangfu Yu is vulnerable and yet invulnerable, in each instance because he is held in an infinite, hierarchical and ultimately benevolent web of human relationships. Colleagues will be 'sacrificed' (killed), but the warfare metaphor is tamed by its confinement within a larger, divine, web of human responsibilities (42).

And yet Huangfu can also be rather stern and unforgiving (130). He is by nature serious, and *feared* citywide, though especially by the crooks (202). This might seem to contradict the image of Huangfu as a benevolent, caring, father figure and bogeyman catcher, except that it so well reflects Chinese ambivalences toward real authority figures, including fathers (see Richard Solomon). Judge Bao was stern, a frightening figure even to the common people who sought his protection. To that extent Huangfu continues the Chinese literary tradition. And, as Liu Zongdai makes a point of showing, Huangfu Yu is unable to flatter people (77), even when such dissemblance might serve him in drawing people out. This, too, seems an inheritance from Judge Bao's personality; flattery, in a bureaucratic state, is so harmful in dealings with uppers that it must be stamped out, even in dealings with equals and lowers.

Apart from the Western martyr syndrome, then, Huangfu Yu shows signs of a return to older Chinese images of the neighborhood watchman, continuous with both the literary tradition and the Chinese social reality of policing, however submerged this may be by modernization and remnant totalitarianism from the Mao era. This post-colonial dialogue with what is still a basically Western detective genre – subgenre police procedural – finds echoes not just in the detective but in his methods. Huangfu Yu operates not only on the basis of clues and procedures but on inspired hunches (99), and he, like any free spirit (but unlike the typical reformist, modernizing cop in a mid-'80s *Woodpecker* story), does not have to apologize for acting on them. On the other hand, Huangfu is wary of having *emotions*; although they humanize the cop in the usual Chinese police procedural, they seem to evoke the old neo-Confucian emotions-vs-reason dichotomy in this novel. Emotions lead Huangfu into a self-acknowledged 'mistake.' Roused by an anonymous phone tip promising information about a secret daughter whose existence he has never heard of, but long suspected, he zooms off on his motorcycle for a secret rendezvous with the caller, thereby allowing himself to be framed for a murder. And yet, morally, concern for this daughter is no 'mistake' – it is even part of the cosmic plan.

Huangfu's divinity-within-humanity is further limned through subtle suggestions of the equivalence of policemen with artists. His two possible mates are artists of sorts, endowed with sensitivity to underlying beauty. The more mature one, who survives, painter Jiang Wanqing, is Huangfu's old childhood flame (before he went into the army many years ago). She remembers Huangfu as a dashing young man who seemed likely to end up as a professional artist. Jiang's foster teenage daughter is a budding pianist who bravely volunteers to catch the 'ghost' and actually plays a role in solving the case, having conceived a desire to become a policewoman herself, just like the 'public security auntie upstairs'. At the end, she is revealed as Huangfu's secret daughter;

unbeknownst to either Huangfu or Jiang, Huangfu's wife had had a baby during her Cultural Revolution custody, just before she was driven to her death, and that baby was switched for the foster child Jiang had thought she was adopting. This of course makes Jiang's family a perfect nest for the lone swan Huangfu Yu, once the other lover dies for his sake; but it also appears that the double entangled helix of artist's and cop's sensibilities pass through the DNA from one generation to the next, making for a heavenly ordained family saga.

By now it should be apparent that not just the hero but the very structure of the novel is a post-colonial, *Chinese* answer to the Western detective story and police procedural. Investigation of the counterfeiting and murders motivates the plot to the end, but the initial hook is the old-fashioned appeal of the ghost story. Liu Zongdai shamelessly exploits the Chinese Gothic tradition. The inhabitants at No. 13 (the address, to be sure, is Western Gothic) provide convincingly eerie stories of ghosts and unexplained deaths at their haunted compound. And Huangfu Yu is after all a reincarnation of Zhong Kui, the ghost-catcher.

Procedure there is, and also much reformist criticism of police practice. Yet, as the police gradually home in on the counterfeiting ring and the murderers (multiple crimes, as in some traditional Chinese novels; while the 'economic criminals' are discovered by the social exposure of the procedural, the murderer is a 'least likely' little old lady, Mother Wu, and this keeps faith with the puzzler tradition), more and deeper mysteries and social conflicts arise to take their place. What comes to center stage is the traditional Chinese interest in interrelations among each of the characters, whose special capabilities, backgrounds, and sentiments are gradually uncovered, on a 'need to mystify' basis. Why does the little old meddling servant lady in Deputy Municipal Party Secretary Lin's household (named Mother Wu) bear Huangfu Yu such a grudge? (She holds him responsible for driving the secretary's daughter mad when, over-privileged cadre offspring that she was, she got mixed up in a criminal conspiracy brought down by Huangfu Yu in a previous novel.) Why is Jiang Wanqing drawn to Huangfu Yu? Why does he feel a strange, paternal love toward her daughter? If they are fated to get together, what will become of the nurse who loves Huangfu? And who learned that Huangfu had a secret daughter anyway, and how? (Mother Wu, who listened in on her boss's Party business and, as a former prostitute under the old society – this *is* a socially conservative genre – retained a few underworld connections of her own.) Above all, as in classic Chinese novels such as *Dream of the Red Chamber*, which of the alternative matches will the hero marry? How will fate arrange it? And will the outcome be happy or sad?

Multiple crimes, revenge crimes years in the making, multiple suspects, multiple villains, all interconnected with each other as neighbors, relatives, and relatives-though-they-don't-know-it – clearly the larger mysteries here are of the big family saga. All the secret relationships must be brought to light; more even than in procedurals where the greatest mystery is the crime, the procedural solution to these mysteries is simply getting people to tell the truth. When the human relationships are clarified, the criminals will expose and destroy themselves, as if by Buddhist divine retribution. Huangfu is matched by a 'mastermind' on the other side, Mother Wu, who directs and then does away with her confederates just as their complicity is disclosed, before they can be arrested. Despite her ruthlessness, she is not really a 'criminal' mastermind like Moriarty, but a bitter woman burning with a sense of injustice who knows where to hurt Huangfu where he's most vulnerable – in the family, a family he scarcely dreamed he had. Mother Wu's diabolical plot is to kidnap Huangfu Yu's daughter, take her down to China's licentious southlands, train her to be a prostitute, then return her a decade later to her loving policeman father a hustler and a whore. There is no better vengeance in the crypto-Confucian, one-child-per-couple nation of China, or perhaps any nation.

Conclusion: Resistance of the Police, or of the Police State?

So much for building up and redefining the Chinese police; is there anything in the texts about limiting them? 'Human rights' is a quintessentially post-colonial discourse, in which post-colonial countries try to reform themselves using Western concepts, often to impress the West, or 'get it off their backs.' By the early '80s the very term 'human rights' was attacked in China as a bourgeois concept from meddling Western cultural imperialism. In 1991 China did adopt and try to co-opt the term – to get the US off its back. Until then, one could hardly expect to find it in stories of and by the police.

Yet, when the rookie cop hero of *The Plainclothes Policeman* objects to the secret surveillance filming of his friends at a political rally, this is a unique statement of a human rights case, even if there is a political explanation: that the demonstration, mourning Zhou Enlai in April 1976 (an occasion coinciding with the first Tiananmen, or April Fifth Incident), later became in the eyes of history 'politically correct' (145–56). To the readers of today, the young cop's derring-do have made of him an underground symbol of the policemen who sided with the protestors at the *second* Tiananmen Incident – and massacre – in 1989 (Lü Haiyan, Interview).

Lü Haiyan's novel also makes a point of the fact that a prisoner (in this case, the rookie hero, Zhou Zhiming) may not be visited by his family while he is being detained, until he is formally arrested (181). It even voices an opinion, by 'law student' characters, that 'political prisoners' should be housed separately from and treated more leniently than ordinary criminals. Lü's very mention of the Western neologism 'political prisoner' (453) must be thrilling to most Chinese readers.

Most of the novel's political criticism, however, even of the police, falls within a long Chinese tradition of moral exposure and bureaucratic self-critique. There are vignettes of tyranny, foolishness, corruption, and cover-ups among the nomenklatura, spicy peeps at the dissolute lives of their sons and daughters, and very seamy scenes of brutality and near starvation in prison farms. Lü Haiyan no doubt pleases many a reader simply by exposing cops who increase traffic fines just because their victims give them back talk. Yet *The Plainclothes Policeman* is terribly popular in police circles, evidently not for its image of the police, but for its expression of certain points that police (particularly young policemen) like to hear for the sake of their in-house bureaucratic struggles: that cases should be solved by police professionals, not by outsiders, army personnel, and Party secretaries up in the hierarchy; that police should have some leeway in making their own decisions; that young employees should be given responsibility of their own; that people whose crimes are not yet fully understood should not be locked up just because a case is politically sensitive; and so forth. Such didacticism goes down relatively easy for the general reader, because gossip about factionalism among an élite is inherently interesting.

The most comprehensive critique of the police is in *Public Security Spirit*, again from within: of scheming bad cops, frame-ups, extorted confessions, and intra-service rivalry – the very stuff of traditional Chinese moralizing, one of whose chief targets was bureaucratic factionalism. Discussion of police torture, on the other hand, something rarely seen in this fiction, would probably reflect a joining of the Chinese fiction with discourse from the West. Most interesting is the novel's depiction of all critical decisions being made by the Communist Party, typically the deputy secretary of the Party Municipal Committee (the committee member in charge of political-legal work), before being passed on to the police professionals. Is this a criticism of the way the police are run? If so, it is a fundamental criticism of the Communist

Party, reflecting sure influence from the Western separation-of-powers discourse. But Communist Party 'leadership' of police investigations is so ingrained that the ideal Party reader may read this simply as realistic social description of the way things work.

And what is one to make of *The Plainclothes Policeman*'s contrast of 'feelings' vs the robot-like following of orders of which Chinese common people evidently accuse them? 'Feelings' are clearly superior, in this novel, to narrow professionalism (159, 365). This resonates with the deep, traditional Chinese privileging of rule by good men over the rule of (arbitrary) law. The values appealed to by this choice are not particularly compatible with modernization.

China may be on the brink of an anti-authoritarian age that will greatly change the role, or the social position, of the police. Already there are works that take hoodlums and ex-convicts as their heroes, and a detective novel in which the sleuthing hero is a lawyer.[15] The more China confronts the problem of modernizing its legal system, the more it will have to confront its different ideas of the past – and the complexities of each of them. The one, post-colonial, is associated with the modern extremes of both totalitarianism and anarchy; the other, 'wholly native,' feels paternal – again, with all the ambivalence that term evokes.

Notes

The author is grateful to St John's University for providing release time to assist this research.
1. Christopher Lupke of Cornell University is applying the concept to Taiwanese literature; for the mainland, Jon Solomon discusses 'colonial discourses.' Chow tap dances around the Chinese semicolonial predicament and that of Chinese women, but without using the term 'post-colonial'.
2. Ashcroft et al., esp. the critique of D. E. S. Maxwell, 24–7.
3. Colonial Taiwan (1895–1945) created a literature in Japanese as well as in Chinese. In English, see Lau.
4. Taiwan publishes a journal called *Tuili xiaoshuo* ('Fiction of deduction,' as the genre is known in Japan), but that, too, is largely filled with foreign translations. Why a native Taiwan detective fiction does not exist is explored by three major writers, Zhang Dachun, Lin Foer, and Ye Yandu (reference thanks to William Tay).
5. Ashcroft 2. 'The Empire writes back to the Centre,' a phrase that inspired the title of Ashcroft's book and some of my phraseology, is from Salman Rushdie.
6. See Victor H. Li, Vogel, Barnett. For comparison, see Bayley.
7. Chinese mob violence is directed against policemen perceived as making unfair arrests, even against whole police stations, as in Hangzhou, 1980: *BBC Summary of World Broadcasts* FE/6519/BII/8, 27 August 1980.

8. Miller imputes this 'policing' function to the old Western realistic novel.
9. Kinkley, *After Mao* 102–5. The term 'preamble' is from Cawelti 82. The cadre who ratiocinates in a rapture is Lao Zao, of Su Yunxiang 40.
10. This is the purpose of Chinese science fiction, according to Wagner. In fact, Jin Ming himself solves cases by making creative connections and even instinctive guessing. On this aspect of the genre, see Eco and Sebeok 11–54.
11. An orthodox example is Ke Yan. But ultimately there were novels about the seamier side of convict life and its failure to rehabilitate people which were sympathetic to the convicts (see Li Jian). Both novels were published by the Masses' Press, which had itself traveled a long road by the end of the decade.
12. Li Di. I know of no police employment experience for Li Di, who resided in Japan while I was pursuing interviews in post-Tiananmen China, but several Peking interviewees volunteered that much of the plot for his story is straight from Ministry of Public Security files (which I understand authors may read on the ministry premises).
13. [Liu] Zongdai. Liu is or was a professional writer and editor, evidently without a police employment history. Despite his national fame and publication by the Masses' Press, none of my police editor friends seemed to 'know' him in 1989–90. One kindly helped put me in correspondence with him when I inquired again in 1992; he added that Liu was now unemployed.
14. The ideograph for 'Geng' resembles the ideograph for 'Di,' and Geng's given name sounds like Di's. On Di Renjie, see Van Gulik.
15. For hoodlums, see Wang Shuo. A novel about an ex-con is Liu Heng. Glorifying a (woman) lawyer: Wang Xiaoying.

Bibliography

Ashcroft, Bill, Gareth Griffiths, and Helen Tiffin. *The Empire Writes Back: Theory and Practice in Post-Colonial Cultures*. London: Routledge, 1989.
Bargainnier, Earl F. and George N. Dove. 'Introduction.' *Cops and Constables: American and British Fictional Policemen*. Ed. Bargainnier and Dove. Bowling Green, OH: Popular Press, 1986.
Barnett, A. Doak. *Cadres, Bureaucracy, and Political Power in Communist China*. New York: Columbia UP, 1967.
Bayley, David H. *Forces of Order: Policing Modern Japan*. 1976; Berkeley: U of California P, 1991.
BBC Summary of World Broadcasts. FE/6519/BII/8. 27 August 1980.
Binyon, T. J. *Murder Will Out: The Detective in Fiction*. Oxford: Oxford UP, 1989.
Cawelti, John G. *Adventure, Mystery, and Romance*. Chicago: U of Chicago P, 1976.
Cheng Xiaoqing. *Huo Sang Tan an Ji* [Collected cases of Huo Sang]. Beijing: Qunzhong chubanshe, 1986–88. 13 vols.
Chow, Rey. *Woman and Chinese Modernity: The Politics of Reading Between East and West*. Minneapolis: U of Minnesota P, 1991.
Dove, George N. *The Police Procedural*. Bowling Green, OH: Popular P, 1982.
Dray-Novey, Alison. 'Spatial Order and Police in Imperial Beijing,' *Journal of Asian Studies*. Forthcoming.
Eco, Umberto and Thomas A. Sebeok, eds. *The Sign of Three: Dupin, Holmes, Peirce*. Bloomington: Indiana UP, 1983.

Fazhi yu renzhi wenti taolun ji [Discussions on the question of rule of law or rule by man]. Beijing: Qunzhong chubanshe [Masses' Press], 1981.

Hay, Stephen. *Asian Ideas of East and West: Tagore and His Critics in Japan, China, and India.* Cambridge: Harvard UP, 1970.

Jenner, W. J. F. and Michael S. Duke. *Worlds Apart: Recent Chinese Writing and Its Audiences.* Ed. Howard Goldblatt. Armonk, NY: M. E. Sharpe, 1990. 177–227.

Ke Yan. *Xunzhao huilai de shijie* [The world brought back]. Beijing: Qunzhong chubanshe, 1984.

Kinkley, Jeffrey C. 'The Politics of Detective Fiction in Post-Mao China: Rebirth or Reextinction?' *The Armchair Detective.* 18.4 (Fall 1985): 372–8.

——. 'Judge Bao, Detective.' *The Armchair Detective.* 21.1 (Winter 1988): 40–54.

——. 'Chinese Crime Fiction and Its Formulas at the Turn of the 1980s.' *After Mao: Chinese Literature and Society, 1978–1981.* Ed. Jeffrey C. Kinkley. 1985; Cambridge, Mass.: Harvard U, Council on East Asian Studies, 1990. 89–129.

Knight, Stephen. *Form and Ideology in Crime Fiction.* Bloomington: Indiana UP, 1980.

Laquer, Walter. 'Julian Semyonov and the Soviet Political Novel.' *Society.* 23.5 (July/August 1986): 72–80.

Lau, Joseph S. M., ed. *The Unbroken Chain: An Anthology of Taiwan Fiction since 1926.* Bloomington: Indiana UP, 1983.

Lazarus, Neil. *Resistance in Postcolonial African Fiction.* New Haven: Yale UP, 1990.

Lee, Leo Ou-fan. 'The Politics of Technique: Perspectives of Literary Dissidence in Contemporary Chinese Fiction.' Kinkley, *After Mao* 160–1.

Leng, Shao-chuan and Hungdah Chiu. *Criminal Justice in Post-Mao China: Analysis and Documents.* Albany: State U of New York P, 1985.

Lewis, John Wilson, ed. *The City in Communist China,* Stanford: Stanford UP, 1971.

Li Di. 'Bangwan qiaomen de nüren.' *Zuopin yu zhengming.* 52 (April 1985): 3–40.

Li Jian. *Nüxing de xueqi* [The bloody flag of womanhood]. Beijing: Qunzhong chubanshe, 1990.

Li Jingchun and Gong Fan, eds. *1984 Zhongguo xiaoshuo nianjian: Zhentan xiaoshuo xuan* [1984 Yearbook of Chinese fiction: Selected detective stories]. Beijing: Zhongguo xinwen chubanshe, 1985.

Li, Victor H. 'The Public Security Bureau and Political-Legal Work in Hui-yang, 1952–64.' Lewis.

Liu Heng. *Black Snow.* Trans. David Kwan. Beijing: Panda Books, 1991.

[Liu] Zongdai, *Gongan hun.* Beijing: Qunzhong chubanshe, 1988.

[Lü] Haiyan. *Bianyi jingcha.* Beijing: Renmin wenxue chubanshe, 1985.

——. Personal interview. Shanghai. 7 August 1990.

Matsumoto, Seicho. *Inspector Imanishi Investigates.* Trans. Beth Cary. 1961; New York: Soho P, 1989.

Miller, D. A. *The Novel and the Police.* Berkeley: U of California P, 1988.

Owen, Stephen. 'What Is World Poetry?' *The New Republic.* 19 November 1990: 28–32.

Slovak, Jeffrey S. *Styles of Urban Policing.* New York: New York UP, 1986.

Solomon, Jon. 'Taking Tiger Mountain: Can Xue's Resistance and Cultural Critique.' *Modern Chinese Literature* 4 (1988): 235–62.

Solomon, Richard H. *Mao's Revolution and the Chinese Political Structure.* Berkeley: U of California P, 1971.

Su Yunxiang. ' "San ke menya" anjian' [The case of the three front teeth]. *Zhong-guo dalu zhentan xiaoshuo xuan* [A selection of Chinese mainland detective stories]. Ed. Cen Ying. Hong Kong: Tongjin, n. d. [1981?].

Sun Yat-sen. 'The Three People's Principles.' From Sun's 'Lecture 6.' *Sources of Chinese Tradition*. Ed. William Theodore de Bary et al. Paperback ed. New York: Columbia UP, 1964. 2: 106–8.

Van Gulik, Robert, trans. *Celebrated Cases of Judge Dee [Dee Goong An]: An Authentic Eighteenth-Century Chinese Detective Novel*. New York: Dover, 1976.

Vogel, Ezra F. 'Preserving Order in the Cities.' Lewis 51–93.

Wagner, Rudolf G. 'Lobby Literature: The Archeology and Present Functions of Science Fiction in China.' Kinkley, *After Mao* 17–62.

Wang Shuo. *Kong zhong xiaojie* [Airline stewardess]. Beijing: Zhongguo qingnian chubanshe, 1988.

———. 'Xiangpiren' [Rubber man]. *Kong zhong xiaojie*.

———. 'Yiban shi huoyan, yiban shi haishui' [One part flame, one part sea water]. *Kong zhong xiaojie*.

Wang Xiaoying. *Ni wei shui bianhu* [Whom are you defending?]. Beijing: Zuojia chubanshe, 1988.

Wang Yonghong. 'Fayi Yang Bo.' Li Jingchun and Gong Fan 444–503.

Weiren [Wei Dongsheng]. 'Xingjing duizhang yu sharenfan de neixin dubai.' Li Jingchun and Gong Fan 564–611.

Wilson, James Q. *Varieties of Police Behavior*. Cambridge: Harvard UP, 1968.

Ye Yonglie. *Hei ying*. Beijing: Dizhi chubanshe, 1981.

———. Personal interview. Shanghai. 23 November 1989.

Zhang Dachun, Lin Foer, and Ye Yandu. *Zhongguo shibao* (China Times), 'Shidai wenxue' (Literature of the Times Weekly Supplement), 28 July 1991.

9
The Traditional Hero as Modern Detective: Huo Sang in Early Twentieth-Century Shanghai

King-fai Tam

I have come to expect the look of surprise and disbelief on my colleagues' faces when I tell them that I am studying Chinese detective fiction. 'Are there detective novels in China, too?' they almost invariably ask. In some cases, this scepticism is built on the belief that present day China, as a communist country, consistently denies the existence of crime in its society. If there is no crime, they reason, there need be no detective, public or private, real or imaginary. That is why when they find out that the author I am studying, Ch'eng Hsiao-ch'ing, was active only in the pre-Communist era, their doubt is quickly allayed, as if this additional piece of information had confirmed their understanding of the communist system.[1]

There are others, usually colleagues in the study of Western fiction, whose curiosity is not to be so easily laid to rest once it is aroused. To them, the knowledge that China has its own brand of detective fiction leads to a series of questions: How is Chinese detective fiction different from that in the West? What is the detective's *modus operandi*? What is the Chinese equivalent of the Cartesian logic that forms the philosophical bedrock on which classical Western detective fiction rests? These questions, if taken seriously, would call for a second look at the critical assumptions behind the reading of detective fiction as a genre.

Yet, it is tempting to conclude from the very little scholarship available on modern Chinese detective fiction not only that the Chinese detective is essentially the same as his Western counterpart, but that the whole genre of detective fiction in China is an import from the West. To a certain extent, such an impression is created by the peculiar historical circumstances under which detective fiction came to be known as a discrete genre in early twentieth-century China. The New Culture

Movement that began in the 1910s brought to the forefront the cultural crisis that had been in the making since the mid-nineteenth century. For close to 70 years, China had suffered a series of military defeats and diplomatic humiliations that continued to erode Chinese confidence. While at first the Chinese could explain away the decline in national power as a temporary eclipse brought about by the backward military technology and the bureaucratic inertia of the Manchu government, it became undeniable by the twentieth century that a much more radical change was necessary for the country to come out of the semi-colonial state to which it had been reduced. To the proponents of the New Culture Movement, the solution to China's predicament lay in a total repudiation of the Chinese culture. Usually equated with the May Fourth Movement of 1919, the New Culture Movement was a complicated matrix of related political, social, literary, artistic, and cultural currents of reform that started in the mid-1910s and continued for decades thereafter. The goal, as envisioned by Western-minded scholars who stood in the vanguard of the movement at the time, was to rejuvenate China so as to bring it into step with the rest of the world. In such a climate, anything that smacked of the traditional culture came under suspicion, and popular literature, for the antiquated values that it was supposed to propagate, was frowned upon.[2]

No sooner had detective fiction been recognized as a genre than it came under the blanket attack directed at all forms of popular literature. Yet, unlike other forms, it has escaped relatively unscathed, owing largely to the fact that the history of modern Chinese detective fiction is marked by a consistent borrowing of strength from the West. Time and again, Chinese detective fiction writers have summoned to their defense the reputation of their better-known Western colleagues from the classical period of detective fiction as a way of gaining respectability. This act of seeking international support has by and large produced the desired result. While love stories were found by New Culture critics to be pernicious because they advocated an outdated attitude towards relations between the sexes, and muck-raking novels because they corrupted the minds of readers with felonious ideas, detective fiction was fortunate enough to encounter benevolent neglect or even acquiescence from critics.

Of course, detective fiction writers have resorted to other measures of self-defense, too, claiming, for example, that detective fiction is a 'science textbook in disguise' (Ch'eng, 'Chen-t'an' 70), that it promotes powers of observation and reasoning, or, in general, broadens the mental horizons of the reader. Similarly, detective fiction is represented as an unobtrusive – and hence, the best – way of inculcating in the mind of the reader a yearning for the rule of law, something badly needed by a country in search of a place in the modern world. To the modern Western reader who picks up a book of detective fiction to while away the time on a plane ride, such defenses might seem overly serious to the point of being ludicrous. Yet, the view that there are practical benefits to be derived from the reading of detective fiction has gained such wide acceptance in the Chinese mind that it alone, of all popular literary genres, is deemed wholesome enough to be the recommended leisure reading for school children in many Chinese communities.

The argument that detective fiction was conducive to the development of both a scientific mind and a lawful society was a powerful one in China, since science and law were two products of Western culture that were held in high regard by the Chinese.[3] Their defense of modern Chinese detective fiction won for the genre a tolerant audience from people who normally tended to point an accusing finger at popular literature in general. The most notable example is Hu Shih (1891– 1962). A declared opponent of many forms of traditional literature and their modern-day reincarnations in various popular genres, he is reported to have spoken favorably of detective fiction.[4] Other unlikely supporters are found in the May Fourth camps, including Liu Pan-nung (1891–1934) and Chang T'ien-i (1906–). This relatively favorable reception enjoyed by detective fiction perhaps accounts for its continued development even after 1949, when, under Communist rule, all other popular genres were pushed into obscurity. However, in response to the political needs of the time, detective fiction thrived in the new garb of *su-fan* novels, where the criminals of yesteryear were now replaced by counter-revolutionaries and foreign spies.

While association with the West has prolonged the life of Chinese detective fiction even under the most inclement political climate, it has by no means been an unmixed blessing. For one thing, it has introduced a foreign perspective to the examination of a Chinese cultural and literary form, with the result that the latter has only developed under the looming shadow of the former. Almost from the very start, studies of Chinese detective fiction have tended to overemphasize its literary debt to the West, sometimes in the face of contrary evidence. Historical accounts often trace its origin to Western authors such as Edgar Allan Poe and Conan Doyle (see Kinkley, Fan 31–7, and Liu Yang-t'i 370). This is true at least in the case of the many Chinese rewritings of Western detective fiction that have appeared in this century, so much so that Fan Yen-ch'iao's 'Min-kuo chiu-p'ai hsiao-shuo shih-lüeh' [A Brief History of Old-Style Fiction of the Republican Period], for example, devotes considerable length to discussion of detective fiction under the rubric of 'translated novels,' even though he also sets up a separate section for detective fiction (258–363). The link between Chinese and Western detective fiction is so strong in the minds of readers that they nickname their favorite Chinese detective heroes after their Western counterparts. Hence, Lu P'in, the detective hero of Sun Liao-hung, is known to readers as the 'Arsene Lupin of the East' and Huo Sang, the detective hero we will study in this paper, is the 'Chinese Sherlock Holmes.'

It is a short step from acknowledging the Western debt to superimposing a reading strategy that is at odds with the creative intention of Chinese detective fiction. As late as 1986, for example, a Chinese detective story published in Taiwan was severely criticized for its sloppy logic and its departure from what was termed 'fair play,' a set of rules derived from classical Western detective fiction (Fu 138–40). However, adherence to these rules was in most cases the last thing Chinese detective fiction writers had in mind.

The unhappy marriage of incompatible critical approaches and literary works is by no means an uncommon mishap in the study of literature. In this case, however, the unfortunate mismatch, a direct consequence of a kind of cultural colonialism, has been allowed to go undetected for much too long. This in turn results in the denial of the presence of indigenous cultural elements in the making of Chinese detective fiction. The example of Huo Sang will illustrate the implications of this culturally biased reading. In the following pages, I will first of all present how, under the collusion of author and readers, Huo Sang has been misrepresented as no more than a Chinese version of the Western private eye. I will then offer what I believe to be a more complete portrayal of the character, taking into account the coexistence of Western and traditional Chinese elements in the characterization of Huo Sang. Finally, armed with this new understanding, I will indicate the presence of a larger cultural meaning of this portrayal of the protagonist, which a lopsided comprehension of Huo Sang's character has served to obscure.

I

Huo Sang is the detective hero in a series of stories written by Ch'eng Hsiao-ch'ing (1893–1976). A native of Su-chou, Ch'eng made a living as a teacher of Chinese at the Tung-wu Middle School in his home town, although he is better known as a writer, translator, and a critic of detective fiction. His most productive years spanned the 1920s to the 1940s, when he authored and translated more than 100 volumes of detective fiction, including *The Fan-shih Cases, The Sheng-tu Cases, The Ch'en Ch'a-li Cases* and *A Collection of Famous Cases in the Detective World.* Considered by his contemporaries to be the best detective fiction writer of his day, he was held in high regard by fellow writers for his intricate and entrancing plots. The 'Huo Sang T'an-an' [Huo Sang's Cases], the most famous of Ch'eng's works, were originally published serially in newspapers and journals from the 1920s onwards, but proved to be such a success after their first appearance that they have been anthologized repeatedly. Some of these stories were made into movies, thus spreading Huo Sang's and Ch'eng Hsiao-ch'ing's fame to the non-reading public. After 1949, when detective fiction was encouraged to include a more pronounced political message, Huo Sang's reputation suffered a brief eclipse. With the relaxation of political and literary restrictions in the late '70s and early '80s, however, the Huo Sang stories were once again reprinted.[5]

In the broadest strokes, the world of Huo Sang can be described as follows. A detective with unspecified private means, Huo Sang lives and works in Shanghai, the most cosmopolitan Chinese city of the '20s and '30s, promising both wealth and vice. He has an assistant by the name of Pao Lang, who is so attracted by the excitement of detective work that he often puts aside his own occupation as a writer to accompany Huo Sang in his many adventures. Their method of operation consists mainly of ratiocination, with a minimum of blows and kicks. The two enjoy the status of social celebrities for their success in combating crime, and their help is constantly sought by people from all walks of life. As the reader follows their footsteps along the streets of this cosmopolitan city, he views a cross-section of Shanghai society.

As mentioned above, Huo Sang has often been perceived as a Chinese version of a Western detective. Nor is this observation unsupported by the stories themselves. Not only does Huo Sang possess an impressive physique – he is 5 ft 9 ins in height and weighs over 160 lb (Ch'eng is very specific about this) – towering over the average Chinese, but his way of life is characteristically Western. The reader learns, for example, that Huo Sang's favorite sport is taking long walks in the morning, a pastime that puts him in the company of European gentlemen rather than other more traditional Chinese heroes. For breakfast, he has coffee and toast. His home is furnished with every Western gadget available at

the time, most notably a telephone and Western-style sofa. His movement around the city is made easy by the constant use of taxi-cabs, again
setting him apart from ordinary Chinese. To the wage-earners who made
up the majority of his readership, all these characteristics were enough
to create the image of a Westerner about him.

To be sure, anyone with comparable means living in Shanghai in the
1920s and 1930s would have found it almost impossible not to pick up a
few Western habits. Yet, Huo Sang's non-Chinese qualities go beyond
the paraphernalia of modern conveniences. Ch'eng Hsiao-ch'ing reveals
to the reader that Huo Sang is a rebel at heart. In 'Huo Sang ti t'ung-
nien' [Huo Sang's Childhood], the tongue-in-cheek biography of his
detective hero, Ch'eng highlights Huo's critical stance towards Chinese
tradition, symbolized here by his turbulent relationship with his father.
In Huo's own confession to his father,

> It is as if I had two minds: the first one wishes to obey your orders, but
> the second one stands in opposition, and competes with the first. The
> result of this competition is that despite myself, my body submits to
> my rebellious mind, and my obedient mind is left in defeat. That is
> why although I never intend to be disobedient, I simply cannot help
> myself. (159)

To his teacher, another spokesman of the tradition, he also raises queries
of the most disrespectful kind:

> How is it possible that what the ancients said was always right? How
> is it that they, as a rule, were more correct than people of today?...
> Why are people nowadays inferior to the ancients? Is it because they
> had one more brain or one more hand? (161)

This questioning attitude towards tradition is given further elaboration in other Huo Sang adventures. Many stories provide opportunities
for Huo Sang or Pao Lang to deliver strong objections to traditional
practices, especially those related to oppressive old-style marriages,
widespread superstitious beliefs, and persistent bureaucratic abuses
('Ch'in-chun' 140; 'He ti-lao' 55).

In place of tradition, Huo Sang advocates studying the best that the
West has to offer. While he is unabashedly ignorant about literature, a
subject traditionally held in high regard, he is enamored of what he
terms 'practical disciplines,' such as the natural sciences, law, medicine,
economics, and philosophy (often narrowed down to denote only the

exercise of the rational mind), all of which were considered by his contemporaries to be the essence of Western learning. He values these branches of knowledge simply because they help him in his battles with crime, which he finds is becoming more technologically advanced all the time.

In this regard, the Huo Sang adventures share with Western detective fiction an inflated faith in science, both in its modes of thought as well as its articulation in scientific laws and laboratory work. In 'Ch'uang' [Window], for example, Huo Sang's calculation of the time of a murder is thrown off by what the witnesses report to be the sound of a window closing in the scene of the crime. Later, however, utilizing his scientific knowledge, he finally deduces that the window is not closed by the murderer at all, as he is led to believe at first. In fact, the servant who discovers the corpse in the room opens the door in such a hurry that he creates a partial vacuum in the room, thus causing the window to close on its own.

To a lesser extent, criminology and abnormal psychology have also won the confidence of our hero, who enjoys quoting the latest theories of both well-known and obscure Western scholars (such as the criminologists H. Cross and Lacassagne and the psychologist G. H. Robinson). It is clear that Ch'eng would have the reader believe that Huo Sang owes his acumen as a detective to his expertise in Western learning, but it must be borne in mind that the 'aura of science' in the Huo Sang stories is as decorative as it is in the West (Knight 86). In most cases, crimes are not solved by the execution of scientific thinking; rather, it is through a combination of the detective's luck and the offender's carelessness that a crime is finally uncovered.

Lastly, Ch'eng's explicit acknowledgment of his debt to Western literature confirms the impression that Huo Sang is an imitation of the Western detective. Compared to his contemporaries, Ch'eng's knowledge of Western detective fiction was amazingly extensive. In his long writing career, he translated and rewrote works by Leslie Charteris, M. Leblanc, Emile Gaboriau, R. A. Freeman, A. Morrison, S. S. Van Dine, Ellery Queen, Agatha Christie, Dorothy Sayers, Wilkie Collins, Anna K. Green, Edgar Wallace, and, most significantly, A. Conan Doyle (Cheng, 'Letter to Wei Shao-ch'ang'). In both his creative and critical writing, Ch'eng compared Chinese and Western detective fiction, and found the former lacking:

In China, detective fictions that follow the workings of the rational mind and refrain from making references to the supernatural and to superstition are as rare as phoenix feathers and the unicorn horn. ('Chiang-nan' 67)

Given the shortcomings of Chinese detective fiction as seen by Ch'eng, it is not surprising that he chose to model many of the Huo Sang stories on the formula of the classical Western detective story (Cawelti 80–105), from the larger sequence of actions down to details such as the idiosyncratic habits of the detective. The pairing of Huo Sang and Pao Lang deserves special mention because it demonstrates the extent to which Ch'eng was willing to learn from the West. As noted, Huo Sang is known as the Chinese Sherlock Holmes, and Pao Lang is jokingly referred to in the stories as the 'Dr Watson of the East' ('Chiang-nan' 67). The narrative functions performed by Huo and Pao also seem to parallel those of their namesakes. Many of the Huo Sang cases open with an episode which is unrelated to the central plot of the story, but is intended to demonstrate the hero's powers of observation and deduction. For example, in 'Chiang-nan yen' [The Sparrow from Chiang-nan] Huo Sang concludes from Pao Lang's suntan, his wind-blown hair, his fatigued but relaxed look, and the yellow-colored earth on his shoes that he has spent the morning rowing (3–4). In this instance, Pao Lang serves merely as a foil to Huo Sang. Just as typical is Pao Lang's role as the intermediary between the detective and the reader when, through his questioning, the reader is given a chance to listen to Huo Sang expound on his method of investigation. In 'Chen-t'an hsiao-shuo ti tuo fang-mien' [On the Various Aspects of Detective Fiction], Ch'eng Hsiao-ch'ing makes a clumsy attempt at providing a theoretical rationale for yet another function of the assistant. He argues that there is a need to narrate the story through Pao Lang, whose main task is to lead the reader away from the right solution. Labeling such a narrative view-point 't'a-hsü-t'i,' Ch'eng proceeds to contrast it with other instances where the narrator is the detective, a narrative viewpoint which he called 'tzu-hsü-t'i' (71ff). While the distinction between the two narrat-ive viewpoints is theoretically sustainable, it is not borne out by Ch'eng's own practice. A comparison between 'I ke shen-shih' [A Gentleman], written in 't'a-hsü-t'i', and 'Pai sha chin' [A White Scarf], written in 'tzu-hsü-t'i', reveals no difference in the strategy of manip-ulating information flow to the reader. It would seem, therefore, that the postulation of these two narrative viewpoints is Ch'eng's way of acknowledging his debt to Conan Doyle, a point that is not lost on readers who are already conditioned to look for Western influences in Chinese detective fiction.

II

Insofar as it is borne out by the text, the observation that Huo Sang is a Chinese imitation of a Western detective is justifiable, except that it has been blown out of proportion at the expense of a fuller understanding of the character. What has been overlooked in this reading are the traditional philosophical and literary elements that went into the making of Huo Sang, which have to be taken into account if a complete understanding of the cultural significance of this group of stories is to be attained. These traditional Chinese elements are by no means disguised or concealed, but with the exception of Fan Po-chün (5) have been ignored repeatedly.

The first of note is the Mo-ist idea of universal love, which is explicitly referred to in 'Huo Sang ti t'ung-nien' [Huo Sang's Childhood]. Mo-ism, named after its founder Mo Tzu (479–38 BC), a late contemporary of Confucius, has been regarded ever since its articulation as a philosophy as subversive to the Confucian ideology of family and state. It advocates a primitive form of equality that threatens to eliminate differentiation of human society by social roles. Although it ceased to develop as a vibrant school of philosophical thought around the first century BC, it has always been a powerful oppositional ideology among the politically and socially underprivileged.[6]

In literature, the Mo-ist philosophy is manifested in the *yu-hsia* figure, a recurrent character type in traditional vernacular fiction and drama. Described by James J. Y. Liu as 'supramoral,' the *yu-hsia* figure is known for his strict adherence to a code of honor and his readiness to help the oppressed. The latest literary reincarnation of the *yu-hsia* figure is found in the proliferation of the genre 'Wu-hsia hsiao-shuo' [Adventures of the Martial Hero] or its cinematic adaptation in kung-fu movies, both of which have yet to receive the serious critical attention they deserve. In many ways parallel to the Robin Hood character-type, the *yu-hsia* casts a figure that is at the same time suave, competent, wise, and just, and fulfills in every way the popular wish for a hero at a time when legal channels cannot be counted on to carry out justice – which, to the many readers of the Huo Sang Cases, appears to be an apt description of Shanghai in the 1930s.[7]

It is to this strong appeal of Mo-ism and the honour code of the *yu-hsia* that the young and impetuous Huo Sang responds when he enters a pact of brotherhood with his peers in 'Huo Sang ti t'ung-nien,' all of whom swear to see each other through hardship for the rest of their lives. It is also for the same reason that he does not hesitate to renounce one of his sworn brothers when the latter is found to have committed a sexual misdemeanor. In this, Huo Sang demonstrates his full understanding of what it means to be a *yu-hsia*: when faced with a conflict between moral goodness and personal loyalty, one should choose the former. Obedience to a higher code of morality accounts for two features of the Huo Sang stories. First, it at times compels Huo Sang to turn against the law. Such an attitude is stated explicitly in 'Pai sha chin' [The White Scarf]: 'We [i.e. Huo Sang and Pao Lang] are not bound by law at all. We observe laws of our own: righteousness and justice' (192). In 'Shuang hsün' [Death Times Two], Huo Sang goes even further. A story of a quadrangular relationship, 'Shuang hsün' begins with Wu Tzu-ch'u's return from overseas as a student to China to marry his fiancée, Mei-hsia. He soon suspects that Mei-hsia has fallen in love with her cousin Yü Hsing-sun during his absence. True to his Christian faith, to which he has been converted overseas, Wu chooses to relieve Mei-hsia of her marriage obligation. He even pretends to be in love with another woman so that Mei-hsia would not be ostracized by society and, more importantly, her stern father. Wu's sacrifice is misplaced, however. While Yü Hsing-sun harbors romantic feelings for his cousin, Mei-hsia has always remained true to Wu. In the meantime, Yü's girlfriend, Hsü Yü-ying, discovers that Yü has had a change of heart. Consumed with jealousy, she tries to kill Mei-hsia, who fortunately survives the small dose of poison put in her food. Realizing that his love will never be requited, Yü kills himself. When Hsü Yü-ying's murderous act is discovered, Pao Lang insists that she be brought to the judgement of the law, but Huo Sang disagrees. He explains to Pao Lang: the law is inflexible; when it comes to judging human behavior, all it requires is that it not be violated. One of the responsibilities of the detective, therefore, is to see to it that human beings do not fall victim to the impersonality of law. Compassion and conscience are the recommended antidotes. In Hsü Yü-ying's case, Huo Sang continues,

> Human behavior is largely determined by our physical and psychological state. Yü-ying is at her prime, and she truly regrets what she has done. As for Mei-hsia, there is still hope that she will get back with Wu Tzu-ch'u. Yü-ying's action has not really caused any harm. We should just let her go. (166)

Secondly, the Huo Sang adventures are marked pervasively by a strong sense of poetic justice. When the law fails to punish a criminal, Huo makes sure that he meets with his just deserts in other ways. Conversely, when a crime is committed in accord with a higher sense of justice, the offender is often given a special reprieve by Huo Sang. Such is the case of 'Mo-k'u shuang hua' [Two Women in the Thief's Nest], a story of ritual murder. He Shih-chieh is a nationally renowned scholar. His professorship at a famous university provides a respectable front for his criminal activities, which include blackmail, kidnap, robbery, and murder. He is murdered by Wang Chen-hua, an ex-student of his, who belongs to a vigilante organization whose goal is to assassinate criminals who successfully evade the law. As he explains to Huo Sang shortly before he dies,

> I know that taking human lives is not usually considered as a sacred act. But suppose the people I kill pose an obstacle to the progress of society and are harmful to the human race, and I do not derive any benefit from assassinating them, should my action be considered as sacred? (126)

Significantly, Huo Sang, who is eloquent at other times, remains silent at the question. When Wang finally dies, Huo Sang not only shows his respect by going to Wang's funeral, but also dissuades the Chief of Police from investigating Wang's gang.

Objections may be raised at this point that the Chinese detective, for all his strict adherence to the 'supramoral' code, is no different from his Western counterpart. After all, Western detective fiction is also full of heroes who will play God and decide who is or is not to be pardoned. What differentiates Huo Sang from Sherlock Holmes, with whom he is often compared, therefore, lies precisely in the anti-establishment slant of the Mo-ist philosophy that informs Huo's action. If, as Ernst Kaemmel and Dennis Porter point out, each from their own perspective, the ostensibly subversive actions of the Western detective hero often end up celebrating the very values of the society they appear to attack (Kaemmel 55–61; Porter 146–88), Mo-ism has consistently remained at variance with the dominant Confucianism, despite the many parallels it bears with the latter. Historically, Mo-ism is condemned, by its intrinsic philosophical opposition to Confucianism in China, to be the ideological guidance of the underclass. Viewed in this way, Huo Sang does not represent the 'heroic qualities of an ascendent middle class' that characterizes Sherlock Holmes (Porter 157), but the spokesman of the oppressed who, under the Mo-ist persuasion, share the view that the interests of individuals or groups can only be entertained in the light of those of the whole society (see Schwartz 138–45).

Another debt that the Huo Sang adventures owe to Chinese literary tradition is their resemblance to *kung-an* literature popular since the thirteenth century (see Ma and Hayden). Usually known as courtroom fiction or drama, this genre of literature features as the main plot an incorruptible judge overseeing the trial of a difficult court case. In the process of bringing the criminal to justice, the judge often has to brave opposition from the court, in whose name justice is supposed to be served. To the modern reader, the plot of *kung-an* literature is frequently marred by the characteristically unlikely coincidences and supernatural interferences. Ch'eng Hsiao-ching, for one, explicitly denigrated it in his 'Lun chen-t'an hsiao-shuo' [On Detective Fiction] (206). Yet, *kung-an* literature nevertheless anticipates the kind of crimes that constitute the majority of Huo Sang's cases, in that, unlike crimes found in Western detective fiction, those in *kung-an* literature have a much broader social ramification if they remain undetected, affecting the society at large. This is due to the nature of the crimes themselves, which often concern matters of great political or social import. George Hayden takes one step further in noting the far-reaching effects of *kung-an* crimes when he declares: '[Crime] disturbs the natural balance at all levels by going against the principle of justice. Disruption in turn may or may not produce supernatural events, but in any case, demands immediate correction' (14).

A comparison between a well-known *kung-an* play, 'Selling Rice at Ch'en Chou' and Edgar Allan Poe's 'The Purloined Letter' should make this clear. In both cases, the crime threatens the security of the country. Yet nowhere in Poe's story does the reader feel the urgency of the impending crisis. In fact, he is not even told how Minister D. might put the purloined letter to his own use. Through this process of aestheticizing crime, the political scandal that could be averted only by recovering the missing letter is pushed into the background. Instead, the point of introducing the political crisis to the story seems no more than to provide an occasion for Dupin to demonstrate his spectacular abilities as a detective. 'Selling Rice at Ch'en Chou', on the other hand, impresses the reader with the enormity of the misdeed at every turn. (An excellent translation can be found in Hayden 31–78.) The play features the legendary incorruptible official Lord Pao. A historical figure, Lord Pao has since the thirteenth century been elevated to a god-like status in the popular consciousness for his sagacity in uncovering crime, courage in resisting pressures from the evil forces, and fairness in settling legal disputes. He is one of the many judges who are the staunch defenders of justice in *kung-an* literature. In 'Selling Rice at Ch'en Chou,' Lord Pao is sent by the court to investigate the work of famine relief headed by the son of his superior, the Prime Minister. There is none of the detective work found in Poe's 'The Purloined Letter' because the crime is plain for all to see.[8] Instead of distributing the relief grain to the famished peasants, the son of the Prime Minister, at the bidding of his father, takes the opportunity to line his own pocket by selling the rice. A moment of delay in the punishment of the crime, therefore, could mean the starvation of thousands of peasants. In the end, the execution of the culprit is presented with a solemnity reminiscent of a cleansing ritual, so much has society been contaminated by the corrupt practices of the relief officers.

This is not to suggest that Huo Sang is called upon to deal only with national crises. While Huo Sang has his share of middle-class crimes and locked-room murders, the reader is constantly reminded of the social and historical specificity of the crimes in Shanghai. In Pao Lang's words, Shanghai is in the midst of 'an eventful time' ('He ti-lao' 1). Frequent references are made to the problems China faced in this period of transition: the clash of old and new values, the proliferation of materialistic culture, the spread of international imperialism, and the threat of internecine warfare all combine to upset the social balance. Time and again, Huo Sang is drawn into political conspiracies and assassinations, and he is brought into direct conflict with gangs that have strong political backing. These crimes, Ch'eng seems to suggest, could only happen in Shanghai. The following passage, coming rather gratuitously at the conclusion of a murder case, reflects Huo Sang's and Pao Lang's tendency to see their work in larger social terms:

> I feel that materialistic culture can on the one hand improve the comfort of our lives, but on the other, incite us to hurt each other... Now that the door to China has been forced open, ... our material poverty is completely exposed. In the face of all these materialistic temptations, it is impossible for us to deny ourselves these material comforts even though we might not be able to produce them ourselves. As a result, average urban dwellers have their eyes on instant gratification, and, accordingly, the society is getting more and more chaotic and our national strength steadily declines.
>
> ('Wu-hou ti kuei-shu' 265–6)

Putting aside for the moment the simplicity of Pao Lang's analysis, one notices in this passage the tendency of the Huo Sang stories to address directly (and awkwardly in some cases) the interconnection between crime and society – clearly a continuation of the *kung-an* tradition. Despite Ch'eng's open disavowal, the two detectives in fact look back to the *kung-an* judge as their model. Even Pao Lang's name suggests as much. His name (literally, Pao the Bright) distinctly echoes Pao Ch'ing-t'ien (literally, Pao the Bright Sky), the name of Lord Pao mentioned above. As far as their conduct is concerned, both Huo Sang and Pao Lang have proved themselves worthy descendants of the moral and social-minded judge.

III

Today, China is still feeling the aftermath of the cultural upheaval that took place in the early twentieth century. The debate is far from over as to what course China is to take in order to restore its once glorious past. While at times tradition appears to remain as unyielding as ever, the sentiments for change can run so deep that nothing short of a complete modeling upon the West is acceptable. The latest expression of this belief is a six-part TV essay/documentary broadcast on national television in China in 1988. With a scope so ambitious that it offers no less than an overall critique of Chinese civilization, 'The River Elegy' turned on its head one of the traditionally revered symbols, the Yellow River. Whereas the Yellow River is usually looked upon as the source from which the glory of China flows, in the broadcast its yellow color is made to symbolize everything that is stagnant, complacent, conservative, and sterile about Chinese culture. The moral of this six-part TV lesson is that just as the Yellow River flows inexorably towards the blue ocean, China should move forward to join the rest of the world. Holding on to the past would simply be an act of sentimental indulgence or even moral timidity.

In retrospect, it can be seen that the defensive rhetoric of Chinese detective fiction and the aggressive gestures in 'The River Elegy' are alike in that they are both informed by a myth of progress. As a motivation for change, this myth accepts in the name of progress the superiority and validity of the Western perspective, and recommends, in various degrees, the abandonment of the indigenous Chinese perspective. 'River Elegy' is ruthless in this regard, while modern Chinese detective fiction reveals a deeper division of cultural allegiance. The old would not be abandoned altogether, but it would have to be carried on in the name of the new, resulting sometimes in the kind of misreading of cultural expressions I described above.

However, when the cultural complexities of Chinese detective fiction are confronted directly, it can be seen that it is by no means simply a clone of the West. For example, instead of being a Western private eye in China, Huo Sang is fraught with cultural ambiguities. Together with other aspects of the stories, such a characterization speaks to a question that must have occupied a central position in the minds of many Chinese, namely, the best direction for China in the early twentieth century. Between the two poles of wholesale acceptance of the West and uncompromising preservation of Chinese tradition, there existed a wide array of possible positions, representing various degrees of negotiation between the two cultures. To the urban dwellers who made up Huo Sang's contemporary readership, this question must have had particular urgency. Faced with a choice between West and East every day of their lives, they, more than other people, were in need of guideposts to help them find their way out of the maze of cultural choices. Vicariously, the readers of popular literature participated in the lives of the fictitious characters, who, during this period, were typically caught between two different historical periods and ways of life. The reading of popular literature, therefore, provided an environment for the readers to try out new ways of life at a safe distance (see Link ch. 6).

What the readers find in the Huo Sang adventures is not too encouraging. To be sure, the West has all its modern conveniences, logical process of thinking, efficacious sciences, organized religions, and rule of law to offer, but the 'progress' it brings is by no means an unqualified blessing. In more ways than one, the Huo Sang cases attempt to dismantle this myth of progress. Many of the stories relate instances of cultural maladjustment, where, for example, honest young girls from the provinces are turned into prostitutes as soon as they arrive in the city. Likewise, as noted above, the narrator's asides suggest that the roots of the most heinous crimes can easily be traced to a sense of cultural confusion. Even the pairing of Huo Sang and Pao Lang, as I argue elsewhere (Tam), represents the give and take between the sciences and humanities, which are temporarily equated with Western and Chinese culture, respectively.

Huo Sang's ambiguous cultural identity, therefore, is part of a larger statement made by Ch'eng Hsiao-ch'ing about Chinese society. It is as if Ch'eng were conducting an experiment, first creating a new hero, then placing beside him an assistant who sometimes agrees with him and at other times challenges him, and finally observing his actions in a new social environment. In this connection, it is interesting to observe that the character of Huo Sang changes subtly but perceptibly from story to story. The experiment, as it were, has to be repeated, each time under varying circumstances.

Notes

The author is grateful for a grant from the St Anthony Hall at Trinity College in support of the research of this article.

1. For a discussion of contemporary Chinese detective fiction, see Kinkley.
2. For a more detailed discussion of the New Culture Movement, see Chow. For the reception of popular literature in twentieth-century China, see Link. For debates between the defenders of and dissenters from popular literature, see Wei and Jui.
3. The two dominant themes of the New Culture Movements are science and democracy, respectively known in their personified Chinese names as Mr Sai and Mr Teh. In claiming that detective fiction promotes science and a sense of the law, the writers summoned to their own defense the two banners under which the rank and file of the Movement marched. That a legal society is equated with democracy in the minds of many Chinese – the former sometimes representing the sole *raison d'être* of the latter – may be lost on the Western readers. Yet, it is a point brought home once again by the cries for the rule of law that immediately preceded the pro-democracy movements in the 1980s.
4. See Ch'eng Hsiao-ch'ing, 'Lun-chen-t'an hsiao-shuo,' 211. A note on the extant edition of the Huo Sang cases, the subject of study in this paper: A succinct discussion of various editions can be found in Wei Shao-ch'ang, 145–50. In the post-Mao years, the Huo Sang cases have repeatedly been reprinted and pirated. The two most notable reprints are *Ch'eng Hsiao ch'ing wen-chi: Huo Sang t'an-an hsden* [The Works of Ch'eng Hsiao-ch'ing: Selected Cases of Huo Sang], Peking: Chung-kuo wen-lien, 1986, and *Huo Sang t'an-an chi* [The Huo Sang Cases], Peking: Chun-chung, 1986. Though widely available, these two editions represent only a very limited selection of the Huo Sang stories. I prefer the Pocket Series edition not only because of its wide selection, but also because the text is accompanied by ample illustrations, which capture rather realistically the aura of life in old Shanghai. Some volumes in this series are not dated, while others are dated 1947. Almost all bear the prefaces written by Ch'eng Hsiao-ch'ing himself in 1944, Chen Tieh-i in 1944, and Yao Su-feng in 1945. References in this paper to the Huo Sang cases are made to this edition. Typically, the title of the story will be followed by the volume number of the series and then by the page number. The Huo Sang cases have not been translated into English.
5. Obvious gaps remain to be filled in our present knowledge of Ch'eng Hsiao-ch'ing's life. Two biographical sketches are available: Yen (550), and Cheng I-mei (388–9), but they are both written in the vague formulaic language characteristic of traditional biographical writings and leave out many specific details, such as important dates in Ch'eng's life that a modern reader expects to find. Even less is known about his life after 1949. Lu Wen-fu in the preface to one reprint of the Huo Sang cases spoke of his friendship with Ch'eng, who was reduced to very straitened circumstances in the last years of his life (1–5).

6. The systematic suppression of Mo-ism can be glimpsed from the *Shih-chi* and *Han Shu*, partially translated by Watson. For a treatment of Mo-ist ideas, see Mote and Schwartz.

7. Space does not permit a full elaboration in this paper of either the Mo-ist concept of universal love or the concept of *yu-hsia*, but James J. Y. Liu, *The Chinese Knight Errant*, Chicago: University of Chicago, 1967, explores rather thoroughly the relationship between these two concepts.

8. While a full elaboration will have to wait for another time and place, it will be noted here that on the whole, there is very little detection worthy of its name in *kung-an* literature. In some cases, the perpetrator of crime is identified right from the beginning, and in others, the process of detection is facilitated by the assistance of spirits and ghosts. Obviously, the primary interest of this early type of Chinese crime literature does not lie in the intellectual process of detection, but in the moral consideration of crime and punishment. In lieu of the 'aestheticization' of crime that one hears so often in connection with Western detective fiction, perhaps it is more appropriate to speak of 'moralization' of crime in Chinese literature.

Bibliography

Cawelti, John G. 'The Formula of the Classical Detective Story.' *Adventure, Mystery and Romance*. Chicago: U Chicago P, 1976, 80–105.

Ch'eng Hsiao-ch'ing. *Ch'eng Hsiao-ch'ing wen-chi: Huo Sang t'an-an hsüen* [The Works of Ch'eng Hsiao-ch'ing: Selected Cases of Huo Sang]. Peking: Chung-kuo wen-lien, 1986.

——. 'Chen-t'an hsiao-shuo ti tuo fang-mien.' Rpt. in Jui He-shih, et al. *Yüan-yang hu-tieh p'ai wen-hsüeh tzu-liao* [Research Materials on Mandarin Ducks and Butterflies Literature]. Fu-chou: Jen-min ch'u-pan-she, 1984.

——. 'Ch'in-chun ju-ong,' *Huo Sang t'an-an hsiu-chen tsung-k'an* [The Pocket Series of Collected Huo Sang Cases]. Vol. 29. Peking: Shih-chieh shu-chu, n.d.

——. 'Chiang-nan yen.' *Huo Sang t'an-an hsiu-chen tsung-k'an* [The Pocket Series of Collected Huo Sang Cases]. Vol. 19. Peking: Shih-chieh shu-chu, n.d.

——. 'He ti-lao,' *Huo Sang t'an-an hsiu-chen tsung-k'an* [The Pocket Series of Collected Huo Sang Cases]. Vol. 30. Peking: Shih-chieh shu-chu, n.d.

——. *Huo Sang t'an-an chi* [The Huo Sang Cases]. Peking: Chun-chung, 1986.

——. 'Huo Sang ti t'ung-nien' [Huo Sang's Childhood]. *Huo Sang t'an-an hsiu-chen tsung-k'an* [The Pocket Series of Collected Huo Sang Cases]. Vol. 19. Peking: Shih-chieh shu-chu, n.d.

——. 'I ke shen-shih,' *Huo Sang t'an-an hsiu-chen tsung-k'an* [The Pocket Series of Collected Huo Sang Cases]. Vol. 30. Peking: Shih-chieh shu-chu, n.d.

——. 'Letter to Wei Shao-ch'ang.' *Wo k'an yüan-yang hu-tieh p'ai*. By Wei Shao-ch'ang. Hong Kong: Chung-hua shu-chu, 1990. 148–50.

——. 'Lun chen-t'an hsiao-shuo.' *Huo Sang t'an-an hsiu-chen tsung-k'an* [The Pocket Series of Collected Huo Sang Cases]. Vol. 30. Peking: Shih-chieh shu-chu, n.d.

——. 'Mo-ku shuang-hua,' *Huo Sang t'an-an hsiu-chen tsung-k'an* [The Pocket Series of Collected Huo Sang Cases]. Vol. 12. Peking: Shih-chieh shu-chu, n.d.

——. 'Pai sha chin,' *Huo Sang t'an-an hsiu-chen tsung-k'an* [The Pocket Series of Collected Huo Sang Cases]. Vol. 15. Peking: Shih-chieh shu-chu, n.d.

——. 'Shuang-hsün,' *Huo Sang t'an-an hsiu-chen tsung-k'an* [The Pocket Series of Collected Huo Sang Cases]. Vol. 23. Peking: Shih-chieh shu-chu, n.d.

——. 'Wu-hou ti kuei-shu,' *Huo Sang t'an-an hsiu-chen tsung-k'an* [The Pocket Series of Collected Huo Sang Cases]. Vol. 7. Peking: Shih-chieh shu-chu, n.d.

Cheng I-mei. 'Ch'eng Hsiao-ch'ing.' Rpt. Jui He-shih, et al. *Yüan-yang hu-tieh p'ai wen-hsüeh tzu-liao* [Research Materials on Mandarin Ducks and Butterflies Literature]. Fu-chou: Jen-min ch'u-pan-she, 1984. 388–89.

Chow Tse-tsung. *The May Fourth Movement.* Stanford: Stanford UP, 1960.

Fan Pao-chun. 'Lun Ch'eng Hsiao-ch'ing ti Huo-sang t'an-an.' *Chiang-huai hsüeh-k'an* [Chiang-huai Journal]. 6 (1985): 31–7.

Fan Yen-ch'iao. 'Min-kuo chiu-p'ai hsiao-shuo shih-lüeh.' Ed. Wei Shou-ch'ang. *Yüan-yang hu-tieh pa'i yen-chiu tzu-liao.* 268–363.

Fu Po. 'Jen-shih t'ui-li hsiao-shuo.' *Wen Hsün.* 26 (October 1986): 138–40.

Hayden, George. *Crime and Punishment in Medieval Chinese Drama.* Cambridge: Council of East Asian Studies, Harvard UP, 1978.

Jui He-shih, et al. *Yüan-yang hu-tieh p'ai wen-hsüeh tzu-liao* [Research Materials on Mandarin Ducks and Butterflies Literature]. Fu-chou: Jen-min ch'u-pan-she, 1984.

Kaemmel, Ernst. 'Literature under the Table: The Detective Novel and its Social Mission.' Ed. Glen W. Most and William W. Stowe. *The Poetics of Murder.* San Diego: Harcourt, Brace, Jovanovich, 1983.

Kinkley, Jeffrey. 'Chinese Crime Fiction and Its Formulas at the Turn of the 1980s.' *After Mao: Chinese Literature and Society 1978–1981.* Ed. Jeffrey Kinkley. Cambridge: Harvard UP, 1985. 91–129.

——. 'The Post-Colonial Detective in People's China.' In this volume.

Knight, Stephen. *Form and Ideology in Crime Fiction.* Bloomington: Indiana UP, 1980.

Link, Perry. *Mandarin Ducks and Butterflies.* Berkeley: U California, 1981.

Liu, James J. Y. *The Chinese Knight Errant.* Chicago: U Chicago, 1967.

Liu Yang-t'i. *Yüan-yang hu-tieh tso-p'in hsüen-p'ing* [A Critical Reading of Selected Writings of the Mandarin Ducks and Butterflies School]. Ch'eng-tu: Ssu-chuan wen-i, 1987.

Lu Wen-fu. 'Hsin-hsiang i-fan tai-hsü' [A Fragrant Heart – as Preface]. *Ch'eng Hsiao-ch'ing wen-chi. Huo Sang t'an-an hsüen* [The Works of Ch'eng Hsiao-ch'ing: Selected Cases of Huo Sang]. Peking: Chung-kuo wen-lien, 1986. 1–5.

Ma, Y. W. '*Kung-an* Ficition: A Historical and Critical Introduction.' *T'oung Pao* 65: 4–5 (1979).

Mote, Frederick W. *Intellectual Foundations of China.* New York: Alfred A. Knopf, 1971.

Porter, Dennis. *The Pursuit of Crime.* New Haven: Yale UP, 1981.

Schwartz, Benjamin. 'Mo-tzu's Challenge.' *The World of Thought in Ancient China.* Cambridge: Harvard UP, 1985.

Tam, King-fai. 'The Detective Fiction of Ch'eng Hsiao-ch'ing.' *Asia Major.* 3rd series, vol. 5, part I, 1992: 113–132.

Watson, Burton. *Records of the Grand Historian.* New York: Columbia UP, 1961.

——. *Courtier and Commoner.* New York: Columbia UP, 1974.

Wei Shao-ch'ang. *Yüan-yang hu-tieh p'ai yen-chiu tzu-liao* [Research Materials on the Mandarin Ducks and Butterflies School]. Shanghai: Shanghai Wen-i, 1984.

—— *Wo k'an yüan-yang hu-tieh p'ai* [My Views on Mandarin Ducks and Butterflies Fiction]. Hong Kong: Chung-hua shu-chu, 1990.

Yen Fu-sun, et al. 'Minkuo chiu-p'ai hsiao-shuo ming-chia hsiao-shih' [Short Biographies on Famous Writers of the Old Style Fiction in the Republican Period]. Ed. Wei Shao-ch'ang. *Yüan-yang hu-tieh p'ai yen-chiu tzu-liao.* 550.

10

Paco Ignacio Taibo II: Post-Colonialism and the Detective Story in Mexico

Jorge Hernández Martín

You don't make poetry with guns. Or do you?
                    -Taibo, *The Shadow of a Shadow* (191)

The history common to all American societies is that they came into being as a result of European conquests and colonization. The eventually independent nations of the American continent and the Caribbean included both colonists and their culture and dominated or exploited social groups that have gradually achieved differing degrees of emancipation. The origin of Mexico is no exception to this pattern of development and, in fact, is a classic model of the phases of colonialism in the American continent. When the word *conquistador* is mentioned, Hernán Cortés comes to mind in an armor-clad, indelible image that signifies militarized violence in the name of plunder. Furthermore, when Cortés made his arrival in Mexico, the history of the country showed evidence of successive conquests, with the conquering people assuming the right to exact tribute from its subjects. The support the Spaniard received from native societies subjugated by the highly developed Aztec empire proved invaluable for the success of his enterprise. In time, European conquest evolved from plunder to more stable forms of exploitation of the conquered lands.

Independence, in the year 1821, found Mexico with a large part of the Amerindian population suffering from at least a partial loss of its culture and with the problem of surviving in some form of servitude to the successors of the European colonial agents. But the sheer numerical proportion of the Amerindian contingent in Mexico made it clear that the pre-colonial past could not be disregarded in the way the metropolis had been able to do in other parts of the empire where the indigenous culture was destroyed by the economic and social forces of colonialism.

What is more, it would be incorrect to affirm that the European group that represented colonial control in Mexico had remained impervious to native culture; it too became 'creolized' through intermarriage and contact with the culture-specific expressions which to this day characterize the area. This was so much the case that the dominant social sector in Mexico today should not be considered a direct descendant of the Caucasian colonial, but rather a racially mixed group that reflects the compositional ethnic features of colonial society.

The nineteenth century is also the cradle of the literary practice of detective fiction. I will not recount in detail how this form, born in England's most important ex-colony in the Americas, is taken up in the metropolis and developed by Collins, Doyle, Christie, Dickson Carr, Innes, Chesterton, Sayers into the twentieth century. In turn, the 'English' mystery would later be reterritorialized in the former British colony by Hammett, Chandler, MacDonald, and many others, to the present day. But it was the 'English' detective story that created a readership for the genre in Latin America. In a personal interview, Paco Ignacio Taibo II, a prolific representative of the new Mexican detective novel, referred to the work of Borges and the generation of the '30s and '40s in Latin America as the 'pre-history' of the genre, if not a downright prehistoric expression of the form. He was indirectly indicating that the tradition advocated by Jorge Luis Borges, who introduced the genre in Argentina, was the puzzle type of detective story, the kind that depended on the reasoner detective and the quaint piece of deduction.

Given the social conditions of Latin America, to expect the kind of stability that would allow for a detective to arrive at a solution through methodology was, Taibo argued, unrealistic, even ludicrous. The current widespread practice of the genre, which favors the 'hard-boiled' or 'noir' tradition of Hammett, Chandler, MacDonald, with their renegade detectives at odds with the cultural mainstream, with administrative corruption, and often in direct and painful confrontation with the agents of the law, would grant the appropriateness of his argument.

His was the generation that galvanized around and participated in the events of 1968, which were marked by a general student strike that lasted 100 days and culminated in the barbarous massacre in Tlatelolco Square in Mexico City. Here the perpetrator was the national government, the same government that later, the very same night of the second day of October, disposed of the bodies of the slain by strewing them onto the deep dark waters of the Gulf. Ernesto – after Ernesto 'Che' Guevara – became the name of choice for the male offspring of the mothers and fathers of this generational group, who favored Julio

Cortázar's short fiction over Borges' because Cortázar sympathized with overtly revolutionary causes whereas Borges did not.

Several clear characteristics of Taibo's important output in the detective genre can be attributed to his generational affiliation with the events of 1968. One is his predilection for the hardboiled detective mode established by Hammett, with its insistent indictment of the system; another is his radical mistrust of the national institutions which appear bent on serving their own machinations of power against the interests of the working class and the population at large; and also the internationalist background of his detective. Taibo's detective, Hector Belascoarán Shayne, is the oldest son of a Basque merchant marine captain and an Irish folk singer. His father, affiliated with the Socialist Party, joined the Republican cause in Spain in 1934, fighting after the amnesty and the fascist uprising as a captain of a socialist and anarchist militia. In Valencia, he met his wife, singing at an International Brigade function. After the Second World War, and having collaborated with the *maquisard* French Resistance, he opted for exile on the friendly shores of Mexico (*Cosa* 171–7).

Belascoarán's younger brother, like an ideologically conscious Mycroft, possesses a wealth of information about labor movements, and is often at hand to point out the implications of the detective's endeavors for the international class struggle and middle-class complacency.[1] The relationship among the siblings of the Belascoarán family is perhaps a notable characteristic of the Hispanic nature of this collection of detective stories. The brothers – and the one sister, who after a disastrous marriage with a Canadian reporter returns to Mexico to sort out her life – share a spirit of camaraderie and mutual support that is rarely found in the genre.

In time, the 'movement' of 1968 would be understood by many of its participants as a revival of the utopian fervor crushed by the fascist triumph in Spain, by the bipolar world order established by the outcome of the Second World War, and later, by the disenchantment with the course of the worker's revolution under the guidance of Stalin in the Soviet Union. But in Mexico, Taibo was one more in the tide of restlessness and indignation that swept the globe and the nation at that point in history. The Mexican student brigades came to feel a solidarity with student unrest in Brazil, with the May Movement in Paris, with the Córdoba students in Argentina, with the events of the Prague Spring, and with the Columbia University students in New York. It was a new development of the old internationalist sparks that resulted from the Bolshevik revolution, taking place without the old communist party cadres to contain and direct the action on the world stage, and without the subordination of the movement in the various postcolonial nations to a European or North American center. Mexico itself took a different existence in the emergent consciousness of the generation. Mexican history became personal, or as García Lorca, the Andalusian poet, might have said, national history became intimate, like a small plaza.

Taibo explains that for his generation, the past, before 1968, 'was an international territory where revolutions and novels took place, not a local and popular territory.... We had little to do with Morelos, with Zapata, with Villa.... at most, they were street names' (*68* 22).[2] The response of the Díaz Ordaz government to the unrest, its unwillingness to enter into public dialog with the strikers, the military mobilization that escalated from beatings and the casualties that resulted from the blowing of the gate at the San Ildefonso school, to parading of light tanks through the streets of Mexico and outright murder, made clear that in the national whodunit being played out in and around the University Town there was only one culprit: the national government and the political party organization that operated through it, forming an entity powerful and shameless enough to disappear the *corpus delicti* of the massacre it orchestrated in Tlatelolco Square in 1968.

The events of 1968 also feed the plots of the Belascoarán novels in specific ways. The individuals and paramilitary units engaged by the forces of repression to contain student unrest appear in the books as either transformed or unassimilated elements in society that pursue their own opportunistic ends in gangster fashion or are discreetly given positions in the power structure. In both instances, these shadowy remainders of the official counter-offensive take the role of 'bad guys' in Taibo's stories. *Some Clouds* [*Algunas nubes*] offers one example in the figure of *The Rat*:

> The movement of 68 offered *The Rat* brief moments of ephemeral glory. He met with the mayor of Mexico City, and through his hands a good amount of money reached the gangster groups that tried to break the first wave of the student movement; but in spite of his good intentions, *The Rat* was swept away by a movement in which hundreds of thousands of students participated, and his efforts did not amount to much. He broke up some meetings, destroyed some automobiles in a parking lot during one of the demonstrations, and he sold some tips to the police, that did not know what to do with so much information.   (*Nubes* 49–50)

In 1970, *The Rat* organizes an 'urban guerrilla' at the behest of the federal police commissioner. Betrayed from the start, 11 misguided individuals who join the group pay with their lives for their mistake. In the mid-1970s, when Belascoarán confronts the character, dirty business of a more lucrative sort occupies *The Rat*'s time and energy. When both characters face off, Belascoarán's repeated question of 'what about the dead?' is as much an instance of account taking of the facts of the case, as it is a reminder of the dead left in the wake of the student movement (72).

In *No Happy End* [*No habrá final feliz*], the detective discovers a former paramilitary group serving as subway security guards. 'The Falcons,' originally deployed against student demonstrators, had killed 40 people in the massive demonstration of 10 June 1968. The scandal caused by newspaper reports indicating the participation of army personnel and members of the police force in the training of the paramilitary unit did not result in judicial action, and 'the files disappeared eight years later' (78). In Taibo's fiction, 'The Falcons' are busy killing civilians who were either involved in their training or were witnesses to their recruitment. In an effort to forestall further killings and what he considers might be a future reappearance of the unit, Belascoarán battles 'The Falcons,' with dire results for his person.[3] The dark and complex network that confronts the Mexican detective is alluded to in the following conversation with his brother and his brother's wife:

'Suppose that you finish off that group at the Metro. Are you going to continue with the Judicial Police? Then with the White Brigade? Then the whole military camp Number One? It sounds absurd, you are going to get killed.' Hector moved his head in the affirmative to all the questions and to the last statement, and then he asked – 'I would like to know why.' 'Why, you son of a bitch, because we are in Mexico' – answered [Carlos' wife] Marina. (105)

One month after the 1968 débâcle, the process of dispersion began for all concerned. Many members of this politicized generation could or would not return to the classrooms where instruction had resumed; some joined urban guerrilla movements that gave rise to the 'dirty war' launched by Díaz's successor, Luis Echeverría. Many others formed neighborhood organizations which represented another form of popular resistance; still others, like Taibo, headed for the factories to investigate the history of the labor movement in Mexico, trying to understand the causes for the unresponsiveness of the workers to the students' strike

(*68* 113). But across the national board, along with the feeling of international solidarity that would rally this generation to condemn the events in Chile in 1973, and to support the Sandinista revolution throughout the '70s, the participants in the events of the late '60s in Mexico found themselves a part of history at a point in the history of the nation. In this, the events that this group catalyzed in Mexican society gave the generation a sense of place, a sense of belonging, that was essentially a form of nationalism.

The detective created by Taibo, Hector Belascoarán Shayne, wears his name, with its double charge of Basque and Irish descent, like a badge; and yet, he makes clear that he is Mexican. Though he is the immigrant son of a couple who never instilled a firm sense of homeland in their children, it is by means of action, the type of action that in the detective's first novel of adventures spells 'going out to the street to walk around, to wait for the other to pounce on his prey, and to let chance find him nearby' (*Días* 64), that makes him feel a common destiny with the people of Mexico, with the country that crime has led him to know:

> That was his way of feeling Mexican. An everyday Mexican, sharing the complaints, protesting over the rise in the cost of corn meal, getting steamed up over the increase in the cost of bus fare, talking back to the abominable news programs on television, complaining about the corruption of traffic cops and government ministers. Cursing the national situation, the deplorable state of the garbage dump of the nation, cursing the the great Aztec stadium into which the country had been turned. Though it might only be through the brotherhood that resulted from the practice of complaining, from the expression of scorn and pride, Belascoarán earned his right to continue being a Mexican, of not becoming a *vedette* or a Martian; complaining was his one opportunity of not losing touch with the people. (*Cosa* 25)

Belascoarán, whom we have heard facetiously addressed as 'colleague' by the sewage expert, holds an electromechanical engineering degree specializing in time and movement that he earned at the National University after his marginal participation in the student revolt. He then married and was a supervisor with the General Electric corporation up to the time when, after watching a screening of *The Case of Justin Playfair*, he decided to leave middle-life comfort behind and become a professional and 'independent' investigator, knowing that in Mexico he would have to go that route alone: 'Héctor. . . had become a detective in a country where logic negated the existence of that role, but where any type of irrationality was at the same time admitted, including that one' (*Cosa* 72). A permit earned by correspondence, the purchase of a .38 revolver, and at 31 years of age the new Mexican detective is on his way.

Taibo's detective shares his office with a plumber who, as a means to lower the rent, subleases sections of the office to an upholsterer and an engineer whose field of expertise is the sewer system of Mexico City. In this context, the detective is one more worker, less skilled than the other two, but each with his own role to play in the urban order; as the sewer engineer reminds Belascoarán: 'You don't realize that the citizens of this capital city would be up to their ears in shit if someone did not concern himself with preventing such a thing' (*Cosa* 36). By means of his detective's working-class relations and sympathies, Taibo neatly defuses the cosmopolitan and exotic connotations of the detective myth.

An aspect of post-colonial society not to be that easily defused by an appeal to class solidarity is the issue of race. Mexican society is largely, as has been stated, a racially mixed society, particularly the dominant sectors, in contrast with other post-colonial entities. In the Caribbean, for example, the dominant social sectors are often of European descent. In these societies, the ethnic and racial appeal of the European is the product of its colonial past and the power associated with the metropolitan institutions, though democratic practice and the political rhetoric of parties vying for voter affiliation have introduced thoroughly creolized and black individuals to all levels of the political power structure. In Mexico, given the relatively undimmed splendor of its indigenous past, European colonial prestige and popular scorn of the foreign *gachupín* make up an ambivalent climate with an underlying current of racial differentiation being practiced in society.

There is no way around the fact that Belascoarán is a white European. However, the degree to which this fact affects the effectiveness of his investigation, the responsiveness of those he questions, the spaces he is able to enter, that is, the racial boundaries that we may assume to be inherently 'there' in Mexican social intercourse, is not apparent in the detective's activities. The absence of these anticipated hindrances could be on account of the ethnic authority represented by Belascoarán. One way in which the detective circumvents the factor of racial difference is by adopting the folk language, as noted in this exchange: 'Hell, this city is magic, there's all kinds of fucking things going on...' 'You never would have used that word when you were an engineer, colleague,' said [sewer system inspector] the Rooster. 'It's part of the magic,' Héctor answered (*Cosa* 57). The word in question is a particularly Mexican expression, and the characters who appear in the Belascoarán novels invariably use many other typical locutions. The detective raises an issue related to the process of national integration at work in post-colonial societies through his adaptation of popular speech. In the detective's usage, ethnic linguistic practice is seen as separate from racial, physical constraints. One might not belong to a particular racial group, but the group's ethnic practices are open to appropriation. The appropriation of cultural expressions enables the user – the detective, in this case – to 'blend into' the structure of ethnicity.[4]

The setting of the capital city of Mexico is of paramount importance in the Belascoarán novels. A city of 14 m inhabitants when the action takes place, in the early 1970s, Mexico City intensifies every aspect of Mexican social conflict. Past critics have pointed out the importance of metropolitan areas to the development of the genre in Latin America:

> The reason that not all Latin American countries have produced detective fiction is to be found, mainly, in the fact that the genre demands a high level of intellectualization on the part of the readers. This readership is often absent, generally speaking, in countries without a great metropolitan center, where the struggle for day-to-day existence does not allow long periods of idleness. These countries are, finally, characterized by a high rate of illiteracy.   (Yates, *El Cuento* 4)

Donald Yates' appraisal of the genre's problematic development is aimed at explaining the acceptance in Latin America of the early detective story. This early expression of detective fiction, highly derivative of the European model, is, according to Yates, 'essentially a type of literature that avoids direct contact with reality and as such offers relatively little attraction to populations whose principal daily preoccupation is the struggle to extract a decent standard of living from the physical circumstances' ('La novela' 6). The critic's account is based on the observation that the principal centers of detective fiction activity in Latin America have been Buenos Aires, Santiago in Chile, and Mexico City (*El Cuento* 7).

It is obviously in reaction to the description of the type that Yates applies to the genre that Taibo elaborates his Belascoarán novels. Whether we accept Yates' hypothesis regarding the influence of metropolitan areas, readerships, and underdevelopment or not, it is a fact that Taibo's relation to the detective genre's past in Mexico is an ambivalent one. On the one hand, the existence of a reading tradition, that is, of a readership predisposed toward detective fiction, however minuscule, makes for a ready-made body of readers who can recognize the modifications implemented by a writer such as Taibo as an evolution of generic conventions and writing practice. In relation to the past, the Belascoarán novels are a bright new national development of the hard-boiled formula. Even the polemics that have developed between the 'new' lions and the 'old' practitioners of the genre, represented by María Elvira Bermúdez, take place in a *Mexican* tradition of detective fiction. On the other hand, as the blurb on the back cover of the third edition of *Days of Combat* (1976) makes clear, Taibo and his fellow writers have their own generational agenda: *Días de combate* is touted as 'the novel with which Paco Ignacio Taibo II founded the new Mexican detective novel.'[5] The audience that this brand of fiction targets is a younger reader, who might not have been interested in the intellectual labyrinths of detective fiction at all, or who might consider the genre to be one more bourgeois cultural artifact.

The difference of approach that 'the new Mexican detective novel' represents is played out in the urban setting of the capital city. The detective is immersed in the capital's culture of crime. In an unprecedented move for the genre, Taibo conscientiously elaborates Mexico City as the hub of a web of intrigue and corruption that spreads throughout the country. The other element exploited by Taibo is the use of the language of the city streets. The representation of this type of language is a strategy the author shares with his character; if the detective is said to utilize language to overcome class differences, the author finds an advantage in colloquial speech in that it allows him to reach an audience that might be beyond the appeal of the intellectual puzzle, but that might recognize an urban reality in the language that makes up his fiction. The people of the city are the reason for whom the detective has taken on that risky profession: 'I am a detective because I like people,' says Belascoarán to a writer named Paco Ignacio in *Some Clouds* [*Algunas nubes*] (103). In fact, in contrast to the detective who reasons in the abstract, Belascoarán adds that his method consists in becoming personally involved in other people's lives (102).

Mexico's capital is the setting for the interpersonal problem solving represented by the detective, but the prevalent metaphor for the city is the sewer. The detective's brother states: 'Business in the Federal District is one big cesspool because there is big money rolling around the country' (*Nubes* 142). Even the sewer system expert, whom we have heard facetiously addressing the detective as 'colleague,' attempts to differentiate himself from the average citizen whom he is busy saving: 'Javier Villareal uses a sort of uniform: jeans, checkered shirt, brown leather jacket. It is a way to vindicate his northern roots and proclaim his status as a foreigner in the Federal District. It is his manner of recognizing himself as a provincial and of reminding others of that fact in a city that blurs and flattens all distinctions' (*Final* 61). In the first novel of the series, the city is described in the following terms, as Belascoarán makes his way through the streets:

> The city opened up to him like a monster, like the fetid entrails of a whale, or the insides of a discarded tin can. In its few hours of sleep, the sleep of a tired man, of a worker worn out by his labor, the city became a character, a subject, signals, and would blow breezes full on strange intentions. The jungle of television antennas was bombarded by wavelengths, messages, commercials. The asphalt, the shop windows, the walls, the cars, the *taco* vendor stalls, the stray dogs all made room for him at the beat of his steps.   (*Días* 25)

Taibo's heterogeneous description brings together Leviathan with the inanimate refuse of consumer culture, the organic with the inanimate, in a disturbing picture of an individual's symbiosis with the urban environment where he, contradictorily, belongs. The intellectual urbanity alluded to by Yates is nowhere in sight except as the solidarity, expressed in the image of the worker at the heart of the city, that the detective feels for the ones who share the burden of production in these strained circumstances. If the rise of the post-colonial modern city gave rise to the conditions that allowed the genre to develop, it now appears as the very negation of the possibility of making sense. In a further description that fuses political reality and fable at the center of the Mexican urban sprawl, Taibo writes:

> Hector, who had never run head first into real power, perceived the State as the great castle of the witch in Snow White, a place that not only had hatched The Falcons, but had also issued the diplomas to the engineers. There were no gradations of shade. Everything was part of an infernal machine from which it was necessary to flee. It was that, or concrete characters against which one could do epic and direct battle. He would go from one vision to the other: from the simplified match of Bakunin against the State, to the simplified match of Sherlock Holmes vs. Moriarty.   (*Final* 102)

Days of Combat [*Días de combate*], the first novel of the Belascoarán series, weds the theme of the devouring city to the one-on-one battle with resourceful and deadly adversaries. On the fateful night when Belas-coarán faces the emptiness of his present circumstances, with his job and his wife, and considers the life of a struggling detective that he has seen on a movie screen, the news of a strangler at large in the streets of Mexico City seals his decision to become a gumshoe. The detective has the curious intimation that the strangler might be the President of the Republic himself: 'Everything might be political. And why not? That was one of the many of the residual ideas left in his mind by his conversation with [his brother] Carlos. Political. A political problem. Why not? In a country that had been awakened to politics by the howling of hyenas, death by strangulation was in the political climate' (45). To set a stran-gler loose in the urban space is a particularly effective way to emphasize the oppressiveness of the modern city. Anyone can be the victim, since until the pattern of order is detected, the difference in the criteria for being a target is overdetermined: is it an occupation, the coincidence of living in a certain neighborhood, a place of origin in a nation riddled with strife, a political affiliation, or is it the unfortunate accident of being at the wrong place at the wrong time that marks the victim?

In the novel, the pattern is gender-determined, an oblique comment-ary on gender relations in a country where traditional roles are still prevalent among large sectors of the population while modernizing factors strain the boundaries of such established social distinction. The novel is unique in relation to others in the series in that the gender factor is coupled with philosophical considerations of the Nietzschean sort that motivated Raskolnikov to perpetrate the murder of his land-lady in Dostoevsky's *Crime and Punishment*. The murderer happens to be an intellectualizing member of the upper class who disavows moral responsibility for his crimes in view of the state of the nation: 'Alright, I have murdered eleven times and I have caused some minor injuries. In that same time period, the State has massacred hundreds of peasants, dozens of Mexicans have died in accidents, hundreds of others have died in brawls, dozens more have died of hunger or cold, and still dozens of others have died of curable diseases, dozens more have committed suicide ... Where is the strangler?' Belascoarán is forced to concur: 'The Great Strangler is the system' (222).

Still, though the detective agrees with the indictment of the system proposed by the strangler, he represents the humanist moral sense rooted in the individual human suffering that the strangler has caused to the victims and to the victims' families.

Belascoarán has visited the grave sites, seen the flowers and mementoes placed there by the family members, and refuses to be drawn in by the nihilist stance of the murderer, whom he sees as one more aberration of the system. With this stance, the detective makes evident the ideological tenets that differentiate the 'new' Mexican detective novel from its 'classical' predecessors. The issue that the novel addresses is one of social content over generic form. If the adventure of detection equates the hunter and the hunted as two parts of the same formula, Taibo stresses the social circumstance, that is, the space and time of the action over the process of detection as the essential difference that allows for the moral superiority of the detective and gives him the right to end the criminal's life. Indirectly Taibo refers to Borges' masterful story, 'Death and the Compass,' by having the detective acknowledge the generic norms of the game – 'others play chess with us' – while expressing disagreement in two particular ways. One, he does not consider the chess players an abstract entity such as a literary tradition that determines a textual repertory of sites and moves, but as a political system that generates all violence and is the ultimate culprit for the facts of the deadly game, and two, death in the detective novel is not the pretext for the hide-and-seek game of the genre; rather, it is a violation of an individual right with reprehensible and moral consequences.

The apparently chaotic nature of the strangler's crimes in the urban setting brings another characteristic aspect of the novels into play. In a city as densely populated as Mexico City, the detective finds a powerful ally for arriving at the solution of the mystery in the mass communication systems. As early as the 1920s, the time in which the events of *The Shadow of a Shadow* take place, with its proto-detectives, spectacular crimes, and incipient trade unionism, Taibo has the protagonists lay journalistic siege to the possible culprits of a murderous plot. Just as it was able to give notoriety and colorful sobriquets to the criminal element by reporting on and characterizing the mode of the crime for their readers, the press of the time was also able, due to the incorruptible nature of some of the reporters, to give voice to the voiceless. In *Days of Combat*, the detective, who has been fortunate enough to appear on a television quiz game show, takes the opportunity to taunt the criminal by choosing the topical category of 'Famous Stranglers.'

An Easy Thing offers a variation on this theme. The detective contacts a former classmate who runs an early morning radio show seeking permission to ask the radio listeners for information over the air and to harass the suspects into the kind of action that would reveal their identities by the same means. Both of the detective's requests are made possible by 'The Raven Radio Show': *'The Raven* is here to serve as a bridge among us all. To mobilize the resources wasted by the city, to establish a solitary path among the denizens of the night, among the vampires of the Federal District . . . Don't be shy. We all have problems, and there are few easy solutions' (*Cosa* 128). Solidarity is the key word in the citizens' strategy for survival. In a city where the forces of order are often the forces of oppression and disorder, citizen action ensures that what needs to be done is carried out with a minimum of waste, self-interest or interference of the profit motive. The speed and efficiency of neighborhood reaction to the disastrous earthquakes that have rocked the Mexican capital city in the '70s and '80s give testimony to the voluntarism and independence which citizens living in these conditions are able to display. In part, this voluntarism is heir to the voluntarism and social consciousness developed in the late 1960s by a generation under fire, but generally, it is the hallmark of the forces of adaptation and responsibility generated by the experience of living in and against one of the largest metropolitan areas in the world.

The Mexican urban context poses other problems to investigative practice. The question that must now be addressed refers, in the parlance of the genre, to the methodology that the detective will follow, or is able to follow, in the course of the case. Belascoarán expresses his predisposition toward the thorough investigative procedure: 'In a city where one would usually settle for "whatever" before the absolute uselessness of doing things right, in a city dominated by the efficiency of appearances over the factual, by the "who gives a" as an answer to cheating and exploitation, doing things right was extremely gratifying' (*Nubes* 115). But does the social context allow him to follow his organizational schemes through to the end? Or is the reader to expect, given the context, innovations in the investigative method?

In a country such as Mexico, where the pre-colonial culture is still a presence, the indigenous past proves impossible to disregard. In fact, the Mexican flag includes the image of an eagle perched on a cactus, a symbol derived from the Mexica myth of the founding of the city Tenochtitlan, the fabled city on the lake destroyed by Cortés. Mexico City itself is built upon the ruins of this ancient Aztec city. Colonial imprecision about the indigenous past, a product of the wanton destruction of Aztec records during the Conquest and the colonial period, has modified the Aztec symbol that appears on the national flag. By means of the Aztec legacy carved into stone, archaeologists have verified that whereas the colonial eagle holds a serpent in its beak, the Mexican tradition represented the symbol for war in that same position. In spite of the distortion – itself a sign of colonial power – Aztec symbols retain prestige with Mexican authorities, perhaps as a way to ensure national loyalty.

As can be expected from an evolved culture, Aztec society did occupy itself with the imparting of justice and the means of attaining it; an interested visitor to the city of Mexico can witness a marketplace 'hearing' in the exquisite reproduction of the *tianguis* at the Museum of Anthropology, one of the finest institutions of its kind in the world. In the scaled model of the Aztec marketplace, one can observe the lords of the market listening to the complaint of a 'plaintiff' before a 'defendant' on the issue of commercial exchange. The criteria for their final judgment, the societal means of investigation of crimes, its investigative agents, or the culture's inclination to investigate rationally on the basis of rules of evidence, and the extent of the process, are facts that remain in the scholarly debate of the anthropologists. The management of justice was one the functions of power appropriated by the European authorities in the business of managing the affairs of the colony. The demise of the indigenous justice system is again an issue to be assessed by ethnographers working with Amerindian native populations and their communal organization system.

It is not surprising, then, that Belascoarán does not take on a particularly Mexican variant of the Western hard-boiled approach to crime investigation. And there is no system offered by the official investigative agencies. Through the character of a crime reporter, Taibo presents a bleak picture of the police force that evolved out of the Revolution in 1922: 'It was good for nothing. The police only solved crimes by absolute chance. And the force's contacts with organized crime were so intimate and extensive that the shadowy zone that separated them had turned into a practically limitless territory where the police and the criminal element cohabited, dedicating themselves to the same activities' (*Shadow* 152). The situation is no better 50 years later, when Belascoarán takes to the street, and the detective is well aware of the fact. He reports the following statistic to a client who suggests they go to the police with their troubles: 'According to a poll taken by Guzman, 76% of the major crimes in this city originate with the police force' (*Nubes* 94).

The Mexican detective's success depends on a strategy akin to showing the trump card that has been hidden under the table. The personages whose crooked game has been exposed reveal themselves in a show of force directed toward the detective, who then has to survive the backlash dealt by the forces of evil. Belascoarán's strategy aims at having the culprits feel enough heat from public scrutiny and the threat of general scandal to make them desist from their purposes and relocate their henchmen to other enterprises. The hope that the reader shares with the detective in this reckless situation is for the desired end to take place before the shadows in the power structure find it necessary to eliminate one of the central characters of the series. Given this *modus operandi,* which is recorded in the eight volumes of Belascoarán adventures, the fact that the detective has been killed twice in the course of his investigations becomes a commentary on the prevalence of violence in Mexican society. Belascoarán might not change the way things are, but since his interest is usually the safety of some threatened character or the prevalence of a cause, the particular, practical effects of being a source of pressure in the system constitute his triumphs.

In conclusion, the new Mexican detective novel can be defined as a type of investigative fiction conceived in opposition, or as an antidote, to the role of the official police force in society. Characteristically, in Taibo's fiction, the search for justice takes place in the face of corruption and the abuse of power. The detective is alone in Taibo's fiction, isolated by the moral responsibility that he feels for his fellows in the inhumane city. The achievement of Taibo has been to ground certain traits of detective fiction on a particular national reality. He does not include the wrap-up solution at the end, for example, as a general feature of his brand of fiction. There are also no butlers, or the dazzling bit of induction on the part of the detective. At best, there are lists of suspects, or of events, that serve both detective and reader to review the complexities of the plot. By means of this practice, the author dismisses the imported divertimento mode of detective fiction that flooded the Mexican book market in the form of the pocket book popular in the post-World War years. The pocket book phenomenon might have created the most extensive readership that detective fiction had had in Mexico, but at the same time it promoted the production in Mexico of derivative, formulaic fiction that can be considered a colonized form of writing. Taibo retains a universal, the criminal act, as the cultural center for his fiction and elaborates it in terms of a national reality, the city, and a typical language, the language of the city, to redefine the readership for the detective novel in Mexico.

In relation to the post-colonial issue that opened this discussion, Taibo points out the complexity of the issue: 'Mexico City today has more movie theaters than Paris, more abortions than London, detective fiction is as popular here as in Detroit, and at the same time, there are more street children here than in New Delhi' (Interview). The frames of contradiction that appear in relation to the setting of Taibo's stories suggest that Mexican 'post-colonial' society is a space marked by high and low stages of development that coexist in a maddening tableau of hope and despair. The detective story reader in a Third World society such as this one, then, is a 'hard' reader no different from readers from First or Second World societies, who demand technical and thematic sophistication from authors of the genre. As a result, it is not surprising to find this new urban detective novel thriving in Argentina, Spain, France, Italy, the United States, as well as in Mexico. Interestingly, the practitioners of the new detective novel share similar liberal leanings and social conceptions that define them as the generational group that actively opposed national politics in the late 1960s. Technical experimentation of the sort found in contemporary Latin American fiction, for example, and the celebration of popular culture, create a national literature, forged with national rules that make it verisimilar to the particular context of origin, and that at the same time can be read in any part of the world as the story of an investigation. The meeting between authors and readers that is taking place at an international level, through actual writing practice within the genre, works to defuse the 'post-colonial' term as a distinction made between an indigenous and an external racial or cultural model.

Notes

1. Carlos Brian Belascoarán Shayne's library contains volumes by 'Marx, Trotsky, Lenin, Mao, Ho Chih Minh, Che Guevara, anthologies of Cuban poetry, Latin American novels, books on contemporary history, an enormous collection of detective fiction, bookshelves full of the classics of science fiction' (*Días* 39).
2. All the translations of the Spanish texts are by the author of this study, unless otherwise indicated by the English title of the work in parenthesis.
3. At the end of the novel, the detective is apparently killed by the group: 'the shotgun blast caught him by the midriff, making him jump through the air, torn and broken' (126). With Holmesian aplomb, Belascoarán reappears years later in a beach resort of Puerto Guayabo, where he has been hiding out while working part time on the city's sewer system. There are indications that in the interim he has been involved in another case that resulted in the accidental death of a child. No explanations are given about his resurrection, and the detective does not seem the worse for his visit to the underworld. The book is, however, more acerbically critical of Mexico and its institutions.
4. One interesting instance that reverses the linguistic assimilation process is provided by the character Tomás Wong in *The Shadow of the Shadow*. A Mexican national who was born in Sinaloa, this descendant of Chinese immigrants affects a characteristic accent that consists of switching /l/ for /r/ in his speech. Wong, who does not speak Chinese, practices this accent as a way to ward off complete assimilation. The action is set in the early '20s, after the

revolution that launched Mexico into modernity. In this milieu, Wong is an anarchist trade union organizer with internationalist sympathies.
5. Among the practitioners of 'the new Mexican detective novel,' Taibo has had notable predecessors, such as Vicente Leñero, author of *The Bricklayers* [*Los Albañiles*], and Jorge Ibargüengoitia, author of *Dead Women* [*Las Muertas*]. These two authors, however, did not dedicate themselves extensively to the genre. Others that could be mentioned are Rafael Martínez Heredia, Eugenio Aguirre, and Juan Hernández Luna.

Bibliography

Borges, Jorge Luis. *Discusión*. Buenos Aires: Emece, 1964.
——. *Oral*. Buenos Aires: Emece/Belgrano, 1979.
Taibo II, Paco Ignacio. *Algunas Nubes*. Mexico: Leega, 1988. Trans. William I. Neuman. *Some Clouds*. New York: Random House, 1995.
——. *No Habrá Final Feliz*. Mexico: Planeta, 1989.
——. *Calling All Heroes*. Trans. John Mitchell and Ruth De Aguilar. New York: Plover, 1990.
——. *Cosa Fácil*. Gijon: Júcar, 1987. Trans. William I. Neuman. *An Easy Thing*. New York: Viking Penguin, 1990.
——. *Días de Combate*. Mexico: Leega, 1991.
——. *The Shadow of the Shadow*. Trans. William I. Neuman. New York: Viking Penguin, 1991.
——. *68*. Mexico: Joaquin Mortiz, 1991.
——. Personal Interview. 21 January 1992.
Yates, Donald A. *El Cuento Policial Latinoamericano*. Mexico: De Andrea, 1964.
——. 'La novela policial en las Américas.' *Temas Culturales* 3 (1967). 124.

Works of Taibo in English

An Easy Thing. New York: Viking Penguin, 1990.
Calling All Heroes. New York: Plover, 1990.
Four Hands: A Novel. New York: St. Martin's, 1995.
Guevara: Also Known as Che. New York: St. Martin's, 1997.
Leonardo's Bicycle. New York: Mysterious P, 1995.
Life Itself. New York: Mysterious P, 1994.
No Happy Ending. New York: Mysterious P, 1994.
Return to the Same City. New York: Mysterious P, 1996.
Some Clouds. New York: Random House, 1995.

11
The Spanish Detective as Cultural Other

Jose F. Colmeiro

Some readers might find puzzling the notion of an essay on Spain's emerging detective fiction among the articles included in *The Post-Colonial Detective*. Clearly, Spain has been one of the biggest colonial powers in modern history, on a scale perhaps only comparable with England and France. Furthermore, historiographic tradition has represented Spain as the essence and paradigm of European colonialism. As an ideological construction, Spain has in fact often been assigned the function of symbolic scapegoat for Western imperialism. Paradoxically, Spain's role as metaphor of European colonization was parallel to its relegation to second-class economic and political status among European colonial nations. Francisco Ayala has explained this peculiar condition in terms of Spain's 'extravagance' and 'eccentricity' in relation to European centers of power, expressions which are etymologically based on territorial metaphors that connote its historic insularity and marginality (21–2).

More recently, the controversial Mexican writer Carlos Fuentes has described the case of Spain's economic dependence and political subordination as the result of Spain becoming a virtual economic colony of Northern Europe during the 16th and 17th centuries, the Golden Age of the Spanish Empire (157). The suggestive notion of the colonizer colonized adds an ironic twist to the whole European colonial enterprise. Colonial situations have indeed existed across Europe, in many instances even within the boundaries of a single nation. The case of Great Britain, where England has held its hegemonic power over Scotland, Wales and Ireland, has its own counterpart in Spain, where for centuries Castile has held its central dominance over the peripheral territories of the Iberian Peninsula, particularly Galicia, the Basque Country, and Catalonia, internal colonies within the colonizer. Post-colonial theories can be particularly appropriate in examining the complexities of cultural production under these eccentric conditions and in bringing to light the emancipatory efforts towards de-marginalization. In this line, Marilyn Reizbaum has shown the great potential of postcolonial criticism in her study of women's writing practices in Ireland and Scotland (165–90).

Most observers agree that Spain has experienced a new age since the end of Franco's dictatorship, a lively reawakening from the 'longa noite de pedra', 'long night of stone', in the words of Galician poet Celso Emilio Ferreiro. The transition from dictatorship to democracy, the full integration in Europe, and the strong renaissance of cultural forces that have taken place in Spain in the last two decades are some of the most obvious signs of Post-Francoism. Many drastic changes have reshaped the map of contemporary Spain: a determination to break with the past and recuperate long lost freedoms, the emergence of women's rights movements, and the self-goverment of autonomous decentralized regions struggling to find their place in a new map of the 'Europe of nations'. These developments signal a new post-colonial landscape, in which the voices of the traditionally marginalized and oppressed have begun to be heard.

During the years of cultural and political transition from Franco's dictatorship to a parliamentary democracy, contemporary Spain has experienced a complete redefinition of its self-identity and its self-representation. The questioning of the old official history of a glorious imperial past has been parallel to the re-evaluation of its literary tradition. Central in both processes of redefinition is the question of representation, of rewriting its political, cultural, and literary histories. Canon formation and colonization are two processes that are closely interrelated, based as they both are on a system of hegemonic dominance. If tradition is a form of cultural imperialism, as Karen Lawrence suggests, then any challenges to this tradition amount to a decolonization of the empire's literary tradition (2). These challenges may come from many sides, as writers openly question traditional assumptions about race, class, gender, and language.

Against this background, marginal literatures as well as marginal literary genres have recently begun to emerge in Spain. In the last two decades after Franco's demise, detective fiction, particularly in its hardboiled variety, has become a popular vehicle to explore contemporary social questions in Spain. My study will focus on three particular areas of Spanish detective fiction where questions of language, gender and ethnicity, closely related to a colonial situation, are explored within a definite post-colonial/post-Francoist framework. The practices under study are not without their problems. As Gayatri Spivak has pointed out, mimicry can be a means of fracturing dominant discourse, but it has some potential traps. Audrey Lorde's well-known maxim 'the master's tools will never dismantle the master's house' problematizes the contradictions this enterprise entails.

Nevertheless, the appropriation and reversal of the conventions of detective fiction (in itself a colonial import and traditionally considered a 'minor' genre) has served to challenge hegemonic forms of colonial territorialization; in the last 20 years Spanish detective fiction writers have managed to empower figures historically marginalized by Spain's dominant culture, relegated to a cultural other, silenced, in fact colonized, marked by their difference (their lack): non-male, non-white and non-Castilian. The emergence of the gypsy detective, the woman detective, and the Galician and Catalan detectives in Spanish fiction in the post-Franco years are material evidence of this post-colonial sensibility.

I will briefly present these particular three cases before a more detailed case study of the Catalan woman detective. The first case is Juan Madrid's saga of 14 novels, already the subject of a popular television series in Spain which has run for two seasons. It features Antonio Flores, a gypsy who has made it to the top of the Spanish police force, as the chief of the élite branch of criminal investigation known as the *Brigada Central* (Central Brigade) – also the name of the series. Interestingly enough, this title implies in its name the centralization of power (always radiating from Madrid, the traditional hegemonic center of political and economic dominance in Spain) but at the same time it reminds us of the struggle for demarginalization on the part of the gypsies, one of the social groups who has suffered the most by the Spanish institutions of power. Indeed, the gypsies, who because of their ethnicity, class, and language are displaced and excluded from obtaining subject status, represent the ultimate form of subalternity in Spain. Therefore, the challenges and obstacles they have to overcome are enormous. The difficulties and cost of such a move as Flores' from the ghetto to the top can be seen in the many contradictions and moral dilemmas experienced by the detective, constantly torn between the strong cultural codes of his gypsy upbringing, traditionally at odds with law and order, and the codes of social order that he now represents and safeguards. With a personal honor code that does not conform to the expectations of the gypsy community, and as one who rejects and exposes police corruption, the gypsy detective is seen both as a traitor by his kin and someone not to be trusted by his peers, who pejoratively address him as 'gitano' (Spanish for 'gypsy').

The empowerment of this marginal figure has a very high personal price: ostracism, isolation, territorial exile (relegated to a provincial secondary post, disintegration of his own family (wife and three daughters), and ultimately, the sacrifice of his career. In the second part of the TV series, developed by screenwriters based on the original character, Flores explores even newer territory. In a move that we will see repeated in the other two cases under study, the detective crosses the national borders to begin a new phase in his career of investigation, literally deterritorializing the practices of detection in the new global economy of interwoven interests. He can now conduct his investigations in Paris or in Colombia on an equal footing with local authorities. It seems as if Spanish detective fiction writers (as well as screenwriters) need to affirm abroad the identity of their fictional detectives and make them prove themselves as equals in the world of detective fiction, while decolonizing detective writing in the process. For Flores, however, while the investigation of international intrigue was successful at a professional level, the return home is again a deeply traumatic personal experience, forever entangled in an identity crisis. Juan Madrid, himself a 'payo' – that is, 'not gypsy' in Caló, the language of Spanish gipsies – can only use the gypsy detective as a marginal instrument for social observation, rather than as affirmation of his cultural identity. In today's Spain, as can be simply attested by following the mass media, gypsies – instrumentalized for centuries as emblematic image of Spain's ancestral past and 'difference'-are still struggling for their identity, caught in the web of modernity in a society that will only accept them as cultural others. Decolonizing the gypsy detective from subaltern status may break a few cultural barriers and allow him to have a voice, but, following Spivak's query, we must ask ourselves in reading Juan Madrid's novels: can the real subaltern speak with his own voice?

It is a well-known fact that Spain achieved its unity as a modern state by means of imposing the hegemonic dominance of one monarch, one language and one religion over other minority groups. It was not a coincidence that this result was accomplished at precisely the same time that its colonial adventure abroad began. The colonial enterprise was the 'natural' extension of Castile's eight-century-long battle for dominance within the Iberian Peninsula (known as the *Reconquista*, or 'Reconquest') at the expense of the expulsion and/or repression of the cultural others (particularly Jews and Muslims). This basic scheme of dominance within Spain was maintained until the latter part of the 20th century – with the brief exception of the Second Republic (1931–39) prior to the Spanish Civil War. Franco adhered to this internal colonial regime with all the might of his military dictatorship (not surprisingly Franco's uprising against the legitimate Republican Government began where the support for his cause was strongest: the Foreign Legion stationed in the Spanish colonies in North Africa, a decisive force of Franco's war victory). In the wake of Franco, however, non-conforming and oppositional voices against a central power have emerged freely in Spain, particularly in those regions with a marked cultural difference and historical claims to autonomous self-government, where repression had been most rigorously exercised.

The battle against the central power in Spain has its most visible symbol in the assertion and 'normalization' of national languages and literatures other than Castilian ('Spanish'), a characteristic feature of the diverse, plurilingual and multicultural life of post-Franco Spain. This process has brought about a rebirth of national literatures written in vernacular languages in all literary genres, and among them detective fiction. As a result of this, it is not surprising that another figure empowered in current detective fiction written in Spain is the non-Castilian detective.

I will focus next on the detective fiction written in Galicia, particularly by Carlos G. Reigosa – *Crime en Compostela* (*Crime in Compostela*, 1984) and *O misterio do barco perdido* (*The Mystery of the Lost Ship*, 1988). These novels are written in Galician, the vernacular language spoken in Spain's northwestern autonomous region of Galicia, where. since the 1978 Constitution, it is co-official with Castilian. Galician has a rich literary history going back to the Middle Ages and is today in the process of validating itself both as an effective communication tool in an age of globalization and linguistic recolonization (where vernacular languages are rapidly becoming extinct), and as a modern and viable literature capable of reaching the general public. Enormous progress towards Galician demarginalization has been achieved since the 1978 Constitution. The emergence of detective fiction in Galician should be understood in the context of the collective enterprise of rebuilding a national modern literature written in Galician, appealing to a wide sector of the reading public and fostering a young generation of readers in Galician. This context might help explain the highly positive reception of Reigosa's novel, awarded the most important literary prize in Galicia, which effectively helped to bring detective fiction into the mainstream as well as to foster the progressive normalization of Galician literature. Before

Reigosa, there had been no other cases of detective fiction written in Galician (although Galician authors had previously written detective fiction in Castilian, before and during Franco's regime, such as Emilia Pardo Bazán, Wenceslao Fernández Flórez or José María Alvarez Blázquez, to name a few).

The results of Reigosa's pioneer efforts are mixed. Some of the difficulties and inconsistencies of his work are illustrated in the contradictory personality of the novels' main protagonist Nirvardo Castro. A perpetual outsider of rural extraction, Nirvardo was obliged to emigrate to Northern Europe to escape misery, later returning to fulfill his military obligations in Spain's last colony in Africa, the Western Sahara (which coincidentally was liberated only in 1975, the year of Franco's death) joining afterwards the Spanish Foreign Legion stationed there. He lived in the US for seven years working in an investigative agency, and during his training as an agent he became acquainted with Taoist philosophy through his Chinese martial arts teacher, a mode of thought which he will put to use in his later work as a private detective back in Spain. In his successive roles as *gastarbeiter* in Europe, mercenary in Africa, and private investigator in America and then Spain (in Madrid and in Galicia), Nirvardo has experienced both ends of the colonizer-colonized dichotomy, and is permanently in search of his roots and his cultural identity.

Reigosa's novels are also in search of their cultural roots and identity, and in their use of detective fiction they explore the possibilities and limitations of expressing one's own culture in a foreign mold. His first detective novel attempts to recuperate some of the glorious Galician pre-modern past, a highly romanticized Middle Ages when the city of Santiago de Compostela, the capital of the old Kingdom of Galicia, was a center of pilgrimage and the repository of European Christian culture symbolized in its impressive Romanesque, Gothic and Baroque cathedral. The old city – and its modern resurgence – is the real protagonist of the novel, having become a living art museum for tourists (modern-day pilgrims), a lively university town, and the seat of the newly restored Galician Autonomous Government. The city is the narrative space in a symbolic search for collective marks of identity through architecture, geography, history, legends, food, and popular customs. In one particularly illustrative metafictional turn, Alvaro Cunqueiro, a well-known modern Galician writer, is tenderly evoked by one of the characters in the novel as having said that his first work of fiction, written at age ten, was a Western story in which his favorite 'Indians', the Cheyennes, spoke in Galician, while the cowboys spoke in Castilian (68). The identification of Galicians with the colonized – mediated through popular culture – is not a casual occurrence in the novel, as it is later reinforced by the suggestive notion of Galicians as Atlantic people who never 'discovered the Mediterranean,' but were discovered instead (perhaps with characteristic Galician irony, since 'to discover the Mediterranean' also means to realize the obvious):

> What happens to Galicia – he had told him – is what happens to all the peoples who have been discovered by other peoples. We Galicians never discovered the Mediterranean, but Mediterraneans did discover Galicia, and it is known that, in this relationship, the discovered is always the victim. (147, translation mine)

New discoveries in the Mediterranean, however, await Nirvardo in his next fictional appearance. Reigosa's second novel is more disturbingly problematic, and, like the second part of Flores' saga, is also a fiction of international intrigue and a (failed) attempt at decolonizing detection. The initial investigation of the disappearance of a Galician fishing ship between the Canary Islands and the Sahara coast takes Nirvardo to North Africa and to the Middle East in the pursuit of an illegal arms ring. The novel explores the hidden links between colonial powers (manufacturers and exporters of arms) and ex-colonies (the recipients and users), in particular Lebanon, the greatest battlefield for the opposed interests of surrounding governments and international colonial powers. Nirvardo's close identification with the Sahara people is counterbalanced in this novel with a noticeable disinterest towards the Lebanese and their cause (perhaps as a consequence of being a Galician from the Atlantic and not able to fully understand other 'Mediterranean people'?). His inability to understand the others becomes painfully clear in this novel, foreclosing the possibility of effectively taking Galician detection into the deterritorialized space of post-colonial detection. The detective fulfills his fundamental role as discoverer of truths and explorer of new territories, but the novel fails to bring into question the relationship between (colonial) knowledge and power.

In the end, Reigosa's two novels are a mixed bag. On the one hand, these works became some of the biggest Galician best-sellers of the decade, proving the viability of a form of Galician detective fiction as well as the awakened interest of the readers. On the other, Reigosa used the conventions of American hard-boiled detective fiction rather mechanically, merely transposing them to local situations, characters and milieux. He even takes to an extreme the traditional misogynist values of the hard-boiled detective in the style of a Sam Spade or a Philip Marlowe. And what is still more problematic is the fact that rather than empowering the Galician detective and bringing him from the margins to the center, his marginalization is in the end reinforced and natural- ized. Reigosa brings Nirvardo from Madrid to Galicia to conduct the investigation and returns him to the capital after the work is done and the truth has been found.The only reason why Nirvardo is able to solve the mystery puzzle is because he has travelled to the metropolis, as Kathleen March has clearly pointed out:

> Not entirely removed from his roots, he [Nirvardo] has accepted the opportunity to reaffirm, or at least reassess them, but then must move ahead to the metropolis that lies beyond their regionalism. In a way, it is possible to connect his success at uncovering the murder mystery to his having overcome the shortsighted perspective of Galicia; he has been to other countries, even to New York, and has settled in the Spanish capital. Only he is capable of revealing to Galicians their own mystery. (210–11)

Reigosa's failed attempt to create a true decolonized detective may be due to his own inability, but it reminds us of the contradiction implicit, as Audrey Lorde has noted before, in the very notion of an emancipatory writing practice effected in an import mold, and it also reflects the difficulties in finding an authentic identity in a mass-mediated global society. Still, Reigosa's works are an important ground-breaking attempt in the normalization and demarginalization process of Galician lan- guage and detective fiction, and at least have sowed the seeds for other later works.

A slightly different situation can be found in Catalonia. Detective fiction in Catalan language can be traced to the post-Civil War period to two pioneer authors, Rafael Tasis and Manuel de Pedrolo (see Col- meiro and Hart). More recently Jaume Fuster and other younger authors have helped to establish a tradition of detective fiction written in Cat- alan. In this case, the author I will focus on is Maria-Antònia Oliver, originally from Majorca in the Balearic Islands, a mini-country within the linguistically unified but politically autonomous 'Catalonian Coun- tries' (Catalonia, Balearic Islands, and Valencia), in which Barcelona, the capital of Catalonia, holds the hegemonic power against a continuing struggle of cultural self-determination on the part of the other commun- ities. As a native of Majorca and long-time resident of Barcelona, Oliver reproduces in her fiction the contradictions and constant clashes between the two worlds of Majorca and Barcelona, playing out the cultural differences between urban progressiveness and rural conservatism, metropolitan dominance and insular unsubmissiveness. Women's issues are central to Oliver's fiction, whether it be sexual harassment, rape, abortion, sexism, mother–daughter relations, or the questioning of patriarchal values. Her strong feminist beliefs also encompass ecological and nationalist concerns, such as the underlying accusation through her fiction of the 'rape' of the Balearic Islands' natural landscape for tourist development.

Lònia first appeared in 1984 in the short story '¿Dónde estás, Mónica?' in Ofèlia Dracs's collective work *Negra y consentida* (a pun involving an old bolero song and the new *novela negra*). Although in embryonic form, it clearly showed promising signs: it was filled with action, irony, a vibrant language, and featured a congenial feminist detective (and lipstick collector). In her first appearance, Lònia skilfully solves the case of Mónica's disappearance, uncovering her lesbian relationship and discovering she was killed due to her opposition to her family's plan for tourist development. Oliver has also published three detective novels to date: *Estudi en lila* (*A Study in Lilac*), 1985, *Antipodes* (*Antipodes*), 1988, both translated into English and published in the International Women's Crime series, and *El sol que fa l'ànec* (*Blue Roses for a Dead ... Lady*), 1994 to appear in English in 1998 (all references are from the English translations).

In addition to her efforts to normalize the use of the Catalan language and the genre of detective fiction, a political position shared with other Catalan detective writers, she embarked upon a different post-colonial enterprise: the creation and empowerment of a Catalan woman detective. Her enterprise is carried out by appropriating and subverting the conventions of the hard-boiled detective genre in the tradition of Dashiell Hammett and Raymond Chandler, through the reversal of its rigid gender roles and stereotypes. The main character is Lònia, a middle-aged Majorcan woman who runs haphazardly a detective agency in Barcelona, a profession and a position from which women, particularly in Spain, have traditionally been excluded. The very idea of a woman as hard-boiled detective is in itself an ironic subversion of canonical genre conventions. Through Lònia, a firm feminist believer, Oliver explores the situation of women in contemporary Catalan society, their new roles, the challenges and obstacles to be overcome, the contradictions and conflicts to resolve both as women and Catalanas. Rather than providing answers, Oliver presents questions open to debate for the reader to solve, like the mysteries investigated by Lònia, which are also open-ended.

Lònia, the detective protagonist and first-person narrator in both novels, is a very particular kind of private eye. She provides the eye of a woman looking at problems directly involving women in a male-dominated society. She is a woman-identified woman, who has renamed herself (her given name was 'Apollònia') to erase the trace of the masculine inscription (Apollo), the symbolic patriarchal marker present in every woman, thus figuratively mutilating the male and devoiding him of his phallic power of domination. In contrast to the solitary *macho* detective of hard-boiled fiction, Lònia engages in close and mutually supportive relationships with other women. In her work, Lònia also enlists the assistance of her women friends, feminists with different degrees of radicalism: Pepa, a worker in an international solidarity group; Jerònia, a Majorcan social worker; Neus, a photojournalist; and Mercé, her gynecologist. Together they make up an informal women's network of investigators, collaborators and confidants which will prove invaluable to Lònia's investigation. In addition, Lònia has no qualms in using her charm among her male acquaintances to advance her investigative quest.

Oliver's detective novels bring to the forefront of the investigation questions of gender and identity. In her first adventure Lònia investigates two different cases, the search for a runaway teenager and the pursuit of three men involved in an art theft from an antique dealer. Although these cases seem completely unrelated, Lònia – and the reader with her – suspects and will eventually discover that the cases are indeed linked. The missing link is finally disclosed as we learn that both women (the teenager and the antique dealer) have been silent victims of rape. The process of investigation parallels the process of Lònia's identification with both women in their roles as victims of violence, particularly since twice in the course of the investigation Lònia herself was almost raped.

Each case presents a distinct set of moral problems for the protagonist, foregrounding the contradictions she must face. On one hand is Sebastiana, the runaway teenager, who is pregnant as a result of rape. Like Lònia, she comes from a rural conservative background in Majorca. Unable to tell her strict, religious family, she runs away to Barcelona. Confused, with a strong sense of shame and guilt, Sebastiana cannot confide in her own family, who she thinks will never understand, and she is unable to decide whether to have an abortion (with Lònia and Mercé's support) or to carry the fetus to term and return to her family (as

Jeronia insists she should do). In the meantime, she takes refuge with Lònia, who acts more like an older sister than a private investigator. Confronted with the imminent visit of her parents to Barcelona, prompted by Jeronia, Sebastiana finally succumbs and takes her life. Lònia's frustration and sense of guilt over Sebastiana's death is carried over to the other case, thus providing a psychological link between the two investigations.

On the other hand, Ms Gaudí, the antique dealer, is a clear-thinking mature woman who has a very precise goal in mind: to take revenge on the men who gang-raped her. Convinced that matters of sexual assault are not appropriately dealt with by the patriarchal legal system, she decides to take justice into her own hands. Ms Gaudí puts into practice the slogan written in the street walls of Barcelona by some radical feminist groups advocating an extreme form of punishment against rape: castration. Lònia, unaware until the end of Ms Gaudí's retributive practice, finally witnesses how her client is about to emasculate her third assailant while he is in a drug-induced sleep. Horrified at first at what she sees, after a moment of reflection in which she puts into perspective some women's experiences, she turns a blind eye to Ms Gaudí's action: 'Sebastiana had slept on sheets stained with vomit. They'd tried to rape me twice at Gòmara's. They gang-banged Gaudí.' (150) Even though she understands Ms Gaudí's violent revenge, still she withholds from Lluis, another detective friend to whom she finally entrusts the case, her mixed feelings towards the outcome:

> 'Haven't you ever noticed the graffiti done in lilac saying "Against rape, castration"?'
> 'Yes, and I think it's barbarous.'
> 'Me too.' I thought of Sebastiana and I wasn't so sure of my affirmation, but I didn't dare argue. (A Study 155)

A Study in Lilac clearly foregrounds some of the basic challenges that women have to face in a patriarchal society (inequality, sexism) and offers an exploration of the implications for women of gender-specific issues such as rape and abortion and the options and choices available. It is ultimately Lònia's feelings of guilt over the two cases that prompt her escape from the scene of the crime, to the other side of the world, the Antipodes, which give their name to the second adventure of Lònia Guiu, a story of international intrigue like Flores' and Nirvardo's before her. In *Antipodes*, what began as vacation turns into another case of personal involvement and originates a profound identity crisis as a

Majorcan, as a detective, and as a woman. Her adventure abroad becomes a journey of self-discovery: '... it was as if I hadn't left Barcelona. Just that the space–time coordinates were on the other side of the mirror.' (4) Her visit to Australia prompts the rethinking of her parameters from a different perspective, the look of the other:

> But of the outsiders, we're the only 'Latins'; we're just about the only ones of that 'race' who get along with the 'Britainoids' (my term). Because here everything is compartmentalized, kid. The city people vs. the bushmen; those from one city vs those from another; the Aussies (another way to say Australian, but nicer) and 'others', and among the 'others,' it all depends – where you come from, what language you speak, what kind of visa you have, and above all, your acquisitive powers. (8)

In Australia Lònia follows the trace of Christina, a Majorcan like herself, who is the young heiress of an important real estate developer, who has fallen into a prostitution ring and become a drug addict. Throughout the investigation the dark side of the 'global village' concept is revealed in all its ugliness. Uncovering a tightly-knit plot, Lònia witnesses the consequences of over-development and ecological devastation in her native Majorca as a result of speculative strategies due to the greed of world tour operators, with tourists being the new agents of colonization and destruction in the island, and the innards of illegal drug trafficking and white trade rings on a global scale, in which women are again the victims of exploitation.

An intriguing process occurs during Lònia's runaway stay in Australia as she submits to a new identity. With a new life, new surroundings, and a new lover, Lònia is soon taken over by Lonnie, a new version of her self, progressively relegated to a submissive role by her Australian lover, who finally takes over the investigation. Lònia is then deported to Spain (by the interference of her lover) and goes to Majorca where, in a trip back in time, she tries to untangle the many threads of the case, while she struggles to recuperate her lost self. In the process of the investigation she suffers again – literally – in her own flesh the degradation of the other young women, who are defenseless victims of coerced prostitution. In her ordeal, very aptly portrayed by Oliver, Lònia loses her sense of time and identity. Confronted with the many ugly truths of her life, Lònia is in a state of total confusion; dream and reality are not easily discerned, as past and present overlap; personal memories and collective memories mingle: the memories of physical punishment in school are mixed with the police brutality of political repression years later; images of sexual assault merge with the violence of criminal thugs. In the end, the experience in Australia is a mirror image of her first adventure. The big island in the Antipodes is only a reflection of her small native island in the Mediterranean, the place of obligatory return. As her friend and secretary Quim points out to Lònia with lucid irony:

> You left here with your head in the clouds, dreaming about fantastic voyages in exotic waters, discoveries of new places and new ways of life, breaking with reality and trips to dreamland (. . .) And what did you find? Everything exactly the same as here. You not only didn't liberate yourself from the problems you have here, you added fuel to the fire. Adventure, my dear friend, is either inside you or not. (103)

Lònia comes out stronger if a little more cynical from her round trip adventure. Her sense of identity is regained and reinforced. Along the way she has to overcome the many obstacles to her affirmation as woman and detective. The problems confronted by Lònia reflect the contradictions of a cosmopolitan Barcelona life-style and a conservative Catholic education in Majorca, and of a woman's desire for self-affirmation in a male-dominated society. Oliver shows great skill in foregrounding these issues against the background of an investigative plot. The conflict that arises from the roles imposed by society, specifically by her Catholic education, and the need to be herself, is a continual battleground. It is in other women that she discovers different aspects about herself that had been repressed, forgotten, or unknown; she explores religious imagery, particularly Catholic mythical figures and martyrs of sexual assault such as Saint Sebastian (the Roman Christian officer shot with arrows commonly depicted in Renaissance iconography) and Maria Goretti (an Italian girl who died to defend her virginity), only to come to terms with her past and finally affirm her true identity.

The most recent installment of Lònia's adventures is *El sol que fa l'ànec* (1994), an untranslatable expression coming from the verses of a deformed Castilian song sung by Catalan-speaking children, which is a clue to the outcome of the mystery. The novel has been imaginatively translated into English as *Blue Roses for a Dead... Lady* and is published by the University Press of the South. Oliver offers in this novel another engaging episode, providing Lònia's clearest defense of her cultural identity and her mother tongue, *Mallorquí*, a distinct variant of Catalan, spoken by all characters in the novel except the Spanish police, who speak only Castilian, characterized as aggressive bullies and contemptuous colonizers. Once again, Lònia is searching for a missing young girl, Júlia, and the investigation takes her and Quim to a travel agency in Germany and eventually back to Majorca, where they discover behind the façade of tourist plot developments, an organized ring of child pornographers and pederasts. In the process, Lònia is physically attacked, almost raped and survives several murder attempts. Oliver forcefully presents a picture of moral degradation, equalling the sexual exploitation of innocent victims with the rape and economic exploitation of the Majorcan environment.

As a woman detective, Lònia's work is constantly being questioned, mostly by her male acquaintances, and especially by other detectives. Indeed, she is a most unusual fictional detective. Her shortcomings as an investigator make her vulnerable, and force her to depend on her friends; at the same time, however, she affirms her own particular style of work (so different from the generic hard-boiled method), impulsive, emotional, collaborative, and not without a sense of self-parody:

> You'll have to teach me a little. A detective who can't take pictures is only half a detective.
> And a detective who can't tell a Citroën from a Porsche, too. And a detective who is afraid of weapons, too. What kind of a detective was I, anyway? Because a detective who gets depressed when she has to spend a few hours waiting isn't a detective, she's a jerk.   (*A Study* 12–13)

Her weaknesses, however, turn out to be her strengths, put to good use by her: 'I did two things at once. I kneed him in the private parts – my specialty – and started to yell at the top of my lungs like a damsel in distress' (*Antipodes* 28–9). Thus, Lònia ironically subverts the stereotype of feminine fragility and helplessness embodied in the 'damsel in distress' figure, which constructs women as dependent on and inferior to men.

In her detective novels, Oliver crosses many conventional genre and gender barriers. The traditionally male-dominated genre of hard-boiled detective fiction, full of strong men and wicked women, misogynist detectives and damsels-in-distress, is subverted with irony. Oliver ingeniously reverses the gender roles enforced by social and genre rules. This objective is implicit in the very title of the first novel, *A Study in Lilac*, a parodic subversion of the quintessential private detective Sherlock Holmes, in his first novelistic appearance in *A Study in Scarlet*. Lilac is, of course, the color used by some feminist groups in their flag, and the title amounts to an ironic declaration of principles. Indeed, it is a woman, Lònia, who is the protagonist in charge of the investigation; she runs her own detective agency with the assistance of a male secretary, thus reversing the traditional and clearly stratified power relations of patriarchal society, delineated in the boss–secretary, male–female roles; their working relationship, in spite of the many intentional jokes, is in fact more like a true partnership. Her network of collaborators is established on mutual trust and a strong sense of sisterhood. Parodying the eccentric hobbies of other fictional male detectives, Lònia's favorite leisure activity is collecting lipsticks, a gratifying act of self-affirmation and fetishistic substitution. Conventional gender identities are also questioned and reversed: instead of the customary 'strong, silent type' of hard-boiled fiction, Quim, Lònia's assistant, is a closet gay man, who finally comes out in the second novel. The result is a true subversion of the patriarchal values embedded in traditional hard-boiled detective fiction.

Of the three authors studied, Oliver is the most successful in her attempt to redraw within her fiction the patterns of dominance affecting both Catalans and women in Spain. Taken together, the three cases show how far Spanish society has come in the last two decades in the direction of correcting colonial attitudes of domination but also how much further this society must yet go. These novels reflect the problematic issues facing contemporary Spanish society at large, where progress is being made but many obstacles remain yet to be overcome. The decentralization of political power and the proliferation of peripheral centers in post-Franco Spain are today the realities of a multicultural plural society. While linguistic plurality has become increasingly 'normalized' – co-officiality of languages at all levels in bilingual regions, particularly in the Catalan-speaking 'nationalities' of Catalonia, Balearic Islands and Valencia and to a lesser extent in Galicia – it is not nearly as widespread in the Basque country and there is still some resistance from the Castilian-speaking majority to fully accept these 'minor' languages. A few authors have been successful alternating languages and thus crossing the linguistic barriers, but neither Reigosa nor Oliver will be found in the national best-seller lists. While women have achieved constitutional equality and significantly advanced their status within the public sphere, the fact is that Spanish society overall remains a sexist one, where more likely than not Lònia would be considered an out-of-the-mainstream radical feminist; and while the move towards integration of gypsies in Spanish society has begun to be perceived as an urgent necessity, racial discrimination and relegation to the ghetto are the reality of everyday life. Success stories such as Flores' are rare and limited to very specific professions.

These obstacles notwithstanding, the continuing process of demarginalization in Spanish detective fiction is clear. The adaptation and acclimatization of the foreign, historically marginalized model of detective fiction presents overt challenges to the insularity of Spanish literary tradition, whose contamination by a foreign and literary debased product is feared by its historiographers and critics, but it also presents challenges to the neo-colonial monopoly of Anglo-American detective fiction, as others begin to enter this carefully patrolled territory. At the same time, the transculturation of detective fiction offers a vehicle for the validation and empowerment of marginal and historically oppressed cultural identities in Spain based on language, gender, or ethnic differences. The legitimization of the gypsy detective, the woman detective, and the Galician and Catalan detectives in post-Franco Spanish fiction are tentative steps towards decolonizing and demarginalizing the subaltern. This search for identity rejects the imposed status of cultural others within the centralist, patriarchal and discriminatory system of hegemonic dominance, but as the irregular results of the case studies previously analyzed show, this is a continuing struggle that will not be over until we can fully accept that cultural others are part of us.

Bibliography

Ayala, Francisco. *La imagen de España*. Madrid: Alianza Editorial, 1986.

Colmeiro, José. 'Stretching the Limits: Manuel de Pedrolo's Detective Fiction.' *Catalan Review* 3.2 (1989): 59–70.

———. *La novela policiaca española. Teoría e historia crítica*. Barcelona: Anthropos, 1994.

Ferreiro, Celso Emilio. *Longa Noite de Pedra*. Sada: Ediciós do Castro, 1989.

Fuentes, Carlos.*The Buried Mirror. Reflections on Spain and the New World*. New York: Houghton Mifflin, 1992.

Hart, Patricia. *The Spanish Sleuth. The Detective in Spanish Fiction*. Rutherford: Fairleigh Dickinson UP, 1987.

———. 'From Knight Errant to Ethical Hero to Flatfoot: The Development of the Detective in Catalan Fiction.' *Catalan Review* 3.2 (1989): 71–93.

Lawrence, Karen R. ed. *Decolonizing Tradition. New Views of Twentieth Century 'British' Literary Canons*. Urbana: U of Illinois P, 1992.

Lorde, Audre. 'The Master's Tools Will Never Dismantle the Master's House.' *This Bridge Called My Back*. Ed. Cherríe Moraga and Gloria Anzaldúa. Watertown, Mass: Persephone, 1981. 98–101.

Madrid, Juan. *Serie Brigada Central*. 14 vol. Barcelona: Ediciones B, 1989.

March, Kathleen. 'Galician Crime Literature.' *Monographic Review/Revista monográfica* 3.1–2 (1987): 202–11.

Oliver, Maria-Antònia. 'Dónde estás, Mónica?' in Ofèlia Dracs, *Negra y consentida*. Barcelona: Alfa, 1984: 117–43.

A Study in Lilac Trans. Kathleen McNerney. Seattle: Seal Press, 1987.

——. *Antipodes*, Trans. Kathleen McNerney. Seattle: Seal Press, 1990.

——. *Blue Roses for a Dead...Lady*. New Orleans: University of the South Press, 1998.

Reigosa, Carlos G. *Crime en Compostela*. Vigo: Edicións Xerais de Galicia, 1984.

——. *O misterio do barco perdido*. Vigo: Edicións Xerais de Galicia, 1988.

Reizbaum, Marilyn. 'Canonical Double Cross' Scottish and Irish Women's Writing' in Karen R. Lawrence: 165–90.

Spivak, Gayatri Chakravorty. *The Post-Colonial Critic: Interviews, Strategies, Dialogues*. Ed. Sarah Harasym. New York: Routledge, 1990.

12

Driss Chraïbi's *A Place in the Sun*: The King, the Detective, the Banker, and Casablanca

Roger Célestin

> You are intrigued by my methods of investigation, eh? I must admit they are not very Moslem.
>
> Inspector Ali

> I am not a crime novel private eye, he began, but a police inspector in real life, here and now. I am sometimes sent on missions to 'brother Arab countries,' as they say, to hide their disagreements. I'm also sent to the West, sometimes. But everywhere it's the same double talk. In order to find my way and keep a cool head, indeed to keep a head on my shoulders at all, I had to have the patience and tenacity of one of our local donkeys. Wherever one lives in this miserable end of the twentieth century, everything has become suspicious: people, feelings, ideologies, religions, words, words especially.
>
> Driss Chraïbi, A Place in the Sun

> Ah, my Lolita, I have only words to play with.
>
> Vladimir Nabokov, Lolita

I write as 'World Cup Soccer 1994' is being played in the United States. The television coverage is as complete on ESPN as it was on CNN for the so-called 'Gulf War,' and, as was the case for the latter, the commentators of the former sometimes momentarily diverge from the immediate theater of action – soccer, like 'surgical war,' comes with its own peculiar tediousness – to provide the spectators with what qualifies as either background material or tantalizing tidbits. During the Gulf War, it was often Saddam Hussein himself, his early life, his 'legendary cruelty,' etc., that provided the commentators with such desultory material. Today, as Morocco meets Belgium on the soccer field, the commentary strays from the two teams' respective merits, the amount of time left to play, or this or that particular sally, to focus on the Moroccan coach's cellular phone: he must, the commentators tell us, keep it on his person at all times lest Hassan II, King of Morocco, Guardian of the Faith ('Commandeur des Croyants'), Shadow of God on Earth (Souhaili 25), call to find out straight from the coach's mouth, as it were, how the team is doing and, perhaps, even to offer some technical advice, kingly encouragement, or reprimand (or worse?). Dixit ESPN.

The ubiquitous presence of politics and political figures in the world of national and international sports is obviously not restricted to Moslem kingdoms. Witness the perennial presentation of assorted cups, plates, and checks by British royalty to unwaveringly white-garbed tennis champions at Wimbledon ('tradition'); the 'ping pong diplomacy' of the Nixonian era ('realpolitik'); or the kiss planted on the cheek of the 7 ft 2 in. Patrick Ewing (now New York Knicks center) by a diminutive and gushing Nancy Reagan sitting on his lap after he had led the Georgetown Hoyas to an NCAA basketball championship and was invited to Ronald Reagan's White House (plain politicking). Sports and politics do mix everywhere. However, the Moroccan coach's quasi-permanent cellular connection to His Majesty Hassan II underscores that particular monarch's own singularly pervasive presence in all aspects of Moroccan life.

This presence is not at all lost on Inspector Ali, operating out of Casablanca in Driss Chraïbi's *A Place in the Sun* (*Une Place au Soleil*), the Moroccan novelist's first foray into detective fiction (all translations from this work are my own). At one point in the novel, Inspector Ali has been making inquiries about a 'suspicious individual' who has affiliations with both 'the forces of law and order' (the police, the army, the secret service) *and* with the armed section of the outlawed Fundamentalist Front; this person has been repeatedly crossing the frontier between Morocco and Algeria (the Algeria of violent fundamentalist action that has resulted in the killing of intellectuals, journalists, and foreigners). In the course of his investigation, Inspector Ali goes to Algeria to see 'the colonel,' 'ex-prime minister of Algeria and ex-director of the fearful Military Security.' There, Inspector Ali collects 'a great deal of information that would be useful one day,' including enough information to identify and even imprison the suspicious individual, 'an insignificant figure, in fact, very low down on the totem pole in the huge game being played out to the finish, with billions of dollars at stake' (25). But the Colonel is shot down, 'along with his son, his brother, his chauffeur, and his body guard half an hour after his meeting with Ali' (27), who now finds himself being interrogated in the 'Big Boss's' ('le Grand Chef') office, the chief of police assisted in this by 'five or six other bosses': Maybe the terrorists followed him to the Colonel's lair? Maybe Inspector Ali is their accomplice? Who told him to sit down? And put out the cigarette! This is the point where the King and the phone (albeit not cellular this time) reappear, in a context quite different from that of a soccer game: Inspector Ali, the supposed fool, the would-be fall guy, the anonymous civil servant, himself not very far from the bottom of the totem pole, requests permission from the snarling sextet interrogating him to call the King on his own direct-access line: 'In the sidereal silence that followed these words, he nonchalantly made his way to the phone' (29). A quick conversation follows – for all present to hear on a speaker – ending with the King's voice assuring Inspector Ali that 'our trust in you knows no bounds' (29). After this conversation – in fact an exchange between Inspector Ali and a few sentences he had recorded, imitating the King's voice, against just such contingencies – he can immediately leave the police precinct bathing in the protective afterglow of royal presence, a voice removed from the vicissitudes of internecine political intrigue. No cellular constraints for Inspector Ali; instead, the elbow-room afforded by this apparent direct connection to a central power that is itself beyond the reach of play (or detection), to paraphrase Derrida (279).

However, doesn't the thing itself that enables Inspector Ali to extricate himself from a difficult situation also contradict the very notion of objective, pragmatic, deductive method that is at the heart of detection and detective fiction? How, in other words, can such a method, and such fiction, posited as they are on the admitted possibility of dismantling mystery itself, be reconciled to a culture in which mystery and limits are perpetually reconstituted in the shape of a monarch 'whose person is sacred and inviolable,' a pronouncement encoded in the Moroccan constitution itself (Souhaili 25)?

In addition, there is the question of whether or not detective fiction as a genre can enable Chraïbi to continue to pursue both the autobiographically influenced and socially engaged projects that have characterized (not enough, according to his detractors) his novels up to this point; can the form initiated by Poe and taken up by an entire tradition ranging from Conan Doyle to Ed McBain by way of Agatha Christie and Dashiell Hammett allow Driss Chraïbi to continue the exploration of his status as an essentially French-educated Moroccan who lives and writes in France but who continues to make the country he was born in the setting and focus of his fiction? As Chraïbi writes in the preface to an earlier novel (*L'Âne* [*The Donkey*], 1956), 'I have already chosen [between staying home and going abroad], but I would so much like not to have to choose anymore ... for if I have chosen to live in France, I continue to partake of that world of my childhood and of this Islam in which I believe more and more (Dejeux 282).' Or does the recent adoption of the detective genre signal, instead, a break? Is it the fulfilment of a desire, as Barthes wrote of his own shift from 'sixties' radicalism' to 'seventies' aestheticism,' a desire to 'leave behind the tyranny of the signified and to luxuriate in the signifier (98)'?

These are some of the questions and issues I would like to address before examining how Chraïbi deals with them in the specific context of *A Place in the Sun*.

In 1926, the Treaty of Fez made Morocco a protectorate, a status that ended only with the departure of the French in 1956. Driss Chraïbi's first and most influential novel, *Le Passé simple* (*The Simple Past*, 1954) is set during those colonial years and is already a reaction against post-colonial Moroccan society's inability to move beyond its resistance to change disguised as resistance to colonialism during French rule. As a contemporary commentator of *Le Passé simple*, Kadja Hadjaki, writes:

> The novelist had relentlessly attacked the traditional, castrating and suffocating family; it had folded back on itself and undergone a kind of sclerosis in order to avoid colonial aggression and alienation. Once colonialism had ended, the causes of this sclerosis should have disappeared and the family should have relaxed its hold. In fact, none of this happened. (331)

It is against this 'sclerosis' and 'castration' that Chraïbi's *Le Passé simple* and all of his subsequent novels are directed. There is, in all of these novels, and especially in *Le Passé simple*, a kind of 'social romanticism' (Hadjaki 13) aimed at the most blatant injustices of post-colonial Morocco: a king who narrowly survives several attempts on his life and, each time, tightens his control even more on all aspects of Moroccan life, with the resulting restrictions on civil liberties and human rights (see Perrault; Souhaili); an important segment of the population whose Islamic faith does not prevent it from being unemployed and from rioting in the streets, with the resulting interventions by an army faithful to the king; an entire society (and a king) poised between the comforts (and injustices) of tradition, and the promises (and cultural dispossession) of (post)modernity. From Chraïbi's very first novel on, this predicament became one of the primary concerns of his fiction on both a private, autobiographical level and on the level of an entire country's dilemma. Hadjaki again:

> His first novel is a transposition of his own dilemma and an attempt to assume it in order to go beyond it: he had written *Le Passé simple*, he says in substance, to settle accounts with life; he had found himself trapped between two doors: the Oriental door he had slammed behind him, and the Western door that refused to open up for him. (313)

During the 40 or so years that separate *Le Passé simple* from *Une Place au soleil*, during those years that followed Chraïbi's resounding literary debut and his departure from Morocco, the 'Western door' did open up for him, as it did for other writers born in the so-called 'Third World,' but living and writing in the West (Salman Rushdie and V.S. Naipaul, both winners of the Booker Prize, and Chraïbi's fellow Moroccan-born resident of France, Tahar Ben Jelloun, winner of the Goncourt, for example). As has sometimes been the case for these writers, Chraïbi has been criticized from the very beginning as an expatriate whose homeland has become a 'fantasy' to him and who has lost touch with its realities. As proposed earlier, the adoption of the detective fiction format could be perceived – in the logic of Chraïbi's detractors – as an indication that he is moving yet farther away from the 'real Morocco.'

A Place in the Sun is in fact not a radical break with the social commentary and acerbic criticism contained in the earlier fiction; instead, it reaffirms from a different angle Chraïbi's connectedness to Morocco. Rather than a move toward an ideology-free or politics-free or culturally neutral or exoticized setting, the world of Inspector Ali constitutes a means for Chraïbi to describe a contemporary Morocco that is far from fantasy; it is also a way for Chraïbi to continue his own 'settling of accounts.'

First, there is a continuation of the blurring of author and fictional protagonist that reflects autobiographical investment. If, about the protagonist of *Le Passé simple*, Chraïbi writes: 'The hero's name is Driss Ferdi. Maybe it's me. In any case, his despair is mine (Dejeux 279),' a prefatory page of *A Place in the Sun* warns us that 'all characters are fictional, with only two exceptions: Morocco, where the story unfolds, and myself, it goes without saying.' But where we would expect this caveat to be signed by Chraïbi, it is instead the words 'signed Inspector Ali' that appear at the bottom of the page. The 'social romanticism' of the earlier novels may be about to be replaced by the simultaneously playful, cynical, and desperate running commentary of the wisecracking Ali, but the focus will remain the same: a passionate dismantling of Moroccan society caught between the 'Orient' and the 'West,' between the glorious past and the turbulent present in which the author himself is implicated.

The continued involvement of a native son living abroad does not, however, overshadow the formal concerns that have also been Chraïbi's from the beginning. And even in this formal realm credit is given to Inspector Ali, who has, 'like Frankenstein's monster, taken on a life of his own and has done [Chraïbi] a favor without [Chraïbi's] even knowing it,' that is to take him to the world of the detective/detective fiction which leads Chraïbi to realize that, 'Yes, the time has come to make this so-called Maghrebi literature, of which I am the ancestor, in a way, go off course, in other directions.'

In other words, detective fiction now provides Chraïbi with a genre he can use to extend his own formal range, to go on to new possibilities without relinquishing his hold on Moroccan reality. The formal characteristics of detective fiction – in this particular version of the Chandleresque hard-boiled novel, Inspector Ali's wisecracking output and his peregrinations through all levels of Moroccan society – provide him with the means to do so.

I refer to Raymond Chandler here with an eye to Fredric Jameson's observations on the author of *The Big Sleep*. Jameson comments on the influence the American-born Chandler's English education and years in England had on his writing, and much of what he says can be applied to Chraïbi, born in an Arabic-speaking culture, but eventually writing in French:

> In that respect his situation was not unlike that of Nabokov: the writer of an adopted language is already a kind of stylist by force of circumstance. Language can never again be unselfconscious for him ... even those clichés and commonplaces which for the native speaker are not really words at all, but instant communication, take an outlandish resonance in his mouth, are used between quotation marks, as you would delicately expose some interesting specimen: his sentences are collages of heterogeneous materials, of odd linguistic scraps, figures of speech, colloquialisms, place names and local sayings, all laboriously pasted together in an illusion of continuous discourse. In this, the lived situation of the writer of a borrowed language is already emblematic of the situation of the modern writer in general, in that words have become objects for him. The detective

story, as a form without ideological content, without any overt political or social or philosophical point, permits such pure stylistic
experimentation. (124)

Jameson goes on to speak of the 'formally satisfying arabesques of a
puzzle unfolding,' thus opposing 'ideological content' or 'political
point' to an aesthetics that has no room for such concerns. For Chraïbi,
however, rather than a pure, historically 'uncontaminated' form, detective fiction becomes the vehicle for a continued *investigation* of Morocco.
As he writes in the preface, *Une Place au soleil* signals for him that 'the
time has come to squarely set foot in the world in which we live.' While
it is possible that as a Moroccan, even if one living in Paris, literature
(and not only the French language) can 'never be unproblematical' to
him, this is not an observation that is to be restricted to writers of a
colonial or post-colonial tradition. Unless, of course, in the specific case
of Chandler and England, we think of the American hard-boiled fiction
writer as a wayward post-colonial son of the British Empire. Whatever
the case may be, Jameson gives a twist to his initial assertion that
detective fiction is a 'purely formal exercise' providing 'satisfying arabesques' to give us a paradox about Chandler's fiction that, once again,
also applies to Chraïbi's:

> A case can be made for Chandler as a painter of American life: not as a
> builder of those large-scale models of the American experience which
> great literature offers, but rather in fragmentary pictures which are by
> some formal paradox somehow inaccessible to serious literature.
> (124)

This is also Chraïbi's Morocco as we see it through the eyes of Inspector Ali: a series of vignettes, fragments, encounters in the small cafés of
working-class neighborhoods or brass and mahogany bars of four-star
hotels, the claustrophobic offices of police precincts or the palatial
houses of government officials, all against the background of international finances, the Arab-Israeli peace talks, multimillion-dollar oil
deals, massive unemployment, and fundamentalist terrorism. The following is one of many 'scenes' strung together by Inspector Ali's investigative (or not) peregrinations throughout Casablanca as he goes
through his day:

> On the corner, a reddish donkey was chasing flies away with its tail.
> Nearby, its master was taking a nap, wrapped snugly in his djellaba.

Housewives were washing the sidewalk with pails of water, gossiping and bursting out laughing. Others took turns around a head of lamb being cooked over a charcoal grill, spicing it with cumin and red pepper. The aroma rising from it made his mouth water and reconciled him with this end of twentieth century devoid of nature and food. (23)

A framed scene and, like equivalent scenes in a Chandler novel, it does not move plot along or lead any closer to the solution of a mystery; it is, like those other frozen moments in American hard-boiled fiction, a scene that stands out against the background of a world gone awry, one in which, like 'slumming angels,' to use Chandler's phrase, Philip Marlowe or Sam Spade or Inspector Ali attempt to follow a personal code of honor that clashes with the ambient corruption and generalized mayhem. In Chandler's noirish America, these scenes are often represented by passing remembrances of small-town life, the farm and family in Kansas, icons of a vanishing, more innocent America left behind by the young man or young woman in big trouble in the big city. In Chraïbi's contemporary Casablanca, these short takes hark back to a traditional, pre-colonial society: the djellabah, the donkey, the sidewalk washed by gossiping housewives. (A more feminist-oriented reading of Chraïbi's novel would easily make a case for the rather male-centered ethic that governs this text. Inspector Ali's wife refuses to cook and has sex with him reluctantly: he will divorce her in good Koranic form and will marry the young and willing protegée of the prime suspect, the banker.) Of course, such things do exist in 'end of twentieth-century' Casablanca, but they already have, for Inspector Ali, the poignant charm of things about to become extinct.

One crucial difference between these American and Moroccan versions of another world left behind is that in Chraïbi's post-colonial Morocco, it is the modernity or post-modernity represented by American civilization itself that threatens to completely overwhelm the Casablanca he once knew. Paradoxically, it is this apparently irrepressible advance of American/Western culture qua planetary norm that, on another level, also recreates artifacts of this vanishing Morocco, even if this recreation is obviously not the 'authentic' Morocco whose gradual disappearance is bemoaned by Inspector Ali. One non-fictional example seen in the summer of 1993: the (kitsch) 'Rick's Café Americain' of Hollywood and Humphrey Bogart fame (Bogart with trenchcoat but not as Sam Spade, private eye) in one of the more luxurious hotels of Casablanca, where waiters wearing Bogie-like trenchcoats and fedoras serve expensive drinks to tourists and well-to-do locals in a decor complete with enlarged stills and softly-played soundtrack from the 1942 Michael Curtiz classic. Sam's piano is on a small stage and, in the evenings, 'As Time Goes By' is a popular request.

What Inspector Ali, himself already a metonymic replay of Humphrey Bogart alias Sam Spade alias Philip Marlowe, seeks amid the detritus of post-colonial, post-modern Casablanca living out its past, present, and future simultaneously, is another, more *authentic* Morocco: the djellaba instead of the Pierre Cardin suit, the head of lamb with cumin and red pepper instead of the fast-food burger, the laughing women with their pails of water instead of the velvet-snooted gazelles (to borrow a phrase from Henry Miller) of the exclusive Hotel Mamounia. These dichotomies are apparent throughout the novel and, more than a solution to a mystery, *A Place in the Sun* is about the way in which contemporary Moroccan culture experiences these oppositions. In fact, the 'end of the twentieth century' that ends the scene described above comes back like a leitmotif throughout, revealing Inspector Ali/Driss Chraïbi's deep and ambivalent nostalgia for another time and another place.

Here, Inspector Ali, following the orders of his superiors, has gone to the home of the Director of the Central Bank (similar to the Federal Reserve Bank), a cousin of the 'minister,' who is at the center of the novel's essential mystery: a dead body with a bullet in its head (a bullet fired by the banker's gun, which has vanished) has been discovered in a garbage bin in the banker's garden. Inspector Ali is waiting to speak to the banker in a living room that takes him back to a past even more remote and authentic than the one symbolized by the scene he witnessed in the streets of Casablanca:

> The music of the water fountains was so soothing. It was as if it washed one clean of the anguish of this miserable end of the twentieth century. How did the alguacils investigate their cases during the time of the Cordoba caliphat? They must have played it by ear, according to the suspect's demeanor; in any case, they must have had a really cushy life. No damned typewriters, no reports to be typed with two fingers. Allah! How simple life must have been during those Middle Ages that frightened the Christians so. (62)

The alguacils did not use the (now consecrated) Western methods of detection: they went with instinct, 'according to the suspect's demeanor'; and this is exactly what Inspector Ali will also do. He will give the banker the benefit of the doubt (and eventually disculpate him) based on their common attachment to a tradition that is both remote in time and above the rapaciousness and smugness of their powerful contemporaries. Their affinity is ostensible not only in their common admiration for long-dead representatives of medieval Arab culture, poets and musicians mostly, among others Zeryab, the fourteenth-century composer 'who made the waters of Cordoba sing' (53), but it is also emphasized by the identical references made repeatedly by both banker and detective to the 'end of the twentieth century' as a closure to their laments on contemporary Morocco. This is the banker's encapsulated history of his country:

> From century to century, from generation to generation, we have known quite a few ups and downs: decline, retreat and isolation, the time of the protectorate, a kind of renewal afterwards. And now, modernity at all cost without a soul, like the Gulf emirates. Of course, I'm a banker, the director of one of the most powerful financial establishments of the kingdom. But should I for all that live solely in the end of the twentieth century and relegate my ancestors to the holy scriptures or even to the oblivion of outdated traditions? (54)

The intended victim of a plot to discredit him, the banker is a crucial figure of the novel: both murder suspect (and thus locus of mystery) and repository of integrity and tradition, it is through him that Chraïbi opts between the oppositions that lie at the center of this revisionist detective novel. Inspector Ali chooses the banker over those who are attempting to set him up because the banker's integrity and sense of tradition are a clear antidote to the machinations of those (among them, government officials, business leaders, etc.) who, to Ali's way of thinking, are ruining Morocco. This is why he does not use the official channels to make his inquiries and relies instead on a variation of Sherlock Holmes's 'Baker Street irregulars,' his 'own guys' picked among Casablanca's poor and unemployed left stranded by 'progress.' At one point, Ali, who is always (facetiously or not) quoting the Koran, communicates with these 'irregulars' at mosque prayer, giving them directions interspersed with Koranic incantations.

The inspector eventually reveals the details of his unorthodox investigation and its equally unorthodox results to the startled banker at the end of the novel where, Poirot-like, he explains everything to the audience (those who may be interested in reading this – after all – mystery novel are advised to skip the long quote that follows):

I played the fool, said Inspector Ali. They wanted to pull the wool over my eyes, I pulled it over theirs. First: the antecedents of the cold meat; I called on other secret services, foreign ones. I gave them some information they badly needed and they did the work in my place. Ali remained unseen and unheard. Second: I took it nice and easy at the Hotel Mamounia these past few days while my own men followed my instructions to the letter. They are not connected to the police in the slightest way. They're just poor souls who, in spite of their poverty, try to live in a decent world. People like that still exist, you know, there are legions of them. They replaced the body with another body, in the middle of the night, at the morgue in the Medico-Legal Institute. Prior to that, they had shot a bullet into its head, using a weapon completely different from yours. They did a beautiful job on his beard, made it look just like the dead guy's, the one found in your garbage bin. They took his picture and put the prints and negatives in the appropriate drawer. They are masters of the break-in, I can assure you of that. The finger prints, you say? I smudged them on the first day of my investigation, at the lab. That's all folks. (140)

Inspector Ali also produces an official (even if censored) typewritten, double-spaced report (he is after all a government functionary and not a medieval alguacil). We are not given the exact contents of this report which does not become an 'embedded narrative,' as is the case in many detective novels. (Rather than these 'embedded narratives' that logically belong to the deciphering of the mystery, *Le Passé simple* is full of Inspector Ali's spicy jokes and shaggy-dog stories that reflect nothing but a luxuriating in language reminiscent of the numerous and unrelated stories of Diderot's *Jacques le fataliste*. See Sweeney.) But we can guess that it will not contain any mention of Inspector Ali's 'irregulars' made up of the 'wretched of the kingdom,' or any mention of their nocturnal activities on behalf of the banker.

Where will this report clearing the banker go? Obviously not to the 'Big Boss' or to other officials, or to the secret service who had orchestrated the entire set-up in the first place. The report will go to 'you know who,' as Ali tells the banker (140). It will, in other words, go to the King, who is the only one who reigns absolutely over the factions competing for power and wealth around him, the only one who can put a definitive stamp of approval on the report.

Which brings us back to our initial question: how does Chraïbi reconcile detective fiction – its reliance on the possibility of justice and elucidation of mystery – with the figure of a king that represents a *removed* position ultimately neutralizing the methods and results of detection? The answer is to be found both in the hard-boiled genre itself that Chraïbi appropriates and in the way in which he dismantles the royal figure within the parameters of that genre.

First, the hard-boiled detective genre itself is already beyond the possibility of civil justice in a stable world: at the end of Dashiell Hammett's *The Maltese Falcon*, a prototype of the genre, Sam Spade delivers a woman he ostensibly loves into the hands of the police, but not because he operates in a world where absolute right and wrong exist; he sends her to jail because of his own, personal code of ethics in a world that has no center, no ultimate right or wrong (Spade himself is described as a 'blond Satan') on which to base objective values, as was still possible in Agatha Christie's English manors, vicarages, and country homes. This is America well beyond Dorothy's Kansas, just as Inspector Ali's Morocco is well beyond the magnificent and regulated Moslem medieval realm.

As for the king, he may be the removed body and voice that gets Inspector Ali out of a tight spot, and the power that authenticates the banker's innocence, but he is, in turn, demystified. His mystery and removed position are undermined and dismantled by Inspector Ali's irreverent and subversive *recycling* of the sounds, images, and texts that are the signs of his pervasive presence in Morocco. We have seen the inspector's use of the king's voice. He makes equally blasphemous use of the daily headlines glorifying the king (a completed highway finished according to His plans and being inaugurated by Him, among other encomia): he makes balls out of them with which he stuffs his new and expensive shoes in order to 'keep up their shape and their morale' (21). As for the pictures of Hassan II that occupy a privileged spot in every public space in Morocco, from the most miniscule spice shops in the most provincial souks to the air-conditioned government offices in the capital, to Inspector Ali they become a means of obtaining figs, dates, honey, and 'a rooster at half the price' from two shopkeepers: he loudly asks the first one why there is no picture of His Majesty in his shop and is diplomatically allowed to leave with the goods without paying, while 'the poultry merchant who was nearby and was blessed with good hearing' (but presumably has no picture of His Majesty in his shop either, or simply wants no trouble from the strange character wearing torn overalls, a club tie, and new shoes) reduces the price of his rooster by half (90).

The shadow of Allah on earth has become the marketable coin of Ali's little business dealings, the banker is innocent, and the detective continues his rounds in Casablanca.

Bibliography

Barthes, Roland. *The Grain of the Voice*. New York: Hill and Wang, 1985.
Chraïbi, Driss. *Une Place au soleil*. Paris: Denoël, 1993.
Dejeux, Jean. *Littérature maghrébine de langue française*. Québec: Editions Naaman, 1980.
Derrida, Jacques. 'Structure, Sign and Play.' *Writing and Difference (L'Ecriture et la différence)*. Paris: Seuil, 1972.
Hadjaki, Kadja. *Contestation et révolte dans l'œuvre de Driss Chraibi*. Algiers: ENAL, 1986.
Jameson, Frederic. 'On Raymond Chandler,.' *The Poetics of Murder. Detective Fiction and Literary Theory*. Ed. Glenn W. Most and William W. Stowe. New York: Harcourt Brace Jovanovich, 1983.
Perrault, Gilles. *Notre ami le roi*. Paris: Gallimard, 1992.
Souhaili, Mohamed. *Les Damnés du royaume: le drame des libertés au Maroc*. Paris: Etudes et Documentation Internationales, 1986.
Sweeney, S. E. 'Locked Rooms: Detective Fiction, Narrative Theory, and Self-Reflexivity.' *The Cunning Craft*. Ed. Ronald G. Walker and June M. Frazer. Macomb, IL: Western Illinois UP, 1990.

Works by Driss Chraïbi

Le Passé simple. Paris: Denoël, 1954.
Les Boucs. Paris: Denoël, 1955. Published in English as *The Butts*. Trans. Hugh H. Carter. Colorado Springs: Three Continents P, 1989.
Succession ouverte. Paris: Denoël, 1962.
La Civilisation, ma mère. Paris: Denoël, 1972. Pub. in English as *Mother Comes of Age*. Trans. Hugh H. Carter. Colorado Springs: Three Continents P, 1984.
Mort au Canada. Paris: Denoël, 1974.
Enquête au pays. Paris: Seuil, 1981. Pub. in English as *Flutes of Death*. Trans. Robin A. Roosevelt. Colorado Springs: Three Continents P, 1985.
La Mère du printemps. Paris: Seuil, 1982. Pub. in English as *Mother Spring*. Trans. Hugh H. Carter. Colorado Springs: Three Continents P, 1989.
L'Inspecteur Ali. Paris: Folio, 1991. Pub. in English as *Inspector Ali*. Trans. Lara McGlashan. Colorado Springs: Three Continents P, 1994.
Une Place au soleil. Paris: Denoël, 1993.
L'Homme du livre. Casablanca: Ediff-Balland, 1995. Pub. in English as *Muhhamad*. Trans. Nadia Benabid. Colorado Springs: Three Continents P, 1998.

Index